WHEN
DARKNESS
COMES

BOOK 2 OF THE OTHEREALM SAGA

W. FRANKLIN LATTIMORE

DIB
DIRECT
IMPACT
BOOKS

Columbus, Ohio

Published by Direct Impact Books
An Imprint of W. Franklin Lattimore
Library of Congress Control Number: 2017935165
ISBN-13: 978-1-7378896-3-2
Visit the author at: www.WFranklinLattimore.com
Also Available in Hardcover & eBook

Cover Design:
Taylor Aldridge
www.TaylorAldridge.com

Author Photo by Christy Brothers
Christy Brothers Photography, Columbus, OH

WHAT PEOPLE ARE SAYING ABOUT THE OTHEREALM SAGA

In *That Dark Place*, Lattimore infuses his characters with emotional depth and spins a plot that keeps you glued to the pages until the last one is turned.
— TOM PAWLIK, Award-Winning Author of *Vanish*

That Dark Place is like a powerful tidal wave that just doesn't stop! This isn't a book for the faint of heart, nor is it one for the reader who wants a book that can be happily tucked away and forgotten. It is one that will disturb the comfortable believer and challenge the prayer warrior. Be careful when you pick it up—you won't want to put it down!
— SHIRLEY AVERY, Editor

Move over Frank Peretti, there's another Frank in town! Frank has written a book *[Deliver Us from Darkness]* that takes you right into the middle of spiritual warfare. Highly recommended!
— ANDI TUBBS, Award-Winning Blogger & Editor

Thank you for writing *That Dark Place* and the best spiritual warfare stories I've ever read! I've spent a lot of time discussing Elizabeth—and her knack for getting herself way in over her head—with my teen daughter and adult son. Your books make for excellent conversations and teachable moments.
— ROBIN NICHOLS, Reviewer

This last book of the Otherealm Saga—*That Dark Place*—was my favorite. W. Franklin Lattimore is a master storyteller; his stories bring you in, and they cannot easily be put down!
— JIM MARZULLO, Reviewer

I found *Deliver Us from Darkness* quite thought-provoking. There were so many wonderful characters from every possible angle and walk of life. I've rarely come across a book that I enjoyed flipping back to a former page (or chapter) to enjoy the moment again and again before heading back towards the finish line.
— D. M. KILGORE, Author: *Call of the Warrior* and *Tales by the Tree* Anthologies

Deliver Us from Darkness grabbed me. The characters and their stories kept me turning the pages. I did not expect this novel to further challenge and teach about spiritual warfare, yet it did. I love a novel that entertains while it simultaneously schools you in something new—something I need to know as I minister to others. Read it to be entertained, informed, and inspired by a God who meets us in the darkest places.

— MARESA DePUY, Christian Blogger and Author of *When God Speaks: One Man's Calling to Save the Children of Uganda*

In *When Darkness Comes*, Lattimore has fashioned a set of new characters just as vivid, faulty, and intricate as the last. His familiar signature of plot twists, clever humor, and spiritual insight provides a book that even a reader who traditionally dreads sequels can excitedly recommend.

— CAROLINE DeARRAS, Writer

Behind the Darkness creates an undeniable need to see what happens next. The book is a game-changer in one's life. You will grow, build on, and delve deeper into a personal relationship with Christ.

— WENDY J. MARSINEK, Reviewer

I felt so *creeped out* reading *That Dark Place!* It felt like watching a wolf stalk a lamb.

— APRIL BILLUE, Reviewer

I hate it when a good book ends! If you want a book that will make you laugh and cry, inspire and humble you, make you search your soul, and is suspenseful enough to have you on the edge of your seat and holding your breath, then *Behind the Darkness* is a must-read!

— SHEROLYN PORTER, Author of the *Reflections from the Sunroom* Devotionals

I finished *Behind the Darkness* last night in one sitting. I was stunned by the last page! After I finished it, I turned over, prayed, and cried into my pillow. I've thought a lot about the story today also. I am very thankful that the author is using his talent to show people God's heart.

— APRIL McCARROLL, Reviewer

ACKNOWLEDGMENTS

The Three-in-One—I am both humbled and amazed by the ability that You have given to me to write these stories and the ones to come. I would say that I appreciate You more than You know, but since You know everything…

Brent Bauer—You are a man of integrity who has chosen to take a stand against the Enemy to fight for the spiritual freedom of others. Your stances and your character are the reasons behind the name Brent Lawton.

Robert Liparulo—A friend and incredible author. I appreciate the amount of time that I got to spend with you at The Ragged Edge in 2011. Your insights prompted the writing of two novels, rather than a single very long one. Your willingness to provide me with additional wise counsel over the past couple of years has been priceless.

Ted Dekker—Someone I've admired from afar for a very long time. Several phone conversations with you inspired a writer. Your 'Ragged Edge' event solidified one.

Mark Russell—Thank you for rooting me on, brother.

Michele Atwell—Thank you for being such a giver of time to my projects. What I have written has only gotten better with your touch.

Lindsay Coy—Taking the time out of your hectic life as a single mom of five children to go through page after page of my books, providing needed edits, has been a true blessing. Thank you.

Sherry Porter—You are the last to touch this book's text. And, as a result, I think there are no longer any rough spots. You have my gratitude for your time and efforts.

The Ragged Blue Monkeys—You are the single-most encouraging group of blue-furred animals I've ever met. "Blue monkeys in a brown-monkey world."

Tammy (Trick) Brant—My biggest critic and a wonderful friend. You were methodic in the picking apart of my novel. It wasn't easy having my creation poked and prodded, but it was your honesty that caused a more worthwhile end product.

Lori Taggart—My friend and editor of one of my early drafts. Thank you for volunteering your 'talentedness'.

To Jerry & Shirley Lattimore
Thank you for the pride you've shown in me.
(Jerry Lattimore, 1939-2018)

PRONUNCIATION GUIDE

Aed (name)
Pronunciation: AYTH (rhymes with "faith")
Note: A common Gaelic name, often spelled "Áed" in Old Irish, meaning "fire."

Airgialla in Ireland (place)
Pronunciation: AIR-yal-ah

Aonghus (name)
Pronunciation: ANG-us (first syllable like "ang" in "angle".
Note: A Gaelic name meaning "one strength."

The Key of **Bridei** (name)
Pronunciation: BREE-jee
Notes: A Pictish name, common among Pictish kings

Cailleach the Hag (name)
Pronunciation: KAL-yakh
KAL rhymes with "pal," while "-yakh" has a guttural "ch" sound, like in "loch" and rhymes with "lock" common in Gaelic.

Ceanannus (place)
Pronunciation: KAN-ə-nəs
Note: A Gaelic name for Kells in Ireland

Cináed mac Ailpin, the Scot King
Pronunciation: KIN-ayth mak AL-pin.

Cruithni (Gaelic)
Pronunciation: KROO-ith-nee
Note: A historical term for the Pictish people, used in both Ireland and Scotland. The "ui" is pronounced as "oo" in "moon." The "th" have been pronounced soft (as in "this").

Eithne (name)
Pronunciation: ETH-nah

Gráinne (name)
Pronunciation: GRAW-nya

Indrechtach (name)
Pronunciation: IN-rekh-takh
Note: An Irish Gaelic name meaning "ruler" or "attack." The "dr" is soft, and "ch" is a guttural sound like in "loch." The final "-takh" has a soft "k" sound.

Lia Fail ('Stone of Destiny')
Pronunciation: LEE-a FAL
Note: Irish Gaelic for the coronation stone, used at Scone in Scotland by 1486. "Lia" is "LEE-a" (stone), and "Fail" is "FAL", rhyming with "hall" (destiny)

Maucht (noun)
Pronunciation: MAWKHT
Note: An ancient Scottish word for power or ability.

Scone (a location in Pictland)
Pronunciation: SKOON (rhymes with "moon").
Note: The historical site in Perthshire, central to Scottish coronations.

Sluag (name)
Pronunciation: SLOO-ah
Note: "SLOO" rhymes with "blue" or "slew," with a long "oo" sound, while "-ah" is a short, open vowel.

Uilliam (name)
Pronunciation: ILL-yəm

PROLOGUE
Present Day

There are certain things a man tries to forget. Things that speak to him only in the silence of a darkened room. Things that make him afraid.

He was reminded, again, of an old Scottish prayer that he'd memorized long ago...

From ghoulies and ghosties
And long-leggedy beasties
And things that go bump in the night,
Good Lord, deliver us!

This was more than a bump in the night, and Brent had hoped he would never have to deal with *anything* like this again.

" ... in times past ye walked, according to the course of this world and after the prince that ruleth in the aire, euen the spirite, that nowe worketh in the children of disobedience ... "

Ephesians 2:2, Geneva Bible, 1599

CHAPTER 1
843 A.D. Pictland
19 Junius
Approaching Midnight

Drosten ran. He had no choice. What else could he do? He wasn't supposed to see. He wasn't supposed to hear.

But he did.

All that he could see now were the branches just before they struck his face. All that he could hear was the snapping of twigs and the rustling of underbrush beneath his feet.

They are dead! All of them!

He had to stop and think. He would, but first he had to find a safe place.

River Tay was to the west. If he could make it, he could follow it back north.

His lungs were burning. He had to stop. He had to catch his breath. He ignored the thought.

I have to protect the key!

Though he tried to press forward, he could no longer take the pain. He'd been running, jumping, and climbing at full speed for too long. He slowed and tried to continue by walking, but ultimately, he fell to his knees, gasping.

He tried to listen. Was he being followed? If his heart would stop hammering in his ears, and his lungs would just relax; he would be able to tell.

Drosten, Keeper of the Bridei Key, focused on controlling his breathing. He stilled his body, closed his eyes, and willed his heart and lungs to slow down.

After a few moments, he was able to hear clearly again. He concentrated on the woods behind him. He could hear nothing. He concentrated on the high grasses to his left. Nothing.

He lifted his chin and breathed in. A scent. *Water! The river is close!* He got up and began to walk toward the last stand of trees that sheltered the wide waterway. Upon breaching the thick woods, he released a sigh of relief. He had reached the Tay.

He recognized where he stood. He was at a large bend that jutted eastward before heading back west. He'd been traveling northward the whole time. Good.

Drosten walked to the bank of the river and knelt for a drink. The cool water from the highlands relieved his parched throat. After taking his fill, he stood and surveyed as much of the land-scape as he could by the light of the moon. Traveling the river was wise, but difficult. Following the waterways, he would make it from river to loch to river, all the way to Loch Ness.

He was more than a week away from completing the jour-ney before him. But a warrior's allegiance is to his king and his people. Because he no longer had a king to serve, back to his people he would go.

The warrior had no illusions about what had happened. In a matter of just a few minutes, the whole world had changed. Drust, king of the Pexa,[1] was dead; betrayed by the Scot King, Cináed mac Ailpin.[2] All seven heirs to the Pexa crown were dead, as well. The Scotti may have finally figured out a way to extend their kingdom into the Highlands without another war.

Even before his ill-fated journey began, Drosten knew that his king—though barely a year into his reign—was already a beaten

---

[1] Turn to Appendix to read about who the Pexa were..

[2] Cináed mac Ailpin later took on the name Kenneth MacAlpin, by which he is most widely known.

man, though the Scot king most likely didn't know that.

King Drust knew that the only chance they had to keep their lands was to bargain for peace and combine their strength with that of the Scotti to defeat the Norse. These raiders from a distant land—these "Vikings"—with their long boats were siphoning away the remaining strength of both kingdoms.

When the Scot king sent messengers to Loch Ness to actually propose such an alliance, King Drust breathed a sigh of relief, and Drosten had seen hope come back into his eyes.

But now...

The keeper of the key closed his eyes, replaying the events in his mind. He would be required to give great detail of what he had witnessed and why he was the lone survivor of Cináed mac Ailpin's betrayal.

The open grounds of Scone had been selected by both parties as an appropriate site to negotiate a treaty of peace. It had been the heart of the Pexa kingdom several times in their history. It was an ancient place, full of legend; a place that Drosten had always hoped to visit. Now it had become a place of agony that he wished he'd never seen.

When the plans had been made to head to Scone, King Drust made it clear to his advisers and the other Pexa nobles that he had no intention of a permanent treaty with the Scot king. He knew that combining the forces of two kingdoms to defeat the Norse would, in the end, leave just the one enemy with which to contend. If the treaty between the Pexa and the Scotti held after the war, it would allow for a period of peace, permitting the Pexa armies to heal and grow strong again. Then, and only then, could they rid Pictland of the Scotti scourge.

Drust, along with the seven earls, had accepted the invitation to meet with King Cináed mac Ailpin. The royals from both sides of the conflict agreed that they would enter Scone unarmed.

The length of time that it took to arrange for the seven royal houses to both prepare and come together for travel—in addition to the time that it took to actually reach Scone—allowed the Scotti the time that they needed to set a devilish trap.

WE ARRIVED CLEAN-SKINNED at the outskirts of Scone. The king made it clear that we were not to cover ourselves with the blue paint that we used in battle.

It was said that some of the Romans whom we had captured in battle years ago were amazed that we even had white skin. They thought we were either covered from head to toe in tattoos or would completely dip ourselves in vats of blue dye. The appearance that we choose for battle is purposeful, and back then, it had placed an additional level of fear into the hearts and minds of the would-be Roman invaders. Tonight, though, we would appear little different than these most recent intruders in our lands—these Scots.

Careful that we would not be noticed until we deemed fit, we took time to eye the encampment of the Scots. A long table with benches on either side stood upon a very large, ornately woven rug. Smaller serving tables surrounded the carpet, with a supply wagon off to the far side. Beyond that was a temporary set of railings that created a makeshift pen where their horses grazed.

Seeing that there were but few of them was an encouragement to my king, but he was still wary. He called for me to ride up beside him as he continued to survey the scene.

"Drosten," he said, "you are to stay here. And you are to remain diligent. Do not let your guard down for a moment."

Turning to me, he looked straight into my eyes. "You are the keeper of the key. Tell me what that means."

The response had been rehearsed by me for years. Each time we rode into battle, each time there was an attempted invasion into our lands, each time that King Drust—and the king before him, Uurad—felt that his life may be lost, I was charged with the security of this holy item that I carry right now. And with that charge, the king required of me to voice my responsibilities. The object in my possession was never kept under lock and key. It was always mobile, in the hands of a warrior loyal to the king.

"I am the keeper of the Key of Bridei. I am to protect it with my life. My life is forfeit if I fail. If my king falls, to the coast the key must go. I am to guard its passage out of the North-land if our lands fall to the hands of the enemy. I will be a warrior, a horseman, a swimmer, a shipman. I will be a snake, a bird, a horse, a fish. I will take on the form of that which is needed to make sure that the key is never touched by evil hands."

The king spoke the ancient Witan[3] blessing over me and then told me to dismount my horse. Because I could not risk my animal being heard whilst in my care, it would be brought into camp as a pack animal so as not to raise suspicion. I was to watch everything that took place in the camp and to watch for any enemy that may be skulking about in the trees.

If my king should fall, I would launch my trek back to the north by foot. I am fast on foot, able to make my way through areas a horse cannot. My journey would take longer, but it would be safer.

After my assurance, the king, the earls, and the attendants made their way into the encampment of the Scots. They were welcomed, not as men at war, but as brothers. I could see the initial hesitation of my king and my brothers, but their trust was soon purchased by the cup.

It became obvious to me that our late arrival would not allow for lengthy formalities, so the Scot king had made arrangements for a time of food and drink to carry them into the night.

Upon the ground, I had sat while my stomach growled with the sight of large portions of meat on spits above fires and the smell of potatoes being prepared with spices. Honey mead by the cask-full was poured and quickly brought to lips. I will tell you; I was envious.

For hours, they ate and drank and told stories of mirth. Laughter abounded. The men were eventually ushered back to the long tables for a final round and a toast. All of my king's men were seated on the long benches. Cináed mac Ailpin's men took up pitchers to fill the cups once more, though it was ob-vious that the Pexa royals had already had too much. Even

---

[3] Turn to Appendix to read a short description of Pecti-Wita witchcraft.

getting back to the tables was a task for each of them. Although my stomach ached for what they enjoyed, I had to restrain a laugh as a couple of our earls tried to lift their legs over the benches to sit down.

The Scot king finally raised his cup in the air. I could not make out what he said in the toast, but at the end, he shouted at the top of his lungs a word that echoed in the night air and sent a chill down my spine.

"Death!"

The word had barely escaped his mouth when his men, standing at the ends of the benches on both sides of the table, pulled out several long sticks or pins from the dirt near where my brothers were sitting. Both benches collapsed at once! Those I knew disappeared … *into the ground!*

I tell you, I do not understand it even now. They were just gone!

The screams echo through my mind and rob the air from my lungs just on the recounting of what I saw. Their bodies fell down onto upward-facing blades. As I stood to my feet, I could see slivers of light glinting out of the backs and bellies of the royals from where the blades protruded.

The Pexa attendants who tried to run were clubbed by the Scots to their deaths. That is when I realized I was alone, alone to my mission.

Listen to me! I am not a coward! I do not run away from a fight. I am Keeper of the Key *because* of my acts of courage! I am fearless in battle. And until this very moment, I thought no enemy could put fear into me.

Listen to me, I say! I do not fear for my life. I fear for the loss of what I carry.

This is the key to the history of my people. Our legacy, our religion, our birthright.

This is what made our people special among the nations of the earth.

This is what will ensure that my people will never die!

CHAPTER 2
Present Day, 2011
Saturday, April 23—10:26 a.m.

B ent sat in the living room with his MacBook Pro on his lap.

He still had a little time to enjoy peace and quiet before the wife and kids got home.

Along with FoxNews.com, he opened up his Facebook page. He had two messages, one notification, and three friend requests that beckoned for attention.

He was admittedly and intentionally a latecomer to the whole Facebook craze. He hadn't wanted any other intrusions on his time. God, family, and work. Those were his daily focus. However, people kept pressing him, both at church and within his own family, especially his sister.

Since she had been stationed at the U.S. Air Base on the Island of Okinawa, Japan, he finally gave in. And now, after the monumental earthquake in Japan, Lydia let all of her friends and family know that she would be posting frequent updates on her page about how things were going amid all of the devastation. Lydia had decided early on to make a career in the Air Force. It was unexpected for the rest of the family, but there was no denying that she loved what she was doing. She was patriotic to her core, and Brent loved that about her.

At nearly forty-three years of age, and after twenty-four years of service, she had recently been promoted to Senior Master Sergeant. She had a goal of becoming Chief Master Sergeant before she got out. Brent knew it was a given.

Brent had also recently been promoted. His present rank sounded a little less lofty than Lydia's, but he was proud to be a sergeant with nineteen years of service on the Millsville Police Department. While others with whom he had gone to high school had been happy to leave their hometown, Brent considered himself blessed to be able to serve the community in which he'd grown up. He knew the people, and they knew him.

It wasn't a big city, or even medium-sized, for that matter, but the 17,000+ residents were enough to keep him and his department busy. While the city had its fair share of problem citizens and passers through, there wasn't a lot of crime—nothing major anyway. Brent was undecided as to whether he preferred the quiet or those infrequent occasions that created some excitement.

Brent took his mouse and clicked on his messages. One was from Galen Todd, his former high-school nemesis. They had reconnected on Facebook. Galen had actually sought Brent out and was excited to find that Brent had finally gotten into the social-network scheme of things. When Galen announced that he had become a Christian, it had blown Brent's mind. He was enjoying a newly cultivated friendship with someone he'd known nearly his whole life.

The second message was from Pastor Jonathan, who was now the senior pastor at his home church. Jonathan's father, Pastor Chuck, had retired about thirteen years prior, but still attended as a member of his son's church.

Brent clicked on Pastor Jonathan's message first.

Jonathan Sagan April 22 at 2:18 P.M.

Hi, Brent. I hope this finds you and the family doing well. I know you've been working the past couple of weekends, but I was hoping that you would be available to meet with me for a few minutes immediately after service tomorrow. If not, maybe you can meet me at my office early next week.

Thank you. Pastor Jonathan

Brent raised his eyebrows for a moment. *Wonder what that's all about?*

After electronically catching up with Galen, he spent the next twenty minutes reading and checking status updates and perusing the latest news updates on Japan and the pummeling of Libya.

You can't be too far off from returning, Lord. Hurry; it's a mess down here.

Finished with the negative news of the morning, he turned off the computer and returned the laptop to his upstairs office. Tara would be home any time now with the kids.

11:03 A.M.

AT LEAST THE SUNSHINE was making up for the still-too-cold temperatures. It was a shame that she was still driving with the heat on. In Tara's mind, the word spring should have meant a fifteen-degree jump in temperatures. *If it's not going to snow, Lord, at least make it warm!* When had God ever answered that prayer in Ohio? She giggled softly to herself.

"What's got you laughing?" asked Jenna, her fifteen-year-old in the passenger seat of the minivan.

"Oh, just trying to get the weather to change."

Jenna rolled her eyes. "Let me know how that works out for you."

Tara just smiled.

Pulling into the driveway, she again hit the depression in the lawn at the corner of the driveway and street, jarring everyone in the van.

"Hey! Watch it!" shot Jamie, the thirteen-year-old.

"Sorry!"

Amy, the six-year-old, laughed.

"At least someone appreciates my driving," Tara quipped.

Jenna retorted, "Mom. Seriously. I'll drive home from now on."

"Ha! Not if I want to keep this latest mailbox!"

Jenna looked away in a huff. It was all Tara could do not to laugh out loud.

That got her.

"Okay, everyone out!" She pressed the button to slide open the side door, allowing Amy and Jamie to vacate. "Jamie...shower."

"Aww, mom! I didn't even sweat."

"Oh. I didn't know that."

"Yep!"

"Shower."

A huff from her boy, now. She smiled to herself.

"Come on out, Amy."

Amy, the Lawton princess—that's how she truly saw herself, with green eyes and strawberry-blonde hair like her mom— stepped out of the vehicle with something akin to a royal air. Her daddy's doing. Those two were quite the pair.

Grabbing a couple of boutique shopping bags from the back of the van, Tara pressed the sliding-door button on her key chain and started for the front door of the house.

Once inside, she watched Jenna walk up to her dad, who was sitting on the couch with a cup of coffee, and give him a quick peck on his left cheek. He smiled.

"You need to shave, Officer Prickles."

"I'll take that into consideration."

Tara enjoyed watching the two of them interact. They butted heads quite often, but next thing you'd know, Jenna would be curled up under her dad's arm as if he was the only man on Earth. She favored him in the looks category. Her hair, just past her shoulders in length, had already gone past the blonde stage and was starting to get dark, though it would never be as dark as her dad's. She'd gotten his eyes, too.

Jenna smiled at her dad, then got up and ascended the stairs, presumably to her bedroom.

Amy walked up to her dad and promptly sat right next to him. He put his arm around her, and she reached up to give him a kiss, as well.

"You need to shave, Officer Prickly Face."

Both he and Tara laughed. Brent gave his daughter a quick embrace and said, "Okay! I'm getting the point." He pushed himself up off the couch while Amy giggled. "I'm going to go sandpaper this face."

"Good morning, Hon," he said as Tara closed the front door.

"Good morning, Officer ..." She paused, allowing the mischievous phrase to just hang incomplete.

Brent walked up to his wife, who placed her right hand on his cheek as he moved in for a kiss. She gave him an appreciatively long one, then whispered, "I actually enjoy your scruffiness."

He gave her a wink and headed up the stairs.

Jamie, in his white karate *gi*, came back into the living room from the kitchen with a glass of milk and a couple of cookies on a napkin and set them down on the coffee table. Turning toward the television, he made a move for an XBox controller.

"Don't even think it, Karate Kid. Finish your snack and hit the shower."

Jamie stood and stared at her for a long moment, probably trying to bend her will with his newly-found teenage attitude.

Somehow, his blonde hair and bright-blue eyes couldn't manage to create any sense of intimidation within her.

Tara smiled inwardly.

"I mean it."

He made to say something back, but Tara gave him 'the look' and he retreated to his cookies.

At least we timed it well enough to ensure that there would only ever be two teenagers in the house at one time.

CHAPTER 3
Sunday, April 24—12:24 p.m.

Pastor Jonathan Sagan, now fifty-five years of age, still had a lean, muscular body. His six-foot frame, thick dark hair with a hint of gray at the temples, and his piercing blue eyes were a combination that gave him a commanding presence. Combine all of that with a double-breasted, dark-blue suit, and he looked more like a model for a clothing catalog than a shepherd. His demeanor exuded confidence, and most who met him were struck that a man of such imposing stature and good looks could be so humble.

Jonathan knew that it was his wife, Jenni, who had kept him grounded through the years. Before she came into his life, he had known how to use his frame and looks to his advantage. But when Jenni and he married, she eventually made a comment that had set things straight ever since.

"Don't forget, Mister, I know your flaws and I have chosen to love you despite them." That single sentence had stayed with him as a constant reminder through twenty-eight years of marriage.

On the platform from which he had just finished preaching,

he looked down and smiled at his congregation. "And before we're dismissed this afternoon, let me add just one more thing. Be careful what you watch…"

The congregation, knowing how he always concluded, took up the phrase in unison. "… Be careful what you listen to, and be careful what you talk about."

A lone, strong voice from the back of the sanctuary yelled out an additional refrain, "… And be careful what you eat!"

The congregation erupted in laughter. So did Pastor Jonathan. "Steve, thank you for that wonderful word of admonishment."

He *really* enjoyed these people.

"Okay, folks, spend some time getting to know each other better. Don't just rush out of here like a bunch of heathens."

Again, the congregation laughed as they started to rise from their seats to head off into the remainder of the day.

Pastor Jonathan walked down the steps leading to the main floor of the sanctuary and was intercepted by a young man with a toothy smile.

"Good message, Pastor. Right on time."

"Thank you, Jeff. I appreciate you saying so."

"Pastor, can I talk with you for a minute?" Jeff asked.

"Sure. I'd be happy to," he answered. "But you'll have to excuse me for a few minutes. I've got to catch someone before he leaves."

Putting a hand on Jeff's shoulder and giving it a squeeze, he turned his attention to searching the crowd.

He found the man he was looking for and repeatedly excused himself as he cut through the throng of people.

"Brent," he called out. "Brent!"

Brent was in his uniform—crisp white shirt, navy blue pants and tie—standing with Tara at the rear of the sanctuary, talking with another couple. Neither Brent nor Tara had heard him.

"Yo, Brent!" Pastor Jonathan called again.

This time he was heard. Brent turned his attention down the aisle looking for the owner of the voice calling out to him. They made eye contact, and Brent excused himself.

Walking toward his pastor, Brent, with a wry grin, asked,

"Are pastors actually allowed to say, 'Yo'?"

Pastor Jonathan chuckled. "Only in extreme situations."

"And I'm guessing this somehow qualifies," said Brent.

"Well, in a manner of speaking, yes. I've got a question that I need to ask you. Got a minute?"

"Yes. Sure, Pastor. What is it?"

Jonathan put his right hand on Brent's left shoulder and began guiding him toward the hallway that led to the church's office area. "Come with me to my office. I'd rather ask you in private."

Brent's countenance changed. Jonathan knew that Brent had seen through his smile to the periphery of a matter of some importance.

Once inside his office, Jonathan closed the door. He didn't waste any time. "Brent, forgive me for pulling you away like this. But something is weighing on my mind. And I'm hoping that you might be able to shed some light on it."

Brent's face was now serious, reflecting the demeanor of the man before him. "Pastor, whatever I can do to help."

"Good. Thank you." He paused momentarily before asking, "While out on patrol, have you, or any of your officers, heard any rumors, or been made privy to any evidence, alluding to occult activity taking place in the area?"

Jonathan knew that Brent would be his best resource for answers. Brent had been patrolling the streets of this community for many years. As a police officer for the Millsville Police Department, he heard things. Saw things. *Encountered* things.

"No, sir," came Brent's reply. "I haven't heard about any activity since way back to Tara's deliverance. But now you've got me curious. What's going on?"

"I've been hearing rumors." Jonathan stopped, wishing he could give Brent something solid to follow up on. "It comes down to a sense. I've been approached three times in as many weeks by individuals who, as far as I know, do not know each other—telling me that there's something in the air."

He stopped. He knew that he was about to sound ridiculous. But before he could continue, Brent stepped in.

"Something in the air ... as in something demonic?"

"Yes. That's what I'm getting at. Now, I don't want to sound like a man searching under rocks for something to…"

"No, pastor. You don't have to finish that thought. If you think something's going on, I trust that. And trust *me,* I know what it means to be sensitive to things demonic."

"I know. And that's one reason that I wanted to ask you about this."

"Frankly, Pastor, I wish I could help you out with some sort of answer."

"Yeah, me, too," admitted Jonathan. "Do you still have my cell number?"

"Of course."

"Brent, I personally have not discerned any demonic activity. But I do believe in the gift, as you well know. And I also know these three individuals pretty well. They are not given to flights of spiritual fancy. They are all biblically grounded."

"I understand," said Brent. "How about Jenni?"

"I've got her praying about it, but she's not picking up on anything." He paused for a moment, pondering. "Here's the thing with the gift of discerning of spirits; every time that I've heard that God revealed something, it's been in relation to a specific individual, not some general feeling over a population center."

Another thought occurred to Jonathan. "Brent, part of a Scripture verse just came to mind. 'Principalities and Powers.'"

It was obvious Brent didn't like where the conversation was headed. "

Here? Over Millsville? Aren't they more concerned with places like Babylon and Persia?"

Jonathan understood Brent's point. "It was just a thought, Brent. But it's something that I'm going to ask God about."

"Well, I will keep my eyes and ears open. And I'll also start asking God to give me the gift of discernment."

"Good. I'll ask the same thing for you, then. Now, this may sound like I'm splitting hairs, but I want you to consider adding two more words to the end of what you'll be praying for. The Bible calls the gift 'discerning of spirits',[4] not just discernment.

---

[4] Turn to Appendix to read about "Discerning of spirits."

I'm not even sure there is such a gift as just discernment. It certainly isn't mentioned in Scripture. So, let's both pray for things in a way we know to be biblical. Agreed?"

"Agreed."

Jonathan walked back around his desk and extended his hand. Brent took it.

It was obvious that Brent was expecting a simple handshake, but Jonathan liked playing this little ruse at times, disguising his intention to lead someone into an unexpected prayer.

"Father," Pastor Jonathan began after closing his eyes, "we come to you in the name of your Son, Jesus. What Brent and I just discussed may be much ado about nothing, but I don't think so. I think there is something to these claims of spiritual unrest. And we come to you, now, for answers."

Jonathan could hear Brent quietly voicing agreement to his requests.

"Lord, if there is a spiritual darkness out there that is planning to hurt this community, beyond what we might normally encounter, make us aware. Help us see with eyes of discernment the works and intentions of these evil spirits.

"If something needs to be done, if a battle needs to be fought, please show and give us your wisdom to know how to advance. In Jesus' name we ask. Amen."

"Amen."

"Well, you're in uniform. Going to, or coming from, work?" asked Jonathan.

"Going to. I've been putting in some overtime to help out an officer whose wife just brought a new addition into the family."

"Ahh, yes. I'm sure he's experiencing some sleepless nights. Well, I don't want to keep you. Go and keep this community safe."

"Pastor, you do the same. God bless. Oh, and tell Jenni I said hello."

"I will. And you tell Tara I said the same."

With those words, they shook hands, and Brent departed the office, leaving Pastor Jonathan Sagan hoping that all of this *truly* was 'much ado about nothing.'

5:03 P.M.

BRENT SAT IN HIS cruiser watching traffic drive by. He was parked in the lot of a long-ago-closed gas station about a mile out of the center of town. Rarely did sitting with his radar gun pointing up the road amount to any tickets being issued. Everybody in town knew this to be the 'danger zone' for speeding. Brent didn't mind, and neither did the department.

During Brent's high school years, there had been five major accidents, one causing the tragic death of a teen from another city. All of the accidents had been caused by taking the downhill curve leading into the intersection too fast to either react to the light change or to avoid vehicles making right turns into the flow of traffic ahead of them. As far as the department was concerned, the more people who knew or believed a cop was sitting in the lot with a speed gun, the better.

The setting sun of a chilly, early spring caused him to have to squint at traffic coming down the road from his left. *Winter's supposed to be over*, he thought.

Just thinking about the coming of summer and the ever-increasing temperatures was enough to bring him out of his cold-weather melancholy.

Why did I take on a job in Ohio? I could have moved somewhere that was always warm after the academy. Brent sighed. It was a thought that had come to mind every year since his graduation from Summit State College. It was also a thought that was never seriously taken into consideration, because Tara loved the snow. And with the kids, snow meant escape from school and winter fun.

He sighed. *Oh well... Small price to pay.*

On the flip side, though he hated the Ohio winters, he sure loved its summers. There were certainly more positives than negatives about staying.

Brent looked at his watch. He had another four hours before his duty day was done. Not that it mattered. Rarely was there a day that he didn't look forward to going to work. Though most days saw little more than the occasional traffic ticket, the anticipation of the eventual next call for assistance always kept him coming back for more. And besides, a boring day on patrol always beat any day in the office.

The weekends and evenings away from home while Officer Marshall was mastering daddyhood were another matter. He'd be glad to get back to a regular five-day shift that allowed him to spend evenings with his family.

Staring off into the distance, he thought about the Facebook e-mail he had received from Galen. Never in a million years would he have thought the two of them would develop a friendship. The fact that it was a Christian one was even more amazing. He shook his head with a laugh. The memories...

How far they had all come. He thought back to college and the events that had led to marrying a former black-magick-practicing witch. A grin lifted the corners of his mouth. Who could have seen that coming?

How he loved that woman.

Outside of my salvation, she's the best thing that's ever happened to me.

His other college friends had moved on. Eric had moved to California. Terry had accepted a job transfer to Cincinnati. Karen met a guy just prior to graduation, got married, and moved to Wyoming, of all places.

And, Marta...

He didn't really know. He kept up to date with the other three through Facebook, but try as he may, Brent could not find a Marta Liliana Rosales Rivas, or any combination of those names that turned out to be his old friend.

She probably married, he mused. *The name change is making it impossible to locate her.* He'd thought about using his resources in law enforcement to track her down. However, not only was that illegal, but a breach of her privacy. So, he let it be. The last time he had seen her was immediately following their graduation ceremony. The months prior had made it obvious that things were starting to get serious between Tara and him. Marta had never shown the slightest twinge of jealousy, only sincere friendship to both of them through their entire final year of college.

After the diplomas had been presented and the mortarboards had been thrown into the air, Marta had caught up with him while standing outside in the plaza with his parents and sister.

She approached them with a big smile on her face and tears welling up in her eyes. Walking directly up to him, she gave him a big hug, kissed him on the cheek, and whispered in his ear, "You two are going to be so happy together, and I need to respect that."

When she pulled back, he could see a tinge of sadness touching her eyes. She turned from him and walked away.

Though he called out after her, she didn't stop.

He never saw Marta again.

When he had told Tara later that day, it had brought her to tears. Oh, how things had changed between the two women. They had become more than friends; they had become sisters.

What a great reunion Heaven will bring, he contemplated.

The thought of Heaven brought his mind back to what he and the pastor had talked about earlier: A demonic force; a prince and power of the air.

I sure hope not.

5:18 PM

BRENDAN, STEPHANIE, AND DAVID sat around the kitchen table of the large farmhouse, drinking coffee. Decisions needed to be made regarding the upcoming gathering at the farm of the recently established Society of Bridei.

David McNeill had been a member of the Home Coven since 1985, at the age of twenty-two. He had been eager from the start. A graduate from Oberlin College, he had already earned two bachelor's degrees; one in archeology, the other in anthropology.

Based on Brendan's genealogical research, the probability had been strong that David's roots ran back to the Picti people. The final proof had come through the discovery of a distant relative that connected his mother's heritage to one of the known bloodlines.

After being inducted into the coven, he was the fourth member by that time—David had been groomed for a specific task within the group: Find both the scattered pieces of the Picti Key Stone as well as the Key of Bridei, itself. No small task, even for the self-described "research nerd."

He and his work had proved invaluable, not to mention that he was extremely faithful to the cause. His twin sister, Donna, though, was an altogether different story.

She was the big question mark. Brendan thought she was a risk, while Stephanie thought of her as an "aloof nuisance." Either way, she didn't want anything to do with her Picti heritage, though her brother never seemed to stop trying to find ways to create an interest within her.

The Village of Pittston, where the Home Coven was based, was not the ideal location to gather, but it was the best that could be arranged without raising suspicion.

The influx of people into the U.S. for vacations in the warm months would draw less attention than groups of foreigners flooding into some small village in Scotland.

The less that the local authorities knew about their gathering, the better. Travelers flying into Cleveland-Hopkins International Airport would be commonplace come June. Lake Erie, the islands off of Sandusky Bay, and Cedar Point amusement park always drew large numbers of international visitors. The half-hour drive to Pittston would also prove convenient for most of those arriving.

So far, 221 of the 325 current members had confirmed their attendance. Flights were being booked, as were hotels throughout the surrounding area. It would be ideal if all of the members would attend, but Brendan knew from a purely logistical standpoint that it was unlikely. Some of the members had not yet received their passports, and others just didn't have the financial means or the time to travel abroad. The latter two, in

Brendan's opinion, were damned-poor excuses.

Getting people onto the farm without raising suspicion was really going to be the trick. Fortunately, though, the local police issue was already handled, and they still had a couple of months to consider how to disguise the gathering.

The discussion this afternoon centered on the ceremony. How much was too much or too little? From a practical standpoint, the core of the Society knew that little to no ceremony was needed in order to conjure spirits or conduct spell casting.

The practice of true *magick* only required a few consecrated tools and materials, the proper environment, correctly recited incantations, and discipline within the members present. These things would garner the attention of the ancient gods of the Picti.

For many of the members, though, practicality was not going to cut it. The resurrection of the old religion almost begged for *ritual* ceremony. Brendan had a flashback to the movie, Indiana Jones and the Temple of Doom. That ridiculous headpiece and stupid costume of the high priest were, more than likely, nothing at all like the clothing of those who had originally worshiped the Goddess Kali.

He sighed.

"Yes?" asked David.

"I'm still torn. Will we truly be disrespecting the ancient gods by *not* wearing some sort of historical garb? Would we truly be disrespecting our people? I'm very close to deciding that we just go with blue jeans and T-shirts. Forget trying to meet people's preconceived ideas."

"Our forefathers were mostly naked for ceremonies," countered Stephanie.

"Yes, and ideally that would work for us, as well," responded Brendan. "But, even if we did do that, what of our plain skin? Do we ceremonially—obviously temporarily—dye ourselves blue? Do we ink our skin with tattoos? I must admit, if there is anything that I don't like, it's the idea of unnecessary additions to what should be the simplest of ceremonies."

"I say we go all the way," said David. "Give them what they're expecting. I can't imagine traveling thousands of miles to just hang out in summer clothes."

Brendan's face pulled into a deep-seated frown. He was frustrated. "I don't *want* a carnival event!" He slammed a hand down on the table and got up from his chair.

Startled, Stephanie and David watched as Brendan began to pace with his right hand at his forehead.

"This is not for entertainment," he continued, reigning in his emotions. "This is to be taken with the utmost solemnity."

He stopped pacing and looked at the two, still seated. "We respect the old religion. We do not mock it. Those in attendance must be warned of the sanctity of the gathering. We are going to be resurrecting a religion that has been dead for almost twelve hundred years. If any of the attendees do *anything* to mock this, I will deal with them most severely."

Stephanie stood and approached her lover, her long blonde hair highlighting her statuesque frame. Though they never married—something too Judeo-Christian for either of them to stomach—they had become "sealed" in their relationship; a covenant relationship, that was the first of what would soon be many dozens in the Society.

"Brendan." She reached up with her left hand and caressed his face. "We are behind you completely in this. We make sure that all who attend know how hallowed the event will be." She raised herself on her toes and kissed him lightly on the lips. "David is right, though. While we honor the gods in our hearts and with our words, we must do our best to *show* them with our practices, including our appearances. To that end, allow me to propose an idea."

Stephanie guided Brendan back to his chair. He sat. She did not.

With both men staring at her, she suggested, "Prior to the Appeasement Ceremony, we shall have a tattooing ceremony involving only the leaders of the twenty covens. With ink or another substance that can later be easily removed, we will take time to cover one another's bodies in Pictish symbols. Those who wish to be naked may do so, while those who are reluctant may remain clothed, exposing more modest areas for the ink. It will be a quiet ceremony. No words spoken."

Brendan looked to David, who smiled and nodded.

He looked back at Stephanie. "Ailene, my love, you prove to me again the smart decision I made to make you mine. Your thoughts are inspired."

As the conversation continued, they agreed that the amount of ceremonial formality would be dependent on the wishes of the priests of the varied covens around Europe and the U.S. As long as the gods were respected and the beliefs were held in common, they would not allow the small things to distract from the larger picture.

The *Olde Faithe* of the Picti people had been deeply ingrained in the worshipers of antiquity. The power they held in common had been the glue of their society in the northern regions of Pictland, where the *Christlings* had not yet violated the land.

Brendan's belief, based on his years of research, was that the rift between the Picts of the North and the South was along religious lines more than a desire for self-governance. Somehow, the *true* faith had been laid down for a lie in the South. No wonder MacAlpin had been able to trick the Picts into offering up their king. A cancer had begun to spread throughout Pictland, making them unsure and weak. They gave up *true* power for an impotent god who died on a cross. A *criminal*, of all things!

What they had set aside for their repugnant god of "peace" was peace in their own lands! It should be a lesson to all people: kneel before Jesus of Nazareth and lose your ability to reason!

The Picts of the South had once had the same power as those of the North, and that they had traded it in for weakness... It was beyond Brendan's ability to comprehend.

The Picts were hardly immortal, to be sure, but they had immortal power; power beyond anything that had been seen anywhere else in the world. They had power over the elements. They could cause the weather to change at will. They had the power to keep the mighty armies of Rome from conquering the North of Britain!

Rome had been forced to end the seizing of new territory because of the Picti people! What did *that* say about their strength? Raw, unconquerable power!

That power would be known again. That power would be *unleashed* again!

And the only thing required to move toward that day was a little bit of sacrificial revenge; just a one-time spilling of "special" blood.

CHAPTER 4
843 A.D.—Scotia
(Ancient Ireland)
18 Julius, Midday

Drosten stood atop an as-of-yet unfinished stonework defensive tower, part of what was once the hill fort of Ceanannus. Leaning against a makeshift wood railing, he surveyed the campus of this, renamed, Abbey of Kells. It was obvious to him, now, why this place had been selected to protect the Key of Bridei.

Selected outside of my control, he thought. *Why here, amongst the Scotti? How could this have been the solution to keeping the key safe?*

His body ached. It was difficult to believe that his journey of more than a month had come to an end. What was he to do with himself now? He could go back to his homeland and... He sighed. Could he? This abbey may well be the place where he would die. He could not foresee another end.

Pictland was grieving the loss of a king. The Scotti were certainly, by this time, amassed for a push north, and the Pexa were in chaos.

The infighting to determine a new king of the Pexa was already raging by the time he had left Loch Ness for Inverness. By the time he had boarded a boat to travel north in Moray Firth, to the Tarbat Peninsula, the heaviness in his heart had convinced his mind that he would no longer have a country, a people, to return to when his mission was complete.

The boat ride to Tarbat had been uneventful. The owner of the boat, in fact, was of good cheer, reassuring Drosten that things would soon return to normal.

"That Scot king will soon find that retribution is both painful and final," he quipped.

Oh, that it could be true, he'd thought. But what he already knew—with certainty—was that a *new* normal would overtake the land; a normal that would shatter everything that the Pexa held dear.

Drosten's eyes hurt. It wasn't a typical soreness from lack of sleep; this pain came from behind his eyes. It hurt to move them. Closing them didn't help.

He heard footsteps approaching from the stairs inside the tower. He turned to see a monk, many years older than himself, appear in the sunlight. The sight of the man reignited a curiosity within Drosten. The monks of Scotia had taken on a different form of *tonsure* from their brothers in Britain and Pictland.

When Drosten was a youth and had first seen the oddly-cut hair, he had been told by one of his elders that it had become the mark of priests within the Roman religion. The design of the hair seemed to have been formed by placing a small bowl on the crown of the head, and the only hair that was allowed to remain was that which was *not* hidden under the bowl.

These monks in Scotia, though, along with the monks he had met at Iona during his journey, had done something different altogether. The hair was left on the back of the head, but starting with one ear, they shaved an arc forward, still leaving hair above the brow, then arced back toward the other ear. It was like a quarter moon had been shaved onto the front half of the scalp.

"Greetings, friend! Pax vobiscum," said the monk.

Drosten bowed, thinking that some outward sign of respect was due.

"Greetings, …" He realized that he didn't know this man's title, so responded in kind. "… friend."

The man smiled. "I am Abbot Conall."

Drosten dipped his head in acknowledgment, now realizing that he stood before the man in charge of this abbey.

"So, then, I am told your name is Drosten."

"It is, your… your…" Drosten sputtered to a stop again. "I'm sorry, but I still don't know how to respectfully address you."

"*Tch-tch*. Let us not get wrapped up in pretense, young man. I am not royalty. You may call me abbot or simply, Brother Conall."

Drosten dropped his eyes. "You ask me to call you brother, but I cannot. After all, it is your Scotti cousins who are at this moment killing my *true* brothers."

The abbot dropped his eyes, as well. "Yes. Yes, of course. I understand."

Drosten looked up again. "In fact, I do not even know why I am here, or where, for that matter."

"First, the where," replied the abbot, meeting Drosten's eyes again. "You are in the Abbey at Kells, within the boundaries of Airgialla. You have heard of it, have you not?"

Drosten shook his head.

"Ah, well… we are about two days north of the Hill of Tara."

"My people know of Tara. It is where your kings are made. An ancient place of power, akin to that of Scone."

Dreadful flashbacks of his one visit to that ancient place of kings began to flood Drosten's mind. He shook the mental images off.

Somewhat off the subject, he asserted, "I have seen the power of our religion strike men down and even raise them back to life again. The right words, the right time, the right stone.

"You, too, have a stone at Tara that provides power to the kings of this land."

"You, of course, speak of *Lia Fail*, the 'Stone of Destiny.'" Again, the abbot clucked his tongue. "That pillar of stone has no true power. Its *only* ability is to keep people blind to truth."

Drosten stared at the abbot. *No power?* But before he could bring the question to his lips, the abbot continued.

"Now, *why* you are here... you are here to be saved," said the abbot. "You have come for protection, and so it is offered."

Fatigue, combined with growing frustration, began to peak within Drosten. "Yes, it is offered. But *why?* We are enemies! You are Scotti! I am Pexa!"

"*You*, Drosten, are a *man!*" chided the abbot. "You may be someone's enemy, but you are *not* mine!" He huffed and turned around to find a bench, and finding it, sat down.

"Good." The older man nodded. "We speak plainly from the start. This is good."

Drosten stood looking at the man. He was perplexing. The 'brothers' at the abbey on the Isle of Iona[5] were perplexing, as well, but at least they were known to have befriended the Pexa generations ago. Some of the Pexa who had converted to their religion—about some god who died and came back to life—had even become part of their order. In fact, they had built a building to worship this god on the peninsula of Tarbat. But after generations of having stood, it was violently destroyed by the Pexa King Caustantín some fifty years prior so as to reclaim their original spiritual heritage.

Caustantín wanted to wield the legendary power of their own Pexa gods. It was said that this power had kept the Romans at bay for hundreds of years, and the king was not going to be denied his place among the legends.

For possibly this very reason, all those who dwelt within the abbey at Iona considered themselves free of kingly allegiances. Drosten wondered what could be said about this cloister of men at Kells.

The abbot continued, "Today, you and Abbot Indrechtach brought with you two objects that are also in need of protection. One of them, an inscribed stone, so I am told."

Drosten nodded.

"The other, a copy of the Blessed Book; as much a work of art as it is the written words and accounts of our risen Lord, Íosa. Between King MacAlpin's bent for conquest and that

---

[5] Iona is a small island (3.4 square miles) of the Inner Hebrides off the West coast of Scot- land, North of Ireland.

of the Viking raiders, it was thought best to relieve the Abbey at Iona of the burden for their safety."

The Pexa warrior stood mute for a moment. The abbot just gazed upon him. *So ... what now? Stay? Return home?*

"Abbot, if I may rest here for a few days, I would be grateful."

"Of course. You may stay as long as you would like."

"I will not overstay my welcome. I intend to head back to my home..."

"Drosten." The abbot pursed his lips and stood up. He walked over to the railing, folded his hands, and then gazed out toward the northeast. His next statement came after a protracted sigh. "Drosten, you are a man without a nation."

Drosten began to object, but the older man closed his eyes and held up a restraining hand.

"I fear that I must be the bearer of ill tidings. From what Abbot Indrechtach has told me, the resistance put up by the Pexa against MacAlpin's forces was feeble at best. With the petty squabbles and rifts that led to a new, yet weak, Pexa king, your people fell into disunity, which allowed for only a very weak defense of your homeland, if defense it could even be called."

Abbot Conall let his words sink in before continuing. "Drosten, my son, Pictland is no more."

The abbot turned from the railing. Drosten faced him and searched his eyes, looking for traces of deception. He couldn't see it. He clenched his teeth. An emotion—an amalgam of anguish and hatred—boiled up from deep within. "Lies! You speak *lies*, priest!"

But Drosten knew. Deep inside, he knew that the words were true. He'd known the impending reality from the moment he witnessed the spikes pierce his king's body.

"Why did the abbot of Iona not say something to me, *if* what you say is true?"

"Whether right or wrong, he felt it best that you be safely transported from Britannia before anything was revealed. Perhaps he feared you would run back to your people once more, only to die a pointless death. Maybe he feared that the mission—the sacred trust—to which you had been appointed, would be abandoned."

The warrior whirled away from the abbot as moisture began to cloud his vision. He looked out over the countryside and stared toward the horizon; toward the northeast, toward his home. It was then that the horrible finality of it all struck his heart: He would never see his beloved Pictland again.

22 JULIUS 843 – MIDDAY

"SO, WHY THE NEED of a key?" asked the young monk apprentice. Aed, a boy of sixteen or seventeen years of age, sat on a high stool from which he had just given Drosten a verbal tour of the facility in which he now stood.

As he walked throughout the structure, the Pexa warrior learned that much of the work of the abbey centered around this small stonework building, with its thatched roof, high writing tables, writing quills by the dozens, vellum paper, and vats of colored inks. Self-feeding oil lamps allowed the men of this cloister to work at all hours to accomplish projects.

Drosten came to know that there were three stations of work. The first was an area where certain monks smoothed and chalked the vellum paper, preparing it for writing. The second area was where another group of monks ruled the writing surfaces and did the actual copying of the texts. Each copyist had his own desk that was partitioned from the others, allowing him to work uninterrupted. The third area was where the remarkable artwork on the pages—the *illuminations*—took place.

Aed had explained that the focus for many of the monks was the production of copies of their *Biblia Sacra* as well as other books they felt worthy to send to the heads of their *Ecclesia Catholica Romana*. Some were also sent to other abbeys or places of instruction.

However, as Drosten was unable to read any of what was being inscribed, he could only stand amazed at the attention that was given to the artwork in their most sacred of texts. The chief of these texts turned out to be the very one that had traveled with him from Iona.[6]

This day was a weekly-appointed time of peace without work—*Dies Dominica*, the monks called it—the Lord's Day.

The brothers spent much time in prayer and singing what they called psalms of praise to their god.

Four days had passed since Drosten's arrival in Kells. He felt out of place and without a purpose. Little that these people did made sense to him. They prayed to an unseen god who was once a man and somehow still was. This god-man died because *he* chose to out of a sense of love for the very ones who would put him to death. It nearly made him dizzy to think about it. A crazy religion. It didn't surprise him that it was Roman. They seemed to want to conquer the world with all sorts of idiocy.

Still, these *brothers* did seem to know how to love differently than most. They were strong men, for the most part, who chose to lead lives showing compassion on the pitiful, providing instruction to the illiterate—several times they offered to teach him to read and write their language—and giving attention to the sick. They appeared to live their beliefs without hypocrisy.

"I've noticed," responded Drosten, "that you have many crosses that surround the abbey, most of which have inscriptions and carvings."

The young monk-to-be snickered. "Aye, but that doesn't answer my question about why you need a key."

A smile came upon Drosten's face. "No, it does not. But it will. The figures on the large cross to the west, do they have a meaning?"

"Aye. They do. The man with his arms outstretched is *Íosa Christus Rex*. The two men on either side are soldiers who put him to death. One spear pierces our Savior's side to assure the Roman soldier that he had truly passed."

Drosten accepted the description, though he now found it a marvel that the Romans killed the god whom they continued to worship.

"The standing stones in my land have messages on them,

---

[6] Turn to Appendix to read about the *Book of Kells*.

as well. They are not representations, such as yours, but they do have meanings. You write a language in your books that can be read by those who know that language. We write a language on our stones that is kept secret from the rest of the world."

"Is it the language that you speak? The Pexa language?" Drosten didn't know how to answer the question directly, so he asked, "The language that you are inking into that book right now, is it the language of the Scots?"

"No," Aed responded. "It is the language of the Mother Church. It is called Latin."

"So, you write a language onto vellum that is not your native tongue."

"Aye."

"We, too, put into stone a language that we do not speak. It is not a language that all of the Pexa know. But all Pexa know that it is a language that tells a secret. This key allows the Pexa to look at the images on the stone and know their meanings in the language that we speak."

"Ahh! It is a *runa* language! A secret or hidden language, heh?"

"That, it is!"

The young monk reflected on that a moment, then the excitement left his eyes as he came to an uneasy conclusion.

"Drosten, if your people are no more, as it is said… If soon no one will know how to speak the Pexa language… How will anyone know how to use the key?"

The realization struck Drosten hard. To have escaped Pictland with the key may have served no purpose at all!

If he were to be one of the last of his people to read and write his native tongue, then no one following would be able to use the key to discover what the great stones throughout Pictland meant.

Even if some still could speak the language of the Pexa, what about the *writing?* How long before the written language disappeared altogether?

He had in his possession the Key of Bridei. The Key Stone, the large standing stone into which the Key of Bridei fit and interpreted the *runa* language, was in hiding near Inverness in his homeland.

Should the two ever be brought back together... with no one remaining who knows how to read or write the Pexa language... this... this whole mission will have been pointless!

Drosten couldn't come up with a response to the monk's question. Eyes big with realization, he just walked out of the scriptorium and into the heat of the midday sun.

The years of carrying and protecting the key... The escape from the murderous Scots...

The weeks of seeking safety for the key...

All of it had come to this: With his death, be it soon or a long way off, would also come the death of the knowledge of his people's very existence.

LATE EVENING

IT WAS WELL INTO the dark of the evening when Drosten sat over a cup of wine relating his dismay to Abbot Conall, Abbot Indrechtach, and a few others of the order. The hall in which they sat had two long tables lined with benches on either side and was used for feeding the men of the cloister. The evening meal was long past, but seven of the men sat to both listen and give counsel to an inconsolable foreigner. The warrior had not eaten, but was willing to drink to dull the pain that attacked his emotions.

It was at this time that Aed came running into the building, out of breath.

"Drosten!" he shouted as he entered. Seeing the two abbots seated with him, the boy became contrite. "Abbot Conall... Abbot Indrechtach... My apologies. I didn't realize that you were still here." He bowed his head and looked to the hardwood floor.

Abbot Conall answered. "It is okay, son. You may approach."

As the young apprentice came near, the abbot looked to his elder. "Brother Indrechtach, this is Aed. He was deposited here at the abbey some thirteen or fourteen months ago by his grand-mother. His family was murdered by Viking marauders some two years ago.

"He's proving to be quite the hard worker and is very intel-ligent!"

Turning back to the boy, he queried, "What is it, Aed, that has caused you to see fit to disrupt this morose occasion?"

"Again, master, my apologies," he began, still excited and out of breath. "It's just that I think I've come up with a way to help Drosten complete his assignment with victory!"

"Go on, my son."

Aed walked up to the table across from where Drosten was positioned. The warrior looked up at the boy with a look of cu-riosity more than hope.

"Well, I was thinking that while Drosten's native tongue may one day be gone, there is one language that will be around forever. Latin!"

Drosten looked at the boy with a furrowed brow, still not grasping what was being conveyed. He looked at Brother Co-nall and shrugged. "I do not understand."

The abbot shook his head. "Nor do I. Pray continue, Aed."

Looking at Drosten, Aed asked, "May I see the Key of Bridei?"

Drosten stared at the apprentice for a long moment, then simply said, "Yes."

He stood to his feet, and the others at the table did the same. All of the men ventured into the cool and damp evening air.

Aed asked if Drosten would retrieve the object and bring it to the scriptorium, where the men would wait.

Upon returning with the key, Drosten saw the group nod-ding with smiles on their faces.

"Drosten!" proclaimed Brother Conall. "The boy has saved the day!"

The enthusiasm in the room was catching. Drosten couldn't help but smile, though only slightly. His eyes revealed optimism, yet remained grounded in caution. "What? What is it?"

"Aed, explain again what you've just told us," prompted one of the monks by the name of Lasrén."

"May I see the key, Drosten?" Aed extended his hands to accept the flat, polished stone that was hidden within a leather bag cinched at the top with a leather drawstring.

Once he had it in his hands, he walked to one of the tables used to stretch the cleaned animal hides for scraping and their eventual transformation into vellum. Setting the bag down and pulling the object out, he set it down atop the pouch.

Turning to look at Drosten, he asked, "The words on the face of the stone, they are of the language of the Pexa. Aye?"

"Yes, my native tongue."

"So, you will have no problem reading these aloud to us. Aye?"

"Aye… Yes." Drosten looked around to the other men gathered around, hoping someone would just spit out what the lad was maddeningly delaying.

The elder abbot, Indrechtach, just smiled and extended his right hand back to the boy, bidding the warrior to redirect his attention so he could continue.

Aed looked back down at the stone. It was circular and approximately sixteen inches in diameter. It was divided into six equal sections by what appeared to be spokes emanating from a central hub. In between each spoke near the hub was a small symbol. Just above the symbol were words of the Pexa language. Above the writing were two more symbols followed by more writing. Each division contained a total of thirteen symbols, with an accompanying amount of writing.

"These symbols that separate your Pexa language, these comprise the *runa* language that you told me about. Aye?"

"Aye."

"Then each of these symbols is something like a *futhark*, a letter in the alphabet of the *runa* language," Aed surmised.

The monks who had not yet seen the stone marveled at the intricacy of the engravings. It was just as much a piece of artwork as anything that they produced within their own walls.

The intricate etchings of the symbols were more out of a need to conserve space than to impress anyone who looked upon it, but it was obvious that a master hand had crafted everything that they saw.

The young apprentice flipped the stone over. The back of the stone was free from any markings. The only thing noticeable was the hub that protruded two or more inches from the center and had a diameter equal to its length.

Pointing it out, Aed asked, "This is to position the key correctly into the Key Stone, aye?"

"Aye." The Pexa warrior was beginning to enjoy saying the Scotti word himself. "Then it is dialed to match symbols in the Key Stone itself. The spokes on the front of the key stretch to match the spokes on the Key Stone."

"Would anything placed on the back of this key prevent it from working?"

Drosten knit his brows together, revealing that he didn't understand.

Aed expounded. "If I were to, let's say, engrave symbols or some words on the back of the key, would it in any way prevent the key from working correctly?"

"I cannot see how it would. But why would you do that?" The boy grinned and looked at his elders and mentors, who smiled back and nodded. Brother Conall even winked at him.

"Drosten, even if your language dies off, the language of the Mother Church will not. What if we transcribe what is written in the Pexa language into Latin, then etch it word-for-word into the backside of the key, with the same spokes? In the future, anyone who can read and write in Latin will be able to understand what is written in your language on the front. They, in turn, will be able to interpret the symbols, and the key will once again interpret the Key Stone of your people!"

Drosten's lips parted. His eyes grew wide as he stood there, the realization of the answer permeating his spirit. Tears of joy and relief began to well up in his eyes.

He had done it. With the help of a pup, wise beyond his years, he had done it.

He *had* ultimately protected the history of the Pexa people.

He had not failed his king after all.

CHAPTER 5
Present Day
Monday, April 25—8:17 a.m.

Tara sat at their breakfast table in the kitchen, waiting for Brent to grab his second cup of coffee. He was stirring the cream and sugar into his cup just a little too loudly.

There was obviously something on his mind, and now that the kids were off to school, they would be able to sit and talk without interruption. She wondered whether he would volunteer what he was thinking or if she was going to have to "convince" him to come clean. Either way, she knew her husband well enough to know his little ceramic music performance was a voluntary hint that he did want to talk about something.

Brent sat down in front of her with his hot cup of vanilla hazelnut coffee, a favorite of hers that he tolerated. He preferred a richer blend.

He looked down at the light-brown, steaming content.

Okay, it's going to take some prompting, she thought.

"It's supposed to be a warm day."

"Yeah," he said." Good thing. Just wish the rain would hold off."

"Getting an early start on those May flowers, I guess."

"How sensitive would you say you are to spiritual things?"

Whoa. Didn't see that coming. "I'm sorry. What?"

"Pastor Jonathan and I had a disturbing conversation yesterday after service."

Men and their far-too-silent internal processing!

"About?"

Brent scooted his chair back, picked up his cup of coffee, and took a sip. He stood and walked away from her toward the stove, then turned around and leaned back against it. "Hon, this is one time that I hope that Pastor Jonathan is wrong." He stopped and seemed to be processing another thought.

Tara was at the edge of her patience. She got up as well and walked over to stand in front of her husband.

"What is it, dear man of my life?"

The right side of Brent's mouth pulled into a grin for a few seconds, then released.

"Pastor thinks that something may be going down in Millsville, or somewhere in the surrounding area. Spiritually, that is."

Tara gave him a confused look. "Going down?"

"Yeah. As in something dark about to strike our community. Apparently, several people, who, to the best of Pastor's knowledge, don't know one another, have approached him to say that they are sensing something looming on the horizon. Something evil."

Tara looked into Brent's eyes, searching for more. "Is that it?"

"That's it. Could be nothing to it." He looked at his cup, then took another sip. "Could be something. Dunno. But I think we need to start praying. Together."

Unfortunately, it had been a while since Brent had suggested such a thing. At the beginning of their relationship and for several years in, nothing had to prompt Brent to take her hand and just start praying, about nothing specific sometimes. Every once in a while, he'd just walk up behind her while she'd be cooking or folding laundry and rest his hands on her shoulders. Then he'd lean his head forward until it touched the back of hers, and he'd just whisper a word of thanks to the Lord.

After they had children, things began to change. It was

fatigue. The spring in their spiritual steps seemed to quiet down into just surviving each day and night. The nighttime feedings and diaper changes, the runs to the store, working extra shifts or doing off-duty work to offset some of the hospital costs and other new expenses.

Of course, all of this should have caused them to focus more on the Lord, but both of them had allowed the spiritual things to slip into mundane, daily habits and ineffective religious rituals.

Now, they still attended church, of course. And, certainly, they both still prayed; they just no longer did it together. Grace at the dinner table didn't quite count.

Life never let up, so they never changed their spiritual habits. They just tended to sometimes glide, sometimes drag from one day into another, never really asking the Lord for much in the form of help.

Now Tara stood there looking at the man that she still loved more than life itself, seeing a new form of concern in his eyes. Slight fear, maybe?

"Okay. We've been long overdue anyway, so maybe this is a good thing."

He looked at her with raised eyebrows.

"I don't mean 'good thing' as in *good* thing. I mean sometimes God uses what the enemy means for evil to also accomplish some good."

He winked at her. "I knew what you meant."

"So, it must be weighing heavily on you," she said as she turned around and walked back to the table and sat down.

He slowly walked back and sat down, as well. "Something the Pastor said... I can't get it out of my head. And it's *that* which scares me a little bit."

Tara felt a slight chill course through her body before he said his next sentence. It was as if a confirmation was penetrating before she had anything to confirm.

"What was it?"

"He didn't come out and say that it was going to happen, but I saw his eyes when the thought occurred to him. It unnerved him. At least momentarily."

"What was it, Brent?"

"He said that there was a possibility that a Principality or Power has taken station over our area. Or *will*."

Tara thought back to her days in the craft. She had never used those exact words, but she knew that there were powers in the heavenlies that dominated areas. But a Principality or Power over a city as small as Millsville? She knew the pastor's phrase from the Bible, of course, but never gave it a whole lot of thought regarding her own life since her salvation.

In fact, unlike Brent, she had never been tasked by the Lord to get involved in the rescue of another individual who was participating in the occult, let alone having to worry about the protection of a city. Was all of that about to change?

"Okaaay," she replied, dragging the word out, "Umm… okay, then we take it seriously. We begin to pray together, again, like we used to."

Brent sighed. Tara knew what he was thinking. *Like we used to.*

"Hey," she said, giving him a closed-mouth smile, hoping that it reached into her eyes.

He took that moment and looked deep into her soul. Her heart skipped a beat. *That wonderful spark!*

Her lips parted, and she felt a broad smile light up her face.

"Let's get back to who we used to be."

She gave a little nod. A smile reached his eyes, too. *I love seeing that!*

He reached across the table and took her hands in his. With his next few words, he maintained eye contact, and then they both dove in with all of their hearts.

"Father, we love you! Welcome us back into your throne room as we welcome you back into our daily lives."

3:47 P.M.

BRENT WALKED INTO HIS captain's office before heading out on patrol. The thought occurred to him that maybe someone in the department or in other local-area departments may have heard of some strange goings-on in the surrounding communities.

"Come in, Brent. What's going on?"

Captain Morelli was just a couple of years older than he. A genial man most of the time, he was someone who garnered trust among everyone on the force, and he was as capable an administrator as he was an officer in the field.

The thing that Brent probably appreciated most was that he took time for his men; he never just dismissed them out of hand, which was saying a lot, considering how sometimes he probably should. Maybe just like this time.

"Afternoon, Captain. Just wanted to stop in before getting into that old jalopy I've been driving."

The Captain smiled at the jab and held up his hands in mock defense. "I know! I know! We're getting there. The mayor is submitting the purchase of new cars to the town council tomorrow."

That took Brent by surprise. Pleasant surprise. "Well, now. That's great to hear."

"Now you can go patrol in peace."

Brent chuckled. "Well, sir, as much as I do want those new vehicles, that's not why I interrupted your day this time."

"Oh? What, then?"

"Okay, this is going to sound a bit strange. And, no, I don't have any hunches, and I've not seen anything. But a few concerned citizens have been remarking lately that they…"

Brent closed his eyes and sighed.

"I'm listening."

"… that they've been sensing something in the community. Something that's not quite right. They can't explain exactly what they're feeling; they're just troubled. I was wondering if you had heard anything similar, or if another department in the area may have hinted at anything."

The captain cocked his head and squinted his right eye at

Brent. "You're serious?"

"Yes, sir. I'm serious."

"Well, no reports of hobgoblins or gremlins as of late."

Brent gave a forced laugh. "Good. That's good to hear. Thanks for your time, Captain." Embarrassed, he turned for the door.

"Sergeant, if I hear anything similar to what you've just said, I'll let you know. Especially if you're wanting to be on the cutting edge of any paranormal police work." He chuckled.

Brent walked out the door. *No, Sir,* he thought. *That is the* last *thing I want on my plate.*

CHAPTER 6
**1486 A.D., Easter Ross on the
Tarbat Peninsula of
Northern Scotland
Thursday, August 23
Three Hours After Sunset**

Eighteen sets of leather-shod feet trekked onto the shore. Fourteen men remained in each of the three boats that had transported them.

The cloud cover was good for such an important raid.

It had only been a matter of weeks since the discovery of the legendary Key of Bridei's location in Ireland. But for the key to ever be worth stealing from another country, Clan MacKay had to first steal the standing stone that the key would fit into … from their own people.

But not from their own blood.

Known simply as the 'Key Stone,' it was of such importance that these eighteen souls would risk their lives—give them, if need be—to retrieve it. If things should begin to go awry, the remaining forty-two men would rush into the village to their aid against the damnable Clan Ross.

Clan Ross was as Scottish as they came. They still sang songs of the defeat of the ancient Picti people and how they had played such an important role in that carnage. Clan MacKay, on the other hand, could trace its lineage back to the Picts. The MacKays were considered one of the "mongrel" clans, being Scottish only through having been conquered. They had no hold on nobility, and none among them would ever hold a title. That was fine by them, though, as they wanted no part of Scotland, England, Wales, or of Ireland, for that matter.

They considered themselves a people without a nation. But they hoped, now, to be able to rediscover their heritage. Mostly legend and myth, the stories told around their fires about the Picts, also known as the *Cruithni* in the Gaelic tongue, were still rich and caught the imagination.

The *Legend of the Key of Bridei* had been passed down from generation to generation for nearly 600 years. The tale of Drosten the Great could, even now, be told with great attention to detail by many of their children.

The account traced the heroic acts of Drosten, who saved the identity of the Picti people. By some accounts, they had, at that time, been called Pexa. No one knew for sure how accurate that was, though.

What they were sure of was that they once wielded glory and power. They had been a blessed people. Some stories even went so far as to call the Picts enchanted and maybe even related to the "faery folk."

This night, for these men, if they were successful, would be sung about for a thousand years. Soon, the name of Aonghus Roy MacKay would be synonymous with that of Drosten the Great!

Aonghus crept forward on hands and knees over broken shells, pebbles, and rocks. They still had to traverse from where they landed, into the village of Portmahomack, where the stone was being kept. It was no great distance, and the ground was flat. It should take just a few minutes, while hunkered down, to reach the outlying homes.

There should be no reason for anyone to be about within the village. By their reckoning, they should pretty much be able to walk in and take the stone.

The lone problem would be the size and weight of it. And,

from what they had been told, it stood upright in the ground as the centerpiece to the church's graveyard. There would be extra effort required to extract it from the ground.

I'll wager that they look upon it as the grave marker of the Picti people, thought Aonghus. *No matter. That will change tonight.*

Five days prior, three boats ferrying twenty men each had set out northward on the 130-mile excursion via the River Naver, which had first taken them into the open waters of Torrisdail Firth, past Strathy Point, and east through Pentland Firth.

From there, they sailed south, past the bay of the St. Clair nobles and then southwest to the Tarbat Peninsula, finally landing near the village of Portmahomack.

It had not been an altogether difficult journey. Truth be told, it would be the journey home that was truly going to tax their strength.

Within an hour of arriving at Portmahomack, if all went well, they would repeat the same journey in the opposite direction, putting all their effort into distancing themselves from any possible pursuers. The thought of raiding the much-hated Ross clan had inspired many of the MacKays back home in Strathnaver to volunteer for this raiding party, and as a result, they were able to choose men of strength, courage, and endurance for the grueling round-trip voyage.

They had rowed passed Portmahomack to begin their approach to the village from the south. The landing had been easier and quieter due to a small stretch of sandy beach on the western shore of the Tarbat Peninsula. The remaining MacKays in the boats would guide the craft silently to the north and wait for the raiding party to reach them there. The shore above the village would be rocky, and certainly more treacherous to navigate by foot, but if trouble befell the raiding party, launching from the north would keep them from having to pass the village, while in harm's way of arrows and spears, to head back home.

Should the moon break through, all were prepared. They wore blackened metal skull caps so that they would not reflect any light. They wore no leg protection, save black hose, to, again, darken their appearance. Under dark-dyed quilted jackets, they wore light chain mail, as fast movement would be essential. All wore their clan badge—a sprig of great bulrush—pinned to their left shoulders, an extra level of identification if things should come to a head in battle.

Nearly all of the men carried *claymores*. The sword could unleash hellish damage to an enemy. Nearly four feet long and double-bladed, it was the mainstay of any fighter's arsenal. Two of the men, though, carried war hammers instead, handy for striking an opponent and rendering him senseless, then allowing for a more powerful follow-up blow. The spiked side of the weapon could penetrate armor and even tear apart a shield. All carried *dirks* fastened to their belts, daggers of about twelve inches in length and sharpened on one side.

Coming up off the beach, they entered the field south of the village. They all kept low profiles as they went a few hundred feet inland before heading north. When they had come within two hundred feet of the village, they encountered a low stone wall. This was good. It gave them a few minutes to reconnoiter from a short distance. All was as they had hoped. As far as the Rosses were concerned, it was just another calm summer night.

The men separated into two groups of nine, one taking a wide inland route around the village, the other, led by Aonghus, skirted the village itself. Quietly, they approached homes and other buildings, using them for cover as they listened for movement or conversation within. Thankfully, all was quiet.

Aonghus was nearly beside himself with excitement. Never, in subsequent raids, had any raiding party gotten this far into Ross Clan territory without being found out. His heart beat with anticipation. Their goal, the churchyard and cemetery, was within sight.

About a third of the way into the village, and toward the back, was the Tarbat Church. Around it was the graveyard in which their precious Key Stone stood waiting, beckoning to be rescued into the hands of the Picti people once again.

The church and graveyard were also surrounded by a stone wall. Both parties met up again at the church grounds, and carefully, all eighteen men climbed over, being careful not to allow the metal of their *claymores* or *dirks* to make contact with the stonework.

Once inside the graveyard, they searched for their sacred stone. It did not take long to find it. It was tall, wide, and flat. One side, like any number of Pictish standing stones, was ornamentally covered with engravings. The opposite side was engraved, as well, but the bare circle at its center was what made the Key Stone stand out. In the middle of the circle was a hole about two inches wide. Upon its recognition, several of the men patted each other on the backs and shoulders, large grins appearing on their faces.

But it was too early to celebrate in full. They still had to wrest this large object out of the ground. To that end, the two men who had brought the battle hammers began hacking at the ground around the stone with the pick ends of the heavy weapons, careful not to come too close to the stone. After a few minutes of loosening the ground, they moved away and four other men moved in to start scooping away large amounts of grass and dirt.

The work went smoothly, and after they had gotten a couple of feet of dirt removed, the men began to shove the stone backward and forward, breaking the earth's grip.

Then it was done. With the stone having been lowered flat to the ground, ten of the men lifted it into the air like a stretcher. Now was the time of their greatest risk.

The pace at which they moved north around the east side of the village was quick and easy. The only delays were due to two low walls that had to be crossed. Those walls now behind them, they believed they had passed their final obstacle.

They were wrong. Dead wrong.

One of the homes, one of the very last that they had to pass before meeting their boats at the shore, had a wood-post animal pen attached to it. And in the pen, nine hunting dogs. It might have been a muffled cough or the snap of a twig, but whatever caught the ear of the first hound, triggered an event that would be remembered throughout the ages as the *Battle of Tarbat.*[7]

The violent eruption of barking in the dead of night startled the raiders. As a result, the men began to run without regard for stealth. A Ross clansman, out of his home to relieve himself, found that he could see the party at a distance heading through a vegetable garden. In no time, he voiced an alarm that roused the households nearest him. He then began to run south into the village, raising his clarion cry to new levels.

Men began pouring out of their homes, *claymores* in hand. The MacKays stopped their forward progress as they were about to be cut off from the beach. They turned about, thinking to run from the Rosses, but were unsure where to go for cover. One of the men purposely let go his grip on the Key Stone, followed by another who couldn't maintain his. The extra weight in the hands of the remaining eight men caused them all to falter. The stone was put to the ground.

Aonghus, knowing that any attempt to reclaim the stone was going to have to come from the use of the sword, drew his. He turned to face the oncoming group of some fifteen Rosses who were already armed for conflict. The other seventeen men in his party did the same. They still had a chance.

The call of alarm in the village had another effect that was unexpected by the Rosses giving chase. Forty-two men began to disembark from three boats and rush the shore.

At first, the battle that ensued favored the MacKays. But within five minutes, the sixty MacKays were met by a force of men twice that of their own. Then it was three times the size. The men from the boats were being hacked down, while the Clan Ross chief, Alistair Ross, along with a band of forty men, chased Aonghus MacKay and his raiding party back to the Tarbat churchyard.

Having made it into the church, Aonghus and his men fortified the doors against Ross's men in an attempt to organize for a counterattack. None of the eighteen had died yet, but they saw the writing on the wall.

---

[7] Turn to Appendix to read the few known historical details of the Battle of Tarbat.

As Aonghus was evaluating their situation, he heard through one of the windows a command that sent a cold chill down his spine.

It was Alistair Ross, and he had just uttered two words that sealed their fate.

"Torch it!"

THREE DAYS AFTER having put all of the remaining MacKay bodies into a pit and lighting them afire, Alistair Ross ordered the Key Stone to be broken into pieces. He had decided against pulverizing it to dust. Instead, the nine pieces of the stone would be used as a tease.

A lone MacKay clansman, who was spared the sword and fire, was released with the knowledge that their precious Key Stone would be used for repair and construction projects throughout the village.

The news delivered back to Clan MacKay in Strathnaver of the death of their chief, as well as the now-permanently ensconced holy relic *throughout* Portmahomack, would serve as a final warning to never set foot in Ross territory again.

CHAPTER 7
Present Day

Roughly twenty-four years had passed since David Mc-Neill, a.k.a. Cowan Cormack, had discovered the first two pieces of the Pictish Key Stone in Northern Scotland. Since then, modern archeology proved to be one of the greatest assets to the Society of Bridei, leading to the discovery of six more of the nine remaining pieces of the stone.

In 1997, two pieces of the Key Stone were found in what turned out to be the collapsed cover of a stone-lined culvert. Two years later, during the excavations of two former buildings—a "kiln barn" and a "corn drier"—four other pieces, all of which *very fortunately* remained as parts of the original masonry, were also discovered.

Thankfully, the locations of the original two pieces that David had discovered in 1987 were still accessible, though one of the pieces—the now-named and famous "Dragon Stone"—having been discovered by an archaeologist in 1995, had been removed in 1997.

The Pictish relic had been taken from the crypt below the Tarbat Old Parish Church and moved upstairs to be a display piece, under lock and key, in the re-named Tarbat Discovery Centre.

The Society of Bridei's other major asset had been the information superhighway. The discoveries of the archaeologists had been turned into news stories and peer-reviewed research articles that eventually made their way to the Internet, then finally to the computer screens of both Brendan and David. The web also aided in locating the prized Key of Bridei, protected in the archives of a college library in Ireland.

The ease of locating all of the artifacts online had been one thing; the challenge of getting the Key of Bridei and all of the pieces of the Pictish Key Stone back to America had been another thing altogether.

But as it is said, "Where there is a will, there is a way."

It soon happened that newspapers in Scotland and Ireland reported the following criminal activities within their borders:

PICTI RAID IN PORTMAHOMACK

PORTMAHOMACK—Many in the region of Easter Ross, in the northernmost part of Scotland, were stunned yesterday to learn that under the cloak of darkness the previous night, several pieces of historical Pictish history had been stolen from the Village of Portmahomack on the Tarbat Peninsula.

At present, no one knows how the "raid" was pulled off, only that important pieces of the nation's history are feared to be forever lost.

Angus Mackay, Director of the Tarbat Discovery Centre, was said to be "overwhelmed with emotion" as he, the primary caretaker of the artifacts within the centre itself, felt solely responsible. "It's my centre. I was tasked with the protection of the items in this facility. There was little I could do about the pieces at the excavation sites, but this, here, was mine to protect."

When Mackay was asked about the significance of the pieces, he said that it appeared that all of the pieces used to be part of one whole, a Pictish standing stone that had been broken apart sometime in the Fifteenth Century. The standing stone's importance is yet to be confirmed, but some residents of the area believe that it was somehow related to the mythological Pictish stone known as the Key of Bridei.

One source close to the director of the Tarbat Discovery Centre stated that Angus Mackay felt as though he had "let his people down."

Local authorities have begun to investigate at multiple sites where the pieces were discovered missing, but we are told that, so far, there are few clues that have been discovered regarding the perpetrators of this crime.

KELLS TREASURE STOLEN FROM TRINITY COLLEGE

DUBLIN—Rest assured, it is not what you might first suspect. In fact, unless you are familiar with ancient Pictish lore and archaeological finds, you may have never even heard of it. A stone claimed by some historians to be the legendary Key of Bridei was stolen from the Conservation Department located at Trinity College Library.

The circular stone that may have had both secular and religious significance, based on the Pictish symbols and Latin words inscribed upon it, had been transported to the safety of Trinity College alongside one of Ireland's greatest treasures, the Book of Kells, in 1661. Since that time, it has only been put on display for special exhibitions in the Long Room of Trinity College Library. Most recently, it was displayed in 2008, as part of an exhibit entitled "Escape from Iona," but the object was greatly overshadowed by the four bound volumes of the Book of Kells, which is believed to have also traveled from Iona to the Abbey at Kells.

Ms. Sally Megaw, keeper of the Preservation and Conservation Department for the library, said, "Whoever perpetrated this unseemly act knew what he or she was doing. It happened when our facilities were at their most vulnerable. We never announce to the general public when we will be moving pieces around for special attention or for transportation to another location. It would seem, though, that someone with that knowledge was able to smuggle the Key of Bridei out of our facilities when we were making preparations to lend a considerable collection of manuscripts to another library in the United States."

Asked about the value of the Key, Ms. Megaw stated that the object had never been assessed a monetary value, but that it was considered priceless, as it is one of only a few pieces of Pictish history resident in Ireland.

Investigators at the scene were confident they would find the individuals involved and bring them to justice. Asked about clues, we were told that they were not at liberty to disclose any information.

TUESDAY, MAY 24—11:45 P.M.

THE KEY OF BRIDEI was now in the U.S. and en route to Pittston, Ohio, along with all but one of the pieces of the Key Stone. Brendan, David, and Stephanie finally felt as though they had everything required to conduct the high ceremony that would officially usher in the "New Beginning of the *Olde Faithe*"—the long-awaited *Redeeming Age*.

But even as the physical preparations were being made, they knew that individual spiritual preparations must take place, as well. Invitations must be sent out—invocations to their gods. If their plans were to succeed, they would need the ancient deities to aid them and bless their mission.

Each with his and her own oak staff, Brendan, David, and Stephanie walked out of the farmhouse and went to meet the other ten members of the Society's Home Coven at the top of a man-made mound at the center of the farm property.

The evening was cool, in the mid-sixties and dropping.

Through scattered clouds, a little more than a half-moon lit the night sky. Cricket song was loud on the evening air.

Nearing the mound from the west the three were acknowledged by the other members of the coven; five women and five men, all barefoot and clothed to match their leaders in knee-length, white-linen tunics cinched at the waists by dyed-blue linen belts.

Brendon, David, and Stephanie stopped before reaching the upward slope of the mound. It was round, approximately five feet high, and had a diameter of about fifteen feet. Though it was man-made—created by Brendan a decade and a half before—it was covered with grass and looked almost natural to the surrounding landscape.

"Welcome, brothers and sisters of the *Olde Faithe*," began Brendan, a smile on his face. "Tonight, we seek the favor of two of our gods; the Hag, Cailleach, who loves the darkness and is a great worker of spells, and that of Sluag, who is the Host of the Unforgiven Dead. After summoning the Hag and the Host, we will seek protection as we go forward in our mission to return the religion of the Picts to its rightful place amongst the world's religions; a position of power and of dominance."

Brendan extended his arms outward to his sides, palms facing the mound, oak staff in his right hand. The twelve men and women approached and formed a straight line to either side of him, facing the mound toward the East. It was time for the ceremony to begin.

Stephanie, to the left of Brendan, knelt to the ground and laid down her staff, pointing it east. Standing again, she untied her belt, allowing the sides of her tunic to fall open. Lifting the shoulders of the garment above her head, she allowed it to fall to her left side and to the ground. The other five women, seeing this, followed suit, disrobing as moonlight tickled the backs of their bodies. Kneeling once more, the women again took up their staffs.

Brendan kept his face relaxed, though he felt the muscles in his back tense. He had not foreseen this and was slightly peeved by the introduction of this potential visual distraction. One thing became obvious by the act, though, and even produced some measure of satisfaction; the women were in unity. Not one among them had hesitated. They followed their priest ess. And the men, to their credit, though most certainly tempted, kept their eyes eastward.

Brendan continued. "Tonight, upon this consecrated ground we will bring ourselves into submission to the powers of the gods and of the earth. Take time, now, to *center* yourselves."

Each of the thirteen spread their feet shoulder-width apart. Placing the bottoms of their staffs on the ground in front of them, they used the long pieces of wood to create triangles coinciding with the positions of their feet. They then placed their hands, one over the other, atop the staffs and rested their foreheads upon their hands.

Closing their eyes, they began to breathe deeply, feeling the energies of the earth eventually draw up into their feet and legs. Though thousands of miles away from their Pictish homeland, they sought to lure within themselves the power of their ancient heritage as the old Earth saw fit to direct and bless.

As each of the men and women reached a centered state, he raised his head. Brendan was patient as he waited for the last of the coven to finish. There was no rush, and these were good people, good students. Good Picti. He trusted their sincerity and commitment to this great cause.

When the last of the thirteen raised her head, Brendan gave her a nod. He then looked down the line to his left and caught the eye of Brook Shaw, whose pseudonym had become Gráinne Lugos, which meant "she who inspires terror" and was also the name of a Celtic sun god.

Brook gave a slight nod of acknowledgment and began to walk a circuit, a *deiseil* movement—clockwise—around the mound. They all followed and walked at a relaxed pace, holding their staffs before them in both hands, the tops of the staffs held above their heads. They made three circuits around the mound, then the line split in half and circled the mound to the east from both sides. They formed another straight line, backs to the mound, and remained facing east.

Keeping their staffs in both hands and planting them upon the ground, they once again positioned their feet in centering positions. Now they waited upon Brendan and Stephanie to take the lead.

In completing these first ceremonial rites, they had shown their respect to the gods, who would now be open to hearing from any among the coven, should they be summoned.[8]

STEPHANIE BACKED OUT of the line and turned around. She walked to the top of the mound, positioned herself in the middle, and lay down flat on her back on the cool grass, hands at her sides. The moon's glow played on her pale skin, creating an otherworldly shimmer.

She tried to relax her breathing, but she was nervous. She didn't know what to expect from this point forward in the ceremony. She felt led to this station on the mound and somehow knew that another piece of the puzzle regarding her life's purpose was about to be put on full display. She hoped she wouldn't disappoint Brendan.

She closed her eyes and heard the twelve others begin to walk around the mound, taking positions to surround her. Brendan Cadeyrn, Stephanie's high priest, whose name was interpreted as "Prince of War" or "Battle King," began to speak.

"Upon this mound rests a holy servant of the gods of the Picti people. Aileen Lóegaire, do you take upon yourself—and

---

[8] Turn to Appendix to read about the *true* history of these ceremonies.

into yourself—that which the gods wish to bestow?"

Stephanie's breathing quickened, and she struggled to maintain composure as she responded in a firm voice, "May the will of the gods be enacted upon and within me."

"May it be done."

The eleven others repeated the words of agreement and unity. "May it be done."

"May it be done," Brendan repeated once more. He extended his oak staff over Stephanie's naked form, and as he called upon the gods, the others reached forth with their staffs, as well.

"Proud and powerful Cailleach, hag and goddess of our people, hear my voice! This night we call upon you to direct your *maucht*—your power—this way. For a brief moment, turn your eyes from our ancient home and direct them toward us that we may honor you and hear from you. Great and powerful Sluag, god and Host of the Unforgiven Dead, turn your ears this way and grant us our desires. May it be done!"

"May it be done!"

Stephanie whispered the words with no small amount of trepidation. "May it be done." It was one thing to do spellcasting, it was another thing altogether to call upon the ancient gods of the most powerful religion that had ever existed and to offer them full reign within her body.

She could hear her pulse as blood coursed through her carotid artery. Having finally given up trying to control her breathing, she was getting lightheaded and very close to hyperventilation. She felt something cool come down upon her chest. It was the head of Brendan's staff.

For a moment, the coolness lingered, then she felt an intense current coursing through her body. Her back arched off the grass. The shock caused her to gasp, and as she inhaled she felt something—some *thing*—enter through her mouth and nose. Her eyes sprang open with fear. A cry tried to force its way past her throat, but she couldn't make a sound. Her eyes darted left and right, trying to find a rescuing presence, but all that she saw was Brendan's staff as it was pulled away from her.

Then everything went dark.

BRENDAN LOOKED AT HIS Aileen with amazement and a sense of satisfaction that the gods had answered so quickly. While he saw her nearly panic upon the mound, he knew that this was the fulfillment of her purpose, so he didn't intervene. These fortunate twelve sets of eyes would now witness the beginning of the *Redeeming Age!*

Her eyes opened and began darting back and forth as his staff rested upon her sternum. Feeling inclined to back away and rejoin the circle with his brothers and sisters, he pulled his staff from Aileen's body. He watched in amazement as her eyes rolled back into her head.

Her breathing slowed and became deep and rhythmic. Her hands came up from her sides and settled upon her bare breasts. She furrowed her brow and seemed puzzled. It was as if she didn't recognize the touch of her own body. Her head turned to the right, and with white eyes that seemed to burn into Brendan, she spoke, *"Gothnik thenum porlah hùme. Porateth inum murah em. Porateth inum murah em! Miriah oneth herùm sù. Eth pelorum mishteth hie!"*

The hag! Her voice was as menacing as it was old and dry. Brendan had never heard a voice that sounded so … so *dead.* For a moment, it shook his resolve. He heard others around the mound gasp. A few of the women and maybe a man or two took slight steps backward.

Brendan tried to refocus. She had spoken. But what had she said?

Aileen's right hand came off her breast and extended toward Brendan. With her index finger, she directed him to come toward her. He forsook his desire to abscond and instead advanced, climbing the slope and kneeling beside her. His tunic touched her hand.

With unexpected speed and ferocity, her hand rushed up and grabbed the garment at his chest, and pulled him forward toward her face. Brendan's first instinct was to pull free and get as far away as possible, but in the attempt to separate himself from her grasp, he found he lacked the needed strength.

Aileen's face contorted into a twisted smile, and she forced out a dry laugh. The stench that ushered forth from her mouth forced Brendan to start turning his face to gag. But he wasn't permitted that liberty. The hag, Cailleach, launched her hand from his chest to his face and grabbed his open jaw. Three fingers extended deep into his mouth, her thumb clamped under his chin. She drew him closer.

She repeated herself, punctuating each syllable so as to make her point clear. *"Gothnik thenum porlah hùme. Porateth inum murah em. Porateth inum murah em. Miriah oneth herùm sù. Eth pelorum mishteth hie."*

Brendan held his breath as long as he could, considering his heart rate had spiked to three times normal. When he could no longer hold it he exhaled and inhaled quickly to get it over with. The stink was worse this time, and he gagged again. This time, he could not retain control of his peristaltic muscles, and he vomited onto the old hag—onto Aileen. She again laughed as the contents of his stomach streamed down her arm.

What does she want? He wanted to bite down on the fingers in his mouth, but he couldn't—he wouldn't. He tried to think of another means of extracting himself from the situation when the woman spoke again ... in English.

"Few survive the call you have made. You ask for a lot. You ask for a *lot!* But granted, it is. *If* you can divine the stone." She loosed his mouth and he immediately pulled back, losing his balance and cascading down the slope.

As Brendan collected himself, grabbed his staff, and pulled himself back to his feet, he watched as Aileen began to writhe and whimper. She struggled with what was in her. Was she conscious at all of what was happening? Was she hearing or understanding the words coming out of her?

A sound came out of Aileen that horrified the twelve still surrounding her. At first, it was a sound resembling that of retching—dry heaves. Then, as if broken glass tied to the end of a cord were being pulled from deep within her body, a horrifying shriek of pain emanated from within.

Everyone backed away, except for Brendan. He forced

himself to step toward her. The scream ended suddenly, with Aileen bolting upright and bringing her hands to her throat.

Fear laced her features, and she looked around quickly, eyes back to normal. Finding Brendan, she tried to speak, but wincing in pain, she stopped short of forming a complete word. Brendan rushed up onto the mound and took Aileen into his arms.

Pulling his woman close, he rocked her gently and whispered into her ear, "It's okay. It's okay. It's over. You did fine, Aileen. You did it."

That night, over the Village of Pittston, a demon took position; a *Principality*—a prince of evil. A being that thirteen clueless humans naïvely believed was a god named Cailleach the Hag.

CHAPTER 8
Friday, June 3—11:18 a.m.

Stephanie was giddy with excitement. This evening it would finally happen. The Key Stone would be assembled—well, at least eight pieces of it—for the first time in over six hundred years. In a couple of days, the Key of Bridei would be reunited with the stone for the first time in over a millennium! What would happen? What answers would be found out?

Brendan had in his possession photos of all of the known standing stones throughout Scotland that had Pictish writing etched into them. Not only would tonight mark the beginning of the discovery of the *true* power of their religion, but Brendan and Stephanie would step firmly into their roles as high priest and priestess.

The field surrounding the ceremonial mound was full of people milling about in street clothes. Two hundred and sixty-seven people had made it to the Pittston farm from five different countries, most coming from the British Isles, and Brendan was pleased. In fact, he was obviously in his element, shaking hands, chatting, and just milling about, completely relaxed.

The occasion was festive. Fire pits were erected in scattered areas of the field where grill masters prepared fare for the attendees. A special ale was created by a local microbrewery that was as close to historical honey mead as Brendan could imagine. Anticipation was in the air as people laughed, ate, and listened to the sounds of music being piped through speakers situated around the field.

Stephanie walked over to an area just east of the mound that had been cleared of grass and made perfectly flat. A few of the new Picti members were standing and looking at the space, arms folded.

"Hello," said Stephanie as she approached the two men and a woman, whom she had yet to formally meet.

"Hello, Aileen!" said the woman, quick to respond.

The two men slightly bowed their heads in acknowledgment.

Stephanie allowed for the British woman's excitement to trump the respect that was due as their high priestess.

"How are the three of you enjoying your time here so far?"

"Ve are enjoying ourselves greatly, mein priestess," said the oldest of the three, his German accent prevalent. "Ve vere just vondering about dis ... umm ... Vhat's de vord? ... emptiness?"

Stephanie smiled with a nod. "Yes. This space is going to play a very special part in the upcoming ceremonies."
She stopped, not wanting to disclose anything further.

It seemed the English woman was about to ask for more details before catching herself. "We are looking forward to seeing what is to take place here, my priestess."

Another smile, reflecting some appreciation for the acknowledgment of her title, and Stephanie resumed her walk through the throng of Picti believers.

She thought about that barren area of dirt. Brendan had come up with an idea of pure genius that pleased David to no end; they would use the original eight pieces of the ancient Key Stone to create a full-size, one-piece replica of the standing stone. It would look and function very much as it had a thousand years ago.

That I get to be a part of it! What a time to be alive!

For the remainder of the afternoon, she would enjoy

meeting and getting to know their guests, interesting people of such varied backgrounds. It was hard to believe that *all* of them had Pictish blood in their veins. The work that David and Brendan had completed over the years was just astounding. More incredible, yet, was that these people had made it their unified life goal to proselytize the faith. Three hundred-plus people were hardly a blip on the radar when it came to having a religion large enough to be recognized by the rest of the world, but it was a good start.

The *Olde Faithe* would not be presented to just anyone, of course, but as the tracking of bloodlines revealed more and more people who had even the smallest amount of Picti blood, the religion would be introduced. There would be no coercion. It made no sense to have anyone in the faith who didn't have a sincere heart. What did make sense, though, was raising one's own children up in the faith.

These modern-day Picti would be encouraged to make babies. The Islamists of the world had figured out a way to spread their religion with very little bloodshed by simply moving into areas where their beliefs were not yet present and begin procreating in large numbers. Look at Detroit! The Picti would do the same.

Stephanie's stomach began to growl. The scent of sweet meats in the air was more than she could endure. Stepping up to one of the fire pits, Stephanie picked up a paper plate and piled some mutton onto a bun. A little BBQ sauce over the top made her mouth begin to water. Walking over to another of the pits, she took an ear of roasted corn and dipped into a pot of melted organic butter, then salted it.

She sighed. *This is going to be so good!*

She found an open spot in the freshly mowed grass and sat down. A hand holding a clear plastic cup of lemonade reached from over her right shoulder. The hand was attached to a delicate, light-skinned arm that belonged to Donna McNeill, David's twin sister.

Stephanie smiled as she looked up and accepted the cup. She hadn't expected to see Donna here.

"Donna, what a pleasant surprise."

"Hello, Stephanie. May I join you?"

"Of course. Please sit."

Donna took a seat opposite Stephanie, her own cup of lemonade in hand.

"Are you not eating?" asked Stephanie.

"I've just finished, but please don't let me stop you from enjoying your food."

"I've got to admit that I didn't plan on seeing you here today."

"David made another plea for me to attend and meet the people who were coming. I think this was a last-ditch effort to convert me." She laughed easily.

"Not happening, huh?"

Donna shook her head. "I find it all very interesting, to be sure. But truth be told, I've got too many other pursuits right now. I will admit, though, these people sure do know how to throw a party!"

Stephanie smiled as she took a bite of her sandwich. But the levity of Donna's quip fell short of the mark.

This woman should not be here. David has taken too large a risk.

Donna continued. "David said that since I hadn't made your beliefs mine, I could only stay for the festivities leading up to the inaugural ceremonies tonight."

"How do you feel about that?" queried Stephanie, hoping for some more insight into the woman's thoughts.

Smiling, Donna replied, "Oh, I don't really mind too much. Of course, I'd love to see the intricacies of your ceremonies, but I understand. I'm an outsider."

"Your brother must hold you in high standing to extend an offer of such high regard."

"David and I have always been close, and we share many of the same interests. I'm sure it has a lot to do with us sharing a womb."

Stephanie remembered a discussion between David and Brendan a couple of years back about the potential of even more giftedness resulting from the McNeills being twins. It was speculative, of course, but there was a lot of evidence in the scientific community that seemed to indicate that twins had more in common than a birth date to make them special.

"Well, I'm sure that David will be disappointed that you won't be joining us. We all are, dear."

Donna looked at her watch. "I only had a brief period to come by today. I've got a client appointment at one o'clock that I must not be late getting to." Donna got up and looked down at Stephanie. "It was good seeing you again, Stephanie."

"The pleasure was all mine," *heretic.* "I hope you have a successful day."

"I hope the same for you," said Donna before turning and walking away.

David... Stephanie produced a deep sigh. *David, this had better not have turned out to be a mistake.*

5:14 P.M.

BRENT LOOKED AT HIS watch, very happy to have his regular shift back, though his day had been a couple of hours longer than normal. He pulled his patrol car into the driveway of his suburban home. At times, he was glad to have the vehicle to take home at the end of his shifts; it allowed him to keep the mileage off his own, though the 3.7 miles to the police station was hardly a concern. If there was a downside to not driving his own car to work, it was the visibility of having the neighborhood's lone police vehicle parked in the driveway, which, in turn, led to knocks at his door at inopportune times.

Just the previous week he had answered the door to find two ten-year-old boys whose faces were covered with red marks, wearing torn shirts, and covered with dirt from head to toe. He'd come to find out that the boys, after battling it out for several minutes on a ball field at a nearby park, came to the conclusion that they would have the police officer who lived in the neighborhood settle things for them.

Apparently, there was the lofty matter of a missing MP3 player. One had accused the other of stealing it sometime during the course of the day while they played throughout the subdivision. The accuser wanted the thief put in handcuffs and carted off to jail.

Brent had done his best to maintain a straight face while listening to the facts and asking the 'hard questions.'

During the investigation, Brent's probing inquiries led the two to discuss their whereabouts during the course of the day. Most interesting to Brent was the description of their time at a nearby creek.

The two boys had gone wading and searching for crayfish. When Brent asked about it, the recollection led to the accuser going wide-eyed with the realization that he had taken it out of his shirt pocket and put it next to a tree on the bank of the creek to keep it from getting wet.

As the accuser hurried off to reclaim his lost goods, Brent called him back, reminding him that a false accusation is a very serious offense and that he needed to immediately ask his friend for his forgiveness in the matter. Brent then encouraged them to shake hands to firm things up. The next moment, the boys were best friends again.

Of course, not all of the knocks on the door were so easy to fix, but he and Tara accepted it as part of the job. Thankfully, the after-hours interruptions were very infrequent.

Brent gathered his gear and got out of the car. He could hear kids playing in the backyard. Opening the door to the house, he was immediately tantalized by the delicious scent of spaghetti sauce—homemade! *Oh, yes! That's what I'm talking about!*

Brent let out a call. "I'm home!"

One of these days, Tara is going to come out to greet me at the door in a casual dress, an apron, a pair of pumps, and with a perfectly made-up pair of lips and eyes, just like June Clever from that old black-and-white TV show. He laughed at the thought. *Yeah right.*

She did come out of the kitchen, though, and met him in the living room. She wore a pair of pink sweatpants and a T-shirt from their trip to Disney the previous year. But Minnie Mouse's smiling face was the only one to greet him this day.

Tara looked defeated.

Without a word, he put his gear bag on the floor and opened his arms for her to enter. She walked into his grasp willingly and pressed her head against his chest. Brent felt her strong arms wrap around his torso while she let out a deep sigh.

Brent's right hand found its way up to the soft, strawberry-blonde hair that he still loved to smell and play with, and he began to knead the back of her neck. For a few moments, neither of them spoke until she decided to break the silence.

"Thank you for coming home to me."

"Bad day?"

"No," she said with a pouty expression.

"But it looks like…"

"Shush. Just hold me and love me, and everything bad about my day will go away."

And that's what Brent did. He held his wife in the middle of their living room and didn't say another word about it.

After what seemed like only a few wonderful moments, Tara raised her head and looked Brent in the eyes. She smiled and said, "I sure hope you're hungry. Because when I'm having a day I'd like to forget…"

Brent finished the sentence with a smile, "… you start cooking everything."

She giggled. "You got it. Tonight, it's a combination of spaghetti and meatballs and pork chops."

"Well, there's a combination we've never had before."

Brent loved his life.

CHAPTER 9
Friday, June 3—6:00 p.m.

So many differences. So many reasons in the minds of these people for driving hundreds, or flying thousands, of miles to this village called Pittston, to attend a gathering that few fully understood. Brendan, David, and Stephanie knew that the lifestyles of those gathered were not the only things that varied in great degree, but also the mindsets. The food, fun, and frolic of the day had been an opportunity for the thirteen men and women of the Home Coven to mingle with and get to know these individuals, who they were, their beliefs, and why they had ultimately decided to become a part of this reestablished culture group.

As predicted, the findings proved to be important.

While the hundreds of Picti had been given leave to enjoy the farmland or to head out into the Pittston community, the Home Coven, along with thirty-five other men and women from the domestic and international covens, had gathered in the farmhouse, away from the rest of the *hopefully* faithful.

They managed to squeeze into the large living room area of the farmhouse. The furniture and folding chairs were filled, with some sitting on the floor and others sitting on the stairs leading down from the second story.

The festive mood was gone. All of those gathered knew that this discussion would set the tone for the remainder of the gathering. And the first thing that needed to be discussed was the mindsets—the paradigms—of many of the attendees.

"There are still many of these people who think this is just a fun getaway; an opportunity to visit the U.S. for several days," said Jim Connor, the Pittston police chief, a.k.a. Uilliam Agar—his adopted Pictish name. "I don't know if they have the mental discipline to accept some of the *'events'* planned over the course of the next several days."

Brendan didn't comment. He just raised his eyebrows and scanned the eyes of the leaders of the covens. He saw a few heads nodding.

"Aye. I've observed the same." This came from one of the Scottish priests, Hugh MacEarnan, sitting on the stairs. "Forgive me for saying so, Brendan, but many of them are from the U.S. and Canadian covens. That's not to say that there aren't some from the homeland, but for the most part, the Scottish Picti know more about the history of our people and the brutality that tried to end our bloodlines."

One of the Canadians spoke up. "If you're claiming that we're not taking our parts seriously in all of this—"

And so began several minutes of clamoring. Brendan just allowed the discussion to take flight, measuring his leaders. There was a lot of self-importance in this group; pride that could cause a lot of division if left unchecked. Unity was essential. Though the contention wasn't entirely unexpected, it was still disappointing.

Brendan finally interrupted and asked them pointedly, "What is more important to all of you, being right or being unified? If any among you are here for a power grab because you think you've got the most important covens or because you thought this would be a fun way to spend your summer vacations, I ask you to immediately excuse yourselves from these proceedings." Again, he looked around the room. All became quiet.

Brendan got up from his chair and knelt on the floor in front of it. His eyes became devices of pleading. "My heart aches. I've not done all of this work to bring us together just so that we can have something akin to another Masonic organization or some new wave of contemporary witchcraft.

"For hundreds of years, my family has passed down secrets—some of them, probably, with only a wisp of truth in them—that revealed that we had once been much more than we are now. Our people had once been the world's royalty, the single most important culture on the planet. We were more than warriors, more than a unified society. We were the *elite!*

"We held secrets that no one else in the world could understand. Some say that we were—that we *are*—related to the *Faery Folk* of legend. These people weren't miniature people like mythical leprechauns or little winged creatures who sprinkled pixie dust. The *Faery Folk* were long believed to be those fortunate few who had escaped the destruction of ancient Atlantis. They were tall, beautiful, powerful people. Think of it, my friends! While we are certainly Picti, we may also be the only blood remaining of an even more ancient and powerful culture!

"Please, let us set aside pride. Let us come together so that we can thrive as a people once again. As for me, I am certainly not the greatest among you…" Brendan paused with a sigh. "*But* I am fully dedicated with my heart, spirit, soul, and body to the resurrection of what I hold most dear, the faith of my forefathers.

"One day, I shall pass from this earth and enter the blessed realm of *Tír na nÓg*.[9] When I do, this mantle of leadership will fall to another. That person's heart must be as faithful to the wellness of our people as is mine. Let this *never* be about power. Let this *never* be about popularity. Let this only *ever* be about whom we once were as a people and whom we will become once again."

Stephanie, who had been seated next to him, now joined her leader and lover on the floor. She rested her right hand upon

---

[9] Tír na nÓg is the most popular of the Otherworlds of Celtic mythology. Its literal interpretation is "The Land of the Young."

Brendan's left shoulder. All those gathered watched as tears streamed down Brendan's face, his eyes moving from person to person in the room.

One of the men toward the back of the living room left his seat, as well, and fell to one knee. With a voice of true humility, he spoke, "I bow my heart and my will to you, my priest. I will give my all, and dedicate my life, to the *Redeeming Age* of our people and our religion."

One after another, each of the priests and priestesses went to one knee and gave their allegiances to Brendan and the *Olde Faithe*.

None of it had been planned; none of it scripted. But it was surely going to be the event that would shape them forever.

They had just become a unified people.

The Picti of legend were coming back to life.

9:00 P.M.

WITH THE DAYTIME festivities behind them, torches had been lit and placed for the evening's ceremonial gathering around the mound. Street clothes had been exchanged for white tunics supplied by Brendan and Stephanie.

The financial contributions of the faithful over the years had been stockpiled for this event and were now being returned in the form of food, ceremonial clothing, and printed materials that needed to be studied when all returned to their distant homes.

Brendan and Stephanie stood atop the mound and looked out over their hundreds of followers. The two of them were satisfied with the decision not to hold the remaining, *darker* ceremonies before the majority of attendees. Instead, the bloodletting of the initiation rites would be performed only before the Home Coven, the thirty-five domestic and international coven leaders, and those special few hand-picked to attend with them.

Tonight would be an evening of light hearts and hope for a magnificent future for their people. Not unlike a motivational rally, the evening's events were crafted to create a unified excitement among the many in attendance and an enthusiasm to push forward for the greater cause.

Stephanie scanned the crowd and then raised her hands into the air. The murmuring of the throng quieted.

"My people," she began, "tonight I have the honor of presenting to you your high priest. For three decades, I have followed him. I have dedicated my life to him and to the cause that he champions. He is more than just a man, though he would never claim to be so.

"He loves all of us with a never-ending love. His hope for us as a people is inspiring, and his love for each of you as individuals is endearing. I give to you now, the High Priest of the Picti Faith, Brendan Cadeyrn!"

The people cheered and clapped. Brendan smiled and began to laugh, looking over at Aileen. After a moment, he lifted his hands, as well, to quiet the crowd.

"I am humbled. Thank you. Know, from my own lips, that I do love you. I love our people, and I am extremely excited about our future."

Stephanie stepped down from the mound to watch Brendan with the others. Brendan began to walk the edge of the mound, the night's stage-in-the-round, to speak with the Picti.

"Tonight, we want to remember and extend a great honor to one of our familial bloodlines." That established, he shouted, "Are there any MacKays in the crowd?"

What sounded like fifteen to twenty individuals sent a cry of affirmation into the air.

"Greetings and welcome, my dear friends! I would like to have all of you gather in front of me at the base of the mound."

Brendan picked up his staff and extended it over the heads of the gathered MacKays. "May the MacKays, from this night forward, always be recognized as the most noble and most honored of the Picti tribes. Forever your names will be remembered for their quest over 600 years ago to revive the memory and religion of the Picti people. Their heroic sacrifice at the Battle of Tarbat, in an attempt to reclaim the great Picti Key Stone, will not be forgotten. May you who are gathered with us tonight *always* bring honor to the name MacKay."

There was an excited murmuring in the crowd as Brendan brought his staff down to his side. "My people, from this day forward, this mound that I stand upon shall be called MacKay Hill as a tribute to those who gave their lives that we may one day again live."

The crowd let up a loud cry. Dozens of people patted the shoulders, heads, and backs of the astounded MacKays who stood before them.

Later that night, it would bring a smile to Brendan's face to hear so many of those gathered claiming to have MacKay blood running through their veins, as well. Maybe they did.

The ceremony transitioned from one of tribute to one of reverence as the eight pieces of the Picti Key Stone were ceremoniously brought forth from the farmhouse. The procession to MacKay Hill included the Home Coven, along with the priests and priestesses of the international covens. Each piece of the Key Stone was carried by four individuals as though it were a miniature casket which lay atop a swath of white linen. They were followed by Uilliam Agar, the Pittston police chief, who carried a chromed shovel.

The crowd parted as Brendan directed everyone's attention to the forty-six men and women who approached, led by David McNeill. Upon reaching the top of the mound, the men and women holding the stones spread out equidistant around the hill and knelt facing the faithful. They rested the stone pieces upright upon the ground. Some of the people gasped in amazement; smiles all around. The atmosphere was electric!

Brendan spoke again. "Most of you know that the search for these eight pieces of the Picti standing stone, called the Key Stone, took years to find and get into the United States. Would you say that the time and effort were well spent?"
A shout of acclamation went up from the crowd.

"Most of you also know that to be complete, the standing stone needs a ninth piece. Many among you have voiced disappointment that it was not found along with the rest. But there was a reason why it was never found; a reason of which not even your dear High Priestess, Aileen Lóegaire, is aware."

He looked down at Aileen, who looked at him with sheer curiosity. He gave her a wink and continued.

"Over three decades ago, I came to this country with a mission. I wanted to see a people group called the Picti reestablished to its rightful position of power and respect. I knew that it was going to take time and money to accomplish. I used my then-limited business knowledge to create some wealth to carry me along, and I began my search for an individual with a special bloodline that I'd traced to this country. The result of that search is your High Priestess. Unbeknownst to Aileen, or anyone else, was that I already owned the first piece of the puzzle that is to be reassembled tonight."

The high priest turned and called for Uilliam to hand him the shovel. Upon receiving it, he moved to the center of the mound and began to dig. After a few minutes of effort, he knelt at the edge of the newly created hole and began to clean away loose dirt. The crowd watched with rapt attention as he, with the help of Uilliam, grasped and finally pulled out a large section of flat stone.

It took the strength of both men, but they managed to lift it out and stand up, holding it at an angle for the people to see. They walked around the top of MacKay Hill, presenting it to the now-cheering crowd.

Brendan looked down to see Stephanie staring up at him, stunned, mouth agape. He grinned. She smiled and mouthed the words, "You have some explaining to do."

After making one full circuit of the mound, the two men set the stone down. Uilliam—Jim Connor—kept it standing upright.

"My dear Aileen says that I have some explaining to do." The people laughed. "That I do, my love. That I do. Now, though, we have a Key Stone to assemble!"

Once again, the crowd cheered their high priest.

Instead of just loosely piecing together the nine sections of the Key Stone on top of the mound, with the mounting circle for the Key of Bridei facing the sky, as was originally intended, they would fully reconstruct the ancient Key Stone. The throng of Picti faithful followed Brendan, Aileen, and Cowan to the flat dirt area that had been prepared a short distance from MacKay Hill.

As the people gathered to watch, all of the coven leaders carefully brought the segments of the standing stone off the mound. They laid them gently onto the dirt surface surrounding a solid-wood frame—a rectangle that measured two feet high by nine feet long by five feet wide.

Within the frame, Brendan and the other men of the Home Coven worked to correctly piece together the nine pieces of the Picti Key Stone, and using sculpting clay, filled in the relatively small gaps and chips that had been created long ago, when the large stone had been maliciously broken apart.

Moist, "green" casting sand was then compressed around and over the stone. This would both protect the back side of the Key Stone that would later be cast and create an exact impression of the front side of the stone that would be filled with plaster.

The process of creating the two full-size, front-and-back plaster replicas of the Key Stone took several painstaking hours and involved some amazing effort and ingenuity. When completed, the two reinforced plaster casts were bolted together back-to-back, creating a replica standing stone that was a little thicker than its ancient predecessor.

When the plaster creation was finally hoisted upright for the first time, a cheer went up from those who had elected to stay to watch the entire process. Brendan smiled and congratulated his co-workers on the masterful piece of work. It was certainly something of which the Picti people should be proud.

Even so, they were not yet finished.

The full plaster replica would now be used to create one more cast, this one made of rebar-reinforced concrete. Upon its completion, the concrete version of the Key Stone would stand erect on the very ground on which it was cast as a permanent monument to the beginning of the *Redeeming Age*.

It would be the first enduring reminder to an ignorant world that the Picti people were about to come back with a vengeance.

Quite literally.

10:19 P.M.

THE EVENING HAD BEEN full, starting off with a squirt gun fight. An exhausted and waterlogged Brent had been no match for his son, Jamie. After quickly drying off, he made a jaunt to Discount Books & More with Jenna, something that the two of them enjoyed doing to spend some additional time together. Then, to cap things off, he managed to make it home in time to read a bedtime story to Amy.

Now, with the two kids in bed and Jenna spending the night at a friend's house, he had the opportunity to sit down with his wife.

He, with his feet up on a small pillow on the living room coffee table, and she, cuddled up under his right arm, had passed the last several minutes just talking about the day. Brent had learned a long time ago that it didn't take a Cleveland Indians or Browns game to give him an evening of satisfaction and relaxation. It could come in moments like this, spending time, even after all these years, getting to know more about his wife.

Over the years, in their alone time together, Brent and Tara had come to play an undefined game. The challenge was to find out if there was at least one more detail about the other's past, so one or the other could have the bragging rights to say, "And after all this time, I thought that I knew you!"

Brent uttered that phrase a lot, usually to find that it was something he had already been told, but had forgotten, or so Tara would claim.

Tonight, there were no *Ah-ha!* moments between them, but the conversation was still pleasant. Tara took advantage of a moment of silence to steer the conversation to what had been on her mind for most of the day.

"So, it's been a week and a half. Seen anything around the city that lends credence to the conversation that you had with Pastor?"

Brent shook his head. "Not a thing. Maybe I'm not looking for the right things. Not sure. Heck, I've got no idea *what* to look for."

"Have you spoken with him since?"

"No. But maybe I should. I'd like to find out if anyone else said anything to him. I'll try to talk with him Sunday."

"I've been praying about it, but all I can think to do is pray against 'Principalities and Powers.' You'd think that with my background, I'd understand what those are."

Brent thought a moment and looked at Tara. "Well, why don't we find out?"

"Huh?"

Brent withdrew his arm from around Tara and started to get up. "I'm going to grab my laptop. Let's do some research, shall we?"

Tara smiled. "We shall!"

Brent went upstairs to his office and brought down his MacBook, and placed it on the coffee table. Opening Firefox browser, they Bing searched "principalities and powers" and were faced with 907,000 hits.

"Wanna look at 'em all? I could call off sick-and-tired in the morning."

Tara laughed. "How about we see if we can get our answers with the first few clicks of the mouse. Okay with you?" Brent chuckled.

With a couple of clicks, they had found a Wikipedia article dealing with the hierarchy of the angelic realm. While it didn't address the demonic, it did give a breakdown of some of the rank structure of angels.

Apparently, *powers* were higher-ranked than *principalities*, also known as *princes*.

Principalities "appear to collaborate, in power and authority, with the Powers (Authorities). Their duty also is said to be to carry out the orders given to them by the Dominions and bequeath blessings to the material world. Their task is to oversee groups of people. They are the educators and guardians of the realm of

Earth."[10]

Another site that they clicked on seemed to confirm this by referencing not only Ephesians 6, from which Pastor Jonathan quoted, but also Colossians 2:15, which read, "He stripped the evil spirits—these principalities and powers—of their authority while shaming them publicly, displaying his triumphant power."

The author of the site indicated that demons appear to have kept the same ranking structure that they had prior to The Fall, but with an allegiance to Satan in a grand conspiracy against their Creator and the Creator's creations.[11]

After reading several pages of information, Brent said, "Based on what we've been reading, principalities are subject to powers, regardless of whether they are angelic or demonic. The princes have governance over groupings of people, whether religiously or politically.

"I think that if Pastor is right, then it's a prince or principality that we need to be concerned with."

"Okay," said Tara, "being concerned is one thing, but doing something about it is another. Maybe we'd better be doing some looking into spiritual warfare, just in case."

After Bing searching "spiritual warfare", and ending up with a jaw-dropping 24,900,000 hits, their first click took them to a site that dealt not only with what spiritual warfare is, but also took time to explain false practices that were a misrepresentation of spiritual warfare.

Link after link that they clicked and found that they needed to grab a Bible in order to verify that Scripture wasn't being taken out of context.

"Hmm," began Brent. "I guess that I had always thought that spiritual warfare was all about forcing the Enemy to do what we command them to do. This guy says that true spiritual warfare begins with living a pleasing to God—living a life that the 'accuser of the brethren' cannot hold up before God and

---

[10] en.wikipedia.org/wiki/Christian_angelic_hierarchy
[11] www.icr.org/article/principalities-powers

say, 'See? This one is disobeying you, therefore I have the right to invade his life.'"

Tara found that same paragraph catching her attention. "'Abiding in Christ' keeps Satan from having any legal rights to mess with us. So, our first defense against the Enemy has to do with just having a proper relationship with the Lord."

Brent sat back. "Okay, what does that mean to you?"

Tara smiled, and Brent knew that she was enjoying this. Several weeks prior, she had told him that his willingness to encourage her to think and provide her own opinions, rather than just being told information, was highly appreciated.

She took a moment to formulate her thoughts, staring at the keyboard of the laptop. "I think that for so many Christians, it means not committing sins, but unfortunately, too many of us think that refraining from something bad is the same as being a good follower of Christ. In actuality, *following* Christ means allowing him to lead. So that means that simply removing wrong things from our lives doesn't make up for having omitted the things that we are *supposed* to be doing.

"An actual *relationship* with Christ means loving him, obviously, but it also means moving when he says move and stopping when he says stop. It means being willing to hear him lead us *into* things, not just *out* of things." She turned to look him in the eyes. "How was that?"

Brent laughed. "Said it better than I could have! Show off."

Tara leaned into him again, so Brent brought the MacBook off the coffee table and onto his lap. "This is interesting. He says that too much of the Church is fixated on dealing with unholy spirits in the territory in which they have legal rights, the heavenly or spiritual realms. That when we start trying to mess with evil spirits in *their* territory, we are almost surely inviting spirits to come and mess with us." Brent scrolled down and found the author was quoting the often-quoted Ephesians 6 passage. He read it aloud.

> "Put on the full armor that God provides, so that when evil approaches, you will be able to stand your ground with firm footing. When you've done all you

can do, stand firm. Utilize the belt of truth strapped around your waist. Fasten the breastplate of righteousness into place, and prepare your feet for movement, spurred on by the gospel of peace.

"Add to these things the shield of faith; it is effective to extinguish the flaming arrows fired by the evil one. Place securely onto your head the helmet of salvation, and take up the sword of the Spirit, which is the word of God.

"Make sure to pray in the Spirit regardless of what's going on, with all kinds of prayers and requests.

"With all of these things in mind, remain alert, always remaining prayerful, for the whole of our family in Christ." Ephesians 6:11-18

"I guess when we look at this as a blueprint for spiritual warfare, we're shown that the *effectiveness* of the warfare we perform is heavily dependent on the intensity and dedication we show to God and our dedication to his Word, not to mention the Holy Spirit. [12]

"Truth, righteousness, the gospel of peace, faith, salvation, the Word of God, and Spirit-led prayer."

Prayer was essential. One thing that Brent was still convinced of in his past dealings was that a closed mouth did little good.

"I think that in this type of warfare, we should be praying out loud, not silently. There is something about the spoken word that has power."

Tara nodded.

They continued to read and talk into the early morning.

---

[12] Turn to Appendix to read about Brent & Tara's Spiritual Warfare Research

CHAPTER 10
Sunday, June 5—1:37 p.m.

Pastor Jonathan, Jenni, Brent, and Tara enjoyed a relaxing lunch together after supervision. The Lawton kids were at home under Jenna's attentive watch. At least that's what Tara kept telling herself. She hoped that upon their return home, they'd find that Jamie and Amy had been kept from wrecking the place.

Conversation amongst the four friends had been pretty casual up through dessert, which had included a *delicious* piece of raspberry-chocolate chip cheesecake. *I'll be working overtime to keep* this *off my body*, Tara thought.

As a fresh round of coffee was poured into their cups, Brent brought up what they all knew they were there for.

"Pastor, when we last talked, you told me that individuals had been approaching you about out-of-the-ordinary feelings or perceptions that something bad might be on the horizon for our area. Has anything happened in the past two weeks that would seem to confirm that?

"Yes. More of the same. As you know, we hold intercessory prayer meetings every Thursday evening. I wasn't there for this one, and neither was Jenni due to unfortunate obligations elsewhere, but I did call the prayer leader that night—You both know Bob Stiller—to ask how the evening went. He said that, while they did begin praying for the needs of individuals who'd made requests, the mood shifted after about half an hour.

"He said that several of the twenty-seven who were there stopped praying and noticeably began looking around at the others.

"Turns out that they didn't want to speak up right away and sound foolish by bringing up the idea that they needed to interrupt praying for people in that moment and turn their attention to demons."

Tara spoke up. "Okay, I think we're coming to understand that something's going on, but did any of them have a clue that others had been approaching you about a seemingly imminent spiritual battle?"

"Yes," said the pastor. "One of those I had mentioned to you in my office, Brent, is a frequenter of that prayer group. But, according to Bob, the prayer group leader, she hadn't mentioned her conversation with me until after they had wrapped up for the evening.

"So, there you have it. Yet another confirmation that something is approaching."

Tara looked to Jenni. "Have you seen or heard or felt anything odd?"

Jenni produced an apologetic shake of her head. "I'm afraid not. But I've stepped up my prayer. In fact, I'd been thinking about calling you to see if you had any insights, considering *your* background."

Tara's thoughts flashed back twenty-four years. While she had certainly been an open-eyed participant in the demonic realm, she had been so far removed from it for so long that she doubted that she could offer anything of benefit, and she told Jenni so.

Pastor Jonathan rebuffed the idea. "Tara, just because you don't recall much or haven't been practicing the occult for a long time doesn't mean you lack value in this area. You have eyes that are probably better suited to perceive things than the rest of us. In my experience, I'd have to say that God has a tendency to use the errors of our pasts to provide answers in the future.

"If the things that people are sensing right now will have a community-wide impact, I wouldn't be surprised if something from your past *is* used by God to help figure things out. Hopefully, there won't be the need, but start asking God to provide opportunities to have your past become a blessing here in the present."

A feeling of nervous excitement passed through Tara at that moment. "I'll do just that, Pastor."

Pastor Jonathan turned to Brent. "How about you? It's been two weeks; anything interesting taking place on the streets?"

"Not a thing that I've been able to notice, and trust me, every day I've been watching with all of this in mind. Frankly, though, I don't have a clue what I'm watching for. It certainly would be a lot easier if a group of black-robed Satanists were caught on camera spray painting occult symbols on tombstones. But all I've been seeing lately is a reduction in speeding tickets."

"Well," began the pastor again, "I'm certain that I did the right thing in bringing you into my confidence regarding all of this. I know that God wanted me to talk to you two weeks ago. It wasn't just a whim. That said, let's refocus our prayer and intuitive efforts to come up with some answers.

"The Holy Spirit is waking people up to some sort of danger, and it's now our responsibility to be vigilant. If a dark time is coming for our community, we are not going to be caught unaware."

"Amen," said Brent.

"Amen," said Tara and Jenni.

"Another thing," Pastor Jonathan added, "As God has obviously specified that you were to be alerted to all of this, Brent and Tara, I want you to be careful. Our enemy is cunning, and he knows your pasts. He knows that God uses our pasts for his glory and will attempt to prevent that. I'll say it again, be vigilant."

Understanding the urgency of what lay ahead of them, Tara's thoughts on weight management were tossed into the back seat.

Funny how that had been my crisis just ten minutes earlier.
She wished she could laugh at the irony.

1:39 P.M.

BRENDAN STOOD IN the garage that sat back from the farmhouse. The main garage door was open, allowing a flood of natural light to invade the normally dark edifice. He looked at the
piece of artwork that had been leaned up against the wall before
him. The plaster form of the Key Stone had turned out perfectly. It stood approximately nine feet high, and since it would
never be sunk into the dirt like its concrete twin, it didn't require
an additional four feet of unmarked surface at its bottom. Every
bit of the imagery from the actual stone pieces could be seen.

Unexpectedly, the plaster cast revealed even more detail
because now, the human eye wasn't being tricked by discolor-
ations from centuries of abuse, ranging from airborne particu-
lates, mud, water, and mortar.

Yesterday, they had taken the dried cement cast and erected
it in the soil near MacKay Hill. It, too, looked great, and with
the concrete having been reinforced internally with the rebar,
it would stand proudly for many years to come. It appeared to
do more to hallow the ceremonial grounds than all the religious
rites they had conducted. Many of the Picti had been flocking
to it as a place of meditation or ritual observance to the gods.

Since the real Picti Key Stone and the Key of Bridei could
never be safely returned to Scotland, it would seem that this unknown little spit of a city in America would become their Mecca,
at least for the time being.

Brendan foresaw annual gatherings taking place on this
property. That meant a lot of work would have to be performed
to upgrade and add to the facilities and grounds.

Brendan knew he didn't have to focus attention on any of
that for the time being. It could wait. During the coming

evening and the next, there would be general sessions with all of the Picti faithful.

He had rented out a large number of chairs for the events of the gathering, and now several of the followers were hard at work, creating a sort of amphitheater facing one side of Mac-Kay Hill. At dusk, he would begin to explain, in detail, their over-arching purposes as a religion and talk about future recruitment efforts.

Throughout the following day, they'd discuss techniques for proper indoctrination and the practice of true *magick*. The evening would conclude with an anticipatory look ahead to Tuesday's big event, the placement of the Key of Bridei into the Key Stone; something that hadn't happened in over fifteen hundred years.

Though determined to maintain the same self-restraint he'd shown in delaying the translation of the Latin and Pictish on the Key of Bridei, it was taking all of Brendan's mental stamina not to place the key into the plaster replica of the Key Stone. He just knew that they would fit together perfectly.

He sighed and walked out of the garage. His excitement and long-delayed gratification would come to their zenith alongside all of the Picti who yearned to witness the event. He deeply desired a holy and reverent observance filled with awe.

What would Tuesday hold? What secrets would be unlocked? What beliefs would he become privy to that the ancient Picts had worked so hard to protect?

He and his people would know soon enough, and in the not-too-distant future, the rest of the world would, as well.

CHAPTER 11
Monday, June 6—3:49 p.m.

Pittston wasn't an everyday destination for Tara and Jenna, but it was certainly a lovely destination when they desired to browse little boutiques. For some reason—maybe it was the beautification project that the downtown had recently gone through—little mom-and-pop-type restaurants, cafes, and niche stores began to flourish, bringing what appeared to be thousands of visitors to the storefronts each day. And this day's beautiful skies and warm temperatures had apparently made it the perfect place to be for everyone in Ohio!

The downtown was much more crowded than usual, which would probably make the day feel a little less relaxed, but Tara knew it would be no less special for some great mother-and-daughter time. This was something important for both of them; another opportunity to bond and be women together.

Jenna was at the age now where boys were taking much longer looks at her and doing double-takes. The teenager was thrilled. Mom and Dad, a little less so, but it was what it was. They couldn't hide what nature was producing in their "little girl."

Tara took solace in the fact that Jenna loved God. The two

of them had a very open relationship with one another, and Tara was overjoyed that Jenna was asking her the questions that so many teens asked of one another to garner advice and direction.

She and Jenna had had several talks about sex, and boy, was Brent happy to hear that! Tara trusted Jenna as much as any mother could, but there was still that nagging desire to send spies out to watch her every move. Tara's own sin-laden past was now revealing more of its consequences, and one of those was knowing that she hadn't been worthy of the trust that she was hoping she could keep firmly placed in Jenna.

Tara sighed. *If only I could go back...*

They walked down Strawberry Lane, where they had found parking, and turned right onto Main Street. Tara glanced at Jenna. She had the beginnings of an uncontrollable grin. The girl had sixty-two dollars in her purse that she felt she couldn't spend fast enough.

To that, Tara felt a need to say something. "Restraint, young lady."

Jenna just looked at her and gave a playful roll of her eyes. Just a block away was Jenna's favorite destination, *Christy's Place*, a little boutique of purses and fashion accessories. She had been saving for a particular handbag for weeks, and now, forgive the pun, it was within her grasp.

"Mom, after I get the purse, how about we go to *Carson's* for ice cream?"

Instantly, Tara thought about that piece of cheesecake from the other night. *Oh brother.* "Sure, why not?"

Jenna smiled.

Twenty minutes and fifty-two dollars and sixteen cents later, they walked into *Carson's Ice Cream Parlor*. It was packed. If they were going to sit down after getting their order, it was probably going to have to be outside somewhere.

They waited in line for almost fifteen minutes, which gave Jenna ample time to make sure that all of the other customers had a good view of her new handbag. Finally, they were at the counter and ready to order. Tara ordered a single scoop of "Crave Chocolate" in a cup, while Jenna got a double scoop of

"Razler Chip" in a waffle cone.

As they walked out of the parlor, Tara commented on Jenna's choice. "Raspberry chocolate chip, huh? Just had that in cheesecake form the other night."

"And that surprises you? Tell me one thing that you like that I don't."

"Your brother."

That caught Jenna off guard, and she laughed with a snort. A quick look around assured her that no cute boys had heard that exit from her general direction.
Tara laughed. "You're too much."

They found a small table with two chairs that had just become vacant and quickly made it their own. As they sat and enjoyed their cold and delicious weight-gain products, Tara caught something out of the corner of her eye. Had she just seen what she thought?

Trying to remain inconspicuous, she turned to look at a couple sitting at an adjacent table. A young woman, maybe in her late twenties, was wearing a turquoise tank top that revealed her shoulder blades, and though she couldn't be completely sure, Tara was convinced that she was looking at a *triskele* tattoo, very much like her own. A slight twist of the woman's body confirmed it. *Wow. What are the chances?*

Then it struck her. What *were* the chances? Slim? None? Her heart began to race.

Within a couple of minutes, the couple got up. As they began to walk away, the man with her, wearing a blue T-shirt, put his arm around the woman, revealing another *Triskele* tattoo under his left arm, just below the armpit.
Oh, dear God! Could it be?

She glanced at Jenna who was licking away at her cone. *Okay, relax. Just relax. Eat your ice cream, don't do or say anything to get your daughter wondering about your sanity.*

They finished their ice cream and Tara suggested that they just walk around and window shop a bit. Jenna was more than agreeable to the idea. Tara, though, wanted the extra time to see if she could find that couple again. She didn't know what she would do if she saw them, but she couldn't just let the possibility go.

Tara was looking at everyone around her and didn't take any serious glances into any of the windows they walked by, except to see if the couple could possibly be seen through them. "Mom, did you see that?"

Jenna's question broke through her thoughts to catch her attention. "See what?"

"That woman. She has a tattoo just like yours." Tara's heart jumped. "Where?"

Jenna pointed at three women standing near a trolley stop. The woman that Jenna was referring to was in shorts and wearing a bikini top. *Another?!* She and Jenna strolled casually by, and they both got a good look at the tattoo. Almost an exact copy. Then something else caught her attention.

The Scottish accents.

4:58 P.M.

THE DRIVE BACK to Millsville required a phone call to Brent. At this point, Tara chose not to hide anything from Jenna.

"I'm very sure, Brent. I saw three of the tattoos. Jenna said that she thought she saw another as we walked back to the car. Something's going on."

"Okay, why don't you take Jenna back home. I'll be home in less than ten minutes, myself. We'll try to figure out what this could mean."

"Okay. I'll see you in a few minutes. Love you." "I love you, too."

Tara pressed 'End Call.'

"Mom? What is it? What's going on?"

Tara expected the question from the moment she dialed Brent's cell phone. "We don't really know yet, hon. But those tattoos that we saw? They mean something. Something not good."

Tara stole a glance at Jenna and found that she was being stared at, concern reflected in her daughter's eyes. She reached out her hand and rested it on Jenna's left knee. "I wish I had more to give you. All we have is a hunch and a lot of Christians who are feeling like something is about to happen in our community. Something evil."

"You know you're starting to scare me, right?"

Tara stared at the road ahead and nodded. "Do you want to be included in what your father and I talk about when we get home?"

At first, Jenna just shrugged. A few seconds later, though, Tara heard, "Yes."

5:19 P.M.

JENNA WAS NERVOUS.

She sat in the living room with her parents, her mom having just finished a call to the sitter to find out if she could watch Jamie and Amy for a little while longer. Household chaos on top of this new situation—whatever it proved to be—was not how they wanted to stack things right now.

Her dad sat leaning forward, elbows on his knees, in a recliner that angled toward their living room sofa, where Jenna sat next to her mom. The two of them watched as her dad considered for a moment the request that had been made.

"You're sure, Jenna? This isn't something that you're going to be able to just dismiss from your mind if later you decide it was a mistake to join us.

Jenna responded, "Dad, I have a female brain. I'm already not going to be able to dismiss this from my mind."

Her dad couldn't help but laugh. "Fair enough." He got up and walked in front of the fireplace and back. "Okay, this is serious stuff, though. This stays between the three of us ... and Pastor Jonathan and Jenni. Do you agree?"

Excitement lit up Jenna's eyes. "Yes. I do." She looked at her mom, nearly ecstatic that she was going to be "in the know" regarding what was going on. Her mom, with a somewhat amused look on her face, simply raised her eyebrows.

Both Mom and Dad filled her in on the little bit of information that they currently had to go on, which wasn't much. But they did have the relevance of her mom's tattoo to ruminate on.

Her mom, to this point, had never gotten into the real reason she had such a tattoo, so she filled Jenna in on some of the darker details of her past life. Up to this point in Jenna's life, there apparently hadn't been a need—in her mom's mind—to venture into a lot of her less-admirable history.

From Jenna's perspective, she knew that none of them—she and her siblings—wanted to venture out to touch on topics of their mom's mostly secret past. They were never told *not* to ask questions; it was just a feeling, a sense that there were areas that were off-limits.

Listening to her mom, Jenna's eyes went from excited to astounded! How had she never known *any* of this stuff?

"Yes, my dear," said her mom, "I'm afraid you were born into a family of former witches."

It only took a moment for that to register, at which point her eyes darted from Mom to Dad. "*Excuse* me?"

Her dad produced a sheepish grin and shrugged. "Who knew, huh?"

Jenna let her mouth drop open.

"Just remember, the operative word in your mom's last statement is *former.*"

"Okay, let me get this straight." Jenna's hands went up to her temples. "You both were witches a long time ago. And now, for some reason, God is putting you both back into the middle of it again."

"It's a very real possibility, Sweetheart," replied her dad.

"And to be very honest, I had hoped I would never have to deal with *anything* like this again."

"But that's not the way God works, is it?" asked Jenna rhetorically. "Okay, so what's next?"

"Good question," her father said. "Hon? Ideas?"

"Just one. I think we need to call an old friend."

3:43 P.M. MOUNTAIN TIME

KAREN STANTON—formerly McGlaughlin—sat working on a project at her desk at home. The light of the midafternoon sun came cascading through her office window. The view across the flat vista that was her backyard still caught her attention from time to time. Wyoming. Not exactly where she thought she'd end up after college in Ohio, but it did have a certain charm.

Cheyenne was a famous location in the western United States … if one were a cowboy—or if one loved cowboys—which, of course, Karen did, having married one.

Cheyenne Frontier Days brought in the best cowboys from around the world to compete at the "Daddy of 'Em All" rodeo. Ten days of music, food, fair rides, and, of course, every sort of cowboy—and cow*girl*—competition one could imagine.

Her husband, Steve, was a judge at different rodeo events, having been a champion bronc rider himself, more than two decades prior.

Karen clicked search in her browser window when the very-loud opening strains of Mozart's *Marriage of Figaro* blared from her phone, startling her. She picked up it up and saw that the incoming call was from Tara. She smiled.

"Hi, you!" she said with no small measure of delight. "How are you?"

"Karen! It is *so good* to hear your voice! It's been far too long since we've talked!"

After several minutes of pleasantries and a quick catch-up

on each other's lives, Tara got to the reason for the call. "Karen, I need help, and I'm hoping that your memory can make a twenty-four-year leap backward."

Karen let out a light laugh and said, "You always were the difficult one."

Tara laughed, too. "My tattoo. Do you remember it?"

"The *triskele*?"

"Yep."

Tara was apparently just going to let the answer sit there to see what the undirected response would be.

"Well, I do remember seeing it on your shoulder for the first time when we went backpacking our senior year of college. I may have even commented on it. Did I?"

"I distinctly remember you bringing it up, because I was startled that it had become a focus of your attention. I didn't want it to be something that directed attention to my practice of witchcraft. I can't remember you saying anything about its relevance, though."

"I don't think I did. I think I wanted to see how things played out and if your tattoo was simply a piece of artwork."

"So, even back then, you knew it was an occult symbol?"

"Yes." Karen paused, then said, "Come with me as I go downstairs to grab a book." She got up from her desk and headed down to the small library in her husband's den, as Tara told her the few details that she already knew about the symbol, which wasn't very much.

Book in hand, and back upstairs in her office chair, Karen thumbed through the pages until she settled on a chapter dealing with occult symbolism.

"Your tattoo is *pregnant* with meaning, Tara. Even I had no idea. I'm reading from a book called *A Scottish Grimoire of Celtic Witchcraft*, by Gordon McGowan. On page 247, it details that there are two different components to the *triskele*. The first component is that of motion and represents moving forward, revolution, cycles, competition, action, and/or progress. The second component can be any of several three-piece representations: Spirit, mind, and body; creation, preservation, and destruction; power, intellect, and love; creator, destroyer, and sustainer; past, present, and future..."

"There! Wait! Past, present, future. Karen, do you remember me talking about a woman named Stephanie O'Leary?"

"Yes, she was your mentor in the craft."

"She used to say that what she practiced was all about the past, present, and future. What else does the book say?"

Karen skimmed the page for anything else that may be germane to their conversation. "It says that it must be remembered that the two components relate. So, take a first component like 'moving forward' and couple it with a second component like 'past, present, future' and you'll have a fuller meaning of what the symbol means to those who've adopted it."

"One of the first components was 'revolution.' What if it was taken not to mean spinning, but overthrow? Couple that with 'past, present, and future' and you have ... what?"

"Overthrowing the status quo? Current beliefs? Replacing the way something is done now with something from the past, for a different future?"

Almost as quickly as it escaped her mouth, Karen was struck by something else she had seen in the book. "Tara, the book also says that the *triskele* could mean 'The Otherworld, where spirits, gods, and goddesses live.'"

Karen heard something like a slight gasp on the other end of the phone connection.

"What is it, Tara?"

"Shalinar."

"The spirit guide you had cast out?"

"The *demon* I had cast out, yes. It kept telling me to join him in the Otherealm." A momentary pause, then, "Karen, I love you. I've got to go."

"Love you, too. Don't keep me in the dark for too long. I want to know what's happening so I can pray for you."

"I'll try to call you back this evening and share everything that we know that's going on. Bye, for now."

"Bye, Dearheart."

Karen looked from her phone to the book. Then she looked from her book to God. "Father, I don't know what's going on, but I pray a hedge of protection around the Lawton family.

Give them wisdom and insight into what they're dealing with. In Christ's name, Amen."

6:19 P.M.

BRENT AND JENNA had listened to the one side of the phone conversation intently, gleaning as much as they could. But now that Tara was off the phone, she was apparently fair game for a gaggle of questions. The first question was expected.

"So?"

Tara looked down at her pad of scribbled notes then up to Brent who had remained on his feet for the entire call. "Hon, could you grab me a couple Aleve and some water? I've got a headache coming on."

As Brent went to get his wife the pain relievers, Jenna repeated his question.

"So?"

Having received and swallowed the two blue tablets, Tara looked again at her notes, apparently trying to piece together the best explanation for what she was feeling and thinking.

"Okay, here's the thing. The first time I saw the *triskele*, which is what my tattoo is called, was on a woman named Stephanie O'Leary." She looked up from her notepad to Jenna. "She was my mentor in witchcraft. I wanted to be just like her.

"One day, I was able to clearly see the tattoo that she had on her shoulder blade, and I made my best hand-made drawing of it from memory And after all this time, I thought and took it to a tattoo parlor to have the symbol inked onto me, as well. I had no idea that it held any relevance at the time, except that it probably had some sort of occult meaning, which was just fine by me."

"Why did you keep it? After you got saved, I mean," asked Jenna.

"That, my dear, has been an ongoing mental debate from 1987 until now. I have no love for it, but it does remind me where I came from. And, while I have no desire to keep it, it effectively serves as a great conversation starter that leads to sharing who Jesus is with people."

Jenna accepted this without further comment.

Turning back to her notes, Tara went on. "Karen has a book that deals with Celtic witchcraft and symbology. In it, it says that the *triskele* has different possible meanings. There are two components, each with its own possible interpretations. But certain things that Karen read to me seemed to hit home. Component One: Revolution. Component Two: Past, Present, Future. Then there was an overarching meaning that it could have as a whole: The Otherworld, where spirits, gods, and goddesses live."

Tara produced a sigh and looked up at Brent. Then she said, "We can't know anything for sure, but my gut tells me that we're looking at a group of people who are going to try to start a spiritual uprising, a 'revolution' that has something to do with the past, the present, and the future. It has to do with what I once knew as the *Otherealm,* where this spiritual war that we're getting into will either be won or lost."

Brent pursed his lips and nodded. It appeared as though he was about to speak when Jenna chimed in.

"But why a Celtic symbol? Aren't there other symbols that could represent similar things?"

Good question, my smart girl, thought Tara. She considered the question for a moment, then said, "Brent, do you remember my deliverance night?"

Tara reflexively shut her eyes in a wince, then turned to look at Jenna. "Something else I'll have to share with you later."

"Yes, of course. What about it?" Brent asked.

"Karen had told Pastor Jonathan that she believed everything had to do with my Scottish roots."

"Mom! The three girls with the accents!"

Tara had almost forgotten. "That's right!" She looked back to Brent. "Today in Pittston, one of the girls that we saw with the tattoo was talking with two other girls, and all three had Scottish accents."

Brent sat down again in the recliner. "Okay, now it sounds like we've got a case. Jenna, will you run up to my office and grab two more legal pads and some pens? We need to start piecing things together to see if we can come up with a discernible path to follow."

CHAPTER 12
Tuesday, June 7—8:10 P.M.

The two evenings of general sessions had gone well. There was a new and growing expectation amongst the Picti about who they would become as they advanced their common agenda. There was a definitive purpose, and all now understood the road map to growth—in numbers and in individual and collective power—over the coming months and years. What had yet to be clearly defined were the precise details, the practices, and the true nature of their ancient religion. These were particulars that had been hidden for well over a thousand years. The first step to

those discoveries, though, would come this night.

Stephanie watched as the people once again gathered in the arranged seating area by MacKay Hill. Tonight, the Key of Bridei would be inserted into the Key Stone. Not the *actual* Key Stone, of course, but the plaster replica which earlier this afternoon had been temporarily fixed atop the mound in its proper standing position.

This night they would get beyond guessing and begin hearing from the ancient Picti themselves, about who they were, what they believed, and what they practiced. To Stephanie, it was all still a bit surreal. Decades of waiting had come down to a lingering fifty minutes.

Brendan was in the house. He had asked to be sequestered until he brought the Key of Bridei out. He wanted to submit his inner being to the hag, Cailleach, in the hope of having proper eyes to see and understand all that would be revealed through the uniting of key and stone.

What would be found? Stephanie knew that the coming evening would not reveal the ultimate answer; that there would be more ceremony than revelation. The reuniting of the stones would be just the first step of several required to fully understand what they had their hands on. Those steps would include a lot of translation work.

Step one would be deciphering the Picti language on the front of the Key of Bridei using the Latin inscribed on its backside; something that Brendan could have done with relative ease, considering how well-versed he had become in Latin. Instead, he opted to share in the crowd's excitement and anticipation. He would translate the key's ancient text in person before his Picti followers.

Step two would involve lining up the key's six spokes with the six corresponding divisions on the standing stone. He would then be able to interpret the *rune*—the hidden language on the standing stone—by using the newly-translated Picti language on the key. The rune language had obviously not been the common language used by the Picts, but it was still exclusively Pictish.

The third step would take the longest: translating hundreds of Pictish standing stones throughout Scotland. While many still weathered the elements, others were preserved in various museums throughout Scotland and elsewhere. Brendan and David had spent many weeks overseas traveling from place to place, carefully photographing each of the standing stones to create an always-accessible information database in the United States.

The inscriptions discovered on the standing stones of ancient Pictland would provide—so they hoped—valuable information on their heritage, not to mention their religion.

Stephanie walked up to the men working as technicians for

the event. She asked that they make sure that the lighting units facing the mound, not create any deep shadows on the surface of the Key Stone, nor upon Brendan's face. He would need the best lighting possible to do the first level of interpretation of the *Rune* language before the onlookers.

She stepped to the top of the mound and knelt before the key stone. She called down, "Okay, turn them on!"

The lights came on. Though the sun was still casting its own illumination upon the stone, Stephanie could see how the ground lighting would affect Brendan's ability to see the images properly. She called back and had them swing two of the lighting units forward a little bit and raise two of the others.

Satisfied, Stephanie walked down from the mound and back to the farmhouse. She would change into her tunic, as would both Brendan and David. No one else was required to do the same this evening. Once changed, she would sit on the front porch waiting for Brendan to end his seclusion.

9:00 P.M.

BRENDAN, STEPHANIE, AND DAVID approached the amphitheater, Brendan taking the lead. Stephanie followed, carrying the Key of Bridei on a large, blue velvet pillow trimmed in gold. David took up the rear carrying a leather-bound blank journal, into which would be written all of the translations over the next few weeks or months.

The moment the three were sighted, the crowd of Picti rose from their seats with great applause. The ovation lasted until they stood atop MacKay Hill side by side.

"My dear brothers and sisters of the Redeeming Age," began Brendan, "this marks the fourth day of our assemblage. I hope that this gathering has, so far, met with your approval and expectations."

Again, the crowd cheered.

"Tonight, we gather for our final night of formalities. Tomorrow will be our farewell feast and celebration, and the following day, most of you will be on your way back to your homes. I am pleased to have your priests and priestesses remain one additional night with us before rejoining you in your homelands. They will be a part of a special rite of initiation into the Picti faith.

"Do not forget what you've seen and learned here. Take your knowledge and plant it into fertile soil that it may yield an even greater harvest for next year's gathering.

"Much of what the Home Coven learns from the ancient Picti standing stones throughout Pictland over the next several weeks and months will be disseminated to your respective priests and priestesses. Respect them. Honor them, for in doing so, you honor Stephanie, me, and the Home Coven.

"Do not allow our enemies to come between you and your destinies. Christlings, Jews, and Muslims will hate what we stand for, as much as Muslims hate Christlings and Jews. You will hear from them that we are an illegitimate religion. But the fact of the matter is that we will now have ancient writings that are older than those that established Islam. I believe that when we've compiled all of the information from the Picti standing stones around Scotland, we will have a holy book that rivals that of the Torah and New Testament. You will all be able to hold your heads high knowing that you have one of the most accurately translated books of religious and cultural writings to ever exist.

"Be patient with us, though. With hundreds of stones to translate, we may not have it ready next week."

The crowd let out a rumble of light laughter.

Brendan turned to Stephanie and gave her a big smile. She returned it in kind. Walking to the outstretched blue pillow and taking the Key of Bridei into his hands, he turned to face the crowd and held the stone high above his head.

"Ladies and gentlemen of Pictland! I give you the legendary Key of Bridei!"

The crowd erupted into shouts and screams and whistles and thunderous applause. A single flash of light came from the official photographer's camera. For the sake of security, no one had been permitted to carry with them any devices capable of taking photos or making recordings. These had to be left in hotel rooms.

Brendan stood there for a good thirty seconds before lowering the key and turning toward the plaster key stone.

Kneeling before the massive standing stone, Brendan reached up and placed the key into the hole at its center. It fit perfectly and didn't require him to hold it in place. He stood and looked at it with awe. For fifteen hundred years, this key had waited to fulfill its destiny for the Picti people. Moving out of the way to allow the crowd to see the joined stones caused the applause to ratchet up another notch. Another flash of light commemorated the moment.

"My Picti family!" shouted Brendan to quiet the throng. "My family! Shh! Please!"

The applause and raucous vocalizations hushed.

"My family, this is the moment that I've been waiting for nearly my whole life." Brendan cleared his throat as emotion began to rise up within him. "From the first realization of who I really was and whence I had come, I have been dreaming of the moment I would become fully alive. This *is* that moment! Please, honor this hallowed event with silence as I strive to do the first translation of the ancient text."

Brendan turned again to the stone. Stephanie knelt at his left, and David to his right. He spoke softly to each of them. "Aileen and Cowan, I am honored to have you both here with me tonight. Cowan, are you ready to document what I speak to you?"

With a smile and a nod of his head, David opened the journal to the first page and responded. "Yes, and with great pleasure."

Brendan's heart was pounding. "Then let us begin."

With those four words, he reached up and removed the key. Flipping it over to the back side, he began to silently read in Latin what he told David to record in English: the titles of each of the six sections.

"Family."

He paused as he rotated the key to read the next title.

"Royalty." A turn of the stone.

"Land." Another turn.

"Warriors." Turn.

"Sea or Ocean."

After turning the stone in his hands one last time, Brendan paused and just stared at the stone. After a few moments, he flipped the stone over to look at the Pictish writing and then flipped it back over again. Brendan's blood ran cold.

No. ... No, no, no, no, no.

His breathing became heavy as his heart pounded in his chest. He fought to keep his composure and not look over to either Aileen or Cowan.

David asked, "Brendan, you okay?"

"Uhh... yes. Sorry. I... I'm okay. Just a little bit of a memory lapse when it comes to my Latin usage." He forced a smile.

"Umm ... the last title is Religion."

Brendan again just stared. *Think, Brendan! Think! You can salvage this situation. It's okay. This can still work.*

Brendan reached up and put the key back into the key stone and made a show of kissing the key. He put a big smile on his face, got up and faced the crowd.

STEPHANIE KNELT NEXT to Brendan, excited to be this close to what was taking place. She looked across to David, who also had a grin like that of a little boy receiving a big, wrapped birthday present.

Brendan ... how to describe him? Giddy? On the verge of ecstasy? She wanted to laugh and give him a big hug.

He began to give David the titles of each section of the key and key stone.

"Family ... Royalty ... Land ... Warriors ... Sea or Ocean." Then he stopped.

Stephanie was already looking up at Brendan when she saw him flinch. *Is that fear?*

"Brendan, you okay?" she heard David ask, but she didn't look away from Brendan's face.

"Uhh... yes. Sorry. I'm okay. Just a little bit of a memory lapse when it comes to my Latin usage." He produced a smile that looked painted on, completely disingenuous. "Umm ... the last title is Religion."

Again, Brendan stared at the stone.

What's going on? She saw perspiration begin to form on his forehead. *Stress!*

Brendan then placed the key back into the standing stone and kissed it. He then turned around with a smile that, now, appeared genuine, though she could tell that he was having trouble controlling his breathing.

She and David both stood and moved to stand at Brendan's sides.

Brendan looked to David and quietly said, "Cowan, would you do the honors of reading the six areas of Picti life represented by the key and key stone? Let them know that each will be meticulously studied and translated."

David followed the request as Stephanie witnessed sweat begin to roll down Brendan's face, down his neck, and into his tunic.

Something terrible has just happened.

Stephanie, too, began to sweat.

CHAPTER 13
Wednesday, June 8—8:11 A.M.

B rent knew that he had to raise a level of awareness in the mind of his captain, so he stood before his closed office door, took a deep breath, and knocked. The man had pretty much mocked him the last time they'd met, and Brent had bit his tongue. What would happen this time?

"Come in!"

Brent walked up to his superior's desk and waited for him to look up from something he was writing.

"Sergeant Lawton, what can I do for you?"

"Good morning, Captain. I'm afraid I'm back to make the same inquiry I made the last time I was in here."

"Oh? Are you talking about your request to check the area for hobgoblins?" The captain sat back in his chair with a smirk that revealed he was pleased with his own sense of humor.

Brent wanted to contest his boss's remark, but fought the urge. "So, you haven't heard of anything strange, maybe occult-oriented, happening in the area?"

"You mean happening in *this* city, don't you, Sergeant?"

"In Millsville, yes, but also in the surrounding communities. Maybe news coming out of Pittston?"

Captain Morelli sat forward again, bringing his hands together and clasping them on his desk. "Pittston?"

Brent could tell that he wasn't curious, but rather on the
edge of becoming quite perturbed.

"Yes, sir. One of my neighbors had been out in Pittston yesterday." Brent felt a pang of guilt as he 'stretched' the truth. "He
said he overheard some people claiming to be involved in some
ritualistic occult activity there. I thought it might be wise to look
into it, just in case something might start crossing the city line
into Millsville."

The captain bored a hole into Brent's skull with his stare for
a few seconds, then picked up the phone. He pulled out a lam-
inated card from a desk drawer with the names and direct lines
to the heads of local police and sheriff's offices in the surrounding area. He punched in a phone number and waited.

"Chief Connor, Captain Morelli in Millsville."

Pause.

"Doing well. You?"

Pause.

The captain chuckled. "Not that I'm willing to admit. Listen, I've got one of my sergeants in my office." He rejoined eye
contact with Brent. "He's telling me that he's gotten a complaint
or two from visitors to Pittston; something to do with supposed
occult activity.

"I'm sure it's nothing to be worried about, but for the sake
of my citizens, I felt an obligation to place a quick call to see
if you've heard anything."

Pause.

"Mmm-hmm. Okay. I appreciate that. Thank you, Chief.
Have a good day."

The captain hung up the phone.

"Well, Brent, according to the chief over there, there's been
no malicious activity that can be attributed to occult practices.
He said that there are several people from Scotland staying at a
hotel in town for a family reunion, but other than that, nothing
out of the ordinary."

Brent was deflated, but refused to let his captain know it.
"Well, thank goodness. Sounds like my neighbor has gotten

weirded out about nothing. Thanks for making that call, Captain. Time for me to get into my brand-new patrol car."

"Ahh ... Seen it already, have you?"

"Yes, sir. Thank the mayor for me." Brent began to exit his captain's office.

"Brent."

Brent stopped at the doorway and turned back to look at the captain.

"Do me two favors. One: Stay out of Pittston. And two: Don't break that car."

Brent released yet another fake, my-captain-sure-is-funny laugh and pulled the door closed behind him.

12:13 P.M.

TARA STOOD STARING blankly at the shelves stocked with what seemed like hundreds of brands of pain relievers. She was supposed to be grocery shopping, but after every couple of items she put into her cart, her mind began to fog. She couldn't seem to focus, and her headache from two days ago persisted.

She had almost decided to do her shopping in Pittston. However, she knew she would accomplish little more in that town than a witch hunt. That thought should have struck her as funny, but nothing involving the word 'witch' was going to come close to producing a smile.

Instead of Pittston, she stuck to her favorite local store in Millsville, where she ... *stared*.

A faint awareness of a woman coming up beside her and looking for something on the same set of shelves was enough to bring her focus back.

Okay, Aleve? Maybe the store's generic...

"Excuse me."

Tara turned to see a pretty woman, maybe a few years older than herself, with blonde hair and fair skin, looking her over.

"I'm sorry," the blonde said, "but did I get the chance to meet you Friday morning?"

Tara tried to think back to what she was doing on Friday

and realized that she hadn't left her house until that afternoon.

"I don't think so, unless we saw each other some other time in the day. But, to be honest, I don't recognize you."

"I'm sorry. I just figured you must have been at the religious gathering I attended."

Tara thought back. Maybe this lady is mixed up on the day they may have been in the same location.

"Do you attend my church?"

The woman released a little snicker. "No, I don't go to church. I'm sorry. My mistake. I just thought that since you had the same tattoo, you must have been with the others that I met in Pittston."

Tara's heart felt like it seized. "Pittston? You were at a religious event Friday morning in Pittston?"

"I probably shouldn't have called it a religious event. It was more of a meet-and-greet cookout that my brother talked me into attending. The actual religious ceremonies were that evening, and I wasn't invited."

Tara had to somehow keep this woman talking. "That sounds interesting!" She played embarrassed and said, "I'm so sorry." She stuck out her hand. "My name is Tara Lawton."

The woman laughed. "I'm sorry, too! My name is Donna McNeill."

"It's great to meet you, Donna. Do you live here in Millsville?"

"No, I actually live in Parma Heights, but I've got a client here in Millsville, so I thought I'd stop here to pick up a few things."

"What do you do?"

"I'm an assisted-living attendant. I work for a company that dispatches me to different people's homes who need special care. Most of them are seniors, but I have a few—like the lady here in Millsville that I'm heading to see—who are young but enduring circumstances in which they're unable to fend for themselves."

Tara was honestly impressed. "What a blessing you must be to people, Donna! Wow! And what a heart you must have."

Donna smiled. "I'm just me. Sometimes I fall short in how

I'm able to help. But at least most of my clients are glad to have me knock on their doors."

"Do you have a business card?"

"I sure do!" Donna pulled her purse off her shoulder and dug for her business-card case. Opening it, she took one out and handed it to Tara. "That's my cell number on the card."

"Thank you. Would you mind too much if I gave you a call later? I'd really enjoy talking with you some more."

"I'm free after 3:00 PM today, if you'd like to give me a call after that."

"Donna, expect a call."

"Good meeting you, Tara. I look forward to talking with you again."

"Same here."

Donna smiled, grabbed what she'd been searching for, and walked away.

Tara watched her turn a corner and walk out of sight.

Looking up to the ceiling, she whispered with a smile on her face, "Lord, did you just set me up?"

3:07 P.M.

WHILE SHE DIDN'T want to seem anxious, Tara couldn't wait any longer to give Donna a call. She had an idea that would hopefully help her gather more information in a relaxed setting. Maybe she could invite Donna over for some coffee. She just hoped Donna was still in the area.

Grabbing her cell phone off her dining room table, she dialed the number on Donna's business card. It rang.

"Hello? This is Donna McNeill."

"Hi, Donna. This is Tara Lawton, we met at…"

"Hi, Tara! I was just talking about you."

That struck Tara as a bit odd. "You were?"

"Yes, with my brother, David. I told him how weird a coincidence it was to meet someone with the same tattoo that wasn't involved with their group."

Oh, no, Tara thought. "What did he say?"

"He kinda shrugged it off. He said that as far as Celtic art goes, the tattoo you have isn't all that rare."

"Well, there you go."

"Yep, there you go."

Tara enjoyed the woman's light sense of humor. "The reason I called was to ask if you had plans for dinner."

Dinner? Tara rolled her eyes. *Where'd that come from?*

She ventured forth with, "I was planning an early meal and thought that if you were still in Millsville, you might enjoy an opportunity to relax after a hard day's work.

"I would love to get to know you better, and with my husband coming home early, I was already planning something quick and easy."

Tara realized that she was rambling and probably overplaying her hand for an opportunity to talk again.

Shut up, Tara, and just let her answer you. Goodness!

"Would you like to be my guest for dinner? I mean, our guest... here at our home?"

Donna let out a giggle. "Well, I am still in town, and if you hadn't offered, it would have been another day of fast food. Tara, I'd enjoy that very much. What is your address?"

Tara gave her the address, and they got off the phone. Now she had to come up with a quick dinner idea ... that *wasn't* fast food.

Oh! And she had to call Brent!

Brent answered on the first ring. "Hi, babe!"

"Hi, Brent. When..." *That was out of the ordinary.* "Did you say 'babe'?"

Brent laughed. "Just flew out of my mouth for some reason. So, what's up?"

"First, you haven't called me babe in a long time. But I think I approve." She smiled. "Second, how fast can you get home?"

"Okay... First, good, I'm glad. Second, I'm just wrapping up some arrest paperwork. My shift is over in ten minutes. Why?"

"You are *not* going to believe who I ran into today!"

CHAPTER 14
Wednesday, June 8—3:19 P.M.

Brendan hoped that these two seemingly unrelated pieces of information were just that. Uilliam had called and indicated that some police sergeant in Millsville may be snooping around, and now, Cowan called to let him know that his sister had just run into a local woman with a tattoo that appeared to be just like that which most of the Picti had adopted as their symbol of faith.

It really could just be coincidental timing.

But he couldn't afford to risk it. Not now. Especially when they were about to take their greatest risk. Even now, David was preparing for tomorrow night's initiation and appeasement ceremonies—the blood-letting rite that would be performed, in part, as homage to Cailleach, the Hag.

He paced back and forth from the living room to the kitchen. Stephanie sat in the living room silently, but her eyes were on him every time he stepped back into her presence. The rest of the Home Coven and Picti were either enjoying the weather out on the farm property or taking advantage of their open schedules to go investigate some of the interesting sights and sounds of Ohio. Tonight, would be the final celebration of their new beginning. The Home Coven would pull out all the stops when it came to prepared foods and entertainment.

After walking back into the living room for probably the seventh or eighth time, he finally came to a stop before Stephanie.

"Aileen, we may have a problem."

"Who?"

That was pretty perceptive, Brendan thought. "Cowan's twin. He told me that he got a call from her. She was apparently quite excited and called to relay that she had a chance meeting with a woman who has a *triskele* tattoo just like ours. The woman didn't seem to know anything about our gathering. But if she were posed with a question or two about it, she certainly does now!

"Aileen, we can't have things like this happening! That damned woman opened her mouth and has potentially put at risk what we're doing."

Stephanie disagreed. "David—*Cowan*—is the one who put us at risk. That woman is just being an average, everyday dimwit. You can hardly blame her for this."

Brendan knew she was right. "I'll talk with Cowan. He needs to rein in his sister."

"Okay, now that that's somewhat settled," said Stephanie, "what's going on with you?"

Brendan knew instantly what she was talking about, but wasn't willing to admit it. "I'm sorry?"

"Last night on the mound, in front of the stone… What happened?"

"Nothing, Aileen. It was as I said. I grew frustrated by my lack of ability to remember some of the proper Latin translations."

"You couldn't remember the Latin word for *religion?* Come on, Brendan, talk to me."

"*Damn* you, Aileen!"

Brendan's blood began to boil. This was not a subject that would be discussed this day. In fact, this was a subject that he'd intended to *never* have discussed.

"There is nothing to talk about! Take me at my word!"

With that, Brendan walked out of the living room, threw open the front door to the porch, and marched off into the fields.

3:38 P.M.

BRENT PULLED UP to the house in the shiny, new cruiser and parked the vehicle in the street. Though his SUV was parked in their garage, the driveway was occupied by Tara's minivan and the champagne-colored sedan of her new friend.

Brent had little doubt that this was going to be one very interesting meal.

As he walked through the front door, he nearly tripped over two backpacks: those of Jamie and Amy. Tara must have seen him come in.

"Sorry about that, hon. I'm the one who told the kids to put them by the door. Nana and Papa are coming to pick them up for hamburgers, a movie, and an overnight."

Nicely done, my bride, he mused. "That sounds great! I'm sure they're going to have a blast."

Walking into the dining area, he came upon an attractive, middle-aged blonde who was sitting in one of the dining room chairs and facing the kitchen where Tara was preparing their dinner. He said a passing hello as he walked up to Tara. "Hello, babe."

Tara giggled. "Hi, baby."

It was all he could do to keep from laughing, but he couldn't prevent the big grin that he now displayed.

"Brent, allow me to introduce my new friend, Donna McNeill. Donna, this is my husband, Brent."

"It's a pleasure to meet you, Brent," she said as she stood and extended a hand.
Brent took it and said, "The pleasure is mine." Turning back to Tara, he said, "Hon, that smells good, whatever it is."

"Braised chicken breasts in a cashew sauce, green beans, and salad."

"Wow." He looked to Donna with raised eyebrows and

playfully uttered, "You need to come around more often."

Donna laughed.

"Well, if you'll excuse me, it's time for civilian clothes."

THE KIDS WERE ON their way to the movies, and Jenna came home at just the right moment to join them for the meal. Over the last twenty minutes, as they ate and talked, Brent struggled to keep from introducing the subject that three of the individuals in the room were most interested in.

"Donna, why don't you tell my husband what it was that brought us together today?"

Donna went on to tell Brent and Jenna about the amazing fluke that Tara would have the same tattoo that she had seen inked on hundreds of others just the other day. "Of course, in my mind, she *had* to have been part of the group out there. Right?"

Brent played dumb. "What kind of group?"

"A religious group. They call themselves the Picti."

Brent knew the name, but couldn't place it. "Picti?"

"They were an ancient warrior culture in what is now Scotland. My brother, David, and I were out there several years ago.

"We actually got to know quite a bit about them. In fact, one of the neat things that we learned was that he and I are both from one of the Picti bloodlines."

"So, you're not a part of this Picti group?" ventured Jenna.

"My brother is. He's been trying to convert me," she said with an easy laugh, "but I'm frankly just not interested in resurrecting some long-lost religion."

Brent and Tara looked at each other.

"That's very interesting," he offered. "So, they're having some sort of convention out in Pittston?"

Donna furrowed her brow. "Yes, but how did you know they were in Pittston?"

Brent didn't want to say that Tara had called him up to tell him. He didn't miss a beat, though. He sported his best confused look and explained, "I'm a cop. The communities around here are loosely interconnected. Cops talk to cops."

"You must know Jim Connor, then."

Brent didn't, but thought it odd that Donna would know him.

"Chief Connor? No. My boss does, but I've only seen him a couple of times."

"Real nice guy."

"How do you know him?" Brent wondered. His gut told him the answer before she uttered a word.

"He's one of the local members of the Picti."

At that moment, Donna's phone rang. She removed it from her purse and looked at the screen.

"Speak of the devil," she said with a giggle. "It's my brother!"

BRENDAN STOOD NEXT to David as he called his twin.

"Hey, Sis. How's it going?"

Pause.

"Good. I'm fine, too." He looked into Brendan's angry eyes. "Say, I was wondering if you had dinner plans this evening. I'd enjoy getting to spend some downtime with my favorite sister."

Pause.

"Oh, that's right, you *are* my only sister."

Brendan, again with the eyes.

Pause.

A spark of fear drained the color from his face. "Say that again. You're having dinner with *who* right now?"

Pause.

David looked at the ground. "I see. No. Don't worry about it; I'll catch up with you later. Bye, Sis."

Brendan didn't wait two seconds after the connection was broken before demanding an answer. "What has she done now?"

David took a couple of breaths before looking up at

Brendan's brooding stare. "She's having dinner at this moment with her new friend in Millsville; that woman with the tattoo and her cop husband. She said the woman's name is Tara."

Brendan's lips began to part as his mouth went dry. *That name! It's not the same...*

"Follow me," he commanded, and made for the farmhouse. Upon reaching the door, he called out, "Aileen!"

Not hearing an immediate answer, he yelled her name. *"Aileen!"*

"Yes?" she responded from the top of the stairs. "What is it?"

"That little strawberry-blonde from years ago... Tara. Remember her?"

She thought for a moment. "Tara Baker?"

"That's the one." He walked halfway up the stairs and stopped. "Think carefully. Did she have a *triskele* tattoo?"

"I ... I don't know. I don't think she did. Why? What's going on?" She looked to David, then back to Brendan.

"That wench, if it *is* her, just befriended Cowan's sister!"

"Okay," she replied. "Even if it *is* her... so what?"

"Her husband's a cop. A *cop*, Aileen! Do you think this might be related to Uilliam's information about being contacted by the Millsville Police Department?"

"Oh, Jesus." The name escaped her mouth before she could contain it.

"Oh, *what,* Aileen? Oh, *who?!*"

She tried to recover. "It was a slip, Brendan."

It didn't really matter to Brendan. But between last night's revelation and today's morass, he'd reached his limit. He spun around on the stairs and charged down toward David. Grabbing him by the collar of his T-shirt, he screamed, "You fool! You damnable fool! Do you have any idea what you've done? You just *had* to bring your sister here, didn't you? You couldn't leave well enough alone! This is *your* fault!"

Brendan released David, and his hands flew up and interlaced on top of his head. Beginning to pace again, he continued his rant. "What are we supposed to do now? Hmm? We've got three hundred people on our property!"

He dropped his arms and rapidly crossed back to David, getting in his face. The man flinched. "We're going to deal with your sister, Cowan. She's got a big mouth."

Looking up the flight of stairs again, he directed his next words at Stephanie. "You, Aileen, you find out if this Tara is the same one. If it is, she's going to need to be contained, along with her cop husband! Losing her all those years ago was *your* fault! You're just as guilty as Cowan!" Walking into the living room to retrieve his cell phone from its charger, he asked of neither in particular, "Is Uilliam here at the farm?"

David answered. "No. He's still at work."

"The two of you had better pray to Cailleach that we get this contained, or both of your heads are going to roll!"

CHAPTER 15
Wednesday, June 8—6:25 P.M.

Donna suggested that they look at some of the pictures that she had posted on her Facebook page of her trip to Scotland. Brent was having his patience stretched as he learned about the amenities of the bed and breakfasts in which she and her brother stayed, the interesting differences in dialects, and even how certain words mean different things in Scotland than they do in the United States. There were interruptions in the monotony, though. Several pictures featured her and her brother, providing Brent a good look at another of the Picti followers.

Donna stopped at a picture of David talking on his cell phone. "I couldn't believe how much time he spent on the phone while we were there. I told him it was going to cost him a fortune calling to—and receiving calls from—the States. I think most of his calls were with Brendan." "Brendan?" asked Jenna.

"Yes, Brendan Cadeyrn. He's the leader of the whole organization. Though I don't think that's his real name."

"Really? Why would you say that?" queried Brent.

"Well, I'm not sure how many of the people that I've met over the years have identified themselves to me with their *actual* names. Seems like my brother had referred to Brendan once as…" She let out an exasperated sigh. "Oh, I don't remember. Something Baird, I believe. It seems that everyone—everyone here in the States, anyway—has taken a pseudonym."

"Your brother included?"

Donna laughed. "Yep. I don't much like it. Makes him sound like some kind of diseased animal."

Jenna laughed, looked at her mom, then asked, "Well, what is it?"

Donna said the name slowly, almost mocking it. "Cowan Cormack"

"Cowan Cormack? Does the name have any special significance?" Brent wanted to know.

"You know? I'm not sure. I never really thought about it."

"Well, let's take a look," suggested Tara. She turned the laptop on the dining room table to face her and pulled up Bing.com. She typed in the name and clicked the search button.

The closest to the name was a man by the name of Cormack Cowan, who worked in the movie industry. Outside of that, it turned up nothing. She searched for "meaning of Cowan," and her attention was immediately caught by a link to a witchcraft site, which defined names.

Though aware that it might make Donna uncomfortable, she clicked on it and found that the name meant an intruder or someone faking his identity. Another link with Scottish first names showed that it meant "co-birth".

"That's it!" Donna exclaimed, probably excited with the opportunity to rid the minds around her of any relation to witchcraft. "Co-birth! David and I are twins!"

"No kidding?" asked Jenna.

"No kidding."

"That's so cool!"

"Well, of course it is," Donna chortled. Then her phone chirped. Lifting it from the table she saw a reminder and sighed.

"I'm afraid I've got to run. My ever-dependable calendar is reminding me that I've got a senior-care presentation to give tomorrow. I've got a lot of preparing to do tonight."

All four got up from the table and, with genuine smiles

reflecting appreciation for her time and company, walked her out to her car.

After getting into her car, she rolled her window down to say a final goodbye.

Brent took the opportunity to hand her one of his business cards without comment. She accepted with a thank you.

As Donna drove away, Jenna remarked, "I really like her."

Tara smiled. "So, do I. We're just going to have to have her back here sometime."

Brent folded his arms and faced his two ladies. "Well, that was certainly an information fest. Let's go inside and talk about what we believe we understand."

BASED ON THE EVENING'S conversation with their new friend, Brent, Tara, and Jenna compiled a list of things that they thought worthy of further investigation.

- Members have fake names.

- Fake names may represent who they are, maybe their roles in the organization.

- Leader's name is Brendan Cadeyrn (aka ??? Baird). Bing search revealed his name to mean:

      - Prince of War

      - Battle King

- Picti were a warrior culture.

- There was something about their trip to Scotland that was important to Brendan Cadeyrn.

- The word "witchcraft" didn't trigger a response from Donna.

- Pittston police chief is member of group.

- *Pittston police chief, Jim Connor, lied to Captain Morelli.*

- *Tara's tattoo seems significant somehow.*

- *There's a gathering taking place in Pittston, but we don't know why.*

- *David's phone call to Donna during their conversation may have resulted in the Picti group knowing that they were being looked at, and by whom.*

"Anything else?" asked Brent.

Neither answered. All three just stared at the list for another moment.

"Oh!" cried Jenna, startling her mom. "She said that they were *resurrecting* an ancient religion, not just practicing a religion."

"Bingo," said Tara quietly. "It comes down to them believing that they can bring back a religion that has been dead for, what? A thousand years? Fifteen-hundred?"

"Well," prompted Brent, "we've all got our own personal laptops. How about some quality family time together ... on the couch ... surfing the web?"

"I'm getting a warm fuzzy feeling just thinking about it," said Jenna with a smirk.

6:45 P.M.

"THE BLOOD-LETTING rite takes place tonight, immediately following the farewell feast. We can't afford to wait until tomorrow. We have to get these people out of here as soon as possible."

Brendan was trying to remain calm; Stephanie could see that. But she was certain he was panicking. The farmhouse was beginning to feel claustrophobic, the living room walls seeming to close in on her. She wanted to get out. If David had been in the room with her, he'd at least be sharing some of the weight.

"The sacrifice is going to have to be delayed. We cannot help that now. Having the police involved…" He sighed and pinched the bridge of his nose.

"Can't Uilliam help?" inquired Stephanie. "He's kept *his* officers at bay thus far. And it's not like the police in Millsville can just waltz in here outside of their jurisdiction. Besides, we haven't done anything worthy of a criminal investigation."

"You mean beyond the fact that we stole priceless ancient artifacts and smuggled them out of two different countries to get them here?"

Stephanie sighed with realization. "I guess there is that to be concerned about."

"Are you *also* forgetting about the appeasement ceremony? Have you forgotten what *that* entails?"

Duly put in her place, she answered, "You're right, Brendan."

"We cannot have *any* suspicions cast our way. But because of you and Cowan, that may already be too late."

His statement bit deep into Stephanie's emotions. She tried to offer some sort of remedy for the immediate concern.

"Then we move the appeasement ceremony to another location. We still appease the gods, but we do it somewhere outside of Pittston."

"That is *not* acceptable, Aileen! Not acceptable at all! We chose this location because of its privacy. It is private property, and the authorities cannot check anything here without a warrant. The bad thing is that it could be the county sheriff's responsibility, not that of the Pittston P.D., to issue that warrant. We have no pull with them."

Brendan walked away from her and the conversation.

Stephanie watched as he became rigid and stared through the lace curtains of the living room picture window. He stood silent for too long. In response, she took a chance and walked up to him from behind. She tried to wrap her arms around his waist, hoping to lend him some of her calm. It had been far too long since they had last touched.

The moment her hands made contact with his waist, he

whirled around, and what she saw in his eyes chilled her to her core. His eyes burned with hatred.

"Don't touch me," he warned in a low, measured tone. "My reign is in jeopardy, and you think that your *touch* is going to cure something?"

Stephanie pulled back. She didn't know what to do or say. In all of their years together, he had never spoken to her like this.

"Brendan, I… I'm just trying to reassure you."

"Don't! I don't need anything from you. Before you even existed in my life, I was working to reconstruct this religion. Because of stupid mistakes that two of my most trusted followers made, my dominion could collapse before it hardly had a beginning!"

Stephanie just stared.

"Stephanie O'Leary, you are not *nearly* as important as you think you are. This is *my* work! I'm the one who made this happen!"

He used my name! My real *name! What does that mean?* Stephanie's emotions were becoming so intense and confused that she wanted to run upstairs to her bedroom and slam the door closed, but she stood still. She attempted an appeal to his heart.

"My love, you know that I have always…"

"Don't you *'My love'* me, Stephanie! Don't you *dare!* So, help me, if this all collapses around us, you'll wish you had never known me!"

And with that pronouncement, Brendan stormed out of the house. The door slammed, providing an emphatic exclamation mark to his threat.

1:37 A.M.

STEPHANIE LAY IN bed alone, staring at the ceiling. The faint glow of a nightlight in the hallway reluctantly passed through the bedroom door that she kept open just a crack. Even light, it seemed, didn't want to be near her.

Tears wet her pillow where they had rolled off her cheek

and nose. It had been years, many years, since she had last cried. Until today she had lived in a constant state of purpose and safety. She knew that it was all tied to Brendan, and she had never minded that one bit. A sick feeling struck her as she wondered if she was supposed to start calling him Brian Baird. His real name seemed foreign to her, but not as much as her own name did the moment it was spat out of his mouth like so much phlegm.

Her heart ached. She tried to provide herself some solace, believing that in a matter of hours, maybe even as they both woke to a new day, he would again speak her name, the name he had given to her, with passion and love.

It was inevitable, right? Hadn't they just spent the past almost three decades pledging their love to one another? Weren't they married?

A niggling thought crossed her mind. *Were* they married? There had never been a ceremony performed by clergy or a justice of the peace. They had never even gone to the state for a marriage license. They had, at least, a 'common-law' marriage ... right?

Are common-law marriages recognized by the State of Ohio?

She sighed into the darkness. She knew that Brendan— Brian—*whoever*—was right, though. What had she *really* contributed to the cause—*his* cause? She had, what, groomed a couple of women that *he* had identified to be a part of their inner circle? So what?

Stephanie began to realize her lack of relevance amongst those that Brendan kept close. She could look at everyone in the Home Coven and see why they were made a part of this assemblage. All were chosen to fulfill a purpose here.

What had *she* been chosen for? To be a trophy? Sex?

Her heart sank further with that last thought. Could it have been just because he needed someone to satiate his physical desires? Yesterday, she was his queen. Tonight, she felt as though she may have only been his whore.

Her pulse quickened as she heard footsteps ascend the stairs. She squelched the desire to sit up and watch for the door

to open. With her back to the hallway, and on the opposite side
of the bed, she watched more light enter the room as the door
opened.

His shadow on the wall before her was imposing.

He took a few steps into the room, then she heard a drawer
slide open. She knew it was the one in which he kept his journal. Each night, he would sit with his back against the head-
board and pen at least a line or two about his day.

Stephanie waited to feel his weight upon the bed. Her heart
beat hard with anticipation. Then she heard him cross back to
the door and pull it closed behind him. She didn't even need to
wonder if he had remained in the room as she listened to his
feet descend the stairs.

She buried her face in her pillow and wept. Each footfall
was another nail struck by Brendan's hammer; another nail
driven into the coffin in which lay her dying heart.

6:34 A.M.

AFTER A FITFUL NIGHT and very little sleep, Stephanie reluctantly extracted herself from the bed. Truth be told, she would
have gotten up an hour earlier except that she feared leaving
the bedroom. But, she knew she couldn't remain inside it all
day, and now was as good a time as any to face whatever new
harshness Brendan might have in store for her.

It was possible that he was in a better mood this morning.
Surely, he had become remorseful over his words and actions
of the day before.

With that slight hope, she crept down the stairs in her pajamas, thinking she might find Brendan asleep on the couch or
maybe in the kitchen eating a bowl of cereal. Halfway down
the stairs, she saw a vacant couch; no pillow, no blanket. Reaching the bottom of the flight, she turned right through the living
room and hesitantly walked into the kitchen, where disappointment again struck her soul. A look at the sink and the breakfast

nook added to the realization that he had not stayed in the house the previous night.

A look out the kitchen window facing the garage showed that his truck was gone. Had he left right after taking his journal? Where had he gone to spend the night?

Maybe she was overthinking things. It might be as simple as Brendan taking one or two of last night's initiates to breakfast or to some coffee joint before they left the country. But when had he ever done anything like that? She sighed.

He had been so angry; angry enough to spit poison at her, anyway. But he had been amazing, yet again, during the initiation—the blood-letting ceremony.

There had been no pomp and circumstance. It had been, more or less, a swearing-in ceremony.

AFTER THE CELEBRATION feast, all of the initiates, once again wearing tunics, gathered outside in front of the porch, even as the hundreds of others departed the property for the final time. These were the priests and priestesses of all of the covens, domestic and international.

Each man and woman was handed a length of rubber surgical tubing, a sterile wipe, a piece of gauze, and a large hypodermic syringe as he passed through the front door of the farmhouse and into the living room. All of the furniture had been pushed out of the way, allowing the large room to accommodate the forty-plus initiates.

The floor had been covered with transparent Visqueen, a self-adhering plastic sheeting, to protect it from any spillage or splatter that may occur. A single round coffee table was at the center of the room. On it were six lit candles surrounding a large ceremonial bowl covered in Pictish symbols. Also, two decanters, one filled with water another filled with isopropyl alcohol, sat to the outside of the candles.

Brendan stood in the living room and greeted each individual by name as he and she entered. He kept a solemn look upon his face, which kept the atmosphere both somber and quiet.

When all were in the room, including Stephanie, David, and the whole of the Home Coven, Brendan asked the faithful to form two concentric circles around the table, leaving enough room for him to walk around the table and in between the two human rings.

Brendan walked around the table and spoke while looking into the eyes of each individual. When he came to look into Stephanie's she was sure she was provided with a purposefully icy stare. She tried to shake it off in order to pay attention to the rite of passage.

"My people—my brothers and sisters of the Olde Faithe—tonight is a night of submission. This is a branding of loyalty, and each of you must take it of your own free will.

"There is an old joke that is used sometimes when someone is entering a contract that is causing the signer some measure of trepidation. The contract holder attempts to assure the signer that things will be just fine by saying something along the lines of, "Don't worry, it's not like I'm having you sign in blood."

"Tonight, however, that's exactly what I'm asking you to do. It will not be signatures on paper, but rather something even more personal and binding. You will be signing on the souls of each of your brothers and sisters in this room.

"First, though, I want to have your verbal commitments. I will walk the inner circle, followed by the outer. I will look you in the eyes seeking your answer. If you offer yourself freely to the Olde Faithe, you will affirm so as you look me in the eyes."

Brendan reached down to the table and picked up his sterile wipe and cleaned an area on the inside of his left elbow. Then he called upon Eithne and Mùirne to come stand before him. One was a member of the Home Coven and a phlebotomist, the other was from one of the covens in Ireland and a full-time nurse.

He handed Eithne the surgical tubing, which she tied above his left elbow. Then, after handing her his syringe and gauze, she proceeded to insert the needle and siphon blood to the amount of five milliliters. Withdrawing the needle, she placed the piece of gauze over the insertion point and indicated to Brendan to hold it in place by lifting his hand up toward his shoulder. She then handed him the syringe.

Brendan turned to the table and held the needle over the ceremonial bowl. He pressed the plunger into the syringe and forced into it the contents. Setting the needle on the table, he produced a wry grin and said, "Nothing to fear."

"Eithne and Mùirne will come to each of you and perform what you've seen done with me. Once all have been attended to, you will be asked to come forth and mix your blood with that of mine."

Brendan turned around and looked into the eyes of the closest individual, a woman, and said, "Ceana, do you pledge your heart, your mind, your body, and your livelihood to the cause of the Picti? Do you commit yourself to the Olde Faithe, with a willingness to give up your very life for it? Do you consign your soul to the Pictish gods of old?"

"I swear that I do," she said without hesitation.

Brendan lifted his right hand and laid it upon her head for a moment before moving to his right to ask the same question of the next initiate. Over and over, he asked the questions, looking each individual in the eyes; each of them affirming his and her allegiance to the faith. As he moved from one to another, Eithne and Mùirne leapfrogged each other, making sure that each initiate's blood-letting took place quickly.

After all of the affirmations and the shedding of blood were complete, all of the faithful made their way to the ceremonial bowl, mixing their vials of life with that of the others. That complete, Stephanie stepped to the table to take on her pre-assigned duty.

She lifted the bowl of blood into the air and called upon the deities. "Gods of the Olde Faithe of the Picti people, we call upon all of you this night to take this blood offering and consecrate it for your use. Let this be forever remembered by each person in this room as a blood oath, an oath of service to you, our people, and to our ancient lineage. May it be done."

"May it be done," echoed all in the room.

Stephanie put the bowl onto the table and took the decanters of water and alcohol, one in each hand, and poured an equal amount of both into the ceremonial bowl, both diluting and making the mixture safe for the next element of the rite.

"I want everyone in the room to find someone that he or she did not know prior to coming to Pittston and then face one another."

There was a rustle as everyone, including Brendan and Stephanie, shifted from one location to another to find someone unknown to him the week before.

Stephanie did not know whether what she would say next would be true of the Picti warriors of old, but she had heard it was true of some Native American tribes as they had prepared for battle. Regardless, her next statement would hopefully make things a bit more comfortable for each man who was paired with another man.

"It is said that Picti warriors would prepare each *other* for battle; that each warrior would offer another his own courage and will to live. That warrior would paint upon his brother his promise of faithfulness and loyalty in battle. That is what we do here tonight.

"It does not matter what Pictish symbol or image you choose; it is enough that you are taking your blood, and the blood of your brothers and sisters, and making an oath of faithfulness to the one before you. Draw the symbols over each other's hearts with your fingers. After tonight, everyone in this room will be tied together by the blood of everyone else; a bond of Picti blood."

Stephanie untied the sides of her tunic and lifted the article of clothing from her shoulders, and discarded it on the floor. As she stood naked, the others in the room understood her cue and removed their tunics as well. Stephanie was paired with a large man, tall and a few pounds overweight. She could tell that he was struggling to keep his eyes from roaming her body.

Turning to the table and the bowl, she dipped two of her fingers into the bloody mixture and stirred the contents. Taking them out, she drew a Celtic comb over his heart. She again turned to the bowl and brought it before the man. He dipped his fingers in and drew over her heart a symbol that on many standing stones appeared to be a mirror. She smiled and gave him a nod.

Stephanie then carried the bowl to each pairing in the room, allowing them to dip their fingers and perform the rite of fidelity. Not a single word was spoken, though there were many smiles and no small amount of nervous energy.

At the conclusion of the rite, Brendan picked up his tunic and placed it back over his muscular form. After securing the sides, he spoke as the others in the room also donned their clothing. "Tonight, we have become one people. We are now *truly* our brothers' and our sisters' keepers. We will protect each other. We will correct each other. We will connect with each other. Protect, correct, and connect."

Brendan paused. Stephanie saw what probably no one else did, a twinge of frustration that struck his features.

"Everyone in this room knows about the ceremony that did *not* take place tonight. Rest assured, though, that the Picti will soon have their vengeance for the betrayal that led to the extinction of our culture and religion. The appeasement sacrifice *will* take place. I promise you that. I'm only sorry that you will not be a part of it.

"Brothers and sisters of the Picti faith, go now and lead your people well."

With those final words to the group as a whole, he walked to the front door and opened it. All in the room exited the house with words of affirmation from their leader. That is, all but two: David and Stephanie.

STEPHANIE STILL STOOD in the kitchen. The morning sun was creeping over the trees in the distance to fill the room with natural light. Again, she sighed and moved to begin her day without her lover.

She wanted to be positive about all that the two of them had accomplished over the past few weeks. She wanted to believe that she was important to all that would take place moving forward.

Today, all of the Picti would begin to travel the long distances to their respective homes and commence the formal reestablishment of the Picti as a unified people. Maybe one day the Picti would even have their own homeland again.

Stephanie knew she should have felt ecstatic, but instead she felt abject sorrow and dread. She felt that she had gained the whole world, but lost her soul in the process.

CHAPTER 16
Thursday, June 9—8:43 A.M.

Tara stood with her back turned to the bedroom vanity. She lifted her hand-held mirror before her to get a good look at her tattoo. *If I had gotten rid of it years ago, I might not have been thrust back into the middle of all of this.* She turned around and put the mirror down. *But ... what this tattoo has brought me into is no coincidence, is it?*

She finished getting ready to take on her day. She felt a sense of adventure, an exhilaration that quickened her pace. Maybe today would be another day of revelations, maybe it wouldn't. Regardless, just knowing that something big was going on around her and that God was seeing fit to use her... Well, it made her want to do more! But what would that be?

As she left her bedroom and began walking down the stairs, she felt a light dizziness that caused her to stop and grab the banister. Her headache was coming back, too. She sighed and made her way downstairs and into the kitchen to take a couple more pain relievers. Maybe a combination of Aleve and Tylenol would do the trick.

Grabbing one of each and downing them with a bottle of water, she walked into the living room. A wave of intense nausea coursed through her midsection, and she immediately ran into the bathroom, barely making it to the commode in time. Sweat broke out on her forehead and shoulders, and she began to shake. *What's going on?* She rested on her knees for a few minutes and caught her breath. She felt weak and suddenly tired.

Feeling *relatively* sure that she wouldn't expel again, she got up, flushed the toilet, and washed her face. She felt a little better. Or did she? Her headache intensified.

Tara walked to the pantry and pulled out a box of saltine crackers, grabbed another bottle of water from the fridge, and two more pain relievers from the cabinet. She walked to the living room and sat on the couch.

Maybe her day of adventure was to consist of a day of *Gunsmoke* and *Bonanza* on TV Land.

9:07 A.M.

BRENT SAT AT HIS desk, looking over reports that were left from his third-shifters. *Just another typical night in the burbs*, he mused. Looking up, he saw Tracy Larkin going about his day.

He'd known Tracy for over ten years and had a lot of admiration for him. Despite that, he still periodically wondered what kind of parent named a boy Tracy. Larkin took his job seriously and garnered a lot of respect from the other officers.

Brent was suddenly struck by a thought. "Corporal Larkin!" Tracy looked over to Brent, who waved him over.

"I thought we knew each other well enough to be on a first-name basis," Tracy said with a coy grin.

Brent smiled. "Got a minute?"

Tracy pulled a chair back from the front of Brent's desk and sat down. "What's up?"

"Chief Connor in Pittston. Know him?"

"I've encountered him a couple of times at cop functions and at Batterson's funeral."

Brent recalled that sad day. The Pittston police officer, Kevin Batterson had been shot point-blank by a man from Fairborn, Michigan, after pulling the man over for a simple broken taillight.

"Know anything about him? On a personal level, I mean."

It showed on Tracy's face that he didn't know where this was going. "Nothing. Why? What's going on?"

"Just found out that he lied to Morelli during a call that the captain placed yesterday."

Brent filled him in on the details, including the evidence of occult activity in the town. Aside from the fact that Connor had blatantly lied, Tracy wasn't overly concerned about what might be happening in Pittston.

"First of all, it's none of our business," Tracy began. "Second, who cares about a bunch of religious nut jobs—present company excluded, of course," he concluded with a laugh.

Brent smirked. He enjoyed the banter the two of them had; he'd been sharing his faith with Tracy for years. Brent knew that Larkin was at least willing to respect his beliefs, though he refused to ascribe to the idea of a literal Heaven and Hell. That had led to some interesting conversations over the years.

"Do you have any friends on the force over there?" Brent probed. "I'd really like to get the scoop on this religious group."

"John Eldredge works first shift out there." Tracy looked at his watch. "I'm sure he's out on patrol right now." He looked at Brent for a moment before asking his next question. "Brent, you're not doing an end-round, are you? Is this off-the-record stuff, or does the captain know you're investigating something out of our jurisdiction?"

Brent pursed his lips, which gave Tracy his answer.

"Don't do this, Brent. This is the kind of thing that ends badly for a good cop."

Brent combined his pursed lips with a nod.

Tracy sighed and pulled out his cell phone. "Here's Eldredge's phone number. I think he'll keep quiet about your call if you ask him to."

12:13 P.M.

BRENT PULLED INTO his driveway. Jenna had called to let him know that Tara was laid up on the couch in the family room. Brent couldn't stay away.

Entering the house, he nearly bumped into Jenna, who was on her way out, her new purse slung over her shoulder.

"What's going on with Mom?" he asked.

She shrugged. "Headache and dizziness. She said she's going to be okay and told me to get out of the house and not to worry. So, Kara Parker and I are going to the mall."

Brent kissed Jenna on the top of her head and smiled. "I'm sure she's right. I'll see you later this afternoon. Love you."

"Love you, too, Daddy."

As Jenna left, Brent walked into the family room at the rear of the house. His wife lay on the couch with a cold compress on her forehead.

"It's not a migraine, is it?" he asked as he strode into the room.

She rolled her head and opened her eyes into a squint. "How would I know? I've never had one before." She forced a smile. "No, it's just a strong, regular ol' headache."

"Jenna said you're experiencing dizziness, too." He sat down on the edge of the oak coffee table.

"She worries too much. I'm fine."

"This just struck you out of the blue this morning?"

She glanced up at him with a look that said he wouldn't like her answer.

"Out with it."

"It's the same headache that I've had for the past few days, only this morning I also threw up. I felt really wobbly coming down the stairs, too."

He could see that a thought struck Tara with the force of a freight train, causing her to sit bolt upright. Brent watched as she squeezed her eyelids together, apparently weathering another wave of dizziness. Opening them again and focusing on her husband, she said with no small amount of alarm, "I'm pregnant!"

"What?!" Brent could hardly believe what came out of her

mouth. He repeated the word, with no better grasp on the situation. "*What?!*"

"What else can it be? My body's acting weird, I'm throwing up in the morning, and I've got this persistent headache that's telling me that something's going on in me that's out of the ordinary. It all fits!"

Brent stood up and walked a couple of paces, then turned around. "Pregnant?"

They were too old for this! He walked back over to Tara and sat down again.

Both were quiet for a couple of minutes while they digested the possibility.

Brent went through everything in his mind. Of course, it was possible. They weren't *that* old. But something wasn't sitting right. The timing? Something about how she described what she was feeling?

"Tara, what day did the headache begin?"

Tara thought back. "Monday. Remember? I asked you to get me some pain relievers."

Brent's eyes got bigger with realization.

"Sweetheart, your headache began after your phone conversation with Karen. Right after, we dove into this spiritual warfare stuff with both feet. I doubt that it's a coincidence that you started feeling bad right after we started getting some answers about the significance of your tattoo."[13]

"Okay?"

"Let's try something." Brent got up and pushed the coffee table further from the couch, then he got down on his knees beside his wife and encouraged her to lie back down. Then he laid his right hand on her forehead and his left on her abdomen.

Closing his eyes, Brent began to pray. "Father, I come to you in the name of Jesus, on behalf of my wife, Tara. We love you and praise you for who you are and what you want to do in our lives. Right now, I feel as though my wife is under attack from the Enemy. I ask, Father, that you put a hedge of protection around her; around *us*. I plead the blood of Jesus over our

---

[13] Turn to Appendix to read about awareness in warfare situations.

situation. In the name of Jesus, I bind any spirit that is messing with Tara, causing dizziness, nausea, and pain. I cast you aside, by the authority I have in Jesus Christ.

"Father, again, I ask for your protection. Extend it over my whole family while we deal with this darkness that's looming over our local communities. In the name of Jesus, I pray. Amen."

Tara began to blink. Brent watched as a haze seemed to evaporate from her eyes.

"Wow," she began. "Okay. I'm impressed." She took in a deep breath and let it out. "Nausea is gone."

Brent helped her sit up, though it now appeared that she didn't need his assistance.

Tara sat and appeared to be mentally gauging her situation. Then she stood up and again evaluated how she felt. "Have I ever told you that you're my hero?" Brent smiled and drew her close.

"Ouch! My side!"

Brent pulled back to see her hand grab the right side of her belly. *Oh no*, he thought.

Looking Brent dead in the eyes, Tara asked, "Do you really *need* all of that stuff on your belt, or is it just to make you look impressive?"

Brent's heart restarted. He shook his head with a laugh.

2:19 P.M.

STEPHANIE FOUND DAVID in the field, cleaning up the area around MacKay Hill. As she approached, he looked up, and she saw a look on his face that she couldn't readily discern. David put down a trash bag in which he'd been placing the littered aftermath of the celebration feast.

Walking toward her, he said, "Hi, Stephanie." "David."

"Well, it seems that we still find ourselves on the outside of Brendan's good graces."

"Have you seen him?"

"No. His truck's been gone all morning; at least since I got here at about nine."

"He didn't sleep here last night."

David looked toward the driveway, as if to find an answer sitting on it. "Don't know where he could be. But you can bet that he's not here today because of us."

Stephanie crossed her arms and looked at the ground. "We need to do something. I just don't know what. We can't go on like this, attempting to avoid what he believes to be our fault." She looked up to see David nodding, still looking at the driveway.

"Tell me what Donna said about Tara," Stephanie directed.

"You already know what I know."

"It wasn't a request, David."

David put his hands on his hips and looked into her eyes.

She could tell he was trying to muster some form of masculine resistance, but she stared unflinchingly into his eyes until he relented. It only took a few seconds.

Donna met Tara at a grocery store. They talked briefly about a *triskele* tattoo she saw on her right shoulder blade."

Did she copy mine somehow? she wondered.

"Later, Tara invited her to her family's home for dinner…"

"For information, more likely. Go on."

"She's married to a Millsville cop. Their daughter ate dinner with them. That's all I know."

"Your sister didn't provide a description of what Tara looked like?"

Stephanie could see that David thought it an odd question. After all, who just volunteers another person's vital statistics while sitting down over dinner?

"No, not a word was mentioned about the way she looked."

"Call her."

"Call … Donna?"

Stephanie nodded. "Casual conversation. Ask about her new friends."

David pulled out his cell phone and called his sister. "Hey, Sis. How's your day going? Are you with a client right now?"

Pause.

"Good. So, tell me, how was your dinner with your new friends? Interesting people?"

Long pause.

"They sound great. You'll have to introduce me sometime. Wait a minute... Tara?"

Pause.

"Well, I'm just trying to remember. Tara in Millsville. Hey! Does she have short, dark hair?"

Pause.

"Oh well. Not who I thought it was. So, what did you all talk about?"

Long pause.

"Hey, Donna? I've got another call coming in. Can we talk more later? Good! Bye!"

David's face was grim. "This Tara has strawberry-blonde hair."

It is *her!*

"And there was a lot of unfortunate conversation." He sighed, knowing he had to lay everything on the table.

"They talked about our trip to Scotland. They talked about what little she knew about the gathering and about 'all the nice people' she had met."

David paused.

Stephanie identified it as hesitation. "Continue."

"And ... she said it was a 'fun coincidence' that Tara's husband, Brent, knew the Pittston Police Chief."

Stephanie remained stoic. She looked him in the eyes and said simply, "Thank you, David." She turned on her heels and walked back to the house.

Under her breath, she muttered, "It's time for a little reunion, isn't it, Tara Baker?"

FIFTEEN MINUTES LATER, Stephanie walked into the Millsville Public Library. She asked the librarian at the main counter where she might be able to find old wedding announcements and obituaries so that she could do some research on family genealogies.

She was led to a computer room where three of the machines had been tied directly to the library server, which housed all the city's old newspapers, historical documents, and public residential records. She was permitted to use one of the computers for one hour. There were no printers in the room and no Internet access, so any information she needed would have to be written on paper.

Not knowing when Tara got married, or where, Stephanie thought she might turn up little or nothing of use. None of the scanned newspapers could be word-searched by the computer, since they were really just scanned into the system as photos.

After about twenty minutes, she developed a system for combing through the newspapers more rapidly. Thirty-five minutes later, she was rewarded with what she'd hoped to find.

LAWTON-BAKER WEDDING

Mr. and Mrs. Keith Lawton of Millsville, OH, are very proud to announce the wedding of their son, Mr. Brenton Nathaniel Lawton, to Miss Tara Darlene Baker of Branson, MO. The ceremony will take place on Saturday, August 29, 1992, at 1:00 PM at Forest Acres Community Chapel in Bedford, OH.

"Bingo!" she said with a smile. "So, your last name is Lawton, now." Looking at her watch, she found that she still had a few minutes remaining to browse the residential records. Maybe she could find a property listing with an address.

Seven minutes later, she was rewarded with the property valuation of the Lawton home back in 1996 and scored the address.

Stephanie scribbled all of the pertinent information into the small notebook that she had brought into the library with her, then closed it. The little black book had just been transformed into a treasure trove of revenge.

CHAPTER 17
Thursday, June 9—3:55 P.M.

Tara sat on the couch in the family room, looking at the list Brent, Jenna, and she had compiled after talking with Donna. There was one glaring omission. Though her name had never been brought up in conversation, everything on the list, especially the city in which all of this was taking place, shouted the name of her former mentor. "Stephanie," she whispered.

Could she really be involved in all of this? Of course, she could. Good grief, the very last conversation the two of them ever had spelled it out plainly. Stephanie's words had been seared into her brain. They had become her fuel to destroy Brent's and Marta's Christian walks, way back in 1987.

"Wait!" a much-younger Tara had said in desperation. "Please wait. I can do it. I can do whatever it is you and the others want! I was the most advanced and well-practiced in my coven."

"Coven? That wasn't a coven, little girl. That, too, was a test. A qualifier. Trust me, you have no idea what a true coven is. Anything and everything you've ever done is little more than child's play. You are a danger to everything that I—that we—are working to accomplish. I want you out of my house and out of my life."

Until now, Tara would have thought that what they were "working to accomplish" would have been *long* over with. Just how big was this thing that they had built? How far did this reimagined religion reach if it took all these years to bring about?

A thought struck her. And she knew herself well enough to know that she wouldn't be rid of it if she didn't check things out.

She looked at the wall clock; a little after four o'clock. *Brent will be home any minute. If I'm going to do this, I'd better get out of here before he pulls in the driveway.*

"Jenna?" she called out as she walked through the kitchen into the living room.

"Yeah, Mom?" Jenna appeared at the top of the stairs.

"I've got to run a quick errand. Jamie's in the backyard, and Amy's asleep in the chair in the family room. Your dad will be home any time now. Will you watch them until he gets home? And, when I mean watch them, I don't mean go back into your room."

Tara heard a huff, then "Yes, Mom." "Thank you, lovely daughter of mine." "Whatever."

Tara began to walk toward the front door and put on her shoes when Jenna came traipsing down the stairs.

"Umm ... Mom?" "Yes?"

"Where are you going?" Jenna's voice indicated that she knew something was up.

"I told you."

"No, you said 'errand.' You never say errand. You're going to go do something that you don't want Dad or me to know about. Aren't you?"

Tara stared at her way-too-perceptive daughter for a moment, then said, "I'll be back soon," and walked out the door.

STEPHANIE TURNED onto the Lawton's street. She began looking at the mailboxes for the right street number when she saw a blue minivan pull out of a driveway a couple of houses down. As the two vehicles drove past each other, Stephanie's heart skipped a beat. It was Tara!

To make *absolutely* sure, she went to look at the number on the mailbox. The address matched.

She quickly turned her white Toyota Pathfinder around in the driveway and began to tail the minivan from a safe distance.

She hoped it was safe, anyway. She had never done this before.

TARA DROVE THROUGH Pittston, looking for the right street to turn down. She was depending on twenty-three-year-old memories to direct her path. The village had changed, and she couldn't be sure of anything.

Then she came across a welcome sight. *The gazebo!* She'd forgotten that she would use it as her landmark for getting to Stephanie's house. Turning left onto Greenwich Street, she remembered easily the remainder of the way.

"SHE'S HEADING TO my old house," Stephanie said to herself. Amazed almost beyond comprehension, she acknowledged her goddess. "Cailleach, if you arranged this, you're even more powerful than I thought!"

TARA APPROACHED the house that she had once shared with Stephanie. Reaching it, she stopped her car on the street and stared at the old home to her left. She wasn't sure that was a wise thing to do, but she wasn't going to leave without at least knowing if the woman still lived here.

She was about to exit the van when she noticed the name on the mailbox: BABCOCK, in silver-traced black letters. A wave of disappointment hit her. She knew it had been a long shot, but still...

She heard a car door close behind her. Looking into her sideview mirror, she saw a woman approaching her car.

"Oh God," she whispered, both an exclamation and a prayer.

"Why, hello, Tara," an older-looking Stephanie said as she approached Tara's open window. "Imagine meeting you here, of all places."

Stephanie was still an attractive woman. Still blonde, though it appeared that it now came out of a bottle to hide some gray that was, even at the moment, peeking through. And she still had a presence that shook her confidence.

"Hello, Stephanie," she managed.

"Just thought you'd take a drive through the old neighborhood? Reminiscing, maybe?"

Tara had the sudden realization that if Stephanie no longer lived on this street, she had been followed.

"I could ask the same of you, since you don't live here any longer."

Stephanie smiled. "I guess it's plain to see that I followed you. And what timing!" She looked at her watch. "I just discovered where you lived not twenty minutes ago."

"What do you want?" Tara was already wanting to end the conversation, shift her car into drive, and get back home. But what good would that do? The woman now knew where her family lived.

"I hear that you've gained an interest in what's going on in this sleepy little village."

"Have I?"

Stephanie smiled again. "You're no longer the little girl that I taught so long ago. You're not spooking so easily. Good for you.

"So, what brings you to my former home today? Do you want to restart your training?"

That struck Tara as funny, so she laughed. "Stephanie, I've been desirous of a conversation with you for years."

"Is that so?"

"Yes, but I realize now that it was for my own personal vindication. I wanted to rub your face into the fact that you failed to destroy me. That, despite how you shunned me and wanted my failure in life, I had come back as a better person."

"Now, now, Tara. Just because you've got the house with the picket fence, the doggie, and the 2.5 kids doesn't mean that your life is better. In fact, it sounds pretty umm... Now what's the word I'm looking for? Ah, yes ... dormant. I could have given you a life of purpose—of accomplishment. Hell," she said with a grin, "I could have given you that power you always wanted. Still can."

Realization settled into Tara's mind. *She doesn't know that I'm a Christian.* An idea formed in her mind.

"Steph, are you hungry? I'm famished."

The question obviously took Stephanie by surprise.

"Have you ever eaten at Dekker's on the village square?" Tara asked.

Reluctantly, Stephanie answered. "Yes. And I must say that I adore the place."

"Shall we?"

With that, two unlikely dinner companions departed for the restaurant, but not before Tara sent a quick text message to Brent:

Dinner w/Steph. Dekkers on the sqr. I'm OK

"JENNA, WILL YOU come in here, honey?"

She walked into the living room while Brent held his phone before him.

"Yes, Daddy?" she asked with a genuine smile on her face. Normally, this would have easily stolen from him the smile she sought, but it wouldn't happen this time.

"Did your mom say anything to you about where she

was going?"

"Oh, you mean like going out to do 'errands'?" she replied, providing him with a pair of finger quotes.

"So, you didn't buy that, huh?"

"You raised a smart daughter. Must be the cop in you spilling out onto me."

"Well, you and I need to pray. Where are the others?"

"Amy's on a chair sleeping, and Jamie just left the yard with Timmy from next door.

"Why do we need to pray?" she asked, her face reflecting her father's sober expression.

He held his cell phone out so she could read her mom's text.

"*The* Stephanie?"

"*The* Stephanie."

HERE THEY SAT on somewhat equal ground. Stephanie had hoped to rattle her with her unexpected appearance, but the tables had been turned. She had to respect the growth in the younger woman before her. Still, Stephanie knew that she had experience and wisdom on her side. Though she wasn't sure why they might be needed, she had them in ready reserve.

Smart move on her part to keep everything in public. Does she have an agenda? Is she afraid that I have one? Or did she really just want to talk?

Their orders arrived after several minutes of very awkward, hardly casual small talk. As they ate, Stephanie ventured into personal territory.

"So, tell me about your family, Tara."

Tara put a knowing smile on her face and replied, "I'm sure you already know about my family. Tell me about yours instead."

Too early to tell if she's being nasty or just curious, Stephanie thought. But she wasn't sure how to handle the question, especially in light of what happened between her and Brendan.

Don't use anyone's name.

Stephanie decided to take a different tack. "Are you still practicing within the craft?"

"Too impractical."

"Now, Tara, don't let your naïveté begin to show."

TARA WAS FACED with a decision. This verbal sparring could go on indefinitely—or at least until the meal was over— *or* she could reveal where she stood.

She asked her Best Friend to give her wisdom. *Holy Spirit, I'm on solid ground with you, but here, before this woman, I'm at a loss. Please, help me know what to do and say.*

He did.

"Tell me about how happy you are."

Stephanie went momentarily rigid. She recovered quickly, but Tara saw what God wanted her to see.

"You *are* still the little girl, aren't you? Except now you're living in a fanciful world where the 6 o'clock news and Oprah guide your life."

"Stephanie, you don't know anything about me," Tara said with an easy smile. A boldness and confidence rose within her. She knew it was from the Holy Spirit. "You're making some very big assumptions. None of which is true, by the way. And you didn't answer me. Or was your silence the answer?"

Stephanie put down her fork, took up her napkin, and with the mannerism of a woman of societal influence, wiped the corners of her mouth. Folding the napkin and setting it to the right of her plate, she said, "Tara, our definitions of happiness are at odds, I'm sure.

"My life is not spent on the pursuit of happiness. It is spent on purpose, on leaving an indelible mark on both society and history. My *satisfaction* lies in that. It is a byproduct of my work."

"Well said, Stephanie," Tara responded with appreciation. "A very similar statement could have come from my mouth and would have been just as true about me. You and I are not so different."

A sudden, "Ha!" escaped Stephanie's mouth and caught the attention of some nearby diners.

Tara explained, "Stephanie, look at us. We're both attractive, confident women, and we've both been beaten up a bit by the world. We both have aspirations—dreams that push us forward. We are *not* satisfied to just sit back and be average, like most people in this world. And you and I are passionate about what we believe. *But* ... there are differences, as well."

"GO ON. IF YOU CAN," replied Stephanie. She wasn't enjoying the meal as much as she thought she would. She was sure she would have gained the upper hand by now, through intimidation, if nothing else. But before her, in some respects, sat a woman who was every bit her equal. Tara wasn't the peon that Stephanie had anticipated ... or hoped she would be.

"Steph." Tara hesitated. "You're sad. Something terrible is eating at you from within." She paused for a moment. "And ... from the outside, as well.

"You've got misgivings about..." She paused momentarily. "I don't know what. But it's real, and it's deep. You are..."

Again, a pause. It almost seemed the woman was listening for the right words to say.

"You are questioning your purpose and your self-worth."

Stephanie realized that her breathing was becoming increasingly shallow and fast. Tara's words had cut to the quick, and she couldn't just sit at the table and expose anything raw. Without a word, she pushed back from the table, grabbed her purse, and made her way to the ladies' room.

TARA SAT STARING in wonder as Stephanie stood up, grabbed her handbag, and walked quickly to the women's restroom. She knew that the words that came off her tongue had been directed by the Holy Spirit. *Words of Knowledge*,[14] the Bible called them. She had experienced the gift a time or two before, but not with such great impact.

Lord, what do I do? Sit here and wait?

She felt the prompting of the Holy Spirit to follow Stephanie into the bathroom. Tara placed her paper coaster atop her coffee cup, letting their server know she intended to return. She then grabbed her purse, as well, and followed the path of her former mentor.

As Tara pushed the door open, she could hear sniffling in one of the three stalls. She stole a quick glance below the doors and found that she and Stephanie were the only occupants of the restroom.

"Steph, are you all right?"

"It's *Stephanie*. Not *Steph*," came the curt reply.

"I'm sorry. I should not have become so casual. Please, forgive me."

"What do you want, Tara? Did you come in here to find out how well your darts landed?"

"Nothing of the sort. I just wanted to make sure you were okay."

"Well, don't! I don't need you in here trying to be my friend. Our history should make it very evident that we *aren't* friends. We never were, and we never will *be* friends. You were a recruit, and I was a training instructor. Nothing more."

"I know. I never pretended that it was anything beyond that. But I did hold you up on a pedestal."

Tara almost couldn't believe the words that just came from her mouth, not to mention the emotion that was beginning to bubble up.

"You were everything that I wanted to be. You will never know how hard I took it when you cut me loose from your life.

---

[14] Turn to Appendix to read about the gifts of Words of Knowledge and Words of Wisdom.

I fell hard. I lost all balance and self-confidence."

She heard herself sniffle. *God, this can't be right!*

"Stephanie, part of me wanted to kill myself. My spirit guide was encouraging me to end it all and join him in the Otherealm. But I was determined to prove to you that I was worth something!" A sob escaped her throat. "I needed someone to believe in me, to tell me that I wasn't a chess piece. I deeply needed reassurance that I wasn't some sort of trophy or whore."

STEPHANIE TRIED TO stifle a gasp. What was going on? How could Tara have spoken so precisely what had been hidden within her own heart, the *very* fears and feelings of worthlessness she had been dealing with throughout the past two days?

"What do you know, Tara? What do you know about anything?"

Really, Stephanie, that's *your response?*

"You can't *possibly* know what I'm dealing with; what I'm going through…"

And just like that, before she could put a cap on the toothpaste, the words were squeezed out, with no way of putting them back in.

"Stephanie, come out here. Please?"

Stephanie sensed a word of warning within her. Her spirit guide was warning her to use caution and flee the situation. She felt exposed, and she hated that. But she needed to know more. How many of Tara's assumptions could be tied to Brendan and the Picti? Was Tara Lawton more of a danger to the Society of Bridei than even Brendan currently perceived?

STEPHANIE EMERGED from the stall, eyes puffy and slightly red. She held a wad of toilet paper that sufficed as tissues.

Tara's first inclination was to step back, but she willed

herself forward instead. She walked straight up to the woman she'd once emulated and then come to despise. Now a feeling of pity rose, and God was placing within her a love for Stephanie that she would never have achieved on her own.

Tara spontaneously held her arms open, thinking to pass on what was starting to burn within her.

The woman didn't budge. Tara dropped her arms, feeling somewhat stupid for the display.

"Tell me how you knew about ..." Stephanie trailed off for a moment. "... how you knew about my ... condition."

"I can tell you, Stephanie, but you aren't going to like the answer. But it will be the truth."

Tara could see a mental debate taking place by the movement of her eyes. She was scared, vulnerable.

"Tell me," she said again.

Tara had to trust that God knew what he was doing here. She answered.

"He loves you, Stephanie. He loves you passionately. He wants to satisfy your heart, your soul, your spirit."

"Just *tell* me!" she spat.

"God the Father, Stephanie. The Creator of the Universe, the one you call 'enemy.' He wants you as his daughter."

Stephanie stood staring at Tara blankly for a moment, then, without warning, made quickly for the door.

Tara followed her out and watched as Stephanie ran as fast as she could through the restaurant and out to her SUV. By the time Tara made her way back to their table, Stephanie was gone.

CHAPTER 18
Thursday, June 9—6:30 P.M.

Jenna sat on the living room couch, her father at the edge of his recliner, both of them transfixed.

Her mom sat next to her, describing in detail her encounter with Stephanie. When she finished, Jenna heard the cop in her dad come out. He was primarily concerned with one thing.

"Did she threaten you in any way?"

"Not at all. In fact, initially, she seemed amused by the fact that I came looking for her at the same time she came looking for me."

"Okay, that's just freaky," Jenna intoned.

"That, dear daughter, was the Holy Spirit," came her mom's smile-laden response.

Jenna looked over to her dad. He crossed his arms. His stern facial expression appeared to reflect the serious nature of her mom's replay of events. Something was definitely weighing on him; she was just wrong about what that could be.

"Okay, first, I'm glad it all turned out okay," her dad began, "but you took a huge risk.

"Why did you think it was okay to haul off without letting us know what you were doing?"

Her mom tensed. Jenna thought that maybe she should leave the room, and she would do so... *if* she were asked.

Otherwise...

"Brent, I'm a big..."

"... big girl. Yes, I know." He stopped and just stared.

"Let's not make a big deal about this," her mom said. "Not in front of Jenna."

Here it comes. 'Jenna, will you excuse us for a few minutes?'

Her dad looked over and said, "This applies to you, too, Jenna. If you ever do anything this stupid, you'll be grounded for weeks. Understand?"

Jenna just sat there and nodded.

"Stupid?" Her mom's eyes grew intense. "Stupid. So, I'm stupid, now?" she said, with livid matter-of-factness.

"Don't," said her dad, holding up a hand. "Don't even. *You* are not stupid, but your impetuous *decision* most certainly was.

"Tara, going off on your own, while purposely avoiding me and misleading your daughter, makes it clear, don't you think, that your actions were going to be risky even in your own mind? Otherwise, you would have told one of us.

"Isn't that right?"

Jenna could see that her mom was conflicted and apparently didn't want to resign herself to her dad's logic.

"So? I'm not allowed to make decisions for myself now?"

"Decisions? Yes. Decisions that include your daughter and me knowing your intentions."

"I didn't want either of you to worry!" Her mom was getting loud. "Don't you get that?!"

Her dad got up from his chair, walked over, and sat between her mom and her. He softened a little bit.

"I *do* get that, Hon. I know you're strong-willed, confident, and capable. But wouldn't you appreciate having all of that backed up with prayer also?"

Her mom looked down at her hands. Jenna could tell

that the wind had been removed from her sails. But her dad was right.

"And if I *had* told you where I was going?"

Her dad took her mom's hand. "I'd have first told you I would go with you..."

"But that wouldn't have..."

Her dad interrupted her mom's interruption. "And if you had said no to that, I would have relented." He paused before wrapping up with, "Probably."

"Really?" questioned her mother, obviously unconvinced.

"It would have, at the very least, allowed me the opportunity to pray with you and to know where you were going to be. Important information, in my opinion."

He took his hand and turned her face toward his own. He looked her in the eyes and said, "Just in case." Another pause. "Okay?"

Her mom looked deeply into her dad's eyes, and with a slight nod, said, "You're right." She looked over at Jenna and said, "I'm sorry, Jenna. Will you both forgive me?"

Jenna could tell the apology wasn't easy for her mom to make. Accepting the apology, she smiled and nodded, and then her dad gave her mom a quick kiss on the lips.

I want a relationship like theirs.

Her dad sat back. "So, now, back to the original conversation. We know Stephanie was caught off guard by your discussion at the restaurant. We don't know if that's going to create some misgivings on her part or if it's going to incite more hatred toward you. One thing's for sure, though, you've been targeted."

Jenna looked hard at her dad, then at her mom. Her eyes widened as she asked, "Targeted? Like *targeted?*" She looked back at her dad. "Is Mom safe?"

Her dad looked her in the eyes as if pondering the answer to her question. Then he said, "Tell me about your relationship with God, Jenna."

Jenna's eyes went from worried for her mom to utter bewilderment. "What? I don't get what you're asking."

"You. Jenna. Your relationship with God. Tell me about

it."

A combination of shock and fear bolted through her chest. She thought that her relationship with God was obvious. Or was it that she hoped that her pseudo-relationship with God appeared real? *I can get through this.*

"It's good," she began hesitantly. "I mean, I love God and I know He loves me."

"Great start. Keep going."

Jenna looked to her mom for some help. She didn't know why she thought she'd get any, but she thought it worth a shot. Her mom looked back at her and cocked her head, as if to say, *"I'm waiting, too."*

Jenna took a deep breath and held it in for a moment, then released.

"I go to church with you. I pray. I…"

"How often?" It was her mom.

What is going on? Her next words sounded as if they were spoken in slow motion. "Every day?" Even she knew her answer sounded like a question.

If there was one thing that Jenna knew for sure, it was that she wasn't putting on a very convincing performance. She must have looked like a trapped, scared rabbit, because her dad let her off the hook.

Sort of.

"Honey, for a lot of people, God is a wonderful person to have around when they need or want something. But when the rubber meets the road, as is the case now in our lives, people who don't have a *trust* relationship with the Lord begin to panic.

"Panic prayers get prayed rather than prayers of faith. And that could mean that they're not convinced that God's heart toward them is good, *or* they might believe that the bad things befalling them are *coming* from God, maybe because they weren't living up to what He wanted.

"The result is that these people end up getting angry with God, or they get consumed with guilt because they believe that they've disappointed God to the point that He no longer cares about them. Possibly both. Does that make sense?"

Jenna looked down at her hands, now folded and in her lap. "So, you're saying that if weird things start to happen or if something bad happens, then I may not have the faith to handle it the right way. Right?"

Her dad nodded and smiled. "That's partly what I'm saying. The other part is that God is always going to be *for* you, even when you're not walking close to him.

"His word says that he will never leave you nor forsake you. You *are* his and always will be.

"But when you do detour from the purpose—or purposes—that he has for you, you need to recognize his chastisement—his discipline—whether it's something you feel in your spirit or by way of a less-than-great circumstance he may choose to use in your life to get your attention.

"So, Jenna," he said softly, "Tell us. How is your relationship with the Lord?"

She paused and swallowed. She had to tell the truth. This was probably one of God's 'less-than-great circumstances' to get her attention.

"Not great." No one said anything, and she didn't want to look up. The silence made her start talking again just to relieve the tension.

"But you don't understand. I don't want to be a freak to my friends."

She looked at her mom, who gave her a look of understanding, then continued. "You know Brinn?"

Her mom nodded.

"Brinn is a Jesus freak. She's *so* not popular because of it. It's like she doesn't care that people make fun of her. Mom, I can't *be* like that."

Jenna's heart began to break. She understood in that moment that she had just denied Jesus so that she could remain part of the "in" crowd.

A look of understanding registered in her mom's face. Again, Jenna lowered her head and this time began to weep. *I'm horrible, God! I so deserve you not loving me anymore.*

Within seconds, her weeping became anguish, and she folded herself into her mother's arms. She knew she had failed God and that she had also failed her family.

TO TARA, THESE were the special moments of being a mother; the life situations in which the title 'Mom' was most endearing.

Her daughter had just bared her soul, and truth had cut her open, causing her to see within herself. The result was a lovely girl who loathed what she had seen. What she didn't realize, though, was that she was simply feeling conviction; a means that the Holy Spirit always used to draw a wayward soul back into the Lord's presence.

Tara held her daughter close to her chest and looked up at her husband, who had bowed his head in prayer. She silently spoke to the Lord, as well. *God, I love my family. Thank you so very much.*

After allowing Jenna to grieve for a minute or two, Tara began to soothe her.

"Shh… Jenna, it's okay."

"No, it's *not*," Jenna pieced together between whimpers.

"Yes, baby, it is. Do you know why?"

Jenna shook her head slightly.

"Because you are still God's favorite."

Tara wondered how that sentence would play in her daughter's brain. After about ten seconds, Jenna willed herself to sit up. Tears and mascara stained her cheeks.

"Huh?"

"It's true, my dear. You, Jenna Lawton, are God's *favorite* daughter."

"That's not really true." Another sob.

"Why not? You're looking at his other favorite."

Jenna was starting to catch on, a smile forming at the corners of her mouth.

Tara pointed at the Bible on the coffee table. "That book right there says that God does not favor one person over another. That means that *you* are his favorite." She gave Jenna a wink.

Brent took the opportunity to speak life into his daughter, as well. "That may not seem like much when you consider that everyone is his favorite, but if you think of it in reverse terms, it may have quite an impact. No matter how bad you feel about yourself, God doesn't feel the same way about you. You have *never* stopped being his favorite."

Jenna's eyebrows pinched together, her lips began to quiver, and tears again formed in her eyes. She collapsed again into her mom's arms for another good, hard cry.

Tara began to pray out loud over her daughter. "Father, I love my daughter. But even my strongest love is only a fraction of the love that you have for her. Let her feel that love right now. Holy Spirit, fill her with an understanding of who you are and who you want to be in her life. Help her love for you grow into a passion that outshines even that of her parents. In the name of Jesus, I pray, amen."

Tara kissed her daughter's head. After another minute or so, Jenna again sat up.

"I get it," she said softly. "But I don't know how strong I'll be when we start school again."

"Do you want to be strong?" asked Tara.

Jenna nodded.

"Then, darling, you've already done some growing in your walk with God."

"What about Jamie and Amy? Do they need to know what's going on, too?"

Tara turned to Brent and raised her eyebrows. "Good question."

"Real good question. I think the answer is yes. They're going to realize something's up eventually."

Turning to look at Jenna, he said, "Leave that up to your mom and me. Okay? We'll figure out the right information to share with each of them."

Brent looked at his daughter. "Now, back to your question. It's not just a matter of keeping your mom safe. It's a matter of keeping the family safe. That is why we need to make sure that we've got strong relationships with God." He paused for a moment, apparently thinking about how to proceed.

"You may think that you're the safest person in the neighborhood because you've got a dad who's a police officer. And while I can certainly be a layer of protection, I don't have the ability to know what's going on at all times. God does. That's why this family relies on his wisdom, his knowledge, and especially his leading. Make sense?"

Jenna nodded.

Tara thought about something she wanted to add. "Jenna, have you ever seen your dad embarrassed to pray or stand up for God?"

"No, I don't think so."

"Neither have I. In fact, if it hadn't been for your dad's prayers and making a stand for God in the first few months that he knew me, I don't know if I would have ever come to Christ.

"One of the results of his prayers for me—and one of the results of him remaining strong as a man of God—is you. You came from his love for both the Lord and me. See how prayer can lead to *incredible* outcomes?"

Jenna nodded again.

"Jenna, become a woman of God, a woman of prayer. Let God show you how big he is. Pray for your dad, your brother and sister, and me. We need what your prayers offer. Wisdom, protection, guidance. Will you do that for us?"

"Of course. You know I will," she responded with a growing smile.

Tara felt Brent place his left arm around her, then he reached over to draw Jenna in. It was time for a greatly desired group hug.

6:30 P.M.

STEPHANIE GOT OUT of the Pathfinder and looked around the

farm property. She sighed. Still no sign of Brendan.

The field was now cleared of chairs, trash, and the fire pits. The standing stone on the far side of the mound definitely gave the spot an air of significance. Stephanie walked back in front of the farmhouse and climbed the three steps to the porch.

It was a chilly but beautiful evening. She sat down in one of the porch's five chairs and looked down the driveway.

The tranquility that normally came with sitting below the overhang escaped her.

Peace seemed completely out of reach. A combo of anger, disappointment, fear, and heartache was on today's menu.

How could she have allowed so much control to escape her? Not only today, but over the past two days? Another realization hit her: Brendan's recent accusations actually pointed to a time when she had lost control some twenty-four years prior.

Tara. Her name had held absolutely no significance for years. Maybe a passing thought of her when looking backward at how far Brendan and she had come. She was just another in a long succession of individuals who had failed to meet her expectations. No one special.

But I was wrong, wasn't I?

Brendan had been right. There were things about this girl—this woman—that she had been too quick to dismiss.

In this situation, she couldn't justify a comment like, *Just water under the bridge.* The water had come back. Like a torrent, it had come back! Stephanie had lost her foothold, and not only was that unexpected, it was now alarming.

She wanted to loathe Tara. In fact, she had loathed Tara, right up to the point when she walked up to Tara's minivan window. Then, loathing morphed into a combination of amusement at how tame she had become. Then, amusement became curiosity at how she was no longer intimidated. Then curiosity gave way to… To what? *Self*-loathing?

Is Tara now the one who is amused? Or am I now a pitiable curiosity?

It seemed that she was losing her standing in everyone's

minds.

Really? I'm having an identity crisis? You have got *to be kidding me!*

Stephanie leaned her head back to try to grasp the events of the past two days. That's when she heard the truck on the gravel driveway.

CHAPTER 19
Thursday, June 9—6:40 P.M.

Brendan saw Stephanie sitting on the porch as he pulled his black F250 up behind her Pathfinder. Parking the truck, he got out and looked over the hood as she watched.

She seems unsure of what to expect. Good.

He turned back and opened the door to the passenger compartment. He grabbed a duffel bag that he had stuffed some newly-purchased items into and made for the front steps.

Stephanie wasn't saying a word and probably wouldn't either.

He could feel her stare as he took each step. He wouldn't acknowledge her yet. She had to understand the deep disappointment that he was feeling.

Opening the door, he walked into the house. The screen door closed behind him with a loud smack of metal against wood. He walked up the stairs to their bedroom and placed his duffel on the bed. Opening it, he retrieved his journal and put it back into the bedside drawer. He left it open.

He would now play a waiting game with Stephanie. He sat on the edge of the bed. It was a waste of time, of course, but it was essential in order to draw her out. She would apologize to him and re-submit to him with the whole of her being. And that would suffice. He would let that be the end of it.

Things were being taken care of in town that would ensure that there would be no entanglements with outside law enforcement agencies. Uilliam, using the authority that came with being the Pittston police chief, would make sure that the Millsville sergeant kept his distance.

Brendan heard the screen door open and close. *Good.* He slouched over, hands clasped before him, elbows on his knees. He heard her footsteps take her through the living room and into the kitchen. He heard the refrigerator door close. She retraced her steps back to the landing, where she apparently hesitated, and then she began walking up the stairs.

STEPHANIE STOOD with a cold beer bottle in each of her hands. She sighed, hoping that his foul temper had somehow been regulated. She began to walk up the stairs. Halfway up, she flashed back to Tara and stopped.

Who am I, really, to this man?

Were the words that both she and Tara had expressed true? Was she just a trophy? A whore? She wanted to turn around and head back down the stairs so she could think things through. But instead, she took a deep breath, released it slowly, and began climbing the stairs once again.

Turning the corner into the bedroom, she saw Brendan sitting, fingers interlaced before him, looking quite depressed. Stephanie's heart began to pound with a combination of anticipation and hope.

As casually as she could, fighting to display no emotion, she reached out her right hand. "Would you like a beer?"

He looked up at the bottle, then up to her. He looked sad. A slight smile lifted the corners of his mouth as he said,

"Sure. I'd like that, Aileen."

Aileen!

She was *Aileen* again! She tried to acknowledge the use of her name with only a soft smile that said thank you, but once again, the rawness of emotion, triggered by her dinner with Tara, began to surface. Moisture pooled in her eyes.

Brendan reached out for the beer, took it, and placed it on the ground beside his right foot. He extended both of his hands out to her. She placed her cold right hand, wet with condensation, into his left and sank to her knees in front of him. Placing her own beer on the floor, she placed her left hand into his right. The warmth of his hands spoke a welcome to her heart.

A tear streamed down her left cheek.

"Now, now, Aileen. None of that. We are strong, you and I. We don't cry."

Stephanie fought back the tears, but a dam burst and she began to sob. She rested her forehead on Brendan's left knee and began to shake.

BRENDAN LET GO of her hands and placed them on Stephanie's head. He wanted her to feel his sympathy, his forgiveness; what little there was of either, anyway.

He considered that maybe all of the troubles that had taken place leading up to this moment had been orchestrated by Cailleach. Maybe Stephanie needed to understand her dependence on him. She needed to know at her core that she wasn't his equal. Important to the cause? Certainly. But never, ever his equal.

"Aileen," he said again. "My love, I've missed you. I needed time, though, to get past my anger. I didn't want to lash out further. You understand, don't you?"

She lifted her head, both cheeks wet with tears. "Yes. I do. I'm sorry for the disappointment that I brought into your heart and mind."

"I know," he soothed. "You need to know that you *are* important to me. Aileen, you are crucial to what we are going to accomplish as a culture and as a religion."

"You're not just saying that?"

"Dear woman, you have no idea how important you are."

Brendan's words couldn't have been more sincere. Her worth was greater than her weight in gold.

STEPHANIE REVELED under the touch of her lover. All of the doubts about Brendan's love and her importance, in which she'd been awash, were now seeping away. How was it that she had actually struggled for the past two hours rehashing the conversation she'd had with Tara?

She was angry at herself now, for doubting Brendan's love and his concern for her. *To think, I had almost been taken by the idea of some ultimate God of love! I have love, and I have it* without *needing to consider something so vile.*

Once again in her priest's embrace, she had all the assurance that she needed.

She could trust in that love to see her through.

She looked Brendan in the eyes. *Surely, I can trust you. Can't I?*

7:16 P.M.

BRENT AND TARA WERE sitting with all three of their children in the family room. The evening light was beginning to wane, the final sunbeams making their way through all of the west-facing windows.

Jenna, Jamie, and Amy all sat on the couch while Mom and Dad sat on the edge of two folding chairs that they had brought in so they could interact in a circle.

"That is why we're going to teach you the things that you most need to know. Not just for now, but for all the rest of your lives." Brent hoped his introduction had helped even Amy to understand what they were going to be learning.

Jamie's eyes lit up! "Sounds scary and cool!"

Brent looked at Tara, who just shook her head and shrugged.

"Daddy?" began Amy, "Is Jesus *really* bigger than the whole world?"

Brent didn't know exactly where that question came from, but he answered. "Yes, Sweetie. Bigger than the sun and the moon and the stars, too."

"But those are all tiny. Is he bigger than Mammoth Cave?"

Tara's hands covered her mouth for a moment as she began to laugh. "Sweetie, I love you," she said.

Brent couldn't help but chuckle. Amy's ability to say things that made him laugh was one of the joys of being a dad.

Though he didn't need to consider the question, he did reflect on the vacation that had taken them through South-central Kentucky and to Mammoth Cave National Park. Lots of lessons had been taught about God during their hike through the monstrous caverns.

"Much, much bigger than Mammoth Cave," replied Brent.

A thought struck Brent at that moment. If she hadn't asked that simple question, he might not have been able to describe the scale of the Enemy that they all faced.

"But, guess what? The devil is much, much *smaller*. He tries to trick us into believing that he's a huge roaring lion."

"Like Aslan?"

Tara took this question. *The Lion, the Witch, and the Wardrobe* was a disc that seemed to have a continuous presence within their DVD player. "He sure wants to be like Aslan, but he will *never* be. He is like the White Witch. Remember her? Remember how at the end of the movie she didn't have the power that she thought she had and wasn't able to beat Aslan or Aslan's people?"

Amy gave a vigorous nod and smiled. "Aslan ate her!"

All of them laughed.

Jenna chimed in. "Jesus is Aslan, and Aslan is Jesus."

Amy's eyes got wide as she looked from her sister to her mom and dad. They nodded.

"Wow!"

"And just like Aslan comes to the rescue of those who love him, Jesus comes to our rescue in the same way."

"Nicely said, Jenna," agreed Brent. "Okay, with that out of the way, all of you need to know that things could get a bit scary around here for a little while. Some people, who don't like your mom and me, may try to be mean to us. And we want all of you to know that you are going to be safe because of Jesus."

Tara added, "If you ever feel anything weird going on, we want you to immediately start praying. Use the name of Jesus like a sword.

"Jenna and Jamie, we can't force you, but we want you to start reading your Bibles. We want you to learn about who Jesus is and who our Enemy is. Begin to pray in the name of Jesus for your own protection and all of us."

Jamie interjected, "What kind of stuff might happen? Are bad guys going to come to our house?"

Amy got a scared look on her face.

"Look," said their dad, "all we're doing is preparing just in case. Remember how we taught all of you how to use the fire extinguishers and to stay low to the ground and how to climb down from the second story if there is ever a fire in the house? Well, a fire has never happened, but you still need to know all of that just in case. Make sense?"

All three of the kids nodded.

"Same thing here. You've also got your awe-inspiring mom and dad here for you." Brent gave them a wink. "We can pray about anything. If you're ever scared, all you have to do is let us know."

Amy's hand went up in the air. Brent smiled.

"Yes, Amy-bug?" "I'm scared now."

"Then it sounds like the perfect time to pray, doesn't it?"

Amy nodded.

They prayed.

CHAPTER 20
Friday, June 10—7:37 A.M.

Brendan lay in bed, staring at the designs in the plaster ceiling. Stephanie was still asleep to his right, her back to him. He pondered the structure of his day and then the important events of the evening. Tonight, the Home Coven would stir up the pot a little bit and send a little "bad luck" over to the Lawtons in Millsville.

He didn't believe in luck, of course, which is to say that he didn't believe in bad luck either. It was maybe the only thing on which he agreed with the monotheists. If there truly are gods, then what people consider "luck" can't possibly be some ubiquitous power drifting about in the universe waiting to settle upon someone at just the right moment in time.

No, he had always made his own luck. And he was good at it. It was time that this Lawton family realized they were in over their heads and needed to step back from things they didn't understand.

Stephanie had confided some of the details of her meeting with Tara. He could tell she was holding other information back, but he didn't prod. The little snippets that he had received from her were enough to assure him that Tara was going to be a non-issue, and Uilliam was going to assure the same of her husband, the police sergeant, this morning. Tara had given up witchcraft. Good. If she hadn't practiced the craft in years, then she was going to be someone who had little power to restrict what they were currently doing, let alone what they intended to do to her family.

Brendan was still put out by the fact that Cowan and Aileen had allowed for so much turmoil. Last night, at least, he had received from Stephanie her pledge to return to the role of the obedient little woman that he had created in the beginning. She had forgotten her place. Ultimately, though, she conceded that she was not his equal, not even his partner. She was his servant of high standing. Far too many liberties had been allowed in the years they had been together. That was over.

He looked over her bare back. Her hair lay against his right shoulder. She breathed steadily. She was still so beautiful. It was no wonder that she had some small amount of power over him. But now things were too close. He had to rein people in.

The thought brought to mind that he still needed to deal with Cowan's sister. It was infuriating that she was traipsing around Northeast Ohio just spewing information out of that mouth of hers. How many others knew about their "cute" little group? Brendan sat up. Time for a cup of coffee and a phone call to Cowan.

7:45 A.M.

BRENT STOOD UP and stretched. He'd been sitting in his office for the past two hours doing paperwork. His desk sat beside Dave Henderson's desk, some ten feet away. Henderson was the sergeant who worked second shift. The two desks faced an arch that opened into a hallway. On the other side of that hallway was the patrol officers' office, a large room that had an expansive common desk that wrapped along the wall on two sides. Chairs and telephones marked the individual stations at which the officers

took care of their own paperwork. Unfortunately, for
Dave and he, neither of the office areas had doors, so interruptions were rather frequent.

Brent grabbed the keys for his patrol car and began to head
out. Time to hit the streets. Best part of the day. No sooner had
he rounded the corner out of his office than Corporal Larkin approached him from behind.

"Brent."

Brent turned around. "Hey, Tracy."

"Captain wants to see you."

"Mood?"

"Crappy."

"Wonderful. Thank you."

"What good am I if I can't be a wet blanket every once in
a while?"

"I'm going to start returning the favor."

Brent turned around and followed Tracy in the opposite direction. Passing the Communications Center, he saw Ron Goodlow in the dispatcher's chair. He tapped on the glass. Ron turned
around with his seemingly ever-present smile. They both lifted
hands in greeting. *Good man.* Brent pushed forward to the captain's office.

He approached the desk of Carol Masterson, Captain Morelli's executive assistant. She glanced up at him and gave him
a look that said, *"You're not going to enjoy it in there,"* then
tipped her head in the direction of the door.

Brent took a deep breath and strode forward. He knocked
and waited.

"Come!"

Opening the door, he started to walk in.

"Close the door, Lawton."

Brent turned, closed the door, and then walked to the desk.

"Take a seat."

Brent sat. "You wanted to see me, Captain?"

"You couldn't leave well enough alone, could you?"

"I'm sorry?"

"This morning, I got a call from Chief Connor in Pittston."
The captain paused, waiting for a response.

Brent shook his head and raised his eyebrows, unsure to what was being alluded.

His captain scrunched his forehead. "You really don't know what this is about?"

"No, sir."

"The chief indicated that you had been investigating the go-ings-on of that religious group in Pittston. Said that you were questioning a relative of someone in that group, seeking information about illegal activities. In his city! Is that true?"

Brent was stunned by what he heard, and it must have shown.

"Captain, let me start off by saying…"

"*Start off* by answering my question, Sergeant!"

"No, it's not true. Well, not completely true."

The captain's head angled down a few degrees while his right hand came up. Placing his thumb and forefinger into his eye sockets, he applied pressure and pulled back to the bridge of his nose, where he hesitated before speaking again.

"Okay. I'm trying to be calm here. But, Lawton, you had better make this explanation worth the effort."

"Sir, my wife was approached at a store yesterday by a woman who was interested in the tattoo she has on her right shoulder blade. She said it was the same design that she saw a lot of the religious attendees—the ones that I told you about—had inked into their skin. My wife became very curious since she had only ever seen the tattoo one time before.

"They hit it off in conversation, resulting in my wife inviting her over for dinner. So, no, I didn't go out of my way to look into what's going on in Pittston. But it did come to my doorstep."

"Want to try telling me why the Chief of Police in another city would call, almost demanding that I tug on your leash?"

Brent momentarily looked down at his hands. "You're really not going to like my answer."

Morelli leaned forward, clasping his hands and resting his forearms on his desk. "Try me."

"Captain, you were lied to by Chief Connor. Or at least intentionally misdirected."

The captain raised his eyebrows at the accusation. "Go on."

"When I was in here with you the day you called him, he

told you that there was some sort of family reunion going on with some Scottish people visiting. Right?"

Morelli nodded.

"Turns out that that was just the first of his deceptions. The woman who came over for dinner is the twin sister of one of the religious faithful over there. No harm in that, obviously. She didn't even know what all of them were practicing, though it's a long-dead religion that this group is trying to revive. Something to do with an ancient people called the Picti, who used to dominate northern Scotland.

"Anyway, she said she was invited to a gathering early on the first day that all of these people arrived. It was a meet and greet and barbecue held at a local farm as a welcome for the attendees.

"There were at least a couple of hundred who showed. And get this... they weren't just from Scotland; they were from all sorts of different countries.

"Ready for the clincher?" Brent leaned forward and clasped his own hands, elbows on his knees.

"I don't think I'm going to like what you're about to say. But, out with it."

"Chief Jim Connor was in attendance. In fact, the man is one of these Picti followers."

Brent's captain pursed his lips and sat back in his chair with a squeak. He stared at Brent without a word. Brent could tell he was not only processing what he had heard, but calculating what to do about it.

After a minute, he spoke. "Doesn't matter."

"What? Captain..."

"I didn't say that I like it, Lawton! But it does *not* matter! So, he lied to me. Guess what? People lie to me all the time. It's not illegal! Neither is participating in some sort of hokey religious nut festival in the middle of nowhere!

"This is none of our business, Sergeant! It's none of *your* business!"

"It is, though, Captain. It is. It came to my doorstep and it didn't end there." Brent was determined to get some leeway.

Morelli frowned. "Okay, I'm still listening."

"Yesterday, unbeknownst to me, my wife went on a self-ordained mission to see if she could find the person that she had originally seen that tattoo on twenty-four years ago.

"As she drove out to Pittston to find out if that woman still lived in the same house that Tara used to visit, Tara was startled to find that she had been followed there from *our neighborhood* by *that* woman! This isn't just a matter of curiosity anymore. This is about the protection of my family!"

"You're telling me that your house was being watched?"

"Not according to the woman. It happened to be a weird co-incidence that had them both seeking the other out at the same time on the same day. Now tell me that wouldn't weird you out a little bit."

"Okay. Okay, I get it. You've got a right to be concerned. But I still don't understand why. Why would *anyone* want to seek you or your wife out just because you were told about some religious freaks?"

"That, sir, is what I would like to find out. But if they're nerv-ous enough to try to keep me from looking into things—and I'm not saying that I am..."

"Mmm-hmm."

"... then there has to be *something* illegal going on. Isn't that the way you would read it?"

Again, the captain stared. He rolled his fingertips on the arm-rests of his leather office chair, then leaned forward again. "Law-ton, I am not going to tell you what you should and should not be concerned about.

"Like you, I'm a husband and a father. You need to protect your family. But that is the *limit* to which you can proceed as a police officer.

"Do you understand me? If you cross jurisdictions..." He shook his head. "Dammitall, I'll take your badge. And I won't have a choice in the matter. Do you *understand* me?"

Brent looked his superior dead in the eyes and said, "You know me, Captain. You know that I've got boundaries. You've never had to worry whether I was going to go over the top with anyone. You know that I'm also a man of faith. You've never criticized me for it, though I know it's not your cup of tea, and I appreciate that. But I'm less cop than I am Christian, and that's something that you're going to have to deal with."

Brent wondered if, with that last comment, he had pushed back too strongly, but he pressed on.

"My family will be protected, but I suspect that something horrible is going on in Pittston. Something that violates everything that I believe in as a Christian. I know that's not enough for me to go out and start looking for answers across city lines, but when that is combined with the Chief of Police in that village telling you and me to keep our noses out of his business...and *his business* means being involved with those Picti people. Well, you tell me what I'm supposed to do. Ignore it?"

Morelli was irritated and made it clear. "You tell me what *I'm* supposed to do! They have done nothing wrong in the eyes of the law!" He momentarily clenched his teeth, then continued, "Yes! I do believe, now, that something is going on over there! But I *cannot* have *any* of my officers going into their jurisdiction! That's it! Period!" He slammed his palm down on the desk to emphasize his point.

With those words, Brent's day was "officially" ruined, because at that very moment, he already knew that he was going to disobey his captain's direct order not to involve himself further.

9:37 A.M.

BRENT SAT WAITING for the light to turn green. As he did, he reengaged the mental debate that he'd been having for the better part of an hour and a half. Should he, or should he not, take the chance of calling John Eldredge? He wondered if any good could come from calling the Pittston police officer.

Tracy said he could be trusted, but he wasn't even sure what questions to ask. Well, he had questions, but would they be too much of an ask from Tracy's friend? What were the chances that Eldredge would look into the leads that he'd been given by Donna McNeill?

For a fleeting moment, he thought of his captain's directive.

What could it hurt? It would be Eldredge doing the investigating, wouldn't it? My hands would be clean. A jab of guilt washed over Brent. *My* hands *would be clean?* He realized that he would be asking someone else to compromise so that he wouldn't be accused of doing the same.

He slammed the palm of his left hand on the steering wheel of his cruiser and let out a frustrated yell. He looked to his left to see a middle-aged woman in a car in the left-turn lane staring at him through her passenger window. He gave her an embarrassed half-smile and wave. She shook her head and looked forward.

He shook his head, too. "This whole situation stinks!" he lamented, slapping his other palm on the steering wheel. The light turned green. He punched the accelerator.

Ahead, he saw to his right the parking lot of TML Motorworks. He decided to pull in. A few minutes were needed to think things through one more time.

One more time, again, he thought.

He parked the patrol unit against the inside curb near the street so that it faced the direction he'd been driving. He figured that he might as well actually do some community service while he continued to weigh things. Terrence, the owner of TML, had given him the liberty to use this area of the parking lot for this very purpose.

He opened the door and grabbed his speed gun. Standing between the open door and his driver's seat, he pointed the gun down the stretch of four-lane road. It was a 45 MPH zone, but with the lack of traffic signals through this area, drivers often felt like they should be allowed to drive faster, and they often did.

43 … 47 … 51 …46 … Brent let the 51-MPH vehicle slip by.

Okay, if I call Eldredge, I could ask if it would be okay *to ask questions; tell him I don't want to put him on the spot; let him know that he doesn't have to say anything he's uncomfortable with.* In his mind, it made perfect sense. No harm could come from just asking for permission to ask questions.

But what of the questions?

Something struck Brent. An idea. *What if we met outside of work hours? We could go grab something to drink and a bite to eat outside of both of our jurisdictions.*

Brent put the speed gun down and grabbed his cell phone. He grabbed the piece of paper from his pocket that he'd written Eldredge's number on and punched it into the phone. Send.

The phone was answered on the third ring. "Officer Eldredge."

"Hello, John? This is Brent Lawton, Millsville PD."

"Hello, Brent. Tracy Larkin gave me a heads up that you might be calling."

Brent hadn't expected that. "Well, good. At least I hope it's good," he said with a laugh.

He heard Eldredge chuckle, as well. "Yeah, well. It's all good. Not during duty hours, though. Know what I mean?"

"Fair enough. Doing anything after work?"

"Just bachelor food."

Brent laughed. "How 'bout I treat you to something a little better?"

CHAPTER 21
Friday, June 10—4:47 P.M.

B rent sat across from Pittston Police Officer John Eldredge. Both of them had had the opportunity to run home after their shifts and put on civilian clothes before meeting in Bedford for dinner.

Melissa's Diner wasn't exactly known for its cuisine, which, truth be told, is precisely why Brent chose the place. All the better for avoiding the people that John and he might ordinarily bump into on a Friday evening out. The diner seemed to always have the scent of something having recently been burned. And by the looks of them, the Formica tables and booth seats should have been replaced fifteen or twenty years ago.

It wasn't a bad place, but it wasn't aesthetically pleasing enough to draw in the populace, that was for sure. Brent guessed that the diner had probably survived the years due to its transient regulars; the truckers that frequented the place primarily because of the diesel fuel tanks across the street and the adequate parking space for their big rigs.

When Eldredge had arrived, Brent immediately apologized for having lured him into the one-and-a-half-star eatery.

Eldredge insisted, "This still beats the TV dinners that have become a mainstay in my microwave."

Tracy was right about this man. He seemed to be a decent guy with an engaging personality. Brent liked him immediately.

The Pittston cop was probably in his mid-thirties, at least ten years younger than Brent. He was about Brent's height, though, with light-brown hair and a strong, rugged appearance.

After a good fifteen minutes of light conversation, each trying to feel the other out, it was Eldredge who broke through the small talk. "So, what is it *exactly* that you want to talk about, or should I be afraid to ask?"

Brent smiled wryly. "Just to be up front, you're going to have every right to feel ambivalent toward me and about this conversation. And I'm sure you'll feel uncomfortable answering my questions. That is, if you *choose* to answer them."

John seemed to stare at Brent's chest as he processed the statement. Then he looked up into Brent's eyes. "I do hold the right of refusal here, so I guess you should just come out with your questions."

"Fair enough. How are the working conditions in Pittston? I mean, in the office around the other cops."

Eldredge tightened his lips for a moment and raised his eyebrows. "Nothing bad to complain about, I guess. Same stuff I'm sure you deal with day to day. In general, I'd say that I have good relationships with the guys."

"How long have you known everyone there?"

"There are a couple of rookies, but other than that, I've known everyone for the full three years I've been there."

It hadn't even struck Brent to ask his next question until now. "You didn't start your career in Pittston?"

"Oh, no. I grew up as a cop in the Columbus area. Hilliard. Bigger than Pittston and a good place to work. But couldn't stay. My niece got sick."

"I'm sorry. I hope she's okay now."

"It was cancer."

John looked down at his plate and took a couple of deep breaths before continuing. When he looked up Brent saw the faintest hint of tears in his eyes.

"She was ten years old. I couldn't bear not being around, especially with the radical treatments she had to go through at the

Cleveland Clinic." He stopped momentarily to maintain his composure. "Sorry."

"No reason to apologize, John."

Eldredge loosed a deep sigh and wiped the tears away before they had a chance to fall. "Anyway, she didn't make it. Passed away last year."

"John, I am so very sorry." Brent wanted to say something meaningful, but could only come up with a feeble, "I can't imagine."

"It's all good, Brent," he said. "She was an amazing little girl. But when the pain became a 24/7 thing, I started asking God to take her home. Guess he heard me." He blinked away the last of his tears.

The obvious question struck Brent. He wanted to investigate the man's faith after his mention of God. But he hadn't come here for that. He needed other answers.

A stab of conviction pierced his conscience. *What is wrong with you? Really?* Had his priorities really gone that far out of whack? *The man gave you an opening to share God, and you're just going to pass on it so that you can go on to other things?*

Brent closed his eyes for a long moment. John must have interpreted it as an aftereffect of the information he had just shared about his niece, because he became the one to apologize.

"I'm sorry. Not what you were looking for, I know."

Brent looked up, feeling worse for putting this man in a position of guilt. "No, John. I was just kicking myself for being a jerk. I was going to skip asking a personal—rather, an *important*—question in favor of one that was a lesser priority.

"Would you mind too much if I divert our conversation for a minute? I want to ask you about something you just said."

"Shoot."

"You said you prayed to God. Are you a Christian?"

Tears began to appear again as John looked Brent dead on. "Because of that little girl, yes." Both elbows came up to the table, and the fingertips of both hands went to his forehead, shielding his eyes.

"She kept praying for me. Dying in that *damn* bed, she was praying for *me!* Told me that Jesus was going to take care of her, but that she wanted to make sure that Jesus took care of me, too."

John's shoulders began to shake, and Brent could hear him sniffling while trying to control his breathing. It appeared that he was losing the battle.

"My sister, Sarah," he continued, voice strained, "told me that Megan—my niece—had been praying for her Uncle John even before she got sick. My sister had gotten religion... well, what I called religion, about ten years ago, when Megan was about three. It was just the two of them up here. Lisa's husband was killed in Iraq." He paused in obvious reflection. "He was a good man."

"So much tragedy," Brent inserted with a whisper.

John nodded. "Yeah. Lisa's really been through it. But with her church family and Mom and Dad's help, she's really been doing well lately. Her faith saved her." He let out a light laugh. "I guess it saved her in more than one way."

John paused a moment, collected his thoughts, then said with a smile, "That was more than you asked for, wasn't it?"

Brent smiled, but didn't say anything.

"Anyway, yeah, through all of that, I guess God got a hand-hold on me. Ended up at Lisa's church for the memorial service for Megan. The pastor said that Megan had asked him to make sure that he told everyone about Jesus when they came to see..." He choked back tears again. "... when they came to see her. He did, and that's when I made a decision for Christ."

Brent was quiet for a moment before responding. "John, I am so proud of you. I don't know you, but I'm definitely proud of you."

"I take it you're a Christian?"

"Without question. It's a pleasure getting to know you, brother."

"Same here."

John extended his hand.

Brent took it.

"So!" asserted John, probably too loudly, "You've got some questions, huh?"

Brent laughed. "A few."

"Well, let's see how many we can get answered for you," he

intoned with a grin.

6:07 P.M.

THE AMOUNT OF COFFEE that Brent and John drank was surely going to affect their ability to sleep later that night. But the information the two of them shared would more than make up for any red eyes Brent would probably have in the morning, though the same may not be said for John.

John had seen Chief Connor leave the offices abruptly from time to time, and he had seen the chief on two occasions with a man who seemed to wield some sort of influence over his affairs.

He went on to describe what he could remember of the man's physical characteristics. Brent wrote them down.

"I had pretty much written the chief's interactions off as none of my business. But now that I'm aware that the chief has been lying to other law enforcement officers…" John shook his head. "I'll keep my eyes and ears open for more information."

"And the farm at which all of the ceremonies are allegedly taking place?"

"I'm familiar with it, as well. But I've never been on the property and likely won't be any time in the future.

"Until you told me about what you suspect is going on, I've been content to believe that it really had been just a large family reunion that had taken place. But now? Well, if I hear of anything going on out there, I'll do my best to scope things out without breaching the law."

That was all that Brent could have asked for.

They were within a few minutes of going their separate ways when Brent's cell phone rang. "I'll bet that's my wife. Forgot to tell her where I'd be. Excuse me a sec."

John smiled with a nod.

Brent looked at the display on his Droid. As he suspected, it was Tara. "Hi, hon. Sorry that I…"

"Brent, Donna McNeill just called. She says that someone's

been following her all day. I told her to get over here right away. She's pretty spooked."

"Okay, but why would she think to call you?"

"Hmm... Remember that police uniform that you wore in front of her?"

"All right, Miss Sarcasm." "Where are you?"

"I'm in Bedford, but I'm going to head home right now. I'll see you in a little bit. Love you."

"Love you, too. Hurry."

Brent slid out of the booth. John started getting up, too.

"Everything okay?"

"That was my wife. She said that Donna McNeill, the woman I told you about, is being followed. She's heading to my house now. I've got to get there to meet her."

"Brent, sounds like things are ramping up. You need anything, you let me know."

Brent took John's extended hand and added his free hand, displaying his appreciation for the man's help and the exposure of his heart.

"John, this whole thing may blow up in my face. But if this ... this religion really is as demonic as I'm being led to believe, then a lot of people's souls are at stake, and as a Christian, albeit a young one, I'm sure you can appreciate the significance of that. I know a false religion isn't illegal, but it is important."

"You're right. And I may be a young pup compared to your years as a Christian, but I take my faith very seriously. I want to protect people from lies as much as you do."

"Good to hear."

"Now get home to your family."

Brent smiled and turned to walk away. He stopped and turned back to face Eldredge.

"You know what gets me about all of this? If the Pittston Chief of Police is working to cover something up, you can bet your badge that something illegal is going on."

"Or is about to," added Eldredge.

6:31 P.M.

BRENT WALKED INTO his house after seeing Donna McNeill's sedan parked in the driveway. As he entered the living room, all eyes turned to him. He saw Donna sitting on the couch, with Tara and Jenna on either side. Jamie and Amy were nowhere to be seen.

Donna put on an apologetic smile and offered, "Hi, Brent. Forgive me for intruding on your family like this."

Tara responded before Brent could open his mouth. "Donna, quit apologizing already. Calling us was the right thing to do."

"Tara's right, Donna," Brent interjected. "But, then, she usually is."

Donna's face showed that she appreciated the humor. Brent looked at Tara. "The kids with their Nana and Papa?"

"I asked Ashley Hahn if she could watch them at her house for a couple of hours."

That was good enough for Brent. It was great having some on-call babysitters close by. He walked over to his favorite chair next to the sofa and sat down.

"Did I miss anything?"

Tara and Jenna both shook their heads. "No, not really. We were just getting comfortable when you walked in," replied Tara.

The police officer in Brent took over. "Excuse me. I want to grab a pen and paper." He got back up, and after several seconds, he returned from the kitchen, notepad in hand. "Okay, let's start from the very beginning.

"Donna, was today the first time you had the sensation you were possibly being followed?"

"It wasn't a sensation," indicated Donna. "I was really being followed."

"I believe you, but I've got to ask the questions that will help me to develop a mental picture of what's going on. So, bear with me. I promise I won't ask any irrelevant questions. Okay?"

It was obvious that she was feeling embarrassed for her defensive tone, but she steadied herself and said, "Okay. And, yes, this is the first time that I've ever had the feeling that I was being followed. I've never had any reason to think that I would be.

Truth be told, I don't know why I was being followed today!"

"Sweetheart," Brent said to Jenna, "will you go get Miss McNeill a bottle of water from the fridge? Thank you."

Jenna hopped up and made for the kitchen.

"You don't have to do that, really," responded Donna to his kindness.

"Trust me, you're going to want it. Questions from a police officer always lead to a dry mouth," Brent stated with a grin.

The statement caused Donna to laugh.

Good, Donna. Relax, he willed.

Jenna returned with the water, and Donna immediately broke the seal, then set it on the coffee table.

"What time did you leave your home today?" Brent began again.

"Umm… I'd say around 9:10, 9:15 a.m. Somewhere around then. My first appointment for the day was at 10:00 a.m."

"Do you always take the same route out of your neighborhood or complex?"

"Yes. My neighborhood is contained within a big loop. I could head either direction to get out, but I always take the same way."

"Nothing unusual? No cars parked on the street that you didn't recognize?

"No one's allowed to park on our streets without permission from the city, so it's rare to have any parked along the curbs."

"Okay, when and where was the first time you suspected that you were being followed?"

"Just after leaving my third appointment." She thought for a moment. "That would have made it about 3:15 this afternoon. I was in Warrensville Heights on Miles Road, about to turn onto Lee Road. I just happened to look up into my rearview mirror to see another vehicle turn onto Miles from East 164th. That's where my appointment was. I didn't think anything of it, really. It was just happenstance that I even looked back to see a car pull out."

"And you're sure that it was *that* car that you saw later."

"Not just later. I'm always stopping off at stores to pick up things that I'll need for a client—as Tara will attest."

She smiled at Tara.

"So, I went to QuickBuy and picked up a couple of things. After I went back to my car and pulled out of the parking lot, I thought I saw the car parked across the street. I *almost* thought nothing of it, but I just had this quick thought that I'd seen the car before. In my rear-view mirror, I saw it pull out a couple of cars behind me.

"I had one last stop I had to make before heading home for the day. I needed to go to the post office to mail in my end-of-week reports and receipts to the home office in Cincinnati. So, I go and do that. When I get out of the post office, there it is, across the street! The same car!"

"What did you do?"

"What do you mean, what did I do? I got in my car and called Tara!"

"Could you see into the car?"

"Yes, there was a man in the car."

"Could you identify him if you saw him again?"

"No. I could only tell that it was a man. The glare kept me from seeing his face."

"No chance it was a woman?"

"Oh no. Definitely not. His head was shaved or cut very close."

Brent jotted that down. "If there was too much glare, how could you see that?" Brent knew the question could sound accusatory, so he appended. "Glare can play tricks on the mind."

Donna answered with no hint of offense, "The building behind his car must have been white or something." She shook her head. "Can't remember. But I could see his head silhouetted through the windshield despite the glare."

"And he followed you again?"

"Yes. He followed me until I got to Millsville, then he disappeared."

Brent looked at Tara. "Well, that's about as big a message as anything we could have gotten delivered to our doorstep."

Tara nodded with realization.

"Message? You mean from me showing up?" Donna asked.

"It was someone from the Picti group."

Donna was taken aback. "What? Who? Why?" she fired in

rapid succession.

Brent went on to tell her about Tara's run-in with Stephanie and the lies that had been told by the Pittston police chief.

"That the vehicle following you would turn away and remain outside of my jurisdiction is *very* telling."

"But why? I mean, my brother wouldn't be involved in anything illegal. The people that I've met... Brendan and Stephanie... You can't be right about this. There's got to be another explanation."

"Maybe there is, Donna. But I doubt it. And if they're keeping tabs on you, then you're a liability to them."

Tara interjected, "Donna, why don't you stay with us tonight?"

Donna looked from Tara to Brent and back. "This *can't* be that serious! It makes no sense that someone would want to follow me, let alone harm me. I'm fine."

She stood up and made to leave, but it was Jenna who tried to calm her down. "I would *love* it if you stayed! It would be like a slumber party. You, me, Mom..." she looked over at Brent.

"Sorry, Dad. Only girls."

Jenna looked back at Donna with pleading eyes. "I don't have any clothes... a toothbrush..."

Jenna stepped through what sounded like a break in Donna's resolve. "We've got extra toothbrushes in the linen closet," she said, looking to her mom. "Right, Mom? And she can borrow some pajamas."

"I think," said Tara with a smile, "that what my daughter is trying to say is, 'Please?'"

Brent could see that Donna's resistance was failing.

"Well," she conceded, "it *has* been years since I've been to a good pajama party."

Jenna yelped with excitement!

Brent could only shake his head.

CHAPTER 22
Friday, June 10—9:58 P.M.

Brendan sat at the dining room table. He held the Key of Bridei before him. Retrospect being what it was, he thought about how he could have avoided the terrible moment on the mound when he had hoped to translate the word "Religion" on the key.

The word *was* there. Sort of.

He had expected to see the word *religio* in Latin inscribed on the back of the key, but instead it read *fides sollemnis*—solemn faith. That hadn't troubled him. What had unexpectedly caught his attention were two other words below those; vile words that had caused the taste of stomach acid to reach his tongue.

The front door opened. In walked Aileen.

He set the stone down on the table. It balanced perfectly on its mounting peg. The question on how to proceed with translating *around* what was inscribed in Latin would have to wait.

"They're arriving," announced Aileen. "Do you want them to come inside, or do you wish that we go to the mound?"

"We'll meet inside. Grab some bottles of water for all of us, will you, my love?"

He could see how his use of the word love played at the corners of her mouth. The right words could move mountains and even greater objects, like hearts.

Aileen stepped back outside momentarily to let the members of the Home Coven know that they should assemble in the living room, then she went to withdraw thirteen bottles of water from one of the two refrigerators that quietly hummed within the confines of the kitchen.

Though tonight would likely not remove from his mind what plagued him now, a little bit of war-making would certainly satisfy a dark craving that had been intensifying for the past couple of days. The right form of spellcasting could transition situations to an acceptable status that had once been dire.

Tonight will be dedicated to the Lawton family in Millsville. It'll be a night they will not soon forget, he mused. The other family that needed to be dealt with, Cowan and his sister, would take a little more thinking … a little more planning.

Apparently, Donna McNeill didn't have a self-stop button. In fact, his "spy" told him that she had fled to Millsville that afternoon. But she wasn't supposed to have fled at all. She was supposed to have gone through the routine of her day and headed back home.

Getting to know how she spent her time outside of her brother's company had been a crucial element in determining the proper course of "discipline" for her. But that got screwed up on day two of the information gathering, apparently because his idiot "hired hand" couldn't keep out of sight.

Brendan checked his watch. Well, Miss McNeill was surely at home by now, and they would deal with her soon enough.

Now, to the issue at hand.

11:07 P.M.

BRENT YAWNED.

He was in the family room. The interaction of the three ladies had become completely tuned out, probably a good hour before.

The discussion of what had driven Donna McNeill to their home had long since transitioned to girl talk. Not a problem. It had allowed for a little bit of interaction with Jamie and Amy before putting them to bed.

He was craving the same thing, now. Heading into the weekend, a good night's sleep would be a great thing.

He got up from his family room chair, where he had spent the past forty minutes or so reading. Even Tom Pawlik's suspense novel, regardless of its intensity, couldn't keep his eyelids from drooping.

Walking into the living room once more, he gave a tired wave and said, "Goodnight, girls. If you hear a rooster crow, you'll know you've stayed up a bit too late."

"Goodnight, Brent."

"Goodnight, Baby."

"Goodnight, Daddy."

Goodnight, John Boy, thought Brent with a smile.

Brent walked up the stairs, peeked in on his two youngest, then prepared for bed.

"BRENT SEEMS LIKE a good man," said Donna. "How did the two of you meet?"

"Umm… That might not…"

"It's a *great* story!" interjected Jenna. "Mom and Dad couldn't have been more different. Well, at least that's what I had *originally* thought. Turns out, they had a more common background than I knew about." Turning to her mom, she said, "Isn't that *right*, Mom?"

Tara closed her eyes, smiled, and shook her head. "My lovely daughter recently found out some details about her dad's and my relationship that came as a bit of a shock." Looking at Donna, she suggested, "Maybe this story would be more appropriate for another time."

Donna was having none of that. "Tara Lawton, don't hold back on me. Give me all the mushy details!"

Jenna grinned from ear to ear as she shifted her attention to her mom.

"I'm not sure how much *mushiness* there will be, but there certainly was a lot of mess."

Tara guarded much of the information from the past that took place between Brent and her. Internally, she cringed at some of the things she had done back then to try to destroy him. While the story was abbreviated, it did contain more details than Jenna had previously been privy to. A good twenty minutes later, she wrapped up the tale.

Donna just stared, mouth slightly agape. Finding her voice, she remarked, "I must admit, I didn't see any of that coming."

Tara's lips pulled into a slightly embarrassed smile and said, "Not exactly a Hallmark Channel romance, huh? But all of that stuff definitely melded us together."

"You two are like blue monkeys in a brown-monkey world," came Donna's response. "I am so far removed from any of your experiences that I hardly know what to say."

"I like that," laughed Jenna. "Blue monkeys! I'm going to have to think up some nicknames for Mom and Dad, now."

Tara's eyes and head swung up to the left, comprising an *Oh brother* moment.

"All of what you said, it really is true?" inquired Donna. Tara didn't blame her for her skepticism. "Every last evil manipulation, and every last profoundly-God work of redemption."

"I think I told you that I'm not the religious type. I've never heard anything like that before." Donna appeared to become momentarily introspective. "I'm not saying that I believe *everything* you just said, but there were definitely some impact moments for me in your story."

"Like what?" wondered Jenna.

"Jenna, be polite," Tara quickly directed.

"Oh, I don't mind," Donna said with a smile. "You described how you had a very emotional experience while traveling home from your backpacking trip. That's *really* what did it for you? I mean, your life up to that point was really … umm *unusual* … to say the least. It sounds like you were really angry and had a lot of hate. I just find it hard to believe that a single emotional experience would cause everything to just turn around to make you who you are today."

"If it were just emotion, I would agree with you."

The three talked for another fifteen minutes or so regarding the dramatic life changes that took place in Tara's life. Tara felt like Donna was starting to understand, while also failing to fully believe, the impact God had on her life.

Tara had just asked Donna whether she had any religious upbringing when she felt a chill that startled her. Her initial response was to consider whether the air conditioning had suddenly kicked on. As a matter of reflex, she looked at the ceiling for a vent, but even before her eyes had reached the plaster, she remembered that all of the house's vents were built into the floor.

"Mom?"

Tara looked at Jenna. "Mom, do you feel that?"

"The cold?"

"I feel it, too," Donna added.

"Yes, I feel it," Tara responded.

"What is it?" Jenna's eyes began darting around, looking for an answer.

Tara stood up and walked around the coffee table into the center of the living room. Her hands were vigorously rubbing her exposed arms.

"I don't..." She stopped. It wasn't just cold. There was a presence. She turned back to the couch. Both Jenna and Donna had begun to visibly shiver.

"Mom!" Jenna demanded her attention.

Tara stared, transfixed, as her daughter's shivering became uncontrollable.

Donna stood, wrapping her arms around herself. Tension and fear were evident in her eyes, and it became obvious that she was on the verge of panic. "W-what-t-tss hap-p-pening?" she managed to get out, her teeth beginning to chatter. Her lips were already beginning to turn blue.

"J-Jee-Jeesusss!" Jenna called out in desperation. Her abdomen had begun spasming, forcing her to double over on the couch.

Donna fell to her knees. "Oh God, oh G-God-dd!" Her right

knee clipped the corner of the coffee table, tearing open a nasty gash in her skin. She hit the ground hard.

Tara's body was on the verge of the same sort of spasmodic fit. She wanted to retch. It seemed impossible how compressed her chest and stomach felt.

She took her daughter's lead. "F-f-fath-ther, help! B-bind yyou … Je…" Before she could get the Lord's name out of her mouth, her throat constricted, forcing her to stop speaking. She, too, fell to her knees, landing forward on her left hand, her right grabbing for her throat.

Tara couldn't breathe. Panic was setting in.

In the back of her senses somewhere, she could hear Donna gasping for air.

Tara had the presence of mind that could only come from being a mother to look at her daughter struggling desperately on the couch. Her eyes were open wide with terror; her face beet-red from her desperate need to exhale.

Jesus! Jesus! Jesus! Help us! Open my mouth, Tara pleaded silently.

Tara tried once again to squeeze air through her voice box. "Jees-us … *name!*"

Instantly, the air that had been trapped in her lungs made a forceful exit; the pressure from her diaphragm caused her to also vomit onto the carpet. She inhaled a ragged breath and immediately let loose a single sentence in the form of a scream. "I bind you all in the name of Jesus!"

Donna began to gasp for air. She continued to tremble un-controllably. Blood was fast creating a pool on the carpet below her right knee.

As quickly as she was able, Tara stood. Grasping her belly, she rushed to her daughter.

"Jenna! Jenna!"

But Jenna's struggle to breathe had not ended. Tara knew she was on the verge of passing out, her eyes pleading to her mom for help; tears streaming down her face.

Tara's hands found Jenna's and took them into a tight grip. "In the name of Jesus Christ of Nazareth! *Let go of my daughter!*"

The words cut her throat like a razor, but they were out, and they were obeyed.

Jenna collapsed forward into her mother as she forcibly exhaled. Tara let go of Jenna's hands and wrapped her arms around her daughter, quickly rubbing her back with a rapid hand motion, creating friction and warmth.

"Jenna…" Tara kissed the top of her daughter's head. "Lord Jesus, take care of my baby."

"Mommy…" Jenna began to cry, but Tara could tell she was all right.

Tara heard Donna groan. She didn't want to, but she had to let go of her daughter.

"Honey, I'll be right back."

"No! Don't *go!*" Jenna pleaded.

Tara ignored the plea, even as it tore at her heart. She quickly went to Donna's side. The woman had pulled herself into a fetal position. Her breathing was faster than normal, yet now unrestricted. But there was fear coursing through Donna, unlike anything Tara had experienced. At least not since the time that she had been brutalized by a demonic force in her college dorm room some two and a half decades before.

She placed her hands on Donna's forehead and abdomen. "In the name of Jesus, I speak peace over you, Donna. Peace, be still, in the name of Jesus."

A thump on the ceiling above the dining room!

No, not on the ceiling … the bedroom floor! *Her* bedroom floor! "*Brent?!*"

She let go of Donna and made her way to the steps leading upstairs. She took the steps two at a time, tripping once and falling to her hands as she made for her husband.

She heard Jenna beg for her to return.

At the top of the stairs, she turned right to head to their master bedroom at the back of the house. She began to pass the doorway to Amy's room when she heard a groan.

"Oh, God … not my baby!"

She was frozen … She didn't know … Brent?!

She rushed into Amy's room. Amy was in her bed, whimpering, tossing, and turning.

A nightmare, Tara realized. She wanted to…

She heard gagging. Then the sound of someone else running up the stairs.

She quickly turned from Amy's bed and ran back into the hallway. She had to find out what was happening to Brent!

Jenna reached the top of the stairs and nearly collided with her. Jenna was terrified.

"Mommy? What…"

"Amy! Help Amy!" With those words, Tara bounded into her own bedroom.

She couldn't see. *Light switch!* She had to force her brain to cooperate with her need. She found the switch and illuminated the room. She looked toward the bed, but Brent wasn't there.

Tara rushed to the other side and found him on his back on the floor. Spittle had become foam in the corners of his mouth, his hands near his throat, but he wasn't struggling. A horrible realization struck her. *He's not breathing!*

"Brent!" she screamed. "Breeennt!" Tears were making it nearly impossible to see now. She started to shake him. *What do I do? What do I need to do?!*

It finally occurred to her that she needed to call on the Lord again. "Jesus! Help Brent! In Jesus' name, help Brent!"

His breathing … it wasn't being restored! "In Jesus' name! Let him go!" she pleaded. Tears were pouring from her eyes now. Her fear was full-blown panic.

Her throat was already raw, but she still let loose. *"BRENT!"* The scream felt like razor blades tearing through her airway. Again, she screamed unintelligibly.

Someone came running into the room. Tara was forcefully pulled backward off of her husband and she began to tremble with uncontrollable anxiety as Donna McNeill rushed to Brent's side.

Tara watched; her arms tightly wrapped around herself in a vain attempt to create even a small measure of comfort.

Donna leaned her left ear over Brent's mouth while at the same time doing a quick check for a pulse. Apparently, finding neither pulse nor breathing, she began chest compressions. They were hard and deep. Tara thought she heard a *snap!* emit from Brent's torso.

His ribs?

"God ... save him!" She began to weep as she watched Donna's heroic effort proceed.

"...7...8...9...10...11...12..." Donna counted to herself just above a whisper with each rapid compression.

Blow in his mouth! Aren't you supposed to blow in his mouth?

"Mooommm!"

Jenna!

Tara's heart seized! She turned her head toward the doorway, then back to Donna. Her emotions were making it impossible to correctly process what needed to be done.

"...15...16...17..." Donna called over her shoulder, "Go! I've got this! ...20...21..."

Tara was on her feet immediately! She ran across the hallway and into Amy's room.

Empty!

"Mommeeee!"

It came from Jamie's room! "Jesus, please!" she pleaded as she ran down to the other end of the hallway and into his room.

Amy was standing just inside the doorway, crying, as she watched with horror what was happening on her brother's bed.

Tara had the restored presence of mind to say to her, "Pray, Amy. Pray to Jesus ... to Aslan." Then she rushed to Jamie's bedside, where Jenna was pleading with Jesus for her brother's life.

"Move out of the way, Jenna. I'm here!"

Jenna backed away, her hands coming to her mouth, unable to control a sob.

Tara looked at Jamie; he was hyperventilating, his stomach making mad contractions that shouldn't have been possible. His eyes were wide open, but focused on nothing. He looked catatonic, completely oblivious to his surroundings.

Tara leaned over her boy and placed a hand on his chest. She would apply the same remedy to this situation. "In the name of Jesus, I bind every demonic spirit over Jamie! In the name of Jesus!" she proclaimed loudly. "I plead the blood of Jesus around him. Father set a hedge, a barrier, of protection around him, in the name of Jesus!"

Her intercession had the hoped-for effect. His breathing began to slow. The stomach contortions ceased. She placed a hand on her son's sweaty forehead and brushed away his wet hair.

A pair of little hands wrapped around Tara's waist from behind, and she felt the chest movement of a little girl who was stricken with fear.

Looking at her son, she said, "Jamie, honey. Can you hear me?"

His breathing was still faster than she would have liked, but continuing to slow. His eyes moved her direction and locked onto her own. Fear was present in them. He didn't speak, but he gave a shaky nod of his head, answering her question.

"Thank God," she whispered and leaned to place a kiss on his forehead.

Brent! The thought struck her with the force of a wrecking ball. She had to get back to him.

She turned around and grabbed Amy into her arms. "It's going to be okay, baby. It's going to be okay."

Tara walked up to Jenna, who had retreated to a far wall to watch her mom deal with her brother.

"Jenna, take Amy. I've got to go back to your dad." She looked directly into her oldest child's eyes and said, "Stay in here. Do *not* follow me."

Fear, mixed with the onset of deep sorrow, filled Jenna's face as pools of tears formed. All she could do was nod that she understood what her mom was conveying.

Having transferred Amy into Jenna's arms, Tara ran back down the hallway and back into her—into *their*—bedroom.

She heard groaning.

Groaning!

An unprepared-for hope caused her to gasp in anticipation as she ran to the other side of the bed.

She looked down to see Donna holding Brent's wrist as she looked at her wristwatch.

A pulse! He's got a pulse!

Donna looked back at her and nodded with a half-smile. "He's okay."

Tara was struck with a feeling of such intense euphoria that she wasn't sure she'd make it the three additional feet to her husband. But she did.

She fell to her knees, and she fell onto him, and she was determined to never, *ever* let him go again!

CHAPTER 23
Saturday, June 11—2:47 A.M.

B rent tried not to hold his rib cage too hard; walking out of the ER was painful enough.

Heading for the minivan in the parking lot, he was flanked on both sides by his family and Donna. Ironically, the boredom of the waiting room seemed to do a lot to still nerves and reduce the overall blood pressure in the group. They had probably been the only ones in it who sat receiving a psychological and emotional break.

Still, the mental reality of the night's experiences would be triggered again, very shortly after leaving the hospital. Fears, real and imagined, would not be easily squelched again this night.

"What, no cast?" asked Jamie, lifting up his father's T-shirt.

"Not how they treat rib injuries, Jamie," Brent replied.

"But that's just tape!"

Brent had four strips of two-inch-wide adhesive tape wrapped from sternum to spine on his left side. The X-ray indicated that his *costal cartilage*, the cartilage that secured the bone of the ribs to the sternum, was fractured in two places.

The tape was supposed to secure the ribs and reduce pain.

Yeah, right.

"I know that, son. It's the best that can be done, though."

"Are you going to need me to remind you to cough?" This, from his smirking wife.

"Do you think I need to be reminded?"

She laughed. "I think you need to be *prodded.*"

This was the worst part of Brent's treatment. The ER doc told him to make sure to cough … *often.*

The idea sounded simply stupid! But, he certainly didn't want pneumonia added to the list of less-than-wonderful things that had taken place over the past couple of hours, and apparently, coughing would prevent the formation of phlegm and mucus in his lungs.

"Hmm?" she prodded.

"Wow, you are persistent! And a bit of a pest, too!" remarked Brent.

"Yes, I am. Now cough."

Brent decided to "man up" in front of his kids and cough. He stopped walking, closed his eyes, and cringed with the effort.

"That's my man," said Tara with a sympathetic smile.

Donna, though, wasn't wearing a smile. The look on her face was apologetic, mixed with a hint of 'What happened tonight?'

"I'm sorry for the broken ribs, Brent," she offered.

"Don't worry. You're protected by Ohio's Good Samaritan Law. I'm an official law-enforcement officer and know these things." He winked at Donna. "I'm sorry about having a coffee table with sharp corners."

Donna's right knee had required seven stitches. Sporting a pair of Tara's jean shorts, she now walked with a little bit of a limp.

"Okay, let's just mutually agree not to sue each other," she quipped.

"Dad?"

"Yes, Jenna-Girl?"

"Can we…" She hesitated. "Can we *not* go back home right away?"

She could hardly be blamed for the question. There was surely not one of the six who wanted to go back into that environment any time soon. He looked at his watch and thought for a moment.

"Well, until the Aleve that they just gave me kicks in, I'm not likely to be able to fall back to sleep. Even when it does, I'm not sure I'll be able to … or even want to try.

"Regardless, I think we've all got a lot to talk about, and a lot of questions to ask." He stopped as they approached the minivan. "How about we go to the Fairlane Diner for an early breakfast?"

"Donna?" Tara asked. "Is that okay with you?"

"A large part of me wants to just go home," she began. "But I live alone and…" She took in and let out a deep breath. "I'm scared. I don't understand what happened or why, and you seem to have some of the answers that I'm going to need for my questions."

That sufficed as an answer to Brent, so they piled into the van and headed out of the hospital parking lot.

3:00 A.M.

STEPHANIE WAS SPENT. She looked into her bedroom vanity and saw the toll that had been exacted.

Tara had been right. They were both beautiful women, but Stephanie had to be honest. The years were catching up—the years and the practice of the craft. No wonder so many witches seemed to age unnaturally.

The conjuring of spirits had taken a lot of spiritual energy, which always resulted in her becoming physically drained. Is that something that would, or even could, change?

She wondered what kind of changes—what enhancements—would come out of learning the true religion of the Picts. Surely, it would be marvelous.

Was the Olde Faithe completely unlike what they currently practiced? Were witchcraft and sorcery just a foreshadowing of true power and knowledge? It could well be that they would have to stop calling themselves witches or 'practitioners of the occult.' After all, the other religions, Islam, Christianity, and Judaism, though monotheistic, do not consider the power and authority that they tap into to be witchcraft or occultism.

If the Pictish faith was going to one day be among the top four religions in the world, they would probably have to *at least* modify what they called themselves as individuals and as an organization in order to be considered legitimate on the world's stage.

She pulled back her hair from the right side of her face, placing the strands behind her ear. She leaned toward the mirror for a closer look. Would the new religion do more to preserve her physically? Why not? If the Pictish faith had previously been the religion of the majestic *Faery Folk* of Atlantis...

Stephanie leaned back and sighed, still looking at her reflection. *Maybe I'm hoping for too much.*

The very thought of what could lie within the ancient Pictish language stirred a growing impatience for the translation of the Picti standing stone. Surely, Brendan and David would soon begin that work in earnest.

First, though, they had to make sure that the Lawtons and Donna McNeill backed away. They were nosing into things they couldn't possibly fathom or appreciate. Hopefully, tonight's spiritcast had taken care of part of the problem.

Time would tell.

She picked up a jar of skincare cream and applied a thin layer to her face and neck. Massaging it in, Stephanie walked to the bed.

Tonight, Brendan would make love to her. He was happy with her again.

3:15 A.M.

TARA SAT IN THE center of the semi-circular booth that was filled now to capacity with six young-to-adult diners. The diner wasn't as empty as she would have thought at—she checked her watch—3:15 in the morning. It must have had staff waiting on a good ten tables.

With their breakfast orders placed—except, of course, for the chicken tenders that Amy and Jamie just *had* to have—conversation about the events of the night began in earnest.

Brent had been doing a great job of keeping the atmosphere as light as possible. It would be interesting to see what paths the conversation would take in the presence of the children. At this point, how much was too much *or too little* to talk about in front of them?

Their dad took the lead. "Amy-Bug? Anything that you would like to talk about?"

Amy looked up at her mom, who she was pressed up against, with eyes that were almost looking for permission, so Tara gave her a nod. She momentarily pressed her lips together and then looked at Jenna.

"You said Jesus would protect me." Her eyes began to blink rapidly, fighting back tears, as the corners of her mouth drew down and trembled.

Jenna's eyes got wide as she pushed her eyebrows up. Her lips parted as if to say something, but nothing came.

"Sweetheart," said Tara, "you don't think Jesus protected you?"

Amy shook her head. A single sob was released before she fought to hold in a second.

"Don't be a baby. You don't see me crying," exclaimed Jamie.

"Jamie! Don't!" his dad warned.

"But…"

Brent cut him off with a hard stare and a slow shake of his head.

"Sorry, Donna," offered Brent.

Donna smiled. "It's good to see something so normal. Normal is definitely good, even if it's just a brother picking on a sister."

Tara empathized with Donna's statement before turning back to Amy.

"Why don't you think Jesus protected you?"

"'Cause the bad stuff happened. I had bad dreams. Jesus didn't stop bad things from happening."

"You know what? You're right. Jesus didn't stop bad things from happening. Not right away.

"Remember Aslan? He didn't stop all of the bad things from happening right away, either. I think that Jesus wants us to understand that there *really* are bad things in the world and that they are dangerous and scary. I think that sometimes we get hurt because we live in a world that has a lot of bad in it. But that doesn't mean that Jesus isn't there. It means that we need to pray to him. We need to call out to him to send us help.

"Remember how using the name of Jesus made the bad things stop happening to Jamie?" Tara looked over at her son, who was still sulking from his rebuke. "Jesus gave us something called authority and his permission to use his name to make the bad things stop."

"Jenna says they're demons," said Amy.

"Well, Jenna is right," Tara responded with a quick glance at her oldest. "They used to be powerful angels, now they are bad angels called demons."

Jamie, setting his sulking aside, got excited and interrupted. "Like in my *GodSend* comic books! Illgate used to be an angel named Aristrong before he and a lot of other angels followed Lucifer in the Prime Rebellion. He didn't lose any of his strength, except that now he lives in darkness. He tries to hurt the humans. But God sends angels like Trilight to fight for us ... I mean them."

Brent smiled. "You were right the first time. To fight for *us*."

Donna interjected now. "Okay, I know you're trying to make the children less fearful, and that's good. But are you honestly trying to get them to believe that there are angels and demons?"

It appeared to Tara that as quickly as the words were out of Donna's mouth, she had realized that her question was undermining Brent's and her authority.

Donna interjected quickly. "I'm sorry. I don't mean to put down what you said, especially in front of your kids."

Brent looked at her for a moment before replying. "Donna, we're laying things out on the table here. You were invited to be a part of this conversation, too. So, no need to apologize. But to answer your question, yes. That's exactly what we believe, and we've got good reason. If you would like, the four of us can, later, get into a deeper conversation about it, and why we are so convinced. Sound good?"

Donna presented an agreeable smile. "I don't know about it sounding good, but I'm certainly willing to talk and listen."

Brent saw the waitress heading their way with a large tray of food. She approached the table, and the conversation came to a standstill. Another, this time a waiter, approached with a second tray and helped to place meals in front of the six diners.

Brent took a moment to pray aloud, thanking God for his provision, and then they began to eat.

Conversation resumed.

Tara turned back to Amy. "It comes down to this, Sweetie; there are good angels and bad demons. Demons hate everything that God loves, and that means they hate people, because we were made like God in a lot of ways. He made us special. The devil—Satan—doesn't want any of us to know God or to follow him. And if we *do* follow God, then that means Satan considers us his enemies, even though he already hates everyone."

She paused for a moment, considering her next words. "What happened tonight was an attack by demons that were sent by some bad people. They were sent to try to hurt us, and they succeeded. But, guess what? Jesus' name was more powerful than the demons that came at us. Right? His name sent them all away and saved us all from worse stuff."

"Amy-Bug," offered Brent, "We learned something tonight that we didn't think about before each of you went to bed. I know that we prayed, but we could have prayed better. Our next prayers are going to protect us better from what happened tonight. We're going to pray protection all around us before we go back to sleep."

"I'm scared to go to sleep," Amy responded.

"I know, honey," said Tara. She looked up at Brent.

"I am, too," Jenna added.

Tara saw that Brent began contemplating an answer to the challenge of getting to sleep for the rest of the night. Within half a minute, he said, "Let's wake up Mom & Dad. There's plenty of space, and with an air mattress, there will be enough beds." He looked at Donna. "That includes you, Donna. Unless I miss my guess, I think you'll be more comfortable sleeping in the home of strangers than in our vacant house or even your own. Of course, I could put you up in a hotel."

Donna looked dumbstruck, not to mention nervous. It was obvious that this was a whole lot more than she had bargained for. She appeared resigned to her situation, though, and said, "I'm going where there is safety in numbers."

Tara smiled. *Good answer!*

"Dad?"

"Yes, Son?"

"Are you going to go get the bad people?"

"I'm going to try, buddy. I'm certainly going to try."

CHAPTER 24
Saturday, June 11—7:49 A.M.

Brent stood outside on the concrete slab that extended from his parents' family room. He looked into the backyard, not looking at anything in particular as he seethed internally.

There were times, infrequent as they may be, that he wanted to ditch his Christianity and deal with things from the same raw, base nature that he saw in a lot of the people with whom he had to contend as a cop.

He wanted to find this Brendan-and-Stephanie pair and stick a .45 semi-automatic pistol in their faces. He wanted to see them with the same terror in their eyes that he'd seen in those of his children.

Who does that? Who attacks people like that? Why?!

Brent interlaced his fingers behind his head as he walked out onto the lawn toward his mom's garden at the back end of the property. Just moments before, he had told Tara that he was going outside to pray, but he *didn't want* to pray! He wanted to hurt someone.

He heard the sliding glass door of the family room open, then close. He figured it was Tara coming out to talk with him, probably hoping to pray with him.

"Good morning, Son."

It was his dad. He dropped his hands and turned around.

"Rough morning?" asked Keith Lawton.

"I'm pretty angry, Dad. So, yes, I guess you could call it a rough morning."

"Guess I can't blame you. Tara said you were out here praying. I don't want to interrupt. Not if that's what you were really doing."

"It wasn't."

"She also said that you were amazing last night, because of how you dealt with things after the attack."

Brent had a lot of respect for his dad, especially because he had held to his relationship with Christ through the years.

In many ways, it had improved their relationship as father and son. No longer was his dad contending with his faith, but instead, was lending godly wisdom gained through the years *to* his faith.

On many occasions, they had gone on walks through the neighborhood or gone fishing just so that they could talk about life, be it child rearing, marriage, or just life in general. They had a common footing, and neither was overly embarrassed about weaknesses or shortcomings.

His dad was being a dad, and Brent couldn't express enough appreciation to God for that.

Brent's mom lent to the strength of father and son, as well. Her faith in the Lord was as strong as that of her husband. Their relationship had superseded that of the two cohabiting daily fighters they had once been. The Lord had drawn the *two* back into *one*.

Several years ago, Brent saw an illustration that had helped him better understand the growing bond between his mom and dad: husband and wife on opposite sides of a triangle, with Christ at the pinnacle. As the two of them grew in their walks toward Christ, they ended up coming closer and closer together. It was impossible not to. Even if one was growing more slowly, they'd still be moving in the same direction, still creating more adhesion between them. If, though, one stopped and the other grew, then there would be pain and more distance.

Over time, his dad had become quite the lay theologian, studying, not just reading, the Bible. He enjoyed reading classic Bible commentators, like John Darby, Matthew Henry, and John Gill. His insights and growing wisdom were valued.

The combination of his dad's knowledge of the Bible and his position as a loving father certainly made him a sage in Brent's life.

In his early seventies now, Keith Lawton still led an active life. He chose to continue working, though it probably wasn't necessary. He just didn't want to remain sedentary. Brent liked that about him. He always had something going on in his life that kept him around people and kept him talking. He'd come a long way from the days of returning home from work to plop himself into a recliner in front of a television.

"Dad, all I did last night was put on a good show. I was furious. If it had only been Tara and me coming out of that hospital ER, I would have told her to go home, and you can bet I would have gone off and kicked in a certain farmhouse door in Pittston."

His dad stepped closer to his left side, put the thumb and forefinger of his right hand around the back of Brent's neck, and began to guide him back toward the house.

"Son, how about we go for a walk?"

Brent couldn't help but smile. He knew that the next twenty minutes or so were going to mean the baring of his heart. His dad seemed to have a way of helping rid him of all the minutiae and bring things back to the basics. Brent knew he was about to either enjoy or, more likely, *endure* an extended talk about how God might be viewing the situation.

But then, he was probably overdue for a change in perspective.

7:53 A.M.

TARA HELD HER CUP of coffee as she watched the men through the family room window.

Looks like Brent and Dad are going out for one of their father-son walks.

She was happy about that. Nothing bad could result from two men walking, talking, and sharing their hearts.

She took a sip of the light-brown morning nectar and returned to the kitchen. In the sunlit, narrow room were both Donna and Brent's mom, each propped up against opposite counters with their own cups of coffee. They both smiled as Tara walked in.

"Good morning, Donna," said Tara. "Sleep okay?"

"Not as bad as I thought I would, actually. Thank you for giving me one of the beds."

"You're welcome. Did I interrupt a conversation?"

"Not at all, dear," offered her mother-in-law. "Just getting to know each other a little bit."

"Mrs. Lawton was just telling me a couple of cute stories about your husband when he was a boy."

"Sharon, please, Donna. You'll make me feel like I'm seventy with all of that missus stuff. Oh dear. I *am* seventy!" Sharon said with a laugh.

What a good woman, mused Tara.

"Donna, do you have to be off on some client calls this morning?"

"No, fortunately. I do have my weekends to myself, usually. Unless there is some sort of emergency."

"Now, what could you *possibly* know of emergencies?" Sharon said with a slight smirk.

The younger two ladies appreciated the humor and allowed the amusement to produce some giggles.

"Mom, can we sit around the dining room table?"

"Why certainly! In fact, let me get us all a few goodies to nibble on while we sip our coffee."

Donna started walking toward the dining room when Tara said, "That woman can bake; let me tell you!"

"Good, my stomach's growling. Even though it certainly doesn't have any right to, after that big breakfast just a few hours ago."

"Trust me. I know how you feel."

As they sat down, Tara asked, "Anything you'd like to talk about while the kids are still out?"

Donna looked a little relieved by the question, though she obviously still had her reservations about such a conversation.

She leaned slightly in toward Tara and whispered, "What about your mother-in-law? Won't a conversation about this stuff, you know, weird her out?"

Tara opened her mouth to reply, but was cut off by Sharon. "What? Weirded out by talk of angels and demons, witchcraft and the occult?" She approached the table with three plates of pastries and cookies. "I'm old, Donna. Not deaf," she added with another of her rich laughs.

"Let me *tell* you about weirded out." Sharon continued. "Weirded out happened when my son came home from a camping trip with this one," indicating Tara with a dismissive wave of her hand and a playful wink. "Told his father and me that Tara would need a place to stay for a few days. I asked why.

"Donna, never ask why, because you just don't know what kind of story you're going to get." She slapped the table with the palm of her hand and just started giggling. "That was funny!"

Donna and Tara fell right in line with their own laughter. How her Mom—and that's sincerely how she viewed this woman—could turn a subject like this into something so funny was beyond her.

Sharon continued with a bright smile. "Tara did *not* want Brent telling us about what had transpired during their several days of backpacking, but the ending of the tale had made it all worthwhile."

Sharon stopped and just sat there with a grin on her face, apparently satisfied with her explanation or not realizing that there was actually more to the story to tell.

Tara and Donna looked at each other, knowing smiles playing across their faces.

Donna took the lead. "Umm… what exactly *did* Brent tell you that day?"

"Oh dear. It's that old-age thing again." That caused her to laugh again. "Sorry about that," she said, trying to rub the tears of laughter from her eyes.

"Whew. Okay. That son of mine told us that Tara was a witch. At first, I was like, 'Nahh...' then I saw how embarrassed and uneasy she was getting. It finally struck home. At first, I didn't really know how to handle it. I'll admit I was uncomfortable with the idea of having a witch—even if she wasn't one
anymore—staying in my home. I took Brent aside to tell him so..." Sharon rolled her eyes upward and sighed. "Let's just say that my argument fell to the ground in front of him."

Donna laughed. "Found out he'd been one, too, huh?"

"Two of my three children..." Sharon paused, then reached out and patted one of Tara's hands. "Witches. Who knew?"

Tara looked from her smiling mom-in-law to Donna, who sat enjoying the most unlikely of conversations *to* enjoy.

"I guess that was a rather long way to say, no, I won't be weirded out by a conversation about witches and demons and the like."

This, apparently, gave Donna the freedom that she needed. Amid a lull in some light conversation while enjoying the pastries set before them, she began to open up.

"Okay, I'm going to try to suspend disbelief for a few minutes and allow for the idea of witches and demons. But with the way that you and Brent talk, Tara, all witches are evil. I may not be the world's leading authority on the subject, but wouldn't that be a rather naïve position to take? I mean, there are some good people out there who believe they are practicing white witchcraft, right? Aren't they just doing what they can to help others? Is it called Wicca?"

"Wicca is a form of witchcraft, yes. And generally, those practicing it believe they are doing good *to* the earth, receiving good *from* the earth, and practicing only a good form of the occult. But it *is* still witchcraft, and witchcraft is, by its very nature, against God."

"But what about their gods? Don't they count?"

"Absolutely, they count," replied Tara. "In fact, they count too much! These 'gods' are toying with those who either worship or merely acknowledge them.

"Those people, like me when I was practicing, are the ones

who are truly naïve. There is only one God; all others who pretend to be gods are really fallen angels who are working to deceive people and to keep them deceived."

"I imagine you're not fans of *Harry Potter*, then," ventured Donna.

Tara couldn't tell if it was a statement or a question, so she answered it as the latter.

"The world hails *Harry Potter* because the book series has gotten children to enjoy reading. Then, when it hit the big screen for the first time, the movie industry knew that it was going to rake in the bucks. But here's the problem—one of them, anyway. The books aren't just engaging kids to start reading; they're also creating a huge interest in the minds of many children to start experimenting with witchcraft. After all, they believe there is a good side and a bad side, and if the hero is Harry Potter, then that's how *they* want to use witchcraft as well … if they can make any of it work."

"Can they?"

"Yes! They can!" said Tara emphatically. "I've got a friend who lives in England. She's told me, on numerous occasions, how *Harry Potter* mania has caused a major surge in occult practice over there! It's alarming, but so few see the danger. Do you want to know why?"

Donna nodded.

"Because the parents are reading and loving the books, too! You see, in England's *very* secularized society, God has been traded in for witchcraft." Tara stopped and evaluated her statement. Donna and Sharon must have seen her struggling for an appropriate sentence to share, because they remained silent.

"I take that back," she said finally. "God was not traded in for witchcraft. Rather, God was first let go by a people who didn't want to have moral or 'religious' absolutes in their lives.

"When they had banished God from their hearts, their schools, and in many cases, their houses of worship, there was a huge spiritual void left unfilled in people's lives.

"Enter J.K. Rowling, the author of the *Potter* series. I do not claim to know whether she had an agenda for writing books for children that make the occult look attractive. That matters little to me. However, the *effect* of what she has written *does* matter to me a great deal!"

Tara looked at her mother-in-law. "Mom, do you have a Bible close by?"

Without a word, Sharon got up and walked into the living room. A moment later, she handed a burgundy-colored Bible to Tara.

"Donna, you and I have different starting points when it comes to evaluating whether witchcraft is bad or not. Prior to becoming a Christian, I had a totally different worldview that almost *encouraged* me to get involved in witchcraft. But now, let me read to you my new starting point. I know you don't believe the way that I do, and maybe you don't give any special regard to the Bible, but humor me for a moment."

Tara opened the Bible up to the book of Deuteronomy, chapter eighteen, and began reading at verse ten:

"Do not sacrifice your children. And don't practice any fashion of magic or witchcraft or fortunetelling. Do not cast spells or attempt to talk to spirits of the dead. The LORD finds these practices repugnant, and that's why He will aid you in destroying the pagan nations occupying this land. Do not make yourself guilty of doing any of these disgusting things! No! Instead, you will go in and take the land from the nations that practice magic and witchcraft."

Tara closed the book. "Does it make where I come from a little clearer?"

"Crystal clear. Okay, I guess I'm pretty satisfied with all of that, but what I'm really concerned about is…" She stopped, as if considering her words more carefully. "If you're right about all of this, then last night was…"

Donna looked right into Tara's eyes. After a few uncomfortable seconds, she shifted her eyes to Sharon and then brought them back to Tara.

Emotion gripped her throat. "Last night, what happened to all of us could partially be…" she said with a hard swallow, "my brother's fault." A trembling hand came up to her mouth as tears formed.

What she said rocked Tara. Her Mom's eyes shifted to hers, a look of confusion forming. Tara had not given this any thought. No thought at all on how this conversation may impact Donna on an emotional level.

Tara's realization reached her lips. "Donna, I'm sorry. All this time, all of your questions… I'm sorry, I didn't even begin to consider that you were thinking about your brother's involvement. I'm so sorry."

Donna pushed back from the table and stood up. Both hands covered her nose and mouth now. Her eyebrows arched in pain as she walked into the living room. She rounded the wall out of sight.

Tara and her mother-in-law looked at each other, not knowing precisely what to do. Tara decided to get up and follow her new friend.

As she rounded the wall separating the dining and living rooms, she watched as Donna made her way to the stairs that led up to the bedrooms. At first, she thought she might be headed for the upstairs restroom, but she stopped, turned, and sat down on the second step.

Donna, trembling hands still hiding her mouth and nose, placed her elbows on her knees. Seeing Tara approach, she lowered both hands and her head.

Lord, help me help her, Tara prayed silently.

"Donna," she began, planting herself next to the grieving woman, "I'm not exactly sure what to say."

"What is there to say? David is involved very closely with the people who have a vendetta against you and Brent. There is no reason to think that he wasn't also involved last night."

"No, you're right. There isn't. It's very possible that David was as involved as the others."

"How am I supposed to process that, Tara?" Donna asked. A mixture of anger and grief emanated from her words. "He's been lying to me. *To me!* We've never had reason to distrust each other."

Tara felt a prompting to say something that, like with

Stephanie, sounded counterproductive.

"Maybe you don't have to worry about him having lied to you. After all, hasn't he been trying to get you to participate *with* them? You said the other day that he had invited you to meet the people at the gathering. It sounds to me like he's a brother who wants to keep his sister at his side."

Her words did make an impact, however slight. It showed in the softening of Donna's eyes.

"You mean like my brother was trying to be nice and invite me into a group of people who hide behind the guise of religion to do harm to other people?" She shook her head, sorrow taking the place of anger. "Why, Tara? Why would a good man like my brother follow these people?"

"It's called the human condition, Donna. The need to feel important, the desire for power, the need for purpose. Those aren't all bad, but sometimes we want them so badly that we'll fall in with almost anyone who seems to be able to grant them.

"Donna, you said that you went to Scotland. You found out while you were there that you were of the Picti bloodline. I think that David took you to Scotland already knowing that."

Donna took that in. "That makes sense. He was doing research for Brendan while also trying to show me how important I was supposed to be. He did make a big deal of it, like it should have both amazed and inspired me."

"Okay, so you weren't inspired and amazed. The love of a brother for his twin sister, shown through an invitation to join him, persisted for years, but fell on deaf ears. I think that God has been protecting you; that he has had his hand on you.

"There's something else I'd like you to know." Tara paused until Donna looked her in the eyes. "I, too, am Scottish."

Donna looked stunned.

"I was recruited by Stephanie back in the mid-80s to be groomed for some group. She would never tell me what it was. Based on everything that has come to light in the past few days, I think it's likely that they had discovered I have Pictish blood coursing through my veins, as well. But I made Stephanie very angry by going against her directive to stay clear of Brent and

Marta. That's the part of the story I didn't tell you."

Donna looked dumbfounded. "That's ... Wait, so you're telling me that you and Stephanie *knew* each other all those years ago, and then, just like that, you've been thrown back into each other's lives?"

"Don't you think for an instant that any of these crossings of paths is a coincidence, Donna. Think about it. Do you think it was a coincidence that you approached me at the store and saw my tattoo—a *copy* of Stephanie's tattoo—just days after seeing hundreds of others with the *same* tattoo? I sure don't."

Tara allowed that to settle within Donna's mind. She had more she wanted to say, but felt a check in her spirit,[15] dissuading her from continuing.

"Okay, if there is a God who protected me from this witch group, why didn't he protect my brother?"

"I can't answer that. I wish I could. All I can say is that I'm sure that God is battling for *you* right now. Step one of whatever his plan is seems to involve you getting to know who he is. You've been singled out for him and *his* purposes."

"So, I'm the *yang* to David's *yin*."

Tara couldn't help but release a soft laugh at Donna's symbolism. "Not exactly the occult metaphor that I would have chosen…"

Donna smiled, but with a hint of confusion in her eyes.

"Never mind. I'm saying that God has a purpose for you. I am *not* saying that David is your opposite or opponent. I believe David loves you, based on all the things you've told me about your relationship. I also doubt that you were supposed to be a target last night. I think you only got attacked because you were in the house with us. I doubt David would have done anything to harm you, at least not on purpose."

"But if I were to accept your God… Sorry, *the* God—the way you've been suggesting, then I would be deliberately aligning myself against David."

"Donna, look at me for a moment." Donna looked back into Tara's eyes.

---

[15] To read about checks in the spirit provided by the Holy Spirit, turn to the Appendix.

"Even if you don't accept Jesus, do you think that you will align yourself *with* David?"

Donna's gaze shifted from one of Tara's eyes to the other, back and forth several times. Tara could see an internal search taking place. And finally, she spoke.

"No. Not after what happened last night. If he were, in any way, a part of that, then David and I have reached a breaking point.

"I know that he thinks of me as sort of flighty." She grinned. "I guess I really am. But I'm not stupid. I can't have anything to do with a family member who participates in such evil."

She hung her head, then said softly, "Even if he is the only family I have."

Donna's revelation stabbed at Tara's heart. She reached around Donna and drew her close. Donna responded by leaning her head onto Tara's shoulder, accepting the friendship and love being offered.

She's a kindred spirit, concluded Tara.

Another conclusion. *We need to start praying for David.*

Donna sniffled. "So, all of this Christianity stuff and demon stuff is real, huh? I mean, it's not like I'm going to be able to disregard it as fanciful imagination any longer."

"It's real, dear one. It's all very, very real."

CHAPTER 25
Saturday, June 11—11:17 A.M.

B rent stood in the center of the living room, having just opened the front door and back windows to allow for some cross-ventilation. The room stank. The carpet was going to have to be replaced. There was just no way all of that blood and vomit was going to come out.

Tara walked in from the kitchen, carrying a warm pail of water with *L.O.C.* and all-fabric bleach mixed into it. Brent doubted that anything could be done about the stains, but at least the smell would be made right.

For all of the chaos the previous night, the house seemed rather indifferent to it all. Not that it should have been screaming, *"Fear this place!"* This hadn't been the *Amityville Horror*, after all.

Not exactly.

"Want to give me a hand moving this coffee table?" Tara invited.

Brent walked over to the "guilty" end of the table and waited for Tara to get into position on the opposite end. Lifting it, they moved it about a foot in her direction, then Tara walked to the curtains of the picture window and pulled them open.

It was then that Brent saw the rest of the blood.

A trail ran from where Donna had fallen, all the way up the stairs to the second floor. He imagined that there must be another major stain in their bedroom like the one a few feet from where he stood. She had lost more blood than he'd initially thought.

Tara knelt down to where she had expelled the contents of her stomach and soaked the area with a washcloth. Brent just stood and watched, feeling disconnected from what she was doing. His emotions had been raw for the past twelve hours; now he felt emotionally barren.

The walk that he had taken with his dad had pulled him back from a ragged edge … at least temporarily.

He needed sleep. Except for the thirty minutes he'd gotten prior to "hell night," he'd been awake since 4:30 the previous morning. He could operate at full capacity on five-and-a-half hours of sleep, which was his norm, but now his battery was drained.

Still staring at Tara on the floor, Brent wondered how she was able to function. He imagined that she could have only gotten two or three hours of sleep while he lay awake next to her on the air mattress in his parents' finished basement.

Thank God for his parents. Their home right now was a safe haven for the kids. Donna was still there with his parents, as well.

Tara had wanted to come back to the house to clean as quickly as possible, and she knew that if Donna knew her intention, she would have insisted on coming to clean up her part of the mess. Tara had told Brent, however, that she didn't want Donna feeling any obligation to help, nor did she want her to be back in the environment right away that had created such an emotional and spiritual upheaval in her life.

Ultimately, Tara made the decision to tell Brent's parents and Donna that she wanted to run some morning "errands" and that they'd be back in a short while. Donna seemed very content to be in the company of Brent's mom and dad, so they extracted themselves before anything could be suspected.

Brent knew that he, too, should have been on his hands and

knees at that moment.

He should have blood on his hands.

11:17 A.M.

BRENDAN SAT WITH David and Stephanie in the living room of the farmhouse. Hundreds of pictures were scattered about the coffee table; all of them were photographs of Pictish standing stones. A few of them had Donna McNeill posing in them for her brother, a tribute to David's love for the woman and memories of their trip to Scotland several years prior.

Brendan stared at Donna in one of the pictures, none too pleased by her image. He *should* just put his attention back to the task at hand, but she remained a persistent mental detour for him.

"Should we group the pictures by symbol?" asked David, steering Brendan back on course.

"Yes. Each of us will take two of the six groupings of symbols on the Key of Bridei and search for standing stones that have at least one of the symbols within those groupings. If some of the standing stones fit into more than one category, then just place it in the seventh symbol pile. I'll determine the best course of action for those as I begin translating."

One symbol, now a plague in Brendan's mind, was one of the most simple of the shapes, looking much like a crescent moon, and was very apparent in the photo he had just picked up: the Invereen Pictish Stone from Highland, Scotland, which presently stood in the Museum of Scotland in Edinburgh. This was the symbol that had been translated into Latin as *solemn faith*. He imagined that the shape was meant to symbolize a cover over the whole of Picti life, similar to an umbrella or an upward-raised shield. He was troubled, though, on how to best work with it. He couldn't just give up determining its real meaning, or that of the others within the category.

Earlier that morning, he had spent several minutes reading all of the Latin that had been etched into the back of the key within the *solemn faith* grouping. The words made him want to lash out and hurl the circular stone across the room and out the window like a discus at a track and field event. Irony being what it was, the discus had been his specialty in high school back home in Scotland.

Brendan forced himself *again* back into the moment. He would get the first five sections translated. His ability to translate the true meaning of the Pictish symbols in the sixth category would come from those.

It had better.

It ended up taking the better part of three hours to get the pictures organized into eight piles; the eighth containing two types of photos: stones that didn't seem to have on them any of the symbols contained within the six categories and stones that had symbols that were just too faint, due to erosion, to determine one way or the other.

For all of Brendan's anger, he was still excited to be delving into his ancient past. No one in over twelve hundred years had been able to understand the stones. Lots of wild guesses had been made, of course, but he, Brendan Cadeyrn, was about to truly unlock secrets that had purposely remained hidden from their sworn blood enemies, the MacAlpins, and the rest of the invading Scots.

The MacAlpins. Yes. Another thing he was looking forward to: the Appeasement Ceremony, which would set things right with the Pictish gods. The Picti had waited far too long for vengeance against Kenneth MacAlpin. Brendan knew that history would not bear it out, but he liked to think that MacAlpin had taken on the name Kenneth to keep his name from being associated with the treacherous, bloody slaughter that had been meted out on the last king of the Picts.

But there would be no hiding. Because just enough evidential history existed about the man prior to his name change to prove he was the traitorous Cináed mac Ailpin. And it was *his* bloodline that would pay for the usurpation of the crown of Pictland, as well as his blasphemous self-anointment as King of the Picts.

Brendan relished the thought of having blood on his hands.

CHAPTER 26
Sunday, June 12—12:18 P.M.

John Eldredge didn't like having to spend his Sundays on the job. But being a cop in a small town meant sacrifices. He was glad that his church held a Saturday evening service. He'd needed that service and some alone time with God to get some clarity on how to handle his new 'work situation'.

Knowing that his boss was an alleged practitioner of witchcraft was one thing; knowing that he was potentially covering up something unlawful *because* he was practicing witchcraft was another.

Brent's evidence had been convincing, or at least the man had been. It was easy to see that Brent was serious about his Christian faith by the way it came up in conversation. What was difficult was getting his mind to knit in the additional information about his boss.

Connor was a decent guy, from the perspective of a working relationship. However, that didn't mean, very obviously, that he didn't have some dirty little secrets.

John drove through the downtown area. The wrought-iron arches, spaced every hundred feet, lent a feeling of sophistication to the Village of Pittston. At night, with the lights turned on, the arches lit up the street and gave the main drag a festive appearance.

There was little trouble in Pittston. Most of the people that he had to deal with during the course of his duties were generally traffic or parking violators. Quite the change from his former home of Hilliard in the center of the state.

The City of Hilliard wasn't a bad place, either. He often missed his former home and colleagues. It was just that Hilliard was larger, and with that came bigger challenges.

He pulled his cruiser to the traffic signal at the main downtown intersection. Looking to his right, he was able to see the police department. The back end of Chief Connor's blue GMC Yukon could be seen in the parking lot.

Hmm. He's not normally in on a Sunday.

John made a right turn and drove to the police station. Pulling into the parking lot, he saw another truck parked alongside that of Chief Connor's. The vehicles were parked so that the two men in the driver's seats could talk comfortably through each of the driver-side windows.

John knew that truck. *The same guy who seems to hold sway over the chief.* There was no turning back once he was spotted coming into the lot. He raised his hand in friendly acknowledgment. The driver of the Ford did the same.

His chief looked over his shoulder, just as John opted to look away. Parking the cruiser near the main entrance to the station, he got out of the vehicle and made his way inside.

There was no reason for him to be inside the building, of course, but he could hardly have pulled a U-turn in the parking lot without looking suspicious. So, inside he went.

The station was relatively quiet, and since all of the glass at the front of the station was tinted, he decided to stand a few feet inside the doors and watch the interaction take place between the two men.

For several minutes, they just talked. Then John watched as the brake lights lit up on the back of the F250. A quick flash of the reverse light let him know that the man had just shifted into drive.

Eldredge could see the chief look around the parking lot, then to the front doors where John stood unseen, before extending his hand toward the driver of the pickup truck. The driver

W. FRANKLIN LATTIMORE

initiated the action first, and in his hand, there appeared to be a small box, about the size of a baseball or softball—hard to determine from the distance. When the chief took possession, the black pickup accelerated out of the parking lot.

Interesting, but not necessarily illegal.

Chief Connor started driving toward the main entrance of the station. Eldredge decided to make his way to the patrol officers' office. Fortunately, he did have a couple of tickets that he could process.

Think of something. What can you come up with?

Eldredge wanted to develop an opportunity—a *seemingly* legitimate reason—for interrupting the chief at an intentionally *very* inopportune time, so as to *hopefully* find out... well, find out *something*. Anything that might incriminate him in this whole Picti-cover-up episode. But John knew that the likelihood of the chief doing something so inept as to reveal a criminal connection was small.

The patrol officer sat himself at an open desk and waited for the Pittston chief to walk through the hallway to his office. He heard the chief's steps bringing him closer, eventually landing him, too, in the same workspace.

"Eldredge, how are things in our lovely community today?"

John turned from the desk to look at his boss. He looked comfortable, even with the small, blue and white, baseball-size box in his left hand.

He's playing it awfully cool for a guilty man.

"Nothing to write home about. Yet, here I am ... writing."

The chief chuckled. "Anything other than tickets?"

"Nahh. The usual." He quickly turned the tables. "Don't usually see you in here on a Sunday. Anything I need to know?"

The chief must have expected the question. "Just forgot to bring something home yesterday. A quick jump into my office, and I'm out of here."

"That's good. Thought for a moment that the guy in the pickup might have been here to report something."

That triggered a reaction. A look in his eye let Eldredge know that he had touched on forbidden, or, at least, unexpected territory.

"Him? Uhh… No, he's not important. That is, he wasn't reporting anything." He feigned a quick look at his watch. "I've got to get running. Keep up the good work."

"Will do, Chief. Have a good day."

Without another word, the Pittston Chief of Police uncomfortably walked out of the room.

That's all I needed to see. That man is up to something.

BRENDAN DROVE HIS pickup back to the farm. Safeguards were now in place to assure that no one would be looking their way on the night of the Appeasement Ceremony. It was great having a loyal member of the police force on their side.

Be that as it may, it was still going to cost a little bit of money to cause the police to deal with another situation far from the farm that night. There was already little chance that problems would arise, but better to have the assurance than to be looking over their shoulders throughout the entire ritual.

Uilliam had made a good call not to have any money exchanged in envelopes. Too suspicious. That little box with a wad of bills would have appeared to be anything but money, should anyone have seen it.

Smart man.

Brendan realized that showing up at the police station probably wasn't the smartest thing for him to do, but he figured that it was better to hide in plain sight. After all, in the eyes of the average citizen—or even the cops—the most unlikely place to conduct criminal activity would *have* to be at the police station with the chief of police. Right?

12:47 P.M.

ALL FIVE OF THE LAWTONS and Donna McNeill walked out of the church and into the parking lot. It appeared to Tara that Donna still had her reservations about the importance of a Savior in her life.

Pleading to God for her salvation during the altar call, Tara was sure that Donna would have responded. After all, who wouldn't, after such a life-changing ordeal, followed by a day with the whole Lawton clan?

Well, astoundingly, Donna.

Tara tried not to let her disappointment show. Normally, Brent and she would have had the same sentiments rising to the surface, but he seemed rather removed from the whole experience, or, rather, lack of one.

Donna did seem to enjoy the atmosphere, however. She mentioned more than once that the people had been so friendly and that she felt such a "sense of well-being" in the building.

God, don't let her drift into that whole "spiritual but not religious" shtick. It irked Tara to hear people use the word *spiritual*. What did that truly mean, anyway?

Typically, it meant that a person was content to create a god—or recreate *the* God—in his or her own image; creating one's own method of worshiping or paying some sort of penance to any number of non-existent gods. "I worship God my own way," she'd heard people say way too many times. *Really?*

Having reached the area of the parking lot closest to their two vehicles, the Lawtons said their goodbyes to Donna. She needed to get home after neglecting "so many things that just have to get done."

Donna couldn't be blamed. After all, she had spent the better part of two days with them. Tara felt confident that a solid friendship was forming. That was certainly a good beginning.

Tara was the last one to part company with Donna, not wanting the separation to take place. Maybe she was being overprotective. It sure didn't feel like it, though.

When she finally got into the passenger seat of the minivan, she heard Amy and Jamie fussing about something in the back seat. That was certainly nothing new.

Brent backed out of the parking space and headed for the exit. The noise created by Amy and Jamie escalated somewhat, but that, too, was not unusual with the two of them always sitting next to each other at the rear of the van.

Reaching the stop sign, Brent jerked the van to a stop. He threw the gear shift into park, unlatched his seatbelt, and whirled around to face his children.

"Hey! I want the two of you to stop it! I've had enough of your bickering! Why can't the two of you just leave each other alone?!"

He turned back toward the front, his eyes momentarily engaging Tara's. What was in them jarred her. There was such intense anger.

The van quieted immediately. Brent put the van in drive and took off.

Tara looked back; Amy was wide-eyed and stunned, staring at the back of her daddy's head. Jamie's mouth was stuck in the open position as he looked at his mom.

Tara mouthed the words, "It's okay," and glanced at Jenna. She was pulling the earbuds from her ears. Whatever she had been listening to didn't seem to be all that enjoyable anymore.

Tara stared through the windshield in the tension-filled van the whole way home.

BRENT WANTED TO YELL. This time at himself.

He hated what he had just done to his family. He knew that Jamie and Amy didn't deserve his outburst. He also knew that he was going to have to apologize.

The problem was that he needed the anger that was coursing through him, and he didn't want to let it go.

So, he didn't.

The van was hushed for the nearly fifteen-minute drive home. He was *very* aware of Tara's quiet presence. And he was sure that she was reserving comment for later, a comment that he would accept without excuse.

While the rest of his family emotionally recovered from their night of demonic attacks, he had done nothing but stew. It began while the events of that night were being explained to him in the waiting room of the ER.

Brent knew it had been a premeditated and deliberately initiated attack, and he knew who the perp was

. It wasn't the first time he'd contended with an attack of this nature. In fact, the first time he'd experienced one, it had been sent by the one sitting in the passenger seat next to him.

He thought back to that night on the campus of Summit State College. He had just left an enjoyable night of laughter with some Christian friends he'd made on campus. Marta and Karen, among them.

He'd walked through the area where the Great Oak stood on his way to the car. It was then that he felt a presence, a *discernible* presence.

He'd known from the outset that it was demonic and began binding and rebuking the spirit right away. That spirit had left without further incident.

A couple of months later, he had discovered that Tara had been the culprit who had performed the spiritcast.

This time, though, he had been asleep.

Asleep!

He clenched his teeth. Unforgivable! Had he just stayed up another half hour, maybe just a little longer…

But no… No, he wouldn't *allow* himself to hang with the girls! It wasn't the *man* thing to do.

Idiot!

He wanted to slam his hand on the steering wheel, but he contained himself … at least that much.

Brent's dad had asked him after the church service if he had taken time to consider what the two of them had talked about during their walk the previous morning. He had said yes.

He hadn't. Not at all.

Love them? That's what he was supposed to do? *Those people tore away the security of my family! They* attacked *my children! You want me to* love *them?!*

"Yes, son, that's exactly what I'm saying. 'Love your ene- mies.' Isn't that what Christ said?"

Yes, that's what Christ said. But there is a difference be- tween loving someone who attacks me and someone who at- tacks those that I care about!

"Yes, Son, there is a difference. But the difference is justice, not hate. Bring them to justice if you're able, but don't let hate for them consume you."

Brent thought through his dad's words again, but it was too late. Or, even if it wasn't too late, he didn't care.

Not one iota.

CHAPTER 27
Sunday, June 12—12:48 P.M.

I'm taking way too many chances, Officer Eldredge eventually acknowledged to himself. *I should have been back on the streets a good ten minutes ago.* But he couldn't stop hoping for the opportunity to see something important.

He had grabbed a copy of the morning's shift briefing, which didn't really have anything significant on it, but it gave him something official to be perusing while standing in the hallway near the chief's office. Come to think of it, there was one thing in the brief that he could ask about if he was caught in the wrong place at the wrong time.

He propped himself up on the left doorpost, looking into the office of the chief's administrative assistant. Beyond her desk was the chief's office; the door wide open. But at this angle, all he could see was the right front corner of his desk. The light was on, and he could hear the movement of the chief's chair.

Behind John, down the hallway, was a mostly empty police station. Thankfully. The dispatcher wouldn't come out into the hallway, and Greg Ballard, another patrol officer, had come in for some reason and already left. As far as he could tell, it was just the three of them in the building at present.

He heard the distinct sound of a cardboard container being opened. A minute later, a piece of paper was crumpled, followed by the audible soft *ting* of a paper wad having been thrown into a brass trash basket. The chief's chair shifted and let out a slight squeak. He was getting up.

Eldredge stepped back out of view, waiting to hear the chief flip the switch to turn off his office light.

Click!

John's heart was beating a little harder than normal as he casually stepped around the corner into the secretary's office. The chief was halfway through the room, heading toward the hallway.

"Oh, sorry, Chief. Got a sec?"

Connor continued into the light of the hallway before answering. "What can I do for you?"

"This morning's brief indicates a need for someone to step into Carrington's shoes as the new *D.A.R.E.* officer."

"Okay. Yes, that's true."

"Sir, did you ever perform that duty?" Eldredge said as they walked toward the front doors. "I don't really want to give up patrol, but I also don't want to give up on something that might be good for advancement. I wanted your opinion."

"Can't say that I have. Filled in one time, and that was my quota," he said with a wry grin. "Frankly, Officer Eldredge, I'd rather have you out in the community and cycle the rookies through our *D.A.R.E.* program here. But I'm leaving that up to Sergeant Strafer and all of you to decide."

The two of them exited the buildings and headed to their respective vehicles. "Thanks for the input, Chief. Have a good day."

"You, too, Eldredge."

The chief got back into his Yukon and left the parking lot.

Eldredge went back into the building and headed to the chief's office.

5:19 P.M.

STEPHANIE LEANED BACK against the wall behind the dining table, arms crossed, watching and listening as David and Brendan continued with the standing stone translations.

They were making pretty good progress, though she was able to see that a certain pile of pictures had yet to be touched.

The important one.

She wasn't sure why Brendan seemed to be purposely avoiding the photos with the Pictish symbol for 'religion' on them.

"So, when do we get to meet her? It is a woman, isn't it?" asked David.

Brendan had kept the identity of the "sacrificial lamb" a secret. Recent lapses in security within the Home Coven had kept this information on a need-to-know basis, and, apparently, Brendan was the only one, to this point, who needed to know.

Stephanie suspected, however, that it would almost have to be the girl whom they had located in the Cincinnati area a couple of years prior. She was the closest, and she was a confirmed MacAlpin.

The Appeasement Ceremony was set to take place in the dark hours of the morning on Thursday, but that was dependent, according to Brendan, on whether Uilliam—Chief Connor—was able to make arrangements for a certain "All-Eyes-Away" diversion to take place. Neither Stephanie nor David was privy to those details either.

Stephanie understood and accepted—for the most part—that she and David were not back on the fully-trusted list yet. It was disappointing, of course. They had gone from being on the front lines of all the planning to waiting on the periphery.

So be it. She, at least, would work to re-earn Brendan's trust. At the moment, though, Brendan looked as though he was pondering how much information to reveal to them.

"Suffice it to say that the woman is identified and is beyond any doubt a descendant of MacAlpin. Uilliam is making preparations for her and for the event that will keep the police from having any eyes in the area of the farm.

" I talked with him in depth about what arrangements need to be made. He's confident that everything will be in order come Wednesday night."

This is where we all find out what kind of metal we are made from, Stephanie thought. *This knowledge alone will be an identifier of Picti loyalty.*

She wondered about the stoutness of the hearts of the remaining nine members of the Home Coven. Wednesday night would not be for the squeamish, to be sure. That night, in the wee hours of the morning, no one in the coven could ever exit back into "normal" life again.

Cailleach the Hag, to whom the entire Pictish nation had sworn allegiance, had made it very clear that the blood sacrifice must take place for the other Pictish gods to rise again to their former standing.

Stephanie imagined it to be akin to a perennial plant coming back to life after a long, hard winter. In this case, though, the gods needed blood and the coldness of death, not water and warmth, to facilitate their return to glory.

"Aileen," Brendan continued, "I will need you to channel Cailleach again. We will need to hear her voice—her instruction—prior to the sacrifice. Are you willing?"

An involuntary chill coursed through Stephanie's body, but she answered without hesitation. "Of course, my priest. Whatever you need from me."

6:37 P.M.

JOHN AND BRENT SAT in the Lawton family room, staring at a photocopy of the crumpled piece of paper that John had pulled from his chief's trash can.

John could tell that the Millsville police sergeant was quite tense. He could also tell that it had little to do with the piece of paper that the man held in his hands. Regardless, both men settled in on the couch to make an attempt at deciphering the five lines of words and numbers on the list.

> Th. a.m. A.C.
> * "AEA": D.M. Rem. Tran. – ABCS
>
> & Arm. Sen. – Approx. 1:00 a.m. *-50*
> * A.C.: S.O. BB/Cad. Pch.
> * Est. Ali.
>
> *-18!*

"Anything about your chief's background that might help in getting some answers to this riddle?"

John shook his head. "Already put my head into that question."

"The minus 50 and minus 18, you think those were hand-written by your boss?"

The short list looked to have been typed on a computer, then printed onto a regular sheet of copier paper, maybe by using a home inkjet printer. It had been cut in half with a paper cutter. Too straight to have been scissors. The only handwritten information on the page was the two numbers.

"I would think so. He often uses a Sharpie to make corrective edits to reports."

"Okay. 'Th. a.m.' That seems to be a given. Thursday morning. Sound right?"

"That's my guess," agreed John. "Any ideas on the rest?"

"Not a clue. Except for maybe the third bullet. Maybe 'Establish Alibi'?"

"Sounds like the thing to do after two prior bullet points of criminal behavior. If that's what they are."

The two of them spent the next fifteen minutes punching word variations into the Bing search engine that was open on Brent's MacBook Pro before them.

"Whoever put this list together—of course, we're assuming it's that Brendan Cadeyrn character—knew how to keep us at bay," decided John.

"No. I refuse to think that he's that clever. We'll get this figured out."

"We've only got three days."

"We will *figure it out*, John," remarked Brent, with maybe a little too much emphasis.

Tara walked in with two plates, a homemade hamburger with fries on each. Setting them down, she remarked, "Let me know when you two need some help." She turned and headed back to the kitchen.

John laughed. Brent, not so much.

"Great gal, your wife."

"Yeah, well…" he started, not wanting to, "… you don't know the half of it. We've been through a lot together. She's the best thing God ever gave me."

"You know," pondered the younger man, "maybe God is the factor that we're leaving out of this. Maybe we should pray for his help and insight?"

With that question, Brent stood up. "I should wash my hands."

Uh oh, thought John as Brent walked from the room.

Tara walked back in with two glasses of iced tea. "Hope you like it sweet."

"The only way to drink it."

"Good. Let me know if I can get you anything else."

"Is Brent okay?"

Tara shook her head without delay. "No. No, he's not. He wants to mete out some payback for what happened to us Friday night. I've been trying to stay out of his way today, hoping he'll just leave the poker in the fire."

John understood the metaphor. Anyone ruled by intense anger was going to make everyone around him uncomfortable.

"Maybe I picked the wrong day to call him."

"No, it was definitely the right thing to do. He's got something to work on now. Without it, he'd likely lash out again."

Tara looked instantly uncomfortable with the statement she'd made. "He's a good man, don't get me wrong. I've just never seen him like this before."

"A vendetta can be as powerful as a drug, and as damaging."

They both heard Brent's footsteps approaching. Tara smiled and turned away.

"Hon," she asked as he appeared from the living room, "anything else I can get you?"

"I'm good, thanks."

He walked back into the family room and, to John's right, sat back down on the couch. "Well, now, this definitely smells good." He picked up his burger and took a large bite.

John closed his eyes and said grace.

CHAPTER 28
Monday, June 13—1:39 P.M.

Officer Brent Lawton sat at his desk. And that was all that he was doing, at least physically.

His mind had done little but contemplate throughout the day. What would he do if ... *when* ... he got his hands on these self-proclaimed Picti people?

Riding his desk had to be as physically painful as sitting in his cruiser, but he knew that his broken rib would just create more problems if he ended up having to deal with someone breaking the law. He was none too pleased with his current state.

Neither was his captain.

Brent shook his head again.

There was no way that Brent was going to tell his boss that his house had been invaded by evil spirits sent by the Pittston chief of police. He'd lose his job for sure with a comment like that. Instead, the explanation had gone something like, "It was the darndest thing. Who knew standing on a chair with wheels, while changing a chandelier light bulb, could be so dangerous?"

He sighed. He couldn't believe he'd even developed the lame excuse.

For the third time in the day, he pulled out his own photo-copy of the list that John had brought over to the house the day before. He had no more clarity today than he did then.

Eldredge and he had racked their brains for another solid hour before the Pittston patrolman had headed home. Even then, Brent hadn't been able to stop trying to break the code. If it was a code.

More than likely, it's just abbreviations and acronyms. I will *figure this out.*

After getting up, forcing a few very unpleasant coughs, and making a dozen copies of Chief Connor's note, he spent the next half hour plugging in more possible solutions for the letters and partial words on the page.

> Th. a.m. A.C.
> * "AEA": D.M. Rem. Tran. – ABCS
> & Arm. Sen. – Approx. 1:00 a.m. *-50*
> * A.C.: S.O. BB/Cad. Pch.
> * Est. Ali.
>
> *-18!*

Brent took out another of the sheets and tried again. Something was going to happen on Thursday morning, and people he knew about—at least one of whom Tara knew personally—were going to be involved.

But knowing meant nothing without proof. Knowing meant nothing if he didn't have jurisdiction. Knowing might also mean nothing if Eldredge couldn't muster the chutzpah to deal with his boss.

The only thing that they had that could break this thing wide open was a bunch of meaningless letters and numbers. For all Brent knew, this could be an abbreviated grocery shopping list.

Was there a lynchpin within the fifty-nine letters and numbers sitting before him? Was one of these lines or numbers all that was needed to crack the rest? Brent stared, willing the answer to come to him.

Tracy Larkin walked into his office.

"Good afternoon, Sergeant Lawton."

"Hey, Trace" responded Brent without looking up.

"How's the desk?"

Brent didn't see the man's smirk. "Just terrific."

"Having a bad day?"

"Something like that." Brent still wasn't looking up.

"Hey, you know what I heard?" said the man in an exasperatingly jubilant tone.

Brent peeled his eyes from the piece of paper. He hadn't been able to concentrate from the moment Larkin stepped into the room anyway.

He sighed. "What is it, Tracy? I'm not really in the mood to—"

"I heard you were feeling a little under the weather, so I brought you a little something."

"Please, don't—"

Tracy walked back to the hallway and grabbed something on the other side of the wall. Bringing it into the office, he displayed two things: An annoying, cheesy grin and a white, folding step stool with a red bow tied to it.

"Some of the guys and I pitched in. Figured we'd be good Samaritans and help prevent another chandelier incident."

Brent looked at the man, then the stool, and back up at the man. He raised his right eyebrow and tried to generate a facial expression that said, *"I'm laughing on the inside, I'm irritated, and I don't want to talk with you."*

"Cute, huh? They had black, but I thought you might trip over that one in the dark and break something else."

The facial expression that Brent had mustered hadn't communicated a single thing he'd intended.

"Cute," he said with a half-smile that would *hopefully* display that he was appropriately humored and would then welcome the man to exit the office.

"What're you working on?"

"You're lousy at reading body language. You know that?"

"Yep. Fully aware. So, what are you working on?"

"Really? This is the way my shift is going to end today?"

"I'm afraid so."

Brent saw his smirk this time. Now he couldn't help but let a small grin of his own escape, as he shook his head.

He picked up one of the photocopies and handed it to Tracy. "What do you make of this? If this were a clue, a prelude to a crime, would you find anything helpful in here?"

Tracy took the sheet of paper and studied it. He looked up at Brent for a moment, then back to the paper.

"This have anything to do with a potential crime in another city?"

"Hypothetically?"

"Hypothetically."

"Yes," confessed Brent. "A hypothetical public servant from a certain hypothetical city … *may* have come across this in his workplace. Something passed from a certain religious group into the hands of …" Brent thought of the best way to conclude his sentence. "… into the hands of upper management."

"I assume, then, that this hasn't crossed Morelli's desk."

Brent shook his head with a hard stare.

Tracy just nodded acknowledgment. "Have you cracked any of this?"

"'Thursday morning,' and the bottom bullet could mean 'establish alibi.'"

Another nod.

"And the two handwritten numbers in here?"

"Assumed to be written by upper management."

"Well, 'A.C.' probably means the same thing in both places."

Brent's turn to nod.

"Can I hold on to this? I do enjoy a good puzzle."

Brent raised his eyebrows.

"Don't worry. Mum's the word."

So, now, all of a sudden, he's able to interpret my facial expressions.

6:37 P.M.

STEPHANIE WAS A MIXTURE of thoughts and emotions. She walked around MacKay Hill several times, just trying to focus and gain some perspective. Things were reaching a zenith, and in a couple of days, everything for which she had been practicing the craft all these years would become a reality. Unspeakable power would be handed down from the ancient gods of the Picti.

Why was she so melancholy, then? Maybe she was just tired. Maybe she just didn't want to go through, yet again, the immense pain that came from channeling such a powerful goddess as Cailleach.

Maybe she didn't love Brendan.

She stopped. Stood still. She looked around as if her thought had been announced through a public address system. Her heart beat hard in her chest.

You're his trophy, his whore. That is not *true!* she rebuked.

He's controlling everything about you. When was the last time you had any semblance of a life of your own?

"Shut up," she whispered. She was losing composure. What would Brendan say if he knew?

See? You fear Brendan.

"Shut up. Shut up!" she said more forcefully. It crossed her mind to call on her spirit guide, Aldinar, for clarity.

She walked over to the Picti Key Stone and knelt before it, the dirt now hard and uncomfortable beneath her knees.

Closing her eyes, she began to whisper, "Aldinar, friend of old, come to me, your thoughts be told."

She waited.

"Aldinar, friend of old, come to me, your thoughts be told."

She waited again.

Nothing?

She tried a third time, then a fourth.

Where are you?

She got up off the ground, dusted the dirt off of her blue jeans, and looked at the concrete standing stone before her. It was magnificent.

It's flat, and it's cold.

Her thoughts were beginning to really startle her. These *were* her thoughts; she could tell the difference. But they were so out of kilter!

She reached her right hand forth and touched the rough concrete fixture. It was warm, contradicting her thoughts. The sun still beat down upon it.

It's flat and cold.

She backed away, staring at the monolith.

The standing stone is flat and cold. You fear Brendan. You're just a trophy and a whore.

Stephanie couldn't take the thoughts anymore. She put tightly clenched fists to her temples and let out a scream—a loud mental and emotional reset.

She rapidly walked from the stone and the mound, making her way back toward the farmhouse. She was still a good twenty yards away when Brendan came out of the house, a look of concern on his face.

"Aileen? Are you okay?"

Do you really care?

Again, she wanted to scream! The first scream hadn't fixed the problem.

"I'm fine, my love," she lied. "I'm just frustrated with my mistakes and how I've let you down."

The right side of Brendan's mouth lifted into a smile. It said, *That you have. Now get back on the shelf, trophy!*

But his actual voice said, "Aileen … all has been forgiven. I thought I made that clear. Anyway, two evenings hence, all will be made right and we'll never have to think about past misgivings again."

Stephanie's visage became contrite. She continued to approach the front porch and looked up at Brendan with eyes that conveyed both appreciation and love.

She climbed the three steps and walked into Brendan's waiting arms. He held her tight. She could hear him as he breathed in the scent of her hair. His hands caressed her back and waist.

"Come inside with me. Let's forget this. We've got some time before Cowan arrives."

She followed his lead and walked into the house.
Trophy! Whore!

6:41 P.M.

"AND FATHER, PLEASE drive it into Stephanie's heart and mind that what she's pursuing for her life is just death and destruction. Open her eyes to what she's giving up for the sake of a power that has all been just a lie from the outset. Make it clear to her that she's being used. I ask this in the name of Jesus. Amen."

Tara got up off her knees and wiped away the tears.

CHAPTER 29
Tuesday, June 14—5:09 A.M.

Tara had had enough.

Enough of the silence. Enough of the avoidance. Enough of the loss of a good man.

Oh, she knew the good man was still in that body somewhere. And it was time for that man to resurface.

She stood in their spacious kitchen, watching the entranceway from the living room at her right. Standing on the opposite side of the kitchen island, she made sure she was directly in front of the coffee maker. Her lower back was pressed against the counter, and she rested the palms of her hands on its edge, waiting.

She knew that when Brent was finished putting on his uniform, he would come down the stairs and make for the kitchen, thinking that he would have his always-uneventful cup of coffee. That routine was about to be disrupted, and she already knew that he wasn't going to like it.

Tara decided that it would prove difficult to present herself as serious while dressed in the pink shorts and tank top that she had worn to sleep, so she waited until Brent entered the shower before rolling out of bed and quickly putting on a pair of black jeans and a long-sleeved, deep-red, button-up shirt.

She was going to make an impression before he had a chance to say a word. And her clothing choice was going to help her say, *"See me. Notice me. I am your beautiful and not-at-all-happy wife. I have something to say."*

Of course, now that she had time to reflect, maybe all it was going to say was, *"Desperate and needy."*

It didn't matter, though. She knew that she just needed to catch him off balance so that she would have time to insert some words of reason before being dismissed as unimportant in the midst of his internal, self-hatred dialogue. He had left her little choice, really. She wasn't about to let him sink deeper into his mire of guilt-induced anger.

The man simply didn't get it. The attack was not his fault, and his inability to do anything during the attack wasn't his fault, either. He had done *nothing* wrong.

Nothing wrong *until now*.

His silence over the past two days, and this third, would soon turn into an unannounced, abrupt word of rebuff against her or another angry lash-out against the kids in much the same way that had occurred Sunday following church.

After he had been home from work for little more than an hour the previous day, all three of the kids knew that Dad was off limits. And that was just unacceptable.

Tara had talked to all three of them before they went to bed, assuring them that everything was going to get back to normal. She prayed with each of them individually in their own rooms. The two youngest prayed emotional prayers for their father, while Jenna prayed to get to the core of the issue.

Jenna's intense prayer developed a resolve within Tara to deal with the issue as soon as possible. Maybe it was a Holy Spirit-developed resolve that burned within her.

She heard Brent's heavy footfall as he walked down the stairs. She straightened herself and crossed her arms, deciding to remain against the counter.

She was nervous.

This is not *right! I should* never *be nervous about talking with my husband!*

Something like righteous anger rose up within her. *"Be angry without sinning."* How appropriate that Scripture verse seemed to be for this moment.

Brent rounded the corner to her right, fully dressed in his uniform, and entered the kitchen. Upon seeing her, he pulled up short. His mouth dropped open a little bit, as a look of confusion crossed his face. He looked her up and down.

"Good morning, Honey," said Tara, taking the initiative.

He found his voice. "Am I missing something?"

"That, husband, is the million-dollar question. Isn't it?"

Brent walked closer, navigating himself halfway around the island, and then stopped. He placed his right hand on the faux-granite countertop of the island, obviously waiting for what was next.

Tara dropped her arms to her sides and tried to appear relaxed. She brought herself full upright and walked up to him. She placed her left hand on his right and felt its warmth. He began to withdraw it, but she pressed down to prevent him. She delicately placed her right palm on the center of Brent's chest, careful not to cause any pain.

She looked him in the eyes and softly said, "I love you, Brent Lawton."

Brent tensed. She could feel it through his hand, and she could see it in his face. His heart started to beat faster under her hand. He seemed to struggle for a moment, but finally allowed words to escape his mouth. "I know you do."

"You know you're everything to me, don't you? You were my reward for turning to God twenty-four years ago, and you are still my reward today."

She could see the muscles in Brent's jaw tense. He wasn't comfortable with what she was saying. She sighed. *Good, we're getting to the heart of this.*

"You are my lover, the leader of my home, and my protector."

Brent pulled his hand out from under hers. He stared at her for a brief moment, then said, "You don't know what you're talking about. I didn't protect you." He stepped to Tara's right, intending to walk past, but she took an angled step back and to her right to prevent him.

With a voice of soft intensity, she said, "You have *never*

failed me, Brenton Nathaniel Lawton. You have never failed *anyone* in this house. Don't you ever believe that about yourself?"

He stepped to her left, and she tried to counter his progress again. But this time, he reached for her shoulders and held her in place, making his way around her to the coffee maker.

Tara turned to face his back. He opened a cupboard, and she could tell that he winced in pain as he reached for an insulated coffee mug and set it down. He pulled the sugar bowl on the countertop toward him, grabbed a spoon from the drawer to his right, and scooped three tablespoons of sugar into his cup. After filling the mug with coffee and placing a cap on it, he turned to venture the other way around the island.

"Oh, no, you don't," directed Tara. She made her way around the opposite end of the island to intercept him before he could head for the front door. She managed to get right into his path before he sidestepped around her and began walking through the living room.

"Brent, stop!" She managed to keep the words quiet enough to hopefully not wake the kids.

He did stop, but he didn't turn around. He was five feet from the door.

"Talk to me about this, okay? Don't shut me out anymore."

The words she spoke swung open a floodgate in her soul. "You want to protect me? Protect me here and now! Make me feel safe *here* and *now!*" She couldn't manage any more words. She brought her right hand up to her mouth and began to sob.

"I love you, Tara." The words sounded contrived, even callous. Without delaying further, Brent walked out the door.

BRENT STEPPED OUT of his house and onto the decoratively curved sidewalk and made his way to the driveway. The front end of his Dodge Charger police cruiser seemed to impersonate the fierceness that coursed through him at that moment.

Opening the car door and seating himself within the

vehicle, he looked up at the front door of the house, half ex-pecting
to see Tara standing there.

She wasn't.

He closed the door, gingerly pulled the seatbelt over himself and secured it, then started the engine and shifted into reverse.

Reaching the street, he put the car in drive and chirped the tires as he drove away.

Why did she have to do that?

TARA STOOD FACING the door, doing what little she could to stop the hurt that wracked her system. She wrapped her arms around herself tightly, her only comfort in this painful moment.

She walked to the couch and collapsed into a sitting position on the soft cushions. Her emotion was threatening her rational-ity, and she desperately wanted to retreat within herself, into a place where she could be insulated from any further suffering.

"Don't do that, Child."

Tara's heart quickened, and she sat straight up, her anguish all but forgotten. Her breathing was heavy, but she tuned her hearing into the silence around her, even cocking her head as if to pick up a sound more clearly.

She knew that voice.

She *had* heard that voice; she hadn't imagined it. She slowed her breathing and listened.

Silence.

"Lord?" she whispered.

Footsteps above her told her that Jenna was now up and about. A slight disappointment struck at her heart. She looked at the clock on the fireplace mantle. 5:35 a.m. She would be meet-ing her bus in just under an hour.

Tara collected herself and stood up. She went to one of the couch's end tables and grabbed two tissues, wiped her eyes, and blew her nose.

Walking to a mirror that was on the wall, left of the

fireplace, she looked at her face. Her eyes were a little red, and so was her nose.

Great. I'm going to have to explain.

She walked into the kitchen. Since she was up, she would make the best of the situation and prepare Jenna some eggs and bacon. It would be a nice little surprise for her and allow Tara to focus on something other than Brent, for the time being.

She grabbed a skillet and frying pan, placed them on the stove, and raised a small flame below each. She went to the refrigerator, grabbed butter, the carton of eggs, and the small portion of remaining bacon.

After just a few minutes, the kitchen was filled with the smell of a country breakfast that was actually starting to cause Tara's stomach to growl. She heard feet lumbering down the stairs.

"Mom?"

Tara could hear the surprise in her voice. She was able to put on a genuine smile before looking over from the stove to face her.

"Good morning, my lovely daughter."

"Umm… You never cook breakfast on weekdays."

"Oh, but I do. I just wait until I'm able to enjoy breakfast all by myself."

"Nice," responded Jenna, with something that sounded like amused disdain. "Seriously, what are you doing?"

Tara had her clothing choice to thank for making her next sentence appear valid. "I've got something to do this morning, so I thought I would take the opportunity to make the three of you breakfast. I'll head out after Amy catches her bus."

"Errands?" asked Jenna with raised eyebrows.

Tara couldn't help but appreciate the humor. She laughed.

"No. No errands. I'm going to have breakfast with Jenni Sagan." *Where did that come from?*

"Pastor's wife? Why?"

"You're too nosy."

"It's what I'm good at," she said with a wry grin. "Because of Dad?"

"Because of Dad."

Jenni, I hope you're available to make a non-liar out of me!

8:31 A.M.

"HELLO?" ANSWERED A friendly female voice on the other end of the line.

"Jenni? This is Tara Lawton."

"Good morning, Tara. How are you?"

"I suppose I could give you the obligatory 'I'm good,' but I'd be lying. And I'm trying to cut back on that."

"I'm thinking about giving that up, too. As soon as I get the Lord's approval."

Tara laughed. This woman always had a fun quip.

"So, you're not having a good morning, huh? I'm sorry, honey. Is there anything keeping you at home this morning?"

"Already have my car keys in the ignition, your home address programmed into my GPS, and my driving goggles on," Tara quipped back.

This got Jenni laughing. "Well, I'm afraid you're going to have to reprogram the GPS. I'm at the church with Jonathan this morning."

"See you in fifteen minutes?"

"I'll be here," Jenni said with a smile in her voice.

It was about ten minutes before nine when Tara pulled into the church parking lot. Except for about eight cars, the expansive lot was empty.

She parked her car and walked into the building. Sarah, the church receptionist, looked up and smiled. "Hi, Tara. Jenni asked me to let you know that she's in Pastor's office."

"Thank you."

Tara navigated three hallways before getting to the senior staff wing. The ministry was growing to the point of having to bring on a pastor who would be responsible for the in-home 'L.I.F.E. Groups' ministry. Brent and she had periodically attended a group that met not far from their home, but they hadn't been to it in probably more than three months. They had allowed life to get in the way.

Life. A little irony there.

She found Pastor Jonathan's office and saw the two of them sitting on a small love seat. They hadn't seen her approach, so she gave a soft rap on the door frame.

"Ah, Tara!" said the pastor as he stood up.

Jenni got up, walked straight over to her, and gave her a tight hug. She had put on just a little bit of weight since they had met back in 1987. She was tall and still very pretty. Her near-dark hair was showing signs of gray at the roots, but she didn't look like she was in her early fifties.

"It's so good to have some one-on-one time with you, Tara! It's been forever." She pulled back and looked into Tara's eyes. "Unless you need some two-on-one time first." Jenni looked back at her husband, who walked up.

Tara looked at both of them with sad eyes.

"Come in, Tara," insisted the pastor. "Have a seat with us."

She walked in, and the pastor closed the door, offering the privacy she might need to expose her heart.

Tara sat down on the love seat that Pastor Jonathan offered, and Jenni followed suit. Pastor pulled a chair from in front of his desk, sat, and leaned forward toward the two women.

"What is it, honey?" asked Jenni.

Tara hesitated, not sure where to begin.

FORTY MINUTES LATER, Tara wrapped up her tale of the Lawton family's foray into darkness.

Jonathan and Jenni looked at one another for a moment. Then the pastor pursed his lips before expressing what was foremost on his mind.

"Brent and I had an understanding. We would keep each other informed about anything pertinent that we discovered in the community. He didn't say a word to me on Sunday."

"He's eaten up with guilt for having been what he thinks was the weak link on Friday night. I don't see his male pride get in the way of common sense too often, but when it does..."

well… you're seeing it."

"Would he mind me calling?"

"Of course, but that doesn't mean you shouldn't. I think he'd rather talk about this with someone he doesn't feel he's disappointed."

"He'll know you put me up to it," the pastor indicated. "So?"

The man chuckled. "Then I'll give him a call this afternoon." He looked to be considering something. "You know, I may not have to let the cat out of the bag after all—the cat being you, of course," he said with a smile. "It's about time I asked him again if he's come across anything suspicious. I'll be able to gauge him by his answer."

Jenni spoke up. "Jonathan, you're being a little bit manipulative. Don't you think?"

"Indeed, I am. But I'm also being wise like a serpent and harmless like a dove." He looked at Tara. "That's Matthew 10:16," he said with a wink.

CHAPTER 30
Tuesday, June 14—4:09 P.M.

The call came as he was heading home from work. He looked at his cell phone and thought he should recognize the number. But he couldn't quite place it. He accepted it.

"Sergeant Lawton."

"Brent. Pastor Jonathan."

"Hello, Pastor. What can I do for you?" Brent asked matter-of-factly.

"Did I catch you at a bad time?"

Brent wanted to say yes, but shunned the temptation. "Not at all. Just heading home from work."

"Good. Can you swing by the church? I know it's a few minutes out of your way, but I'd be grateful. I'd like to get a status update on our community situation. Plus, I've got some additional questions."

Now, Brent wished he had lied. "Sure, Pastor. Be there in ten minutes."

Brent did an illegal U-turn at the next available intersection; one of the perks of getting to drive a squad car, he often mused.

Ten minutes later, he was walking through the halls of Restoration Community Church. He'd been a part of this church for—he did a quick mental calculation—twenty-seven years. *Hard to believe,* he thought. Then he thought about how old he was when he'd gotten saved. *I've been a Christian longer than I haven't been one. Time sure flies when...*

He stifled the rest of the thought.

Reaching the pastor's office, he knocked on the partly-opened door.

"Come on in, Brent."

Brent pushed the door open the remainder of the way and saw the pastor take off a pair of reading glasses and set them on his desk. He got up and met Brent halfway.

"Good to see you. How're things?"

The question seemed suspicious, but Brent downplayed it as a normal icebreaker.

"Not too bad. It's Millsville, after all. How bad could it be?"

Pastor Jonathan just smiled in response.

"How about we have a seat?"

The pastor pulled a chair back a couple of feet from the front of his desk, then walked around to his own.

Brent accepted the invitation and sat down, crossing his right leg over his left.

"It's been better than a week since we had the pleasure of time with you and Tara. That prior Thursday, if you'll recall, we had some spiritual commotion amongst our intercessors.

"Well, it happened again this past Thursday. Frankly, people are getting worried. They're convinced something's about to happen."

Brent nodded, but didn't say anything. *I don't want to get into this, God.* Not exactly a prayer, more of an insistence that God comply.

He didn't.

"What's the news from the streets? Any new details you can share to shed light on all of this?"

Great.

"As a matter of fact, yes. There has been a lot of headway made when it comes to information. Suffice it to say, the intercessors are right to feel the way they do. A week ago, Monday, Tara and Jenna came across some interesting tattoos in Pittston..."

Brent brought the pastor up to speed with everything that had happened. Almost everything. The man didn't need to know about the strain all of this was having on his relationship with Tara ... and the kids.

"You've had information for eight days, Brent? This church, and other churches in the community, could have been praying about this for *eight days!*"

Brent hadn't expected anger to rise in the man. "Not exactly eight days, Pastor. We didn't really tie things together that quickly. Clues, but nothing solid."

Pastor Jonathan got up from his chair and interlaced his fingers behind his head. He was exasperated.

"Brent, so what if it had only been five days? Two days? At what point was it going to be important enough for you to let me know this? This is *not* just a police investigation. In fact, based on what you've told me, it's *not* a police investigation!"

The pastor got out from behind his desk and began to pace his office. Hands still behind his head, he bowed his head slightly, staring down at the floor as he walked. Brent could hear him begin praying in the Spirit, just above a whisper.

Brent felt guilty. Again. Now he'd let his church down. He couldn't handle this. He got up abruptly and began to walk toward the door.

"Brent?"

Brent ignored the man and reached for the door handle. Reaching it, he turned it, opened the door, and walked out of the office.

As he headed for the church's lobby area, he could hear the pastor gaining ground on him. Brent wasn't so immature as to start running, though. Within a matter of seconds, the taller man, with his quick gait, reached him and placed a hand on his left shoulder.

"Brent. Stop."

Brent did. Pastor Jonathan definitely had a commanding presence. He knew how to use the authority that had been placed in his care. The pastor moved to stand directly in front of him.

He sighed. "Brent, talk to me. Something's eating you. What is it?"

Brent was five feet eleven inches tall and still had to look up into the eyes of the older, more sagacious man. He was one of the few men who could actually intimidate him. He hated that about himself, but really appreciated that about his pastor.

Brent put his hands on his waist, just above his gun and utility belt, and hung his head with a sigh. After a moment, he forced himself to meet Pastor Jonathan's eyes.

"Things are not going well at home because of this," Brent finally admitted.

"Because of what, specifically?"

Brent turned away and slowly began to walk, hands still firmly placed at his waist. Now it was his turn to pace. After a couple of turns, he faced his pastor again. There was a little more distance between them this time.

He could see the concern in Pastor Jonathan's eyes. It was genuine. *He* was genuine.

Brent took a deep breath, his fractured ribs painfully objecting, and held it for a moment. Letting it out, he said, "I let my family down." The corners of his mouth involuntarily drew down and began to tremble. *No. Not this.* Tears began to form. He sniffled and took in a rapid, deep breath and exhaled quickly.

"*Woo!* Sorry..." He turned away.

I can handle this. I can manage this.

He finally got enough of a grip on his emotions to continue. "They were attacked by these … *people.*" He did not want to say 'people.' It was too kind a word. "And I wasn't there for them! They took me out first, before I could do a single thing to help!"

Rage was starting to develop within him again; an abhorrence that he had rarely, if ever, internalized during his five decades of life. He turned around and looked straight into Jonathan's eyes. "I hate them, Pastor. With everything that is in me, I *hate* them! "

Another layer of guilt washed over him.

I failed my family. I failed my pastor. I failed my God.

The pain in his ribs was not great enough to outweigh—didn't even compare *to*—the emotional pain he was feeling in that moment. He bowed over. Grabbing his knees, he began to weep in torrents. The pressure on his rib cage forced his right hand to his chest; an avalanche of pain from so many different heights and directions.

"Oh God… Oh God… Oh God…"

BRENT WAS AWARE that Pastor Jonathan was allowing time to think and grieve. The man stood protectively a short distance away. He could hear as others entered the hallway to find out what was going on, but his guardian assured each of the curious that the situation was going to be fine. As they returned to their duties, Brent imagined that the church staff was probably adding extra prayer to their normal routines.

Brent sniffled again. By this time, he was crouching against one of the walls on the balls of his feet. It was very uncomfortable, but there was stability; the wall behind him lent to that. It felt solid.

His foundation had shifted so much since Friday night that everything in his life, good and bad, had left him off balance.

Brent took in another deep breath and let it out slowly. He looked over to his pastor, who was leaning back against the opposite wall in the same squatting position. But he was praying. Watching Brent and praying.

Upon seeing Brent's gaze, Pastor Jonathan smiled.

Genuine.

The pastor got up and approached Brent, offering his hand to help him get back on his feet. "Feel like you can manage a little more conversation?"

Brent took his hand and allowed himself to be pulled up, wincing in the process. He thought now was as good a time as any to take care of his lungs, so he let out a series of three coughs. They hurt, and it obviously showed.

"You all right?"

"Yeah. Guess I forgot to mention the fractured ribs."

"Ouch."

They walked back into the office and took seats. This time, the pastor made use of the other guest chair in front of his desk.

Leaning toward Brent, he said, "What these people are doing is evil. It's vile and despicable." There was a pause, then he continued. "But, they are just as loved by God as you and me."

Brent's teeth involuntarily clenched.

"I'm serious. And you know it's true. These people, loved by God, are doing unspeakable things. We don't know what the endgame is for this group, but something even more evil is on the horizon that can hopefully be prevented."

"Prevented only if we can crack the code on that note I told you about."

"Brent, don't limit God to your ability to figure things out. He's bigger than that note. He also knows what that note means. Have you asked him for wisdom with regard to figuring out its meaning?"

Guilt.

"No," he quietly admitted.

"It's time to start, because maybe God put that note into the hands of three police officers for a reason. Pray for the officer you work with... Tracy?"

Brent nodded.

"And for John Eldredge, as well. Interesting name, by the way."

Brent smiled in acknowledgment. Another John Eldredge had made a huge impact on his manhood by means of a book he'd written.

The pastor got up and walked to the built-in shelving units behind his desk. He looked through an impressive collection of DVDs before he found what he was looking for. Coming back to the front of his desk, he extended it to Brent to take.

"It's called *'Furious Love,'* and it's important. This documentary was planned to be a God-versus-the-devil smackdown. The documentarian, Darren Wilson, wanted to watch as God showed up in different situations and proved himself against the powers of darkness. There was a sort of spiritual pride that was being brought into each encounter. But God wasn't going to be tempted by Darren or the others he had brought into the mix.

"God did show up, though. Just not at all like Darren had expected. Watch this film with Tara and Jenna. You might want to bring our younger brother, Officer Eldredge, in for a viewing, too."

Brent accepted the plastic case and flipped it to the back. He didn't read it. He just stared as he touched one last subject.

"Pastor, it's going to be hard being the man you're expecting me to be. I may have broken down in the hallway, and I may have listened to what you've said, but I'm still angry."

"Brent, just by saying that, I can already tell you're allowing God to penetrate. Don't stop talking with him. That's what got you into this painful fix to begin with, not those Picti people over in Pittston."

Brent considered that and nodded. He stood up and extended his hand to the man he loved as a brother, maybe even as a second father. The pastor's hand was strong in his own, just as another friend's had once been; one that he missed dearly.

"I sure wish George Chamberlin was still alive."

"Yeah. Me, too, Brent. Me, too."

Releasing Pastor Jonathan's grip, he looked into the pastor's reassuring eyes one last time and made for the office door. Reaching it, he paused and turned back over his shoulder.

"Pray for me. I've got a hurting wife who wants her husband back, and three kids who have to be wondering about their dad."

Pastor Jonathan nodded and flashed what appeared to be a knowing smile.

CHAPTER 31
Tuesday, June 14—6:33 P.M.

They were installed correctly? There can be no mistakes in this. None," insisted Brendan. "Uilliam, this is it. Any mistakes here, and the entire Home Coven has to leave and go into hiding."

The High Priest of the Picti nation stood, leaning over the dining room table of the farmhouse. Before him were the plans—the almost moment-by-moment details—of everything that was about to happen in a mere twenty-seven-and-a-half hours.

"Brendan, I know the stakes. The installation was no problem, and no one saw it take place. As long as she comes exactly where we tell her, when we tell her, the transmitter will do all of the work."

"Well, that's the trick. Isn't it? When has Donna McNeill ever been predictable?"

The Pittston police chief was silent for a moment, then said, "As long as Brook fulfills her part in this, everything will be fine."

"Don't worry about Gráinne. She's dependable."

"She'll need to be *very* convincing during the phone call.

Donna has to believe what she hears about her brother. She has to come *exactly* where we tell her."

Brendan looked at his legal pad. The intersection was remote enough, and most likely, there would be no one around for miles driving that stretch of back road in the early hours of a Thursday morning.

"You're sure her GPS will navigate her into that intersection? The GPS will be able to identify these two specific roads?" Brendan knew he was frustrating the man, but there could be no room for error. Not now. He heard the man sigh.

"The GPS will get her there. I've tested two different systems, and both of them identified the intersection without a problem," Uilliam answered, obviously trying his best to fend off signs of irritation.

"Good. Is there anything else about the planning of which I need to be aware?"

"Just that I'll be the one pressing the button and making the call to police dispatch about the scene. If it's okay with you, I'm going to have Brook—excuse me, Gráinne Lugos—come with me. If there are any loose ends to tie up before making the call to alert the police and fire departments, we'll take care of them.

In fact, now that I think about it, Gráinne will make the phone call, so that there will be no chance of my voice being recognized. I've already picked up another disposable cell phone, so none of the calls from the intersection can be traced. We'll head straight to the farm the moment that the call is made."

"It sounds like everything is in order," allowed Brendan.

"See you tomorrow night."

Brendan set his own disposable cell phone on the table. There could be no trace of any phone calls related to the upcoming events.

A nervous excitement coursed through him, producing a tingle down his spine. Soon, he would have power beyond what he could have imagined. The gods of the Picti people would be satisfied, awakened from nearly twelve hundred years of slumber. Cailleach the Hag had assured him that he was doing everything that was needed to avenge the Picti people.

Soon, the House of Kenneth MacAlpin would pay for its treason. Cináed mac Ailpin's own blood would be spilled for what he did to the last rightful king of Pictland, ushering in the Redeeming Age for which they'd been planning and working for over three decades.

To look into the terror-filled eyes of the chosen woman… That, alone, would make worthwhile of all the preparation and waiting that the Home Coven had endured. Brendan's only responsibility, tomorrow evening, was to make sure that she was present, drugged, and prepared for her important role.

Brendan smiled.

MacKay Hill would soon be anointed with the blood of royalty.

6:37 P.M.

STEPHANIE WAS DOING a little shopping for tomorrow night's 'festivities.' The little lamb that was to be sacrificed needed to be adequately clothed for the event. Brendan had been very specific: get a dress for a woman of medium height and slim build. It needed to be white, pretty, and something that could not be traced back to a specific retailer. That meant a day of meandering through local thrift stores.

She was amazed at some of the quality she had come across. She had no idea that one could find high-end fashion in some of these places. In fact, one of the stores seemed to cater to 'upper-crust' thrift shoppers—if such people actually existed. Though she had initially managed to maintain a strict focus on only the necessary garment, she found herself looking through handbags, shoes, and accessories for herself. She was a girl, after all. It had been a while since she had been around such finery.

Her mother had been a woman of some means after divorcing her father. Taking part of her divorce settlement, she had capitalized on some risky stocks—"sure bets—that had actually turned out to be just that.

Fiorucci, Helmut Lang, and Carolina Herrera had been some of her mother's favorite designers. If it hadn't been for Brendan, she would have probably followed in her mother's footsteps, a life of pretentiousness and lack of purpose. In retrospect, she was glad to have avoided all of that.

The woman did have style, though!

Stephanie found a pair of Prada shoes for $179.00. *Flared heel platform Mary Janes! You've got to be kidding!* Turning them over, she could see the remnants of the original price tag. They had been worn, what ... twice? They were, unfortunately, a size too small.

Finally making her way to the store's area of nice dresses and formal gowns, she rifled through rack after rack until she saw a dress that just might be the one. Pulling the hanger out from amongst the others, she saw that the white dress was quite beautiful. It spoke of an innocence that she hadn't known in thirty years. Lace ran around a neckline that plunged at the front; almost risqué. The dress had obviously not been custom-tailored to a specific woman's curvature, because it had a silk drawstring belt at the waist.

Stephanie looked at the tag. It was a brand she had not heard of, but it was not cheaply made. She located a full-length mirror and held the dress up before her. The hem fell down to mid-calf.

Those Prada heels would have made quite a combo, she thought. *It's sort of sad that the woman that Brendan found was only going to have one opportunity to wear this. Sadder still, I can't take it for myself after the ceremony is over!*

She laughed to herself.

Oh well. Such is life ... and death.

She was about to head to the register when the handbags caught her attention.

Sometimes I love being a little A.D.D.

7:09 P.M.

NOW I'VE HEARD IT all, Tara reminisced.

Brent came home late. Upon walking into the house, he'd sought her out, finding her in their bedroom folding a small pile of laundry. It hadn't *needed* to get done, but the task had consumed some of her otherwise anxious self-time.

He walked directly up to her, took her two shoulders in his hands, looked her directly in the eyes, and said, "I need to talk with you; apologize to you. But can you wait for a few minutes?"

She looked back with a wide-eyed stare that indicated she didn't know how to respond to the question. He'd smiled and walked out of the room.

She, in turn, walked to the doorway and watched as Brent walked to Jenna's room, where music blared, and knocked on the doorjamb. He said her name, and the music volume went down. Tara heard him ask if he could talk with her downstairs in the living room. She said yes. He then asked if she knew where Amy and Jamie were.

Tara already knew that Amy was decked out in her Princess Rapunzel dress—a gift she had received during her birthday party the previous month. Her Nana and Papa were *all about* making sure she had *every* opportunity to make herself look princessy.

That girl had better not grow up to be a spoiled snob, thought Tara with a smile, knowing the very idea was utterly ridiculous.

Brent returned and saw Tara standing in their doorway. He presented her with a smile and a wink, then turned to Amy's room.

"Amy-Bug, are you in here?"

"Yes, Daddy," came a soft response.

"Oh, there you are! What are you doing on the other side of your bed?"

"Being Princess Rapunzel, of course!"

Tara drew her left hand up to her mouth and let out a small giggle as Brent flashed a big grin.

"May I have the pleasure of your company downstairs in the living room, your highness?"

"Uh-huh."

Brent looked at Tara again. Another smile, before heading down the stairs.

Tara continued standing at the entrance to their bedroom as her two daughters came out of their respective rooms and headed down the stairs.

Tara secretively followed behind them to the top of the stairs, then waited. She heard Brent open one of the sliding glass doors in the family room and call out. "Jamie! Can I talk with you, Buddy?

Hi, Tyler! I'll have him back outside in a little while. Sorry for interrupting your game."

After several seconds, Tara heard her two men walk into the living room together.

All four were gathered, and Brent cleared his voice and paused, presumably collecting his thoughts and the words he'd use.

Tara quietly walked partway down the stairs until she was able to see all three of her children sitting on the couch, their backs to her. Her husband was sitting in his favorite swivel rocker, leaning toward them. He clasped his hands.

Tara contented herself with sitting down on the stairs, watching between the balusters as she listened to what happened next.

"I owe all three of you apologies—individual apologies—and I'm going to do that, but I wanted to get you all together first.

"I know that I haven't done much to show it in the past few days, but the fact is that I love all of you very much. You are the greatest kids that *any* father could ever have, and I am very happy and very proud to be your dad."

Tara watched as Jenna's head bowed and her shoulders began to quake. The sight of it caused a spontaneous smile to form on her lips and a slight misting in her eyes.

"Not one of you has done anything in my eyes that has been wrong over the past couple of days. But, then, that's probably only because I wasn't paying attention." Brent paused. "Okay, that was supposed to be at least a little bit funny."

Jamie shrugged his shoulders, obviously not getting the attempt at humor.

Brent feigned a grimace and trudged on. "I'm hoping that all three of you will forgive me for being a rotten dad over the past several days. I am going to start doing a better job. I promise. If I hurt—"

Jenna got up off the couch, cutting off her dad, making it very clear in that moment that she didn't care to hear another word. Tara held her breath. It appeared that her oldest was going to leave the room. But, instead, Jenna walked around the coffee table and over to her dad. She literally collapsed into his arms. Tears were released without restraint.

Brent held his daughter without a sound, though Tara saw him wince at the sudden pressure that had come down upon his chest. His other two children advanced upon him, as well. His grimace made it painfully apparent that he was doing his very best to hold them tightly, while also making everything right again that had been wrong.

It was beautiful. And, yes, Tara had heard it all.

Several minutes later, it became Tara's turn to receive, and her heart was stitched up rather nicely by the man in uniform.

Now she lay with her head in her husband's lap in an otherwise vacant living room, as they communed on the couch. He played with the full length of her hair. She *loved* that. It was soothing and so much more.

Neither spoke for several minutes. Her contented smile and his gentle caresses were conversation enough for both of them.

"Thank you," she finally offered in a whisper.

"For?"

"For being you again."

CHAPTER 32
Wednesday, June 15—11:14 A.M.

Tracy Larkin walked into Brent's office at a fast clip. "Got a minute?"

"Yeah. What's up?"

Tracy held up the half-page of cryptic letters and numbers had been trying to decipher.

"What if they're 10 codes?"

"I don't follow."

"Connor's handwritten numbers. What if they're 10 codes?"

Brent sat up straight and reached to his shrinking pile of alphabet-soup-on-paper, grabbed one, and looked at it. He hadn't even considered the possibility.

"Okay…" But as Brent thought about the meanings of the codes, they didn't seem to hold a lot of promise except, maybe, the '-18'. Well, 10-18 would seem to make a lot of sense."

"Assignment Completed," interpreted Tracy. "It being at the bottom of what may be a list of things to get done."

"A 10-50 doesn't make much sense, unless we're missing something."

"Brent, a '10-50' that means 'Cancel Message' to us, could mean something altogether different at Pittston P.D. It's not like these codes are uniform across jurisdictions."

"Very true!" said Brent, as he pulled out his personal cell phone. He pulled up John Eldredge's number and pressed 'Send'. His call went straight to voicemail. "John, it's Brent. Call me *as soon* as you get this. We may have gotten a break."

He ended the call and looked at Larkin. "We could be wrong. That '18' could mean 'Chasing a Streaker' over there in Pittston."

"Oh, yeah. I'd forgotten all about that useful code," said the corporal with a smile. "We'll know soon enough."

"I think it's time for lunch," suggested Brent. "Can I buy you a burger at Angie's while we wait for John's call?"

"You're on."

ELDREDGE'S CALL didn't come in until 4:07 p.m., after they were both already off duty. Brent picked up his cell phone from the passenger seat of the police cruiser, answering on the first ring.

"Lawton."

"Brent, it's John. First, my apologies. I always have my personal phone turned off during duty hours. Sorry, I hadn't given you my duty cell."

Brent disregarded the apology. "The numbers on our sheet of clues, the ones written by Connor. Could they be 10 codes?"

There was a moment of silence while John considered the question. "A '50' here is 'vehicle accident with fatalities'. '18' is 'Assignment Complete.'"

"John, can you be at my place in an hour?"

"I'll be there."

"Bring a laptop."

Brent ended the call, then dialed through his contacts and found Tracy Larkin's cell.

"Larkin."

"Tracy, it's Brent. The '18' is the same, but the '50' means a vehicle accident with fatalities. Can you be at my place in an hour?"

"See you at five o'clock."

Brent made a final call home to prep Tara on the impromptu gathering that was about to take place.

"Hon, we may have gotten the break we needed in this case. John Eldredge and Tracy Larkin will be coming over at five o'clock. We're going to crack this thing tonight if it kills..." Brent stopped before finishing with something stupid.

Don't go there.

"Anyway ... will you order us some pizzas or something? Call Mom and Dad and ask them if they'd be willing to come pick up the kids. It's your decision on whether Jenna stays or not. But, personally, I think her sharp mind would be a benefit to us. I've got to..."

"Brent! Take a breath!" responded Tara. He could hear in her voice that his spontaneous, high-speed checklist needed to be paused. "I'll call Mom and Dad. I'll ask Jenna to stay. What kind of pizza?"

Even with his adrenaline spiked, he had to laugh. "Get a few pepperonis, one with banana peppers and whatever you and Jenna want."

"Got it. So, what's the break?"

"Hon, I'll tell you once I've gotten there. First, I've got to turn around and go back to the police station for something."

"Okay. See you in a few."

"Oh! Tara, call Karen. Find out if she can fit us into her evening schedule. If she has a webcam, we can do a video conference with her and tie all of us in at the house."

Brent pressed 'End Call' without hearing Tara hang up and without a goodbye.

Forgive me, Hon.

Two minutes later, Brent was back at the police station and walking through the front doors. On his way to one of the office's supply rooms, he heard his name called out from his left.

"Sergeant Lawton."

It was his captain.

Not now.

Brent stopped, momentarily squeezed his eyes shut, and

stepped back to see that the captain was walking toward him from an adjoining hallway.

"Yes, sir?"

"Just wondering what brought you back to the office in such a rush."

As the captain reached Brent, he considered lying about his reason for coming back, but he'd been crossing that line too many times as of late.

"Heading to the supply room. Picking up a whiteboard."

"For official business?"

"No. Personal. If that's okay with the department," he added.

"Not if it's personal and unofficial *police* business. That would make it *not* okay."

Good forehand swing, Captain, Brent conceded. *Ball's in my court now.*

Brent stared into the man's eyes for just a couple of seconds before he turned around to head back to his cruiser, tail tucked between his legs. But he didn't make it two steps.

"Lawton. My office. Now."

Brent stopped and closed his eyes again. Opening them, he turned and followed his superior.

Once inside his boss's office, with the door closed, the captain began. "Are you going to tell me, or are you going to be difficult?"

"Sir, the gloves have come off. That Picti group attacked my family and me Friday night."

He saw his captain's mouth begin to open in response. Brent quickly maintained ownership of the dialogue.

"And before you ask, I didn't report it because there is no physical proof that it was them. But you and I both know that these people know *who* I am, they know *what* I do, and they know *my wife*."

"Your broken rib. It didn't come from falling off a chair. Did it?"

One of those lies he'd told was now coming back to bite him in the butt.

"No, sir."

The captain just stood looking at Brent for several seconds

before relaxing his posture a little bit.

"Brent, I want you to lodge and personally log a formal criminal complaint with the department. Whatever happened at your home... whether it can be attributed to these cult members and that Pittston police chief doesn't matter. You know that someone attacked and injured you. Someone hurt your family. Let this department launch a formal investigation. I'll have Detective Lewis drop whatever he's doing and make your family a priority."

Brent didn't expect this... this benevolence from his captain.

Maybe he was finally getting to the place where he believed his Pittston colleague was riding off the reservation. It made no difference, of course, since they still could not legally cross into that jurisdiction without proof of criminal malfeasance. Even then, they would need a warrant and the backing of the county sheriff and state police before they could cross city lines.

"Thank you, Captain. I appreciate it. But I can't. There is no physical proof. On top of that, without any proof, my lie about falling off a chair and breaking a rib is going to look just as valid a reason for my injury as this new claim. Lewis won't have any viable leads that he can follow."

Brent probably shouldn't have pushed forward, but he said, "Not legally."

"That's right. Lewis is restricted to Millsville. We do *have* a mutual-aid agreement with Pittston, but I seriously doubt that Chief Connor, over there, is going to invite you in or provide a jurisdiction grantor.

"Now, look me in the eyes, Brent, and tell me that you're not going to cross any jurisdictional lines. Tell me, and I'll believe you. I'll even pretend that I didn't see you walk back into this station."

Captain Anthony Morelli had just offered Brent his out. He searched the eyes of his superior and saw within them a plea to just say the magic words, 'I won't cross.' But in those few moments of silence, Brent *found* himself. If nothing else, he was going to be a man of integrity.

"Sir, I can't tell you that."

Disappointment crossed his captain's eyes as he reached out his right hand, palm up.

"I'm going to need your badge, Brent. And your firearm, if it's not your personal weapon."

Brent felt like he'd just been stabbed. He opened his mouth to object, but his now-former boss interjected.

"Don't, Brent," he said softly. "It won't make a difference. I can't take the chance of having the Millsville Police Department's name come under fire because of an order being disobeyed. It's better for all of us, you included, in my opinion, that we cut ties before that happens."

Brent had only seconds to resign himself to his fate. He reached up with both hands to his badge to unclasp the pin that held it in place. He pulled it from his shirt, re-clasped it, and placed it into Morelli's hand.

"I'm sorry I disappointed you, Captain," said Brent with an underpinning of grief.

"I'm not disappointed in you, Brent. I'm disappointed in the situation. You can turn in your uniform tomorrow morning. I'll have your discharge paperwork ready when you arrive."

Captain Morelli did something, then, that would stay with Brent for years to come. He transferred Brent's sergeant badge into his left hand, then extended his right to him again, offering Brent to take it into his own.

Brent did.

"You're a good man, Brent. I'm sorry things worked out like this. Now, go do what needs to be done to protect your family."

Brent, in that moment, was a man without words. He could but nod and turn around.

On his way out of the office, he walked up to the dispatch window and knocked. Ron Goodlow turned around, saw Brent, and gave him his customary big smile. Brent waved him over.

Sliding a glass partition, Ron asked, "Hello, Sergeant. What can..." That's when he noticed the missing badge. His question became another. "What happened?"

"I'm going to miss your friendly smile, Ron." Brent reached into his right pocket and grabbed his keychain. Taking off the keys to his cruiser, the back entrance to the station, and the storage locker, he handed them to Ron.

"Not going to need these any longer."

"Brent, I'm really stuck for words here. What are you going to do?"

"I'm going to go stop some bad guys. God bless you, my friend."

Brent extended his hand, and Ron shook it.

BRENT OPENED THE front passenger door of the Dodge Charger and grabbed his cell phone and Millsville Police Department duffel. He quickly scanned the car for any other personal belongings and then closed the door.

He looked at his cell phone. The mental debate as to whether or not he should make this next call was short-lived.

"This is Larkin."

"Tracy, would you mind stopping by the police station on the way to my place and picking up a large dry-erase whiteboard and an easel? Oh, and you may want to make sure the captain is gone before you do."

"Will do. See you shortly." Larkin disconnected the call.

Brent walked home.

CHAPTER 33
Wednesday, June 15—4:30 P.M.

Of course, the news shocked Tara. How could it not? Her husband had just been kicked off the police force!

They stood before one another in the kitchen.

"He knows me! Us! Our kids!" Tara responded in a stammer. "He *knows* us!"

"Hon, he does not know us *that* well. Relax. It's all going to work out. Don't worry about it."

"Worry? Who's worried? I'm mad! That man just got rid of the best police officer this stupid city has ever had!"

Brent laughed, and Tara didn't like it. She hit him in the chest with the flat of her hand.

"Stop laughing at me!"

His hard wince reminded her of what it was that she should never do; hit another human being's broken ribs.

"Oh, baby, I'm sorry! I'm sorry, I'm sorry!"

Brent leaned forward ever so slightly, trying to find that position that would exhibit the least amount of pain. He raised his right hand as a sign that it was okay. He coughed a couple of times, which intensified the pinch in his chest.

Tara was beside herself. She wanted to touch him. Lessen the pain. Anything! But she stood back, watching as her husband found the will to look her in the eyes again.

"Wow, if I had seen that coming…"

"I know. I'm so sorry," Tara lamented. She bit her lower lip, her face a portrait of sympathetic pain.

"I'm okay, Tara. But, man," he grimaced again, "this rib is obviously not destined to heal."

"What can I do to fix this? I so need to restart my angry rant."

Brent stared at her with a look that said, *'Really?'*

She smiled, then shrugged, then sighed. "I'm sorry, man of mine."

"I know that. How about a couple Aleve?"

"I'm on it," she said, as if she were the nerdy high school girl who had just been asked for a pencil by the school hunk.

She went to the cabinet in the kitchen where they kept their vitamins, supplements, and over-the-counter medications, and withdrew the plastic bottle. A moment later, she walked back to Brent with the two blue tablets and a bottle of water from the fridge.

Brent swallowed the pain relievers, then said, "How do we stand with the pizzas and sleeping arrangements for the kids?"

"You're not serious. You're still going to do this, even though you're not a cop anymore?"

Tara was momentarily stunned. She had just somehow figured that the loss of his job equated to the end of his ability to do something about what was happening.

"Tara, I'm a free man. I'm not tied down by jurisdictional laws anymore. I'll let the guys know when they get here. They can make their own decisions as to whether they still want to continue with this."

Tara looked at him blankly for a moment, allowing the logic to slip into the proper drawers of her mind. Of course, he couldn't stop. This had nothing to do with it being criminal activity. It had to do with the safety of their family and the prevention of something very evil that was on its way.

"I made all of the calls right after we talked. Pizza, Mom and Dad, and Karen. It's all worked out."

"Good. We're going to need to clear this table. The dining

room and this area of the kitchen are going to become our ops center, provided that John and Tracy are still in.

"Can you grab our laptops and tell Jenna to bring hers down, too? Let's start setting things up so we can jump right in when the guys get here. While you're doing that, I'm going to call Pastor Jonathan, so that I don't get rebuked again."

Tara flitted off through the living room, then up the stairs, taking two steps at a time. She checked first to make sure that Amy and Jamie had gotten together the items that were probably going to be needed for an overnight with Nana and Papa. Then she went to Jenna's room.

"Jenna, you and your laptop would be greatly appreciated downstairs in the 'Ops Center.'"

A twinge of excitement was visible in Jenna's face. She jumped up off her bed, where she had already been using her laptop, and started getting things together.

Tara, then, went to the master bedroom and unplugged her laptop that was leaning against the nightstand. Grabbing it, she went into Brent's den—his 'man cave'—and snatched his, as well.

Okay, she thought, *let's make this happen. God, please be in this with us.*

5:11 P.M.

PIZZA WAS BEING STUFFED into the mouths of two still-willing-to-participate police officers. Brent gave all of them—his wife, Jenna, and Karen—who was interacting by video conference—the lowdown on how they would proceed.

"Karen, did you get the clue sheet that I scanned and e-mailed?"

"Opening it right now," she responded; her voice and video stream impressively clear.

"Good. You and Tara are responsible for doing some research on possibilities. We're going to need background on the Picti people—the ancient ones. What is there to know about them? Why did their religion go away? Why is their religion so important to these new Picti that they would be willing to break the law?

"As for *what* they want to accomplish, John, Tracy, and I will be responsible for that research. We've got only *these* clues to work with.

"Jenna, you are going to be responsible for a couple of different things. You can shift back and forth in research. Keep an eye on what both the ladies and the men are doing. Try to mentally piece things together. Nothing is too far-fetched at this point to be ruled out, so as soon as you think you have something viable to add, you let me know.

"Your other responsibility is this whiteboard. It's divided into 'Soft' and 'Hard' information categories. When we are confident that we've figured out a piece of this puzzle, it goes onto the hard side. Any possibilities that we think may have *some* merit ... those will go on the soft side. Got it?"

Jenna nodded quickly, listening, her eyes intense. "Okay, hop to the board."

Jenna stepped to the board and picked up a blue dry-erase marker, opened it, and waited.

"All right, everyone, what do we know?"

"There's likely to be an orchestrated car accident, with the clear intention to kill the driver and/or passenger," answered John Eldredge.

Jenna wrote below 'HARD' Car accident—death.

"At least part of whatever we're trying to prevent is scheduled for around 1:00 a.m."

Jenna looked. That was already on the board, among the list of clues that her dad had placed up there:

- Th. a.m. A.C. **(Thursday morning** – *??*)
- "AEA": D.M. Rem. Tran. – ABCS & Arm.

   Sen. – Approx. 1:00 a.m.

   -50 = **(auto accident with fatalities)**
- A.C.: S.O. BB/Cad. Pch.
- Est. Ali.
- **18! (Mission accomplished)**

Brent looked at them. Having been handwritten, they almost seemed to be a whole different set of clues.

Karen chimed in. "Maybe we should assume that the 'C' in 'A.C.' is 'Ceremony.'

"Jenna, put that in the soft category," instructed her dad. "Anything else that we can know for sure?"

After a moment, Tracy Larkin spoke. "Yeah, we can know for sure that we can't let that 10-18 happen."

A feeling of fear, cloaked in resolve, seemed to rest upon everyone at that moment. All in the room, including Karen, already knew what that -18 meant.

If the words ten-eighteen came out of the mouth of Chief Connor in the morning, it would mean they had been too late.

THE OPS CENTER HAD been abuzz with activity for a little over an hour. Jenna was excited, scared, and aware that she was playing an important role in a life-or-death situation.

She would probably have nightmares about this night, especially if they didn't figure this all out in time. Unfortunately, though, not another piece of the puzzle, hard or soft, had yet found its way onto the whiteboard.

She found that the most important thing that she could do in the midst of all of the activity was to listen. Listen for something that she could enter into the browser of her own laptop and hopefully find a piece of the puzzle.

She was searching, now, for anything to do with "AEA" associated with "accident". Then she tried "AEA" with "car" and then "auto" and then "automobile."

Nothing seemed to be a fit.

She overheard her dad saying, "The A.C., if it is a ceremony, seems to be the key event here, not the accident. It appears in the header, then it follows the accident. So, the A.C. is the climax of what's scheduled to take place.

"Do you want either of us to focus on one or the other?"

asked Tracy.

Her dad thought for a moment. "Either of you have an automotive background at all?"

"My dad is a mechanic," answered John. "Used to hang around with him quite a bit before entering the academy."

"Then you've got the accident. Tracy, I want you on the A.C."

"Got it," both men said in unison.

Jenna was watching her dad with new eyes. He had always been her hero, but now she was watching him do what he did best: be a hero to anyone who needed him, whether they knew they needed saving or not.

She had never been so proud to be a part of this family. "God," she whispered, "please, help my dad and all of us get this done before it's too late."

TARA AND KAREN were trying to coordinate their efforts so that they wouldn't be looking at the same Internet sites. The easiest way to prevent that seemed to be just announcing the name of the site that one or the other had just entered.

So far, they had dug up mostly repeated information. There was far less information about the Picti than either of them had supposed. The whole Pecti-Wita witchcraft thing didn't really seem to go back further than *maybe* a hundred years.

One piece of information that both of them agreed was particularly interesting was a man named Kenneth MacAlpin, who had been the one who defeated the Picts back in 843 A.D. He had also slaughtered the King of the Picts and the remaining heirs to the throne by plunging them into a pit filled with spikes.

In several of the websites, it was repeatedly called "MacAlpin's Treason." They would keep this information at the forefront of their minds as they continued searching for more relevant information about the Picti people of northern Scotland.

Their perusal of site after site after site had also shown that there was a strong connection between the Picti and hundreds of what were called 'standing stones.' They populated northern Scotland, and recently, a group of anthropologists came to a shared belief that the symbols on the stones may actually be the original Pictish language.

MacAlpin came back to the forefront of Tara's mind, yet again. "Jenna?"

"Yes, Mom?" Jenna walked up to her.

"Something for the board. MacAlpin's Treason. See how it's spelled? Soft side of the board."

Jenna nodded and walked to the large whiteboard.

Karen spoke up. "I think you're right about that. Just a hunch. Also, I think I may have found something else. I Bing-searched the year 2011 and Picti, but didn't come up with anything. But when I made it 2011 and Pictish, I got several news articles out of Scotland, England, and Ireland talking about pieces of archaeological finds that had been stolen.

Here, I'll send you some of the links."

Tara received them and began to read the articles.

Hmm… This sounds familiar. But where would I have… Donna! Tara picked up her cell phone and dialed Donna McNeill.

"Hi, Tara! Was just thinking about you!" She sounded as cheerful as always. But then her voice came down to a near whisper. "How are things with Brent?"

Tara had to smile at how her whisper over there was supposed to keep Brent from hearing.

"Brent?" She looked over at her husband, who heard his name mentioned and met her gaze. "Brent's fine. It's all good."

"I'm so glad. I was worried."

"Are you okay?"

"I'm fine. Seems like my stalker's gone, and it's back to life almost as usual. So happy about that! But I'm still concerned about David's activities."

"I don't blame you. Donna, remember when you were talking with us about your trip to Scotland and Ireland with David?"

"Of course. What about it?"

"Just a quick question. Does the Key of Bridei or pieces of

a broken standing stone sound familiar to you?"

"Why, yes! David and I got to see the Key of Bridei at Trinity College in Dublin! He was very excited about it. I have to say that it was the nicest of the objects that we saw on our trip. Well, of the stone objects, anyway. The *Book of Kells* at the college was amazing, too! The artwork. Oh, Tara, you should have …"

"Donna, thank you so much for the information. Something's come up, and I've got to run."

"Oh! Okay, Tara. Have a good evening!"

"You, too, Dearheart."

She ended the call.

"Brent!"

He was there in a moment. "What is it?"

"I think Karen and I just found the first true link to a crime. And we can connect David McNeill to it."

"Tell me."

She had Brent read two of the articles. One dealt with stolen pieces of a standing stone from Portmahomack, Scotland, and another pertained to the heist of an object called the 'Key of Bridei'.

"Okay, what's the connection?"

"David and Donna had visited Trinity College, specifically to look at this key."

"So, somehow, the objects in these two heists are interconnected. What's the relationship between the key and this particular standing stone?"

"We'll search."

"Jenna!" called Brent.

"Yes?" she said with a sly grin, already listening over his shoulder.

"Cute. Go write stuff on the board."

"Got it!"

"Okay, guys," announced Brent, "The girls are winning this race. Let's ramp it up!"

CHAPTER 34
Wednesday, June 15—8:27 P.M.

Stephanie reflected upon all of the activity surrounding the events of the coming evening. The majority of the Home Coven was already at the farm. Several were out at MacKay Hill, prepping the site for the Appeasement Ceremony.

They had dug out a shallow basin on the top of the mound. The freshly exposed dirt would allow blood to quickly seep into the ground. Visqueen plastic sheeting was laid around the basin's perimeter in case of splatter; the *last* thing that needed to be detectable on any of the surrounding blades of grass was evidence of a crime having been committed. Especially a bloody one.

Brendan and David were downstairs in the dining room, going over how to make sure that any and all evidence would be removed from the property.

Chief Connor, Dean McClain, and Brook Shaw were out on the other side of the town on some out-of-the-way stretch of rural road. Somehow, arrangements had been made to capture the MacAlpin girl there and cart her back to the farmhouse property.

Stephanie stood in the third-floor spare bedroom, a cold glass of lemonade in her right hand. The especially warm evening had prompted her to call down to David and request a glass. It was always warmer upstairs in the old house, especially on the third floor, where there was no air conditioning. She could feel the perspiration rising to the surface of her skin. She tilted the glass back, drained the last of its tart contents, and set it down on an old dresser of drawers.

It would be here, in this room, that the MacAlpin girl would be dressed. Stephanie laid the white dress down on the bed, the hem just inches off the floor. *Whoever she is, she is going to look beautiful in it*, she thought.

She felt again a sensation in the pit of her stomach that she had been playing off as just so much nervous energy. She wanted to be done with the ceremony.

But why?

Why wasn't she anticipating it instead? For nearly thirty years, she had given herself to this. It was to be the beginning of everything she had hoped for. Power, purpose, and fulfillment.

Maybe it was about the channeling of the Hag that she was having misgivings. No pleasurable thought there, to be sure. But she had survived it once, and she would survive it this time, too. Besides, if Brendan required it...

Trophy! Whore!

Why could she not *rid* herself of those words?!

Because you're being used, and you know it.

She had to admit that to herself. But it had always been her role. All of them had a purpose. This was hers. Right?

"You were everything that I wanted to be." Tara's voice echoed in her mind; echoes from their dinner together at Dekkers.

"...the one you call enemy. He wants you as his daughter."

"Stop it!" Stephanie hissed, just above a whisper. "Just shut up!" She threw her hands up to the sides of her head as if to create a barrier of protection for her mind.

"God, the Father, Stephanie. The creator of the universe."

Anger cycled through Stephanie; the gnawing replaced with an urge to lash out. She marched down one flight of stairs and into her bedroom.

Walking over to her vanity, she angrily snatched up her cell phone and quickly walked down the last flight of stairs. Reaching the landing, she took care not to slam into the screen door as she exited the house. She didn't want to alert Brendan to her current emotional state.

Standing on the porch, she looked to her left and out to MacKay Hill. Tiki torches were lit around its circumference. It was a mystical sight with the nighttime sky setting in.

But she cared little about that at the moment. She walked down the three porch steps and turned right to go around the house to head back toward the garage. There, she would be afforded some privacy.

She had Tara's home phone number. Though she had doubted it would ever get used, she had still taken the time to program the number into her cell phone. Finding it, she selected it and pressed *Send*.

JENNA RAN TO GRAB the ringing phone on the closest end table in the living room. She looked at the caller ID. Just a number, no name.

"Hello?"

There was silence. "Hello?" she asked again.

"Is Tara Lawton available?"

"Yes, one moment, please. Mom? For you." Jenna walked the phone over to her mom.

"Hello?"

"You do *not* know me, Tara! Don't *ever* assume that you do! Those lies about your God…! You were trying to get into my head. Weren't you?"

"Stephanie?"

That got everyone's attention.

"Just watch yourself, missy. And just leave me the hell alone!"

The call went dead. Tara sat stunned, slowly lowering the phone from her ear. She could hardly process what had just happened.

A perplexed look overtook her facial features. "That was

Stephanie."

"What did she want?" asked Brent.

"Just to chew me out, it would seem. She said something about what I had said to her at the restaurant. She ranted about God being lies and that I was trying to get into her head."

Karen's voice came up out of her computer. "She's lashing out, Tara. She's lashing out the same way that you did. Remember? On our backpacking trip? You wanted everything that I had said to you about God and salvation to be lies, and you made sure I knew it."

The revelation shook Tara to her core. "I'm sorry, everybody. I've got to go pray."

"Yes, you do, dear friend. Be her hero," replied Karen.

Tara got up from her chair and was about to walk away when she heard Karen's voice again.

"Tara, will you face your laptop's camera toward the whiteboard for me?"

Tara took care of that immediately. Looking to Brent, she said, "You know where I'll be." She headed for the stairs.

"Say some prayers for us, too," he called after her.

Brent looked at his watch, then spoke to the room. "Okay, gang, we've got just over three hours to find a very good reason to call in the state troopers. Let's find it. We *can* do this!"

9:00 P.M.

NIGHT WAS DESCENDING upon the rural outskirts of Pittston. Jim Connor watched the blinking red and amber lights above the intersection; Donna McNeill's light was red. Dean McClain's was amber.

Blink. Blink. Blink.

He stood in the middle of the road, facing the direction from which David's sister would be arriving.

Twins. He wondered if David would sense something the moment that his sister perished. He made a mental note to ask him someday.

The Pittston police chief heard Brook race her car's engine behind him. She was ready for another dry run. He looked down the street to his left and saw Dean finish backing his truck into position. He flashed his headlights, indicating that he was ready for another go.

The International F4900 dump truck was used quite a bit on Dean's farm, which was about twenty-five miles to the east in Mantua Corners. It featured a 250-horsepower diesel engine and could get up to speed pretty quickly for something its size.

It sported a short and shallow bucket, which made it light on the back end, but the front was nearly the size of a standard all-purpose dump truck and would put a hurting on any car that ended up in its path.

Dean had called a local repair center about his truck earlier in the day, complaining about a hydraulic leak below the bucket. The owner of the place told him he could bring it in and leave it in their parking lot to have it looked at sometime during the day on Thursday; a valid reason to be driving these back roads late on a Wednesday night. If asked about getting back home, he'd say he'd intended to call a cab to complete the return trip.

Connor gave a wave above his head, signaling the vehicles to approach the intersection again. Dean would be approaching without headlights on. The derelict store on the corner would allow ample reason for not having 'had time' to stop his truck as the car strayed into the intersection without having stopped for his 'right of way.' Unfortunately, the store was also the reason that the timing hadn't been quite right yet.

They didn't matter too much, these practice runs. After all, one could never predict the reaction of Donna McNeill when the impossible happened. Would she hit her brakes? Forget about them as a result of her own fear and pain?

They were banking on the latter. She shouldn't be able to make any rational decisions once the remote transmitter in his pocket was pressed. This was going to prove to be one very interesting display.

The chief backed off the road to watch the two vehicles

approach.

They'd get this timed perfectly. They still had three and a half hours to do so.

He was glad he'd had the forethought to bring a sandwich and a cold beer.

10:04 P.M.

THE TORCHLIGHT AROUND the mound made Aileen's hair shimmer and her eyes sparkle. She was beautiful, indeed. Brendan walked up to her and gave her a kiss on the forehead.

She received it stoically.

"How goes it out here, my love?"

"Everything is ready, Brendan. We await your bidding."

Her emotional distance was uncharacteristic. But then, she certainly had to have been preparing herself for another visit by Cailleach. During her first encounter with the goddess, she'd had the advantage of not knowing how brutal the experience was going to be.

"Very good. It's all coming together just as we planned."

"Just as you had planned," she countered.

"Indeed." *Good, she's still walking ten steps behind.*

"Is there anything further that you require of me?"

He thought for a moment.

"A kiss."

She walked up to him, placed both hands on his cheeks, and drew him into a prolonged kiss that stirred a longing within him. When she released him, she stepped back and put a smile on her face.

"I'm going to head back into the house," she told him. "I'd like to rest before things get … intense."

He momentarily closed his eyes and gave her a single nod, granting her permission. She walked away.

If I hold such sway in a person's life now, Brendan began to wonder, *what will it be like after the gods bless me with even greater influence?*

He knew that he needed to get back into the house, as well. The one thing that was keeping him patient during these hours of waiting was translating the stones. So many more to go, but the culture he was learning about was incredibly vibrant and rich.

Brendan realized at that moment that he was a man who held the world in his hands. The secrets of a lost civilization were coming to light, hundreds of people would turn into thousands who looked at him as their benevolent leader, and soon … *very* soon … he would be endowed with such power that no one would stand in the way of him getting what he wanted.

He was, indeed, a man with a future.

CHAPTER 35
Wednesday, June 15—10:17 P.M.

B rent was getting nervous. He was sure they'd have more of the code cracked by now. They had some assumptions, but nothing solid.

The whiteboard was little more than a giant tease, taunting everyone who looked at it. It whispered with a cold sing-song voice, *"I know something you don't know."*

SOFT:	HARD:
Ceremony	Car accident-death-1:00 a.m.
MacAlpin's Treason	Key of Bridei - Stolen
Gain favor of Picti gods?	Pictish standing stone-Stolen

Karen's research seemed to be yielding the most results. When Brent asked her how she was approaching it, she gave him her path of logic. It ran something like this:

If there is to be a ceremony tonight, why?

Why would anyone be in danger unless it involved harming someone? Murder?

Was it a sacrifice? To whom? Why?

What do these Picti ultimately want? Power.

From where would they get this power? Pictish gods?

What would they have to do to gain the favor of these gods?

Brent had to hand it to her; she had a skilled and analytical mind.

Fifteen minutes earlier, he'd gone upstairs to check on Tara. She was lying face down on the floor of their bedroom and sobbing deeply, interceding like he had never heard anyone before.

Those four hundred square feet of bedroom space had become holy ground, and he'd felt he should not set foot in there. Instead, he'd turned around and come back downstairs, allowing her to do as the Holy Spirit was leading.

He could see that Tracy and John were getting frustrated. He understood what they were feeling; the same thing he'd be feeling if he had been tasked to be the go-to guy for something this important. They felt like individual failures.

He'd had enough experience with police officers to know they had breaking points that, when reached, made them want to start throwing things; usually electronics of one variety or another. It was time for a mental break. But first, he needed to check on Jenna.

She was sitting alone in the living room, laptop on her lap, legs outstretched to the coffee table. He walked in and sat next to her.

"How're you doing, Jenna-Girl?"

She frowned. "I'm not being much help. Am I?"

He put his arm around her. "Honey, all that any of us can do is what we can do. I'm not expecting anything beyond who you are, doing your best. If that translates into solutions? Wonderful. If it doesn't? It's only because you didn't have the information you needed to solve the problem. It's that simple."

She nodded. She felt defeated, and he could see it in her eyes.

"Jenna, why don't you go in and see if Karen could use some help. Ask her to give you her *logic path*, as she calls it."

Jenna produced a half smile, set her laptop aside, and walked into the dining room. Brent followed.

"Okay, guys. Outside."

Both of them looked up at him quizzically.

"Into the backyard. Now."

Both men got up and headed to the sliding door to the patio.

"I'll be out in a sec."

He went into the kitchen and pulled out three energy drinks. All of them could use the B12 boost.

He looked to the table.

"Jenna, want one?"

"Are there any cranberry-grape ones left?"

He grabbed a fourth can and walked it to his daughter. Then he headed outside.

JENNA TURNED HER mother's laptop back around to, once again, face where she had been sitting. Karen must have noticed the movement on her screen and looked up into her camera.

"Hi, Jenna. How are you holding up?"

"Not great. Feel like I'm letting everyone down."

"You can only do what you can do."

"That's what my dad just said."

"Smart man, your dad," she said with a smile.

"Can I help with anything? Dad told me to ask you about a logic path?"

Jenna grabbed a pen and wrote down the mental path Karen had taken.

"Hitch your horse to my wagon, and let's see how far we can pull it together."

The analogy made Jenna laugh.

She looked at what she had written and read each phrase carefully, making sure she understood how each connected to the other. A question came to mind.

"Would the gods be mad?"

"Hmm?"

"The Picti gods. Would they be angry? You asked why they might be trying to gain their favor. Maybe they think they're mad."

Karen's eyes became a little wider, and she sat up a little straighter. Jenna could see that she was evaluating her question, probably along with other things she'd been reading or thinking about.

"Oh … dear Jesus!"

Fear lit up her eyes.

"Jenna, go get your dad. Hurry!"

Jenna leapt from her chair and to the sliding door. She pulled it open and almost screamed for her dad.

"Dad! Come quick!"

BRENT RAN BACK TO the house, followed closely by the other two men.

"What is it, Jenna?"

"Karen!"

He slipped past her and to the dining room table. He leaned into Tara's computer.

"Karen, what is it? What did you find?"

"It was Jenna. She was the catalyst that I needed. Brent, 'A.C.' It stands for Appeasement Ceremony. I'm sure of it! The gods are mad! Angry! Or, at least that's what the group out there believes. They've got to make the gods happy again."

"Okay, but how?"

"Brent, MacAlpin's Treason!" She let out a guttural cry of frustration. "Why couldn't I have seen this earlier?!

"Jenna, you may well be the hero of this night." She tried to calm down.

"More, Karen. I need more," prompted Brent. Jenna could tell that his adrenaline was spiking.

"MacAlpin was a Scot. In fact, he's the one responsible for northern Scotland no longer being called Pictland. His people's blood infected the Picts. Ultimately, they died as a culture through assimilation, not by the sword.

'This group in Pittston… They want to avenge the blood of their people with the blood of a Scot. And I'll bet it's not just any Scot. A group this organized, that has been this patient for decades, to bring all of this to pass would have targeted their sacrifice. They are going to kill someone tonight, Brent; some-one from the bloodline of Kenneth MacAlpin!"

Brent stood up straight, ignoring the stab of pain he had generated in his rib cage again. His breathing was becoming more rapid, his heart thumping hard in his chest. He knew she was right.

He knew she was right, but ...

"It's all circumstantial! We can't call the state police with circumstantial evidence. No judge will issue a warrant on this alone."

Brent walked away from the laptop to look at the board. The clues. There were answers in there that they needed, and they needed them *right now!*

He turned and looked at his team. To his right, he heard footsteps descending the stairs. Tara looked drained as she approached, but determination was in her eyes.

Brent turned back to those around the table. "John and Tracy, swap work. Fresh eyes on this. Jenna brought fresh eyes to Karen's work; it's time for you two to do the same. Ask questions of each other, but ask them quickly. We may now have *two* lives to save this night!"

He turned away and walked over to his wife. She looked so frail. "As for you, my warrior chick, I wish I could pour out in prayer like you've just done."

She laid a hand on his right cheek. "Baby, God gave you and me special gifts, both of which are working at full steam and in perfect harmony. Don't doubt yourself."

She glanced toward the dining room table. "Sounds like something big has just happened."

"Yes. And there's no doubt in my mind that it came about because of what you just did upstairs." He leaned forward and gave her a big, noisy kiss on her forehead.

She laughed. "Go get 'em, tiger."

Brent looked at his watch. 10:35.

10:55 P.M.

STEPHANIE STARED UP at the ceiling from her bed. She would try once more to concentrate—to tap into the Otherealm. She needed Aldinar's insights and wisdom.

Why hadn't he been meeting her? She needed her spirit guide as much now as she had ever needed him. He had always come … until recently.

What was going on? This wasn't the first time in the past few days that he'd been silent.

She sat up and brought her bare feet to the floor. The hardwood was cool beneath her soles. She grabbed her half-finished bottle of water and took another swig.

This time, Brendan was the man who had come to her hydration rescue. He had even removed the top for her. It was small things like that that caused her to doubt her doubts about him.

"You've got misgivings about… I don't know what. But it's real, and it's deep. You are… You are questioning your purpose and your self-worth."

Tara's words again!

Again!

Stephanie felt like she was going mad. She had more voices going through her head than she could catalog, and they were *all* the wrong ones!

"Damn you, Aldinar!" she cursed with a ragged growl. "Damn you for leaving me with *these* voices to contend with!"

She stood up and began pacing.

"He loves you, Stephanie. He loves you passionately. He wants to satisfy your heart, your soul, your spirit."

Stephanie felt suddenly weak. She reached for the support of her nightstand, but missed it. She fell forward, her legs unable to hold her upright any longer. She was blissfully unconscious before her head struck the floor with a crack.

11:15 P.M.

"OH NO."

It was John, this time.

"What is it?" asked Brent.

"I think I just solved another piece of the puzzle." All attention focused on Eldredge.

He continued. "BB/Cad. Pch. It's a body bag."

"And the Cad...?" Tracy began to ask. But before he finished his question, he had already realized the answer.

"Cadaver Pouch." He looked into Brent's eyes.

Brent tried to keep everyone on an even keel. "Okay. I'm glad we can get past that part of the clue. We already knew they were planning a homicide. All we've gained with this is that they're going to try to be careful with the evidence.

"Keep going, guys. We're pushing half-past eleven."

They were exhausted. Brent doubted that any of them had been involved in this much detective work. He knew he sure hadn't.

"Oh, and the 'S.O.'?" prompted Brent.

John pursed his lips and just shook his head.

Brent walked to the board and added the additional information to the clue list. Then he made bold the areas that still needed solving.

- Th. a.m. A.C. (Thursday morning Appeasement
          Ceremony)
- "AEA": **D.M. Rem. Tran. – ABCS & Arm.
  Sen.** – Approx. 1:00 a.m.
  10-50 = (auto accident with fatalities)
- A.C.: **S.O?** BB/Cad. Pch. (Appease Cer./body
                    bag/cadaver pouch)
- Est. Ali. Establish alibi?
10-18! (~~Mission accomplished~~)

Brent drew an angry line through the last statement. They were *not* going to allow that to become a reality.

He walked over to Tracy Larkin. Maybe he could lend a not-so-fresh pair of eyes to the clues he was working on.

Larkin looked up momentarily. "No clue on 'Rem.' I keep thinking 'Tran.' means either transmission or transportation. Both seem related, but I can't make them fit the situation. Transportation seems redundant. 'ABCS'? Anti-*braking something* system?"

Brent was just as perplexed. He sat down at his own laptop and typed into a Bing search window what each man probably had done a dozen or more times before him:

[**abcs auto accident**] and clicked the search icon.
Lots of ABCs, but no ABCS. He tried something else.
[**"a.b.c.s." auto accident**]

Nothing. He pounded his fist on the table, startling everyone.

"Everything okay over there?" came Karen's voice from in front of Tara.

Tara answered, "Just blowing off some tension. We're all right."

Jenna walked back into the dining room from the living room, where she had tried to resume her research. Coming up behind her dad, she leaned over his right shoulder and kissed him on his cheek.

"Love you, Daddy. You're doing what you can do."

Tears welled up in his eyes as he reached over his shoulder with his right hand to keep his daughter's head in place long enough to kiss her cheek.

"You have no idea what that did for me just now," he whispered.

She gave him a soft smile, then another kiss, this one on the crown of his head.

God, you have blessed me greatly. Help me, Lord. Help me to bless the two people whose lives are in danger.

CHAPTER 36
Wednesday, June 15—11:57 P.M.

It was almost midnight, and they were losing.

Tracy was of the mind to call the state police regardless of the evidence. Brent was *almost* of a mind to let him. But he knew that if a single state trooper rolled onto Brian Baird's property, they'd first be asked to see a warrant, then denied admittance and told to leave.

Then the whole thing would be scrubbed, and the murder would just take place somewhere else at another time, with a lot fewer clues to go on than they had now.

At least they knew where the property was, and they knew who owned it. Donna's information during the first night they'd met had given them Brendan's true last name, Baird. It was just a matter of a property records search by one Officer John Eldredge that turned up his full name and location.

A sickening thought struck Brent just then. What if the remaining pieces to the clue they held were just as insignificant as 'body bag'? That string of letters that had finally been solved had done nothing for them at all.

The Ops Center was quiet, but for the sounds of breathing and the soft whirring of laptop fans. Everyone was staring blankly.

He imagined Karen was doing the same thing. All the while, minute after precious minute was ticking away.

There was only one thing left that he knew to do.

Brent reached his left hand out to his wife. She gave him a sad smile and accepted his comfort. He could tell that she was misreading him.

"Hon, take Tracy's hand," he directed.

"Huh?" Tracy didn't know what to think.

"John, take his other hand."

John grinned with realization, and he latched onto the older cop's left hand.

"Now, *wait* a minute," Larkin objected. "I am not going to participate—"

"Jenna? Will you come in here and join us?"

He heard Tara tell Karen in a low voice that they were going to pray.

Jenna walked in, pulled out a chair, and curled a leg under herself as she took her dad's and John Eldredge's hands.

Brent looked Tracy in the eyes and said with a smirk, "This won't hurt too much."

A reverential silence settled upon them, then Brent began to pray aloud.

"Heavenly Father, we love you. Even in the midst of such a heavy burden, we are grateful for who you are in our lives. We acknowledge our dependence on you, and we humbly ask for your help right now.

"Based on what we've learned, Father, there are probably two people out there who are in grave danger. We need your help to save them.

"Father, we've got some clues here that we haven't been able to solve. I'm hoping that they've been worth all of this effort, and if they are, then we ask you to open our eyes and minds to what they mean. Help us to save some lives tonight. We give you the honor and the praise. In the name of Jesus, we ask these things and stand in agreement. Amen."

There was a chorus of "Amens" around the table, including one that was added mainly out of peer pressure. But Brent would take it.

He looked at Tracy and smiled. Tracy shook his head.

If Brent, or any of them, for that matter, had been hoping for some explosion of knowledge to fall down on them at that moment, he would have been deeply disappointed.

John shuffled a couple of papers.

Tracy and Tara looked up at the whiteboard.

And Brent held his precious daughter's hand.

More minutes ticked by. It was now twenty minutes after Midnight.

Then one word was called out with such concern that it startled everyone sitting around the table.

"Donna!"

Brent looked at Tara, who was so stricken with fear that he thought she had seen something.

She had; two letters on the whiteboard.

'D.M.'

"Brent, 'D.M.' is Donna McNeill!"

DONNA WAS STARTLED out of a dreamless sleep by the sound of a phone ringing. A quick look at the clock revealed that it was 12:21 a.m. Her heart skipped a beat, knowing that only bad news came by phone in the middle of the night.

She grabbed for the cell phone plugged in beside her bed. She looked at the display. It was a number that she didn't recognize.

She flipped open the phone. "Hello?"

"Donna? Donna McNeill?" the voice sounded panicked.

"Yes! Who is this?"

"Donna, you probably don't remember me. My name is Debbie Schuck. I met you at the welcome festivities at Brendan's farm."

She couldn't place the name or the voice. "Okay. What is it? What's going on?"

"Donna, it's David. He's been in a terrible car accident.

Police and paramedics are at the scene, but it doesn't look good. They're waiting on a piece of equipment called the 'jaws of life' to arrive so that they can extract him from the car."

Donna was already on her feet. She heard a police or ambulance siren in the background!

"Where are you?!"

"Do you have a GPS?"

"Yes, yes! In my car! Where are you?!" She scrambled for a pen and her journal. She flipped it open, ready to write.

"We're in Pittston. I'm told you're in Parma. Right?"

"Yes, but..."

"Take the Interstate south. Your GPS will do the rest. Here are the names of the cross streets where we are."

Donna wrote them down, ended the call, ripped the paper out of her journal, and quickly threw on a pair of jeans and a dirty shirt she'd worn for cleaning her house earlier in the day.

She left her bedroom and ran down the stairs to the front door, barely remembering to grab her purse. She ran from the house, not caring that she hadn't locked the door.

Her hands shook as she got into the car, started it, and began programming the cross streets into the navigation system.

The GPS began laying in a course as she backed out of her property and took off down the street, hoping desperately to make it to her brother in time.

What she never heard was the sound of her cell phone ringing again. Ringing over and over on her still-warm bed.

BROOK SHAW DISCONNECTED the call with a self-satisfied smirk and looked at Chief Connor. She gave him a wink.

Dean, Brook, and the chief got into their respective vehicles and waited for a lone pair of headlights to light up the night.

TARA TRIED CALLING a third time. Still no answer, and it wasn't going straight to voicemail. Either she had turned off her ringer, or...

She refused to allow the thought to enter her mind. Looking to Brent, she shook her head, giving him—giving all of them—the answer they did not want to know.

"Brent, I'm scared."

Brent turned to Eldredge. "John?"

The Pittston police officer stood up and pushed his chair underneath the table. Placing his hands on the back of his chair, he answered the unspoken question.

"There is absolutely nothing that I can do. We have no idea where this accident is supposed to take place. I'd assume it's in Pittston ... somewhere the chief can control the incident and the investigation. I'm sorry. I'm of absolutely no help with this."

CHAPTER 37
Thursday, June 16—12:40 A.M.

A groan was emitted from Tara's left. It was Tracy. She watched him drop his head into his waiting hands.

"I'm too late." He lifted his head. Eyes, already bloodshot, were now laced with emotion. "I'm too late," he repeated in a strained whisper.

Tara placed a hand on his arm. "What is it, Tracy?"

Everyone was looking at him now.

"That line of clues. I figured them out. I figured them out, and it doesn't matter." An angry left hand smacked the surface of the dining room table. "I figured it out, and it doesn't matter one *damn* bit!"

Brent asked anyway. "What does it mean?"

Tracy tried to collect himself. He was losing that battle, but he was still able to explain the meaning of the abbreviations and the acronym.

"Rem. Tran. It means 'remote transmitter.' I figured that out after I determined what ABCS and Arm. Sen. finally meant.

"ABCS is an 'airbag control sensor'. Arm. Sen. is 'arming sensor.'"

Brent took it in. "They're going to remotely deploy her air-bag. She won't have any chance of controlling the car when she's impacted by it."

Both hands came up to Tara's face, cupping her nose and mouth. Her heart was beating so hard now that she couldn't possibly be the only one who heard it.

"No," she sobbed. "No. I won't let it." She grabbed her cell phone again and dialed Donna's number.

"John," directed Brent quietly, "pull up comscan.net. Let's hear the traffic. Jenna, Tara… the two of you may want to go into another room."

Tara looked at him, tears cascading down he cheeks, hardly able to breathe. She shook her head.

Jenna just put her head down on the table and began to weep.

12:44 A.M.

JIM CONNOR SAW THE headlights far in the distance and turned the police cruiser's light bar on, along with the vehicle's "Wig-Wag" headlights. They would lend credence to Donna McNeill's perception of an accident scene, and it was Dean McClain's cue to start his truck's engine.

It was time.

Connor looked at his watch and back at the approaching car. Impressed with her transit time, he chuckled.

Maybe I should cite the woman for speeding first.

His vehicle sat on a rise in the road, about a tenth of a mile past the impact area. He got out and began walking toward the intersection. He had to make sure he was close enough to trigger the airbag.

DONNA ROUNDED A BEND and saw the flashing lights about a mile down the road.

"Please, please, please be alive," she begged her brother.

She accelerated, now that it was a straight stretch of road ahead of her. She advanced toward an intersection. A single blinking red light warned her that there was a stop sign that needed to be obeyed. She looked left and right as she continued her approach. There was no other traffic. She wouldn't stop if she didn't have to.

A quarter mile away, she realized there was only a single emergency vehicle on the road. Even if the accident was on the other side of the rise, she should still be able to see the moving glow of other emergency responder lights. Shouldn't she?

Did they already get him out?

Donna was quickly approaching the intersection. She looked right one more time to...

An explosion of white pummeled her face. The intensity of the pain caused her body to react and attempt a rapid and deep inhalation. The material across her face prevented it.

Utter confusion. No focus.

A simultaneous involuntary reflex occurred; her right foot mashed the accelerator, giving the car a further burst of speed.

Airbag.

It was Donna's final lucid thought before a massive impact pulverized the driver's side of her car.

A flitter of realization began to form, but it was gone as quickly as it tickled the cognitive processes of her brain.

Milliseconds later, Donna McNeill's senses were clear again. No pain. No car. No light.

She staggered upright, her eyes straining into the suffocating black.

Nothing. No landmarks. No escape. Only void.

A foul odor stung her nostrils, heavy and acrid. Then came the sound—low at first, then swelling, like a wind gathering strength in the distance. Was it rushing toward her... or was she being pulled toward it?

A fiery glow broke through the dark, growing brighter, nearer. With it came heat—searing, suffocating, unlike anything she had ever endured.

And then she knew the stench. Sulfur.

Donna's throat tightened. The scream tore from her before she could stop it. Raw ... and useless.

BROOK SHAW AND CHIEF Connor approached the accident on foot at the same time. The impact couldn't have been more precisely placed. Her inability to steer the car had caused it to veer left into the intersection, and Dean's dump truck struck the woman's door with its left corner, creating even more damage than if it had been a perpendicular hit.

Both vehicles skidded off the road and into a shallow ditch right where the two roads intersected.

The truck's cab door opened. Out of the cab jumped Dean McClain, holding his left shoulder, but looking pretty good, considering the punishment that was just meted out.

The chief walked over to Donna McNeill's car and peered over the hood and into the cab. Her body was a mangled mess. Blood splatter covered a great deal of the windshield.

He walked back to Brook and Dean.

"How are you, McClain?"

"I'm going to feel it in the morning," he complained. Then he reached up, pulled at the collar of his T-shirt, and looked down at his chest and stomach. "I think that's going to need looked at. Pretty bad seatbelt burn."

Brook climbed into the truck's cab, turned on the headlights, and pulled two queen-sized pillows from the floor. The truck didn't have airbags, so he had been forced to improvise.

"I'll take these back to the farm," she said.

"Okay," said Connor, "you know what to do, McClain. If you can get to it, pull the receiver from the airbag's control system, then I want you, not Brook, to make the call. I can't think of a valid reason for her to be out here in proximity to the accident and then not be here when my patrolmen arrive to handle the scene. Brook and I are heading to the farm."

12:47 A.M.

KAREN, TARA, AND JENNA… Brent, John, and Tracy.

The six listened. Waiting for the words that they all knew were coming. Each squawk that came through the Internet police scanner on John's laptop caused hearts to nearly seize.

So far, though, it had only been chatter; just a little bit of late-night back and forth between two patrol officers that John knew.

Brent stood in front of the whiteboard, willing himself to do something other than wait. He scribbled the most recent answers onto the white surface.

> — Th. a.m. A.C. (Thursday morning Appeasement
> Ceremony)
> — "AEA": D.M. Rem. Tran. – ABCS & Arm.
> Sen. – Approx. 1:00 a.m.
> Donna McNeill, remote transmitter, airbag
> control sensor & arming sensor
> 10-50 = (auto accident with fatalities)
> — A.C.: S.O? BB/Cad. Pch. (Appease Cer./body
> bag/cadaver pouch)
> — Est. Ali. Establish alibi?
> 10–18! (Mission accomplished)

Brent realized that everything on the list had been discovered, with the exception of 'AEA' and 'S.O.'

"Tara?" he said quietly.

She looked up at him, but he could tell that she wasn't seeing him. The night was taking a brutal emotional toll on her. She looked awful; her eyes, glassy and puffy. Her nose, red. She had pushed her hair back with her hands so many times that it had begun to stand up in front like a cowlick.

"S.O.," he said. "They have to be initials, too."

Tara looked blankly at the board, then back at the table. She wasn't focusing.

"Tara," he said more firmly. "I need you."

Her eyes seemed to clear, and she looked back at him again. "Hmm?"

"S.O. They're initials, too."

She looked at the board again. Her lips began to part as her eyes focused on the two letters, and realization struck.

Tara swallowed hard. She struggled to swallow again. Bolting from her chair, she rounded the table and ran out of the kitchen. Entering the living room, she rushed for the bathroom to the right, along the wall that divided the living room from the kitchen.

All five of them listened as she expelled whatever contents had been in her stomach. That was all the confirmation that Brent needed.

"Gang, the second person on the list is Stephanie O'Leary."

"The Picti woman?" asked Tracy, a shocked look on his face.

Before Brent could answer, he heard Karen's voice yell through the computer.

"Get to her, Brent! You have to get to her!"

Brent didn't waste another second. "John, you need to make the phone call. Call county and state. Officer needs assistance. Alert them to known criminal activity taking place at the Baird farm. Report it as an abduction, with intent to harm or kill."

He grabbed a piece of paper from near his laptop and handed it to Eldredge. "Here's the address. Who is second in command in Pittston?"

"Lieutenant Given."

"Have his number?"

"I can get it from dispatch."

"Call him. I think he's going to want to be there when Pittston's policing authority drops into his lap."

An anger, this time righteous, rose and burned at his core. "Connor is going down tonight."

Knowing that he couldn't be fired twice for the same offense, Brent decided not to remove his Millsville Police uniform. He ran upstairs to his bedroom and picked up his backup utility and gun belt, his personal .45 ACP semi-automatic, already in the holster.

"Tracy, you don't have to come, but if you do, you're going to want to ask Eldredge if he wants assistance. I think he's now going to have the leeway to grant you a 'Jurisdiction Grantor' via Millsville's mutual-aid agreement."

Brent grabbed his M.P.D. duffel and riffled through it for a flashlight and tactical light. "Wish we had some body armor," he mumbled out loud.

He didn't know that Jenna had moved into the living room behind him until he heard desperation play out in her voice.

"Body armor?" Her breath caught. She finally forced out, "Dad, *no!*"

Tara was out of the bathroom and tracking toward him. "Brent, don't go alone."

"I'm not going to be alo—"

That's when they heard the words. The ones no one had wanted to hear, but all were expecting. Everyone's attention traveled back into the dining room where a loud and clear voice emitted from John's laptop speakers.

"All available units in the vicinity of Abrams Rd. and Rural Route 81, 10-50, multiple MVA. Roll EMS and Fire to location. Code 3."

Brent could see Tara waver. He reached for her and caught her as she collapsed.

Jenna screamed, falling to her knees beside her. "*Mom!*"

Brent had the presence of mind to quiet his daughter. "Jenna, she's okay. She's o-k. She just passed out." He looked over to the couch. "Honey, move your laptop for me."

As Jenna got up and rounded the coffee table, Brent lifted

his wife into his arms. From the kitchen, he could hear Karen's voice calling out. "What's going on? Someone tell me!"

Tracy moved in front of Tara's laptop and quietly began the explanation.

Brent carefully placed Tara on the couch.

Turning to his daughter, Brent gave full, measured instructions so that Jenna didn't have to think things through on her own in her current emotional state.

"Jenna, go get a *clean* dishrag ... and *soak it* ... in *cold water* from the faucet."

Less than a minute passed before Jenna was back. Brent folded the cloth and placed it on his wife's forehead. Tara's eyes fluttered open.

Blinking a couple of times and orienting herself, she finally whispered, "Brent, you've got to go. Go save Stephanie. Don't let her die."

Tears were already streaming down the sides of her face. He nodded, gave her a kiss, and stood up.

"Guys! We've got to roll!"

CHAPTER 38
Thursday, June 16—12:59 A.M.

S tephanie's mouth felt dry; cottonmouth. Her back hurt, too.

Had she fallen asleep on the floor? She tried to open her eyes, but the effort didn't seem worth it for the moment.

As she became more cognizant, she realized that she had a horrible headache. She tried to reach for her head using her right hand, but for some reason, her arm wasn't answering her brain's call.

Sounds were now making themselves evident around her. A soft breeze was rustling leaves not very far away. Something sounded like flames being fanned.

Adding to her growing sense of confusion were the smells of damp earth and the occasional wafting of smoke past her nostrils.

She tried again to open her eyes. This time, she managed to force her eyelids to comply. What she saw made no sense. She was in outer space!

It's beautiful! I've always wanted to be in the stars.

Her reverie was interrupted by a voice. She recognized it, but she couldn't remember from where.

"Aileen, my sweet."

Oh! It's Brendan Cadeyrn. I like him. Don't I?

"Focus, my love. I can't allow you to miss this." Brendan took Stephanie's right hand and patted it.

"Mmm. It's warm," she managed just above a whisper. "Why are we in outer space?"

"Focus, Stephanie."

But my name's Aileen.

She blinked and rolled her head toward the voice.

Brendan was kneeling next to her. But he seemed strangely elevated. She rolled her head further and saw his knees. They were at eye level, but on the ground. That's when the realization struck.

I'm in the basin. I'm on MacKay Hill!

The knowledge startled her. How had she gotten here?

Stephanie looked around some more. All of the torches were lit, encompassing her. The whole of the Home Coven was in its ceremonial white tunics and stood around Brendan.

Stephanie panicked for a moment. Then another realization struck her and put her back at ease.

Cailleach. I'm here to channel Cailleach.

She tried again to move her arms, but she was still unable to do so. It felt like...

Stephanie looked down at her right arm extended alongside her white-clothed body. Her wrist was tied to a wooden stake in the ground. She scrunched her brow in confusion, then looked back up at Brendan.

"What's going...?" She looked down her right side again. Her white clothing wasn't a tunic. She lifted her head and looked down the full length of her body. She was wearing the sacrifice dress!

"Brendan, what—?"

"Shhh." He leaned down and kissed her on the forehead. "I told you that you were important, that you were even *crucial* to what we were going to accomplish as a culture and a religion. Remember?"

He reached his left hand to her brow and smoothed her forehead with his thumb. "How long have you doubted your purpose? Hmm?"

"Brendan, this can't... This can't be right! I'm Picti! We've got to bring the girl. The MacAlpin girl. The one that Uilliam and Gráinne are fetching."

She made sure to use their Pictish names.

"You, my princess, *are* that girl."

"I'm *Picti!*" she screamed.

"Now, now. Don't be distressed. I've treated you well, haven't I? All these years, haven't I treated you like the Scottish royalty that you are?" He thought for a moment. "Okay, well, at least until recently, when you began to think too highly of yourself." He smirked at her. "That's a little ironic. Isn't it?"

Her eyes narrowed with anger. "I ... am ... *Picti!*" she growled.

"You, my dear, are MacAlpin."

She began to panic again. She knew how the MacAlpin girl was to die. She had to convince him that he was making a mistake.

"Brendan, listen to me..."

"Hmm?" Brendan lifted his eyebrows in mock interest.

"Think this through! You're making a mistake! It's the other girl, the one that we've been researching. The girl we located in that suburb of Cincinnati. Blue... Blue..."

"Ah, yes. Blue Ash."

"Yes! In Blue Ash! Tabitha! Tabitha MacAlpin!"

Brendan pulled his lips in tight and shook his head. "I'm sorry, Steph. I'm afraid that whole search was nothing but a ruse." He shifted his weight, and his countenance changed. He was no longer amused.

"You see, when I left Scotland to move to America, I already knew about your family; your mom's side of the family, that is."

"My mom? What does she—?"

Brendan cut her off. "*She*, Stephanie," he continued in a snide tone, "had one of the target names. Your mother's maiden name was Dunkeld. It seemed by the research back then—and trust me, I've confirmed it since—that her father came from an unbroken lineage of Dunkelds..." Brendan moved his head back and forth, reconsidering a thought. "… as far as I'd been able to prove, anyway. And, trust me, Steph, I am an *outstanding* researcher.

"I'm sorry, but you're it. That's just the way it is; the way it was always meant to be."

Brendan looked up, seeming to peer into the darkness that lay beyond the mound, then returned to his thoughts.

"The Dunkelds have a storied history as royalty. You should actually be *very* proud," he said with a nod of his head.

"Anyway, the Dunkeld dynasty came from another prestigious, albeit evil, family bloodline called the MacAlpins. Princess Beatrix MacAlpin, to be precise. And in case you're interested, she was the Heiress of Scone about a hundred-and-forty years after her bad-guy relative, Kenneth, destroyed so many of *my* relatives."

He stood up, towering above her. Brushing the dirt from his bare knees, he said, "And that is why *you*, Stephanie O'Leary, are in a hole in the ground."

As if struck by an afterthought, he crouched down before her again. "I do appreciate all of the, you know, favors over the years. You've been quite pleasurable."

He laughed, got up, and walked off the mound.

Trophy! Whore!

It had been true all along.

Her breathing became rapid as another wave of panic rose within. Tears rolled down her cheeks. She lifted her head and began to plead with the others before her.

"Charlotte? Taran? Please, help me. Cut me loose."

While Charlotte seemed to have a certain amount of pity in her eyes, Taran just laughed. Stephanie used to appreciate his strong, joyful laugh.

Brendan called back as he walked toward the farmhouse. "Ladies! Gentlemen! This way, please. Final prep!" And just like that, Stephanie was alone.

1:09 A.M.

FORMER MILLSVILLE POLICE sergeant, Brent Lawton, and Corporal Tracy Larkin crept up the gravel and grass driveway that approached the Baird farmhouse. Their purpose, for now, was to be on-scene and out of sight. Brent wished, now, that Millsville's police uniforms had incorporated dark, rather than white, shirts.

The trees that lined the right side of the driveway seemed to end about a hundred feet in front of the farmhouse. To the left side of the drive was a thick wooded area that extended as far back as they were able to see in the darkness. Brent took out his cell phone and turned back toward the road, using his body to block the light from its screen. He opened up the GPS app that they had used to get there and saw the final destination still pinpointed on the screen.

He clicked the 'Layers' button and then 'Satellite.' The screen changed from a road map to that of a daylight satellite view of their location.

Zooming in, he was able to get a pretty good idea of the layout of the property. He could see the shape of the house, the garage behind it, and a large clearing to the right.

Brent nudged Tracy, who turned around and looked at the phone. Brent whispered, "Chances are, this field is where they will hold the ceremony."

Tracy nodded and turned back to the house.

They were only about thirty feet from the road and still a good two-thirds of a football field away from the house. The trees to their right were simply too thick to see through, so they really had no idea at all where anyone was at the moment.

"Brent!" said Tracy in a strained whisper. "Move!"

Tracy scampered into the trees, followed by Brent. They pushed in as far and as quickly as they could manage in order to hide their white uniform shirts from the vehicle that had approached and was now turning into the drive.

On their stomachs, Brent again had to force himself to contain a fractured-rib-generated groan. They watched as a dark-blue police cruiser rolled by. Another vehicle followed: a late-model, silver Chevy Camaro.

"Plate," whispered Brent.

Tracy lifted himself and moved close to the drive. After a moment, he came back.

Tracy pulled a notepad out of his pocket. "Light."

Brent lit up his phone screen, providing enough light to write down the plate number and vehicle description.

"That was Connor in the patrol car," said Larkin.

Brent only nodded.

They waited a couple of minutes before extracting themselves from the trees, in case there had been another vehicle straggling behind the first two.

Back into their crouching positions, Brent said, "You're on Eldredge's frequency, right?"

Tracy looked to make sure, then nodded.

"Let him know we're in position and that Connor just arrived. Find out about state and county."

Larkin whispered into the mic on his left shoulder. "Eldredge. 20." He placed his fingers on the volume control, wanting it only loud enough to make out what was said.

Fortunately, the majority of the Ten Codes that the two departments used were the same. All of the codes that should be needed tonight had been discussed on the way out of Millsville.

"Copy you, Larkin. 20 is leaving Pittston P.D. Conferring with upper management to be."

"60 on state and county?"

"Confirmation. They are rolling."

"77 on them and you?"

"State and county, ten minutes plus. Management and I, seven to nine."

"Contact again. Tell them to run hot and silent. No lights.

"10-4."

"4 and out." He looked at Brent. "Did you get that?"

Brent nodded. "Come on. We need to get closer."

BRENDAN WALKED UP to Uilliam and Gráinne as they exited their vehicles in front of the house. He was encouraged by the smiles on their faces.

"Everything went perfectly," said Uilliam. "It was just a very unfortunate accident in the middle of nowhere."

"Excellent!" exclaimed Brendan.

"City resources will be out of our way and focused on the other side of town for a while. Does Cowan know about the … umm … *unfortunate* loss of life, yet?"

"He does. He's inside grieving his dear sister now."

"Will he be trouble?"

Brendan shook his head. "Not at all. He understands that it needed to be done. Regardless, tonight's ceremony will have cemented his dedication, had there been any chance of wavering. I'm also pretty sure that he'd hate to have something so tragic occur in his own path... so to speak. How's Sòlas?"

"He's pretty bruised and raw, but he otherwise came out of it intact. He deserves a big pat on the back when we see him in the morning."

Connor looked over at the mound in the distance. "I see she's awake and aware."

Brendan looked over, as well. Stephanie was straining to keep her neck elevated in order to see what was going on.

He shouted over to her. "We'll be there soon, MacAlpin! Be patient!"

Both of the men, as well as Gráinne, laughed.

"What do we need to do?" asked Uilliam.

"Change into your tunics. We've been waiting on you two."

TARA WAS DESPERATE for news.

She sat in front of her laptop once again. Jenna was just inches away, sitting to her left. They made sure that they could both be seen at the same time as they talked with Karen.

"Karen, I just can't sit here wondering. You've got to understand that."

"That's not the point, and you know it. You are *not* equipped to be in proximity to what's going on out there."

"Maybe not. But I can't think of a reason why I can't be there immediately *after* everything goes down. I've got to find out about Stephanie!"

Karen stared at her through the screen for a few moments. Finally, she said, "Tara, get going. It's not like you're seeking my permission anyway. Right now, though, make a *wise* decision concerning your daughter."

"Aunt Karen, I'm going with my mom. That *is* the wise decision. I need to know about Dad." She looked into her mom's eyes, pleading.

"Tara..." Karen didn't say anything else. The way she said her name was pregnant with meaning and emphasis.

Tara looked at her daughter. "Put your shoes on, and grab some bottled water. I'm going to need it."

Jenna removed herself from the table immediately.

"Tara!" exclaimed Karen. "What do you think you're doing?"

"Karen, I love you. And I appreciate you beyond anything you can possibly understand. But she and I have *got* to do this. Together." Tara continued. "Jenna has been in this with us from the beginning. She's earned her place beside me while I do this."

Karen sighed. "I guess this is goodnight, then. At least on here. I'm going to keep my ringer on, so please call me once everything is settled. Okay?"

"Don't worry. I wouldn't think of keeping you out of the loop. As soon as I know *anything,* I will call you. I love you, Karen."

"I love you, too, Tara."

A shout from the living room. "Love you, Aunt Karen!"

CHAPTER 39
Thursday, June 16—1:14 A.M.

Everything she had believed in for thirty years ended up being a lie.

She whimpered alone in the night. The far-off sounds of laughter and talking were only on the periphery of importance. At the forefront of her thoughts were all of the preparations *she* had made that were supposed to be leading to the death of a different woman.

I'm the woman. I've always been the woman.

For years, she had been orchestrating her own death. And now she lay in a dress that she had jealously wanted to wear herself.

The irony was a stench in her mind.

"It's for the best, my lovely."

Her eyes opened wide with realization.

Aldinar!

"Help me," she whispered. "Guide me from this. Please! I'm not supposed to die."

"From the time you were born, you were predestined to die. Whether by pain or in peace, it's all the same."

"But… I'm supposed to be…" she stammered.

Supposed to be what? she wondered.

She realized that the larger portion of her life had been sequestered from the rest of the world. The friendships that she
had developed existed only within the Picti people.

She hadn't held a job since she was in her early twenties,
and she knew no one in the community, not a single neighbor.
She would never even be missed!

How could I have been so blind?

"Aldinar, you…" She didn't want to finish the question, but
needed to learn the truth. "All this time, you *knew* I was the
appeasement sacrifice?"

*"It has always been your destiny. At the moment of your
birth, I had chosen you."*

"What?" The statement seemed impossible. It *was* impossible!
Unless.

Unless Aldinar had been lying in wait, waiting for the right
time in history to bring all of this together.

"Brendan," she whispered.

"He was meant *to find you, my beloved. You were his
from the beginning. He thinks he found you, but he was led."*

Anger mixed with understanding. She had been naïvely
guided into this position. A twelve-hundred-year-old circle
had been completed; from MacAlpin's betrayal of the Picts to
the Picts' betrayal of a MacAlpin.

*"Very soon, my dear… Very soon, you and I will be face to
face. I hope you enjoy what you see."*

A shiver coursed through her body. Soon she would enter
the Otherealm.

But if everything else had been a lie…

Stephanie pulled hard at the bindings on her arms and legs
and screamed at the top of her lungs!

"*AHHHhhhhh!*"

BRENT'S WEAPON WAS OUT of his holster in a flash. The
scream cutting him to his core.

He and Larkin had made their way to the edge of the tree line and were able to see the ceremonial mound to their right at a distance.

The drawing of his weapon had been pure reflex. He knew that there was no immediate threat to Stephanie, with everyone still congregated at the front of the house.

Jim Connor came storming out of the house with his weapon pointed toward the sky, shoulder height. The normally impressive-looking man looked like a buffoon as he scrambled off the porch in a near panic, wearing nothing but a toga-like dress.

He must have thought they'd been found out. Now that he's had a scare, he's going to be more wary.

As if to emphasize the point, the Pittston police chief looked past his police cruiser and the Camaro in the direction of the driveway. Brent and Tracy pulled back slightly until they could no longer see him. Hopefully, their shirts hadn't been noticed.

A moment later, Brent heard the sound of footsteps behind him; the soft crunching of gravel underfoot. He swung around, aiming into the darkness, his eyes unable to adjust quickly from the lights at the front of the house.

"Stand down!" came a whispered command.

He lowered his weapon as the voice registered in his brain. "Eldredge?"

"And Lieutenant Given"

Brent and Larkin quietly trekked back to the other men. It turned out that there were two other cops with them.

The lieutenant noticed Brent's missing badge immediately. "You're not a cop?" He looked at Eldredge.

Brent answered. "Not as of 4:30 this past afternoon." He wasn't going to get into the details. Instead, he deflected the subject. "This is Corporal Larkin. He *is* a cop."

The lieutenant took the hint. "SITREP."

With that word, Brent assumed that Given must have had a military background. SITREP was a military acronym for 'Situation Report.'

"A woman, by the name of Stephanie O'Leary, is restrained, back to the ground, about seventy to eighty yards to the right of our position. Looks like she's on some sort of ceremonial mound. I haven't gotten a firm count, but there are at least ten people milling about the front of the house.

"It appears that they're about to head out to Miss O'Leary's location to perform some sort of ceremony. I've got reason to believe that they intend to ritually sacrifice her.

"I don't know how many people remain in the house, but your boss just came out with his weapon drawn. Unknown if any of the others have weapons."

"Okay," said the Pittston lieutenant, "we sit tight and wait on county and state. They should be here in a couple of minutes. We go in alone *only* if we know the woman is in imminent danger."

"Yes, sir," replied Brent.

He looked at Larkin, who gave a nod toward the Pittston cop. Brent understood.

"Sir, do we have your permission to be in your jurisdiction for this action?" He needed to have clarification, if only for Tracy's peace of mind.

"I'm giving you and Larkin a 'Jurisdiction Grantor,' Lawton. I'm not sure how that's going to play out with you, though. You're not a cop, and I don't exactly have deputizing powers."

"I understand. I submit to your authority."

Given nodded.

They sat tight.

BRENDAN AND THE REST of the Home Coven approached the ceremonial mound and ascended to the top. They took positions standing in a circle around Stephanie, with Brendan at her head. He watched as the woman struggled, but now she didn't say a word. She was no longer begging.

"No time like the present," Brendan began. "I see no reason for a lot of ceremony for what we are about to do. But we will be calling on Cailleach the Hag. The goddess herself will guide us in this act of revenge and will let us know if the appeasement of the Pictish gods has been accomplished. Then…" A big smile lit up his face. "*Then* we will celebrate! For this is the day of our redemption!"

He looked into the eyes of each of his followers. Smiles and excitement were evident on every face, man and woman alike.

Brendan threw his head back, stretched out his arms, and said with a shout of exclamation, "The *Redeeming Age* is about to begin!"

STEPHANIE STILLED HERSELF as best she could. Her heart raced, and she could not take a steady breath. Her heart raced, and she could not take a steady breath.

This is it. Her whole body trembled uncontrollably. *This is it.*

She gasped for breath. It felt as though she might vomit. Her eyes shot back and forth between Brendan's face and the ceremonial knife, a *ballock* dagger that he was holding in his left hand. It was a long blade with a blue agate hilt. Stephanie had seen it on many occasions. Brendan had once told her that he would pull it out from time to time to remind himself of the importance of what they were doing.

The beautiful and dreadful instrument had been handed down to him from his father's brother. His uncle had created it with the belief that *he* was the one to usher in the Redeeming Age. It was covered with Pictish scrollwork and symbols. Beautiful it might be, but now it was every bit an object of terror.

"Kneel, faithful Picti," commanded Brendan in a steady, calm voice. He was peering directly into Stephanie's eyes as he sank to his knees.

God the Father, Stephanie, came Tara's words again. *The Creator of the Universe, the one you call enemy. He wants you as his daughter.*

It can't be true, she lamented inwardly, unable to pull

her eyes from Brendan's gaze.

He loves you, Stephanie. He loves you passionately.

"Cailleach, goddess of the Picti people!" Brendan began, arms once again outstretched. "We invoke your name and seek your power and guidance. Into your hands I give myself. I am your vessel. Enter. Fill. Fulfill."

All was silent, except for the sound of Stephanie's own pulse and ragged breathing.

Brendan remained kneeling, arched backward, head back.

Though Stephanie had personally experienced what happened next, it still caused her blood to run cold to see it take place.

Brendan's eyes shot open, and his mouth opened wide, as if pried apart. She heard him gasp in pain as Cailleach began to enter. His throat got wide, as if swallowing a softball. He was a snake ingesting an overly large prey. His back then arched further back, into an impossible horseshoe shape.

A softly emitted cry began to form. Whether from pain or from the goddess, Stephanie didn't know, but it grew in intensity. Louder and louder and impossibly long. His lungs couldn't possibly have held that much air.

Stephanie's eyes left Brendan, hoping to find a source of help from those around her. But the Picti were terrified, several of them holding hands over their ears. Stephanie wanted to do the same. She yanked at her restraints.

She pulled at them again with all of her strength.

"PLEASE!" she howled, her scream combining with Cailleach's.

Then it stopped. Silence.

Stephanie arched her neck backward to see Brendan's body become upright once again; his back making popping noises as the vertebrae repositioned. The sound was sickening.

When Brendan's body was back in proper human form, he brought his eyes down to stare into Stephanie's. His face had contorted into an evil scowl.

Then he—*it*—spoke, a voice as old and dry as Death Valley; a voice that less than a month prior had ushered forth from her very own mouth. "Remember... *Few* survive."

CHAPTER 40
Thursday, June 16—1:22 A.M.

Tara and Jenna kept their distance behind the last of the police vehicles that had sped by them, but they still kept pace.

She was grateful that they had shown up when they did because, while she knew what road the Baird farm was on, she was clueless about the address; no idea how far down the road the property was, let alone whether it was on the right or left side.

While there were no sirens, the light bars of the six cruisers and one SUV lit up the night.

According to Tara's GPS, the turn-off that would lead all of them to Baird's property was only another two miles down the road.

Suddenly, all seven of the light bars went dark. Tara hoped that as the police vehicles made the right turn, their van, doing the same, would be perceived as just another responding unit.

They sped up the rural road until the headlights of the seven vehicles simultaneously shut off. Tara almost panicked while she scrambled to do the same. Then the units began to coast, no one using brakes.

They don't want anyone to see brake lights, Tara thought,

also allowing her vehicle to slow on its own.

She looked over at her daughter. She stared forward. Her eyes and face were intense, but she didn't seem panicky.

The police officers rolled their vehicles to a stop, some slightly right of center, others slightly left. Any vehicles that might enter the road behind them would not be permitted to get through.

Using her emergency brake, Tara stopped her van on the right shoulder. No lights.

The police officers and sheriff's deputies were already out of their vehicles and assembling. She could see they were all wearing protective vests, some emblazoned with STATE PO-LICE in white, others reading SHERIFF in yellow.

Tara and Jenna got out of the van and quietly closed the doors. As Jenna walked around to the driver's side, two Summit County deputies ran toward them, weapons out, but not aimed.

"Stay where you are!" called one, short of using his vocal cords.

As they approached, the second deputy, a woman, said, "Hands where we can see them! Who are you? What are you doing here?"

Tara and Jenna were startled, but compliant.

"My name is Tara Lawton. This is my daughter. My husband is up there."

The first deputy spoke again. "Your husband, is he on the farm or is he a cop?"

"My husband is the one who led the investigation. He's up there now."

"Ma'am, show me some I.D."

Tara opened the door of her car to reach for her purse. "Slowly, Ma'am."

She pulled her purse out and set it on the ground, so that the deputy could have a downward look into it. She leaned down and shined her tactical light into the bag. Tara pulled out her wallet and withdrew her driver's license.

The first deputy looked at it and returned it. "Ma'am, you have to stay back here. You can't enter the property. Do you understand?"

Tara nodded her head in disappointment. "But we can stay right here?"

The second deputy responded. "Only if you remain behind our cruiser."

"We will."

After the female deputy gave them a hard look, the two took off to catch up with their team.

THE REQUISITE INTRODUCTIONS had been made. Lieutenant Given made it clear that he was going to maintain jurisdictional authority over the scene.

It was time to set up the raid.

Nineteen total officers made up the team, which included Brent.

Four state troopers quickly and quietly moved into positions on the drivers' sides of the two cars that sat on the right side of the driveway, which included the Pittston chief's car. They brought their weapons up, scoped rifles resting on bipods, and trained them on the ceremonial mound.

As much as Brent wanted to be at the forefront of what was about to happen, he understood his place. Without a badge, his authority was little more than that of a rent-a-cop.

He was told that he would have to stay on the driver's side of either of the two cars on the left side of the driveway. He chose the SUV, closest to the house.

Brent could see that the remaining force of officers, still hidden behind the stand of trees, was formed and ready to assault the mound. Handguns were drawn, rifles and shotguns were positioned.

CAILLEACH HAD ONE LAST comment to make before using

Brendan to thrust the *ballock* dagger into Stephanie's rib cage.

"The power that we grant today comes from the ancients of days. It is ours to bestow and take away. Remain faithful and remain blessed.

"Princes! Powers! Authorities! I prepare for you a feast!"

Brendan's left hand, clasping the dagger, began to rise above his head before finally...

LIEUTENANT GIVEN STEPPED out from the tree line with a bullhorn. He was about to lift it to his mouth when a cry came from the front door of the farmhouse.

"*Noooo!*"

A lone man holding a rifle rushed out onto the front porch and trained it upon the mound. He aimed and fired!

The bullet cartridge's report drew two handguns in his direction, one of them Brent's. And one of them fired, opening a hole in the right side of the man's ribcage, collapsing him to the ground.

With the element of surprise gone, the lieutenant dropped the bullhorn and yelled, "On me!" bringing a force of fourteen men and women around the tree line with him.

Brent and the state trooper who had discharged his weapon ran to the farmhouse to clear the scene. Brent reached the rifle first and kicked it away. The trooper went for the door, bobbing his head in front of it to get quick peeks into the residence. He opened the door and entered.

STEPHANIE HELD HER BREATH and closed her eyes. She would now know what it felt like to have life wrenched out of her body.

I deserve this.

That was the last thought she was granted before she heard someone scream *"Noooo!"* and a gunshot rang out from her right. Then another. She kept her eyes closed, barely distracted from her own imminent demise.

Her lungs were beginning to feel the burn of having air that needed to be expelled, but the anticipation of her death played on. The expected agony, the result of a blade puncturing her skin, breaking of bone, and the rupturing of vital organs, still hadn't happened.

She risked opening her eyes and exhaled. With sight came the realization that not only was the blade still suspended in the air, but chaos had erupted all around her. The Home Coven was scattering into the field away from...

Stephanie turned her head in the direction that Brendan was now facing. *Police! A lot of them!* They were rounding the trees that hid the driveway!

Her heart leapt!

Then it about shriveled within her as she heard Cailleach release a scream of such fury and evil that she thought she might die from the sound alone.

She looked up. Brendan's eyes were on her chest again. No longer distracted by the ensuing chaos, he lifted the blade up further to drive it down with maximum force.

A hole that wasn't there a fraction of a second prior curiously appeared in his right temple. His eyes went unfocused as a spray of pink mist ejected from the left side of his head.

The blade fell from his hand as Brendan collapsed forward, narrowly missing Stephanie's face, landing across her left shoulder.

She screamed.

ELDREDGE AND GIVEN saw their target, and he was running away just like all of the others dressed in white.

Weapons in their right hands, flashlights in their left, the two Pittston police officers had the advantage of seeing where they were going as they gave pursuit across the field.

A glint of reflected light that was periodically visible at Connor's right side indicated that he still had his weapon. If he were to make it into the trees and find a good place to hide, this could get bloody.

Given called out, "Chief Connor! Drop your weapon and stand down!"

The man had obviously concluded he'd been found out, as his pace dropped from sprint to jog, to a walk, then to that of a resigned middle-aged man, hands on hips and out of breath.

As Eldredge continued to approach at a run, he could see the handgun drop from Connor's hand. The chief walked a few steps back in their direction and then assumed the position.'

Dropping to his knees, he interlaced his fingers above his head, crossed his feet behind him, and waited.

John reached him first. "Get on your stomach, Chief," he commanded, his 9MM Glock semi-automatic trained on the man's chest. "Hands behind your back."

Connor didn't say a word. The look on his face was that of a man bewildered. This hadn't been part of the chief's agenda for the night.

Eldredge could hear the sounds of a dozen or more police officers giving chase, making arrests, and plowing through the woods. Dropping his flashlight, John grabbed handcuffs out of one of the pouches on his belt. He waited for Lieutenant Given to arrive and cover him so he could holster his weapon and secure the *alleged* perpetrator of a murder that was already under investigation on the far side of the Village of Pittston.

Eldredge dropped to one knee and placed the chief in cuffs. As he began to help him up, the Lieutenant began to read, *very carefully*, from a small card that he had pulled from his chest pocket.

"Chief James Connor, you have the right to remain silent…"

CHAPTER 41

B rent sat on the porch, his back against the wood siding of the house. He cradled a head with thick, dark hair. The man was having trouble breathing. And for good reason. The state trooper's bullet had pierced the man's right lung from behind and tore a ragged hole through his chest. The oxygen required to enrich his blood and feed his brain was being received in his chest at half-normal capacity. Even that would soon end. There was no way for Brent to stop his bleeding.

He knew who the man was. It was David McNeill. He was older by a few years, but recognizable from all of the pictures that Donna had shared from their trip to the British Isles.

David's eyes tracked upward to meet Brent's. He spoke through a gurgle of bloody red foam that filled his mouth.

"They killth … mah … my shis-ster."

Brent nodded.

"We… wuh wrong. Lied to … ush."

"David, listen to me. Jesus. Call to him. He loves you."

"Hurts… cold…"

"David, listen. Jesus … he will forgive you. Ask him to be your Savior. He *will* forgive you."

David's eyes were getting glassy. Each breath becoming

shallower and further apart. He was departing this realm.

"David, can you hear me?"

David's body stiffened. His breath caught. Brent knew this was it.

One last exhale with one final word: "Jee-zush..."

He was gone.

IT HAD BEEN SEVEN agonizing minutes since Tara and Jenna had heard the three rounds of gunfire. They held each other, mother reassuring daughter that everything was okay. What Tara would give to have someone do the same thing for her.

They stood just left of the sheriff deputies' vehicle, the one they were supposed to be remaining *behind*.

Since the moment they had heard the shots and the screams of a woman that sounded very much like Stephanie, they began inching—quite literally inching—their way forward. How could anyone have been expected to stay put? It was cruel.

Tara heard something. She angled her ear to listen behind them, down the road. There it was again. A siren.

More police?

"Mom, do you hear that?"

Tara nodded, still paying attention to the sound. The low guttural trilling sound of the siren could be heard in short blasts. She recognized the sound.

"It's EMS."

"An ambulance?" Jenna looked into her mom's eyes. "Mom?"

Tara could feel her daughter's breathing quicken. Jenna no longer wanted to be held. She let her go.

Jenna must have interpreted the action as permission, because she turned and sprinted for the driveway.

"Jenna!"

Tara ran after her. By the time she reached her daughter, she realized she didn't *want* to stop her. She wanted to *pass* her. Adrenaline pushed her faster than she thought herself capable.

"Oh, God," she prayed, her voice vibrating with each step.

"Make them be all right."

She slipped on some loose gravel and nearly fell as she made the left turn up the driveway, but she regained both her balance and her momentum.

A police officer jogging back to the vehicles saw them approaching and commanded them to stop. But she ignored him, mother and daughter rushing past. He would have to tackle her from behind *if* he could catch her.

Tara could see the end of the trees, followed by four cars and a house. She pressed forward, not easing up from her sprint.

Tara and Jenna finally reached the end of the tree line and pulled up when they reached the vehicles. One of them was a police cruiser.

Their heads and eyes darted around, taking in the scene. Torches to their right by a hill. Police officers milling about. Two men lying on the porch of the house.

Tara did a double-take and screamed! "Brent!"

She was already moving forward when she saw blood all over his shirt. Jenna's panicked cry added to her need to reach her husband.

Brent's right hand flew up. "Tara, stop! Stop right there!" She did. Just short of ascending the first step.

"Stay down there. I don't want you to see this. The blood isn't mine. I'm okay."

Tara intercepted Jenna by grabbing her left arm as she began to bound up the steps. It caused Jenna to lose balance and fall on the stairs.

"Ouch!"

Tara was out of breath. She let go of her daughter and doubled over, hands on her knees. "I'm sorry, Jenna," she panted. "You heard. You can't."

She found enough breath again to stand up and look into Brent's eyes, deliberately avoiding the body he was cradling.

She had to know. "Who is it? Is it…" She stopped.

"It's David McNeill."

Tara's emotions were about to get the better of her again. "Oh no. Dear God, no." She turned away, her right hand coming to her mouth. It was then that she saw the woman.

Silhouetted by the torchlight from the mound, she was being escorted by two police officers toward the house; one of them wearing a Millsville police uniform, Tracy Larkin.

Tara stepped slowly away from her daughter, who was remaining obedient to her dad's directive, and she walked toward the woman.

It's her. I'm sure of it.

She picked up her pace. The woman was close enough now that the illumination from the porch lights showed her face. It was Stephanie. She had obviously not yet been identified as a suspect, as her hands were still free of handcuffs.

"Stephanie!" she cried. The three came to a stop, and Tara saw Tracy say something to the other officer, granting her permission to penetrate their protective custody.

Tara threw her arms around the one who had been neither her acquaintance nor her enemy for nearly twenty-five years, and hugged her as if she had been reunited with a long-lost best friend.

It took a moment, but Tara realized that Stephanie wasn't responding to her elation, and after another long moment, she stepped back.

"Stephanie, are you okay? Are you hurt?"

STEPHANIE DIDN'T KNOW how to respond. The hug was scaring her. When had anyone ever been so ecstatic to see her? And now that it was occurring, how could it possibly be *this* woman?

Tara stepped back.

"Stephanie, are you okay? Are you hurt?"

She opened her mouth to speak, but before the first word could roll off her tongue, she sobbed and fell to the ground. Tracy and the other officer attempted to catch her, but they were too late.

On her hands and knees, she was now looking at the feet of the woman that she had tried to both mentor and destroy. This was a fitting position for both of them; Stephanie humbled before the one who *truly* was the better woman.

But then, Tara's knees bent and came to rest on the ground beside her. A gentle hand rested upon her head. Stephanie couldn't bear the touch, the outward show of compassion.

Weak from emotional exhaustion, she rolled over onto her side and pulled into a fetal position, and began weeping bitter tears. She didn't care how it looked. She didn't have to be strong any longer.

She heard Tara speak to one of the officers. "Tracy, could one of you see if there's a blanket in the house?"

"You got it," he said.

After a minute, the tears began to subside, but she felt like she was slipping away. Her vision was getting cloudy, and sounds seemed further away somehow.

From somewhere, she heard her name being said. "Stephanie? Stephanie, are you okay? Stephanie!"

TARA WATCHED AS STEPHANIE slipped into shock. "Hurry with the blanket!"

She heard movement behind her and to her right. She looked and saw paramedics rushing toward her.

"Ma'am, please move back." Tara did, and they took over.

She sat on her rump, staring at the scene. A pair of hands gripped her shoulders from behind. She looked up.

It was her husband.

BRENT LOOKED DOWN at his wife. Her makeup was all but gone, her hair was a tangled mess, and she had the appearance of one who had walked through Hell and barely lived to fight another day. But Brent held only one opinion of her in that moment: she was beautiful.

He couldn't have created a greater specimen of a woman

if he had all of God's power and imagination.

They were right for each other. They had chosen wisely.

Movement caught his attention. He looked up to see the approach of three men: Eldredge and Given with Jim Connor cuffed between them. They were headed toward the Pittston chief's cruiser immediately behind Brent.

Eldredge had a satisfied grin on his face, but it was Connor's look that grabbed his attention.

It appeared that the chief of police was gauging the man in the bloodied Millsville uniform. He looked directly into Brent's eyes as the passenger-side back door was opened.

There was a deep-seated loathing that filled Connor's eyes as he came to the realization of who the Millsville cop was.

Brent's mind stirred. He wasn't filled with the hate that he expected to have upon encountering the Pittston chief. Clinging to both his wife and his God, the only thought in his mind at that moment was how pathetic and weak the chief appeared.

Connor was made to sit in the back seat of his own police unit, and the door was closed.

I doubt he's sat back there before.

Both Eldredge and Lieutenant Given approached Brent. He took the lieutenant's extended hand.

"I hear you gave up a lot in the past twenty-four hours, Sergeant Lawton. Eldredge told me about your sacrifice."

"I was part of a great team that included Eldredge. He and Corporal Tracy Larkin were indispensable.

"As for me, I was just protecting the ones I love, Lieutenant."

"Be that as it may, if it hadn't been for you, this community could have been subjected to a whole lot more death and deception over the long term. Please accept my gratitude."

"You're welcome, Sir. And if I may... Thank you for allowing Corporal Larkin and me to work with you. You seem like a good man." Brent smiled. "You've got a new and important job, Lieutenant. I hope you fill it well."

"Frankly, the chief's job was never something I wanted, but I guess now I'm stuck with it." He ushered a mirthless laugh. "I don't think my wife's going to be happy."

With that, the interim chief of police walked around the front of the cruiser and got into the car. He started the engine, performed a U-turn around him, his wife, and the paramedics aiding Stephanie, then drove from the property.

"Quite a night, huh?" said Eldredge as he approached.

"Quite a night, indeed," Brent agreed.

"I've got a long night of ..." John looked at his watch. "Strike that. A long *morning* of paperwork ahead of me. Talk with you later in the day?"

Brent smiled and nodded. He watched as John began looking around the property for whatever else needed to be handled. There were still things that needed to be wrapped up before he, too—with Tracy—could head to their own police station. Except that, when he eventually walked through those doors again, he'd be Tracy's witness. Nothing else.

TARA HAD BEEN CONTENT to sit and listen to all of the interaction. She deeply appreciated the praise that was being lavished upon her husband.

She started to get up.

Brent offered his hand.

Taking it, she was pulled upward to stand before the man that she loved more than life itself. She looked down at his abdomen and the blood drying into his shirt and momentarily hesitated.

Tara stepped into him. She felt his strong embrace wrap around her. A moment later, she felt another arm work its way around her waist. Tara turned her head to see the beautiful hair of her brave, inspiring, blessing of a daughter.

She pulled her right arm out of the mesh and placed it around Jenna, drawing her into them as tightly as she could.

It was an odd thought to have in the middle of a war zone, but this was where she wanted to be. Right here, within the arms of her daughter, and held tightly against the broken ribs of her hero.

CHAPTER 42
843 A.D.—Scotia
26 Julius 843—Mid-Morning

Drosten stood atop the watchtower. He watched as masons continued to add stone around the wooden framework. It would be an impressive structure one day.

His world had irreversibly changed over the past five weeks. He'd lost his king, his country, and probably many of his family and friends, as well. He supposed that the rawness of it would last for a long time.

He had changed, too. Eight days on this island of Scotia had changed him more than the whole of his life in Pictland. It hardly seemed possible. These monks allowed him to be whomever he wished. They did not try to change him.

But change him they did.

Every single day, they changed him.

Hearing the creak of wood behind him, Drosten turned and watched as Abbot Conall reached the top of the stairs.

They met eyes.

The abbot huffed and puffed as he said, "Every time I climb those stairs, I am convinced it will be the end of me."

Drosten smiled. "Have a seat, Abbot."

"That I will, lad. No need to offer." The older man seated himself on the bench of new wood and looked at Drosten curiously. "Seems a repeat, you and I here like this."

Drosten nodded his head in agreement, remembering their first encounter.

"I know why you were up here in these stoneworks the last time we talked," said the Abbot. "Why so this time?"

"It's really no different a reason than the first time. It seems like the right place to rise above everything and reflect." Unlike their first meeting, Drosten walked over and sat next to the old monk. "I miss my home," he admitted.

The Abbot put his arm around the former warrior. "I know you do, my son. I know you do."

"At the same time, I'm growing in the belief that Pictland is, as you've said, my home no more."

"And what of that? Have you made a decision?"

"Aye. I have."

Drosten didn't get the opportunity to draw the abbot deeper into conversation, as a call came from below.

"Drosten!" came a young voice. "Drosten!"

Drosten got up, walked to the wall, and peered down to the yard below.

"Aed! What can I do for you?"

"Come! It is done!"

Drosten's face lit up, and he waved. "On my way!"

He crossed back to the bench where the abbot was already getting up.

"Ach, I should have just called up and asked you to come down!" The old man shook his head with a sigh.

Drosten laughed.

DROSTEN AND THE ABBOT followed Aed into the scriptorium and his writer's cubicle. Resting atop a soft square of calfskin was the Key of Bridei, looking the same as it always had. That is, until Aed turned it over.

The back had been beautifully inscribed, with such care that it rivaled the elegance of his own people's work.

"It is magnificent, Aed!" Drosten exclaimed.

"Indeed, boy! You will be a master before you know it!" echoed Abbot Conall.

"Would you like for me to read it, Drosten?" The boy was beaming.

"With all that is in me, aye!" he said with a laugh.

"Where do I start?"

"You know what I long to hear, but let me hear all of the section headings first."

"As you wish."

Aed sat on his high stool and picked up the key. Resting the weight on his lap, he rotated the stone to its starting position.

"They read as follows:

"*Sanguis*. It means family. *Nobilitatis*. It means nobility, and is the closest word I know to royalty, without using the word for king. *Terra*. It means land. *Militaris* means warriors, and *oceanus* means ocean or sea."

Drosten nodded slowly and appreciatively. "And the last?"

"Here, look." Aed turned the key over so that Drosten and the Abbot could read it.

"Ahh..." intoned the Abbot. "A most wonderful choice, Aed."

"What?" Drosten looked back and forth at both of the smiling monks. "What does it say?"

Abbot Conall looked at the young apprentice who bowed his head in submission and relinquishment.

"Thank you, Aed."

Looking Drosten in the eyes, the abbot explained. "The boy opted *not* to use the word *religio*. Certainly, it would have been an appropriate header for what you asked the boy to inscribe. However, he chose to use two more appropriate words to convey what you are wishing to convey to those who may one day translate the key.

"It reads *Fides Solemnis*, and it means *Solemn Faith*."

The words struck at Drosten's heart and filled him with an even greater appreciation for the boy's wisdom. "They are well chosen, Aed. Thank you."

W. FRANKLIN LATTIMORE

The boy bowed his head in humble recognition. When the boy's head came up again, Drosten saw a big and genuine smile.

"May I read the rest to you?"

"Yes, please. But as we have been spending time learning one another's languages, do you believe you know enough of mine to read what you've inscribed in my tongue?"

The boy's smile began to fade as he, once again, looked at the bottom of the key. His face became the epitome of honor and respect. "I can do that, Drosten."

Drosten lowered himself to his knees, his heart contrite. The words that he had asked Aed to inscribe were truth, and they were holy, and they reflected what his heart now contained.

Aed spoke.

"In these walls of Abbey at Kells, I, Drosten, warrior and keeper of this key, have traded old rags of scarlet for garments white as snow. I pledge my heart and my people to the single God of creation, Christ Jesus the King. May the past be lost and the future forever new."

EPILOGUE
Present Day
Tuesday, September 6, 2011

*W*hat an amazing, adventurous way to spend a wedding anniversary! And seventeen years!

It hardly seemed possible. Then again, why had it taken so long for them to get married in the first place? It had taken seven years between the time they had met and the time they walked down the aisle.

Tara sighed. The answer was obvious. On top of her remaining year of college after Brent graduated, there were a lot of life adjustments that needed to take place for them both.

Thank you, God, that you helped us to be patient enough to wait for each other.

She sat staring out the window of the Scottish Citylink bus as they crossed over the choppy waters of Cromarty Firth. They were on the A9 highway on their way from Inverness Airport toward the Tarbat Peninsula of northern Scotland.

Tara turned from the window to look at Brent, a big grin on her face. "I'm so excited I could almost *scream!*" she said, her voice elevated.

"Yep. Almost!"

Elbow.

He laughed. "That elbow of yours is how we first met."

She put on a playful grimace. "Just had to bring that up, didn't ya?"

Tara stood up to peer over the two seats in front of them. Amy had her face pressed up against the window, looking out.

Jamie, on the other hand, had his precious gaming device in his hands, earbuds in place.

She shook her head. *You'd think...*

She sighed again, smiled, and sat back down.

Stealing a glance across the aisle to see what her oldest was up to, Jenna lifted her head and looked Tara's way. Their eyes met, and Jenna lit up.

"Mom?"

"Yes?"

"I am so excited I could almost scream!"

"Hey, watch it!" chided Tara with a playful smile.

Jenna giggled and returned to looking out her own window. Tara sat back and looked at Brent. "I still can't believe it."

Brent smiled. "I'm sure it'll sink in eventually."

"Part of me hopes not. I love this feeling!"

Brent winked, drew her close, and kissed the top of her head.

Within 40 minutes, they arrived in the town of Tain where they were met by Angus MacKay, their driver, to the small village of Portmahomack, their final destination.

"A fair bit o' attention's been drawn to our wee village these past few months," offered Angus, his accent barely allowing the Lawtons a measure of comprehension.

The whole of the Lawton 'Clan' could tell that he was excited and proud.

"The word o' crackin' the Pictish tongue's brought scribblers from papers and telly folk from all sorts o' lands, plus archaeologists, anthropologists, and crowds o' Scots—hundreds swearin' they're direct kin o' the Picts themselves!" He smiled big. "And tourists traipsin' in from every corner o' the world, too! It's a right braw commotion."

"It sure sounds like it," responded Brent, shrugging. He looked at Tara with a wide-eyed grin and a seventy-five percent lack of understanding.

"You, my dear new friends, are a grand arrival this day. The fact that you, Tara, are Pictish an' all… well, that's stirred up a braw wee fuss, to be sure!"

"We are so honored and grateful to be here," responded Tara, bursting with emotion. "I could hardly believe that you would cover the cost of our whole family to travel all the way from America."

"Dearie, the coin that's come intae our wee community o'er the past couple o' days alone's more than made up for any cost o' travel we've gien ye. Dinnae fret yer bonnie wee head o'er it, hinny."

Tara turned to Brent. "Hear that, honey? I'm a *hinny!*"

Angus and Brent both laughed out loud.

"Yes, you are, my *bonnie* wife. Now don't ye be fallin' in love with the locals and forgettin' aboot yer wonderful husband."

BRENT AND TARA STOOD in the Tarbat Discovery Centre. It had once been the center of worship for a clan of Scots called Ross, the Tarbat Old Parish Church. What a perfect setting for what they were learning—what only the *two* of them were learning.

Jenna and the kids had decided to explore the village. They were being accorded as much recognition as their parents for the recovery of so much of their history.

My three little heroes, thought Tara with a smile.

Their guide within the museum, in which they stood, was none other than their bus driver.

It turned out that Angus MacKay was actually the curator of the Tarbat Discovery Center *and* had *deliberately* and *liberally* poured on the Scottish accent. He had quite a sense of humor, and they were thoroughly enjoying his company.

Equally as obvious as the man's wit was his knowledge. He was certainly a scholar. And what he'd been learning over the past several weeks since the Baird-farm raid in Pittston was the subject he really wanted to discuss with his guests.

And every question that Brent and Tara had, Agnus was zealous to answer for them.

"What of the key? Why would it have been made in the first place?" asked Brent. "How could they have known that it would be needed?"

"Ah, a fine question," replied Angus, with a nod of appreciation. "Our best guess is King Uurad saw trouble comin' and knew it was only a matter of time before the Picts fell to the Scots or the Norse; the legendary Vikings.

"It's known the Scots aimed to wipe out the Picti from the British Isles. Likely, with the makin' of the key and the Pexa Stone—what you've been callin' the key stone—the Picts meant to preserve their heritage and culture—with the means of recoverin' it—if it was ever lost or taken.

"Think of the nation of Israel, God bless 'em. The Hebrew language was near extinct; their culture almost gone. But look at 'em now! A restored people and nation, with Hebrew taught worldwide.

"And the ancient Egyptians, they did all they could to ensconce their traditions, beliefs, and ways for future generations."

Brent and Tara nodded, appreciating the explanation.

"The Picts, it seems, were attemptin' the same with their upright slab stones across the land. But with the Scots and Norse wearin' 'em down, I reckon they made the key and stone out of fear, knowin' they'd be a lost people without it. And, lookin' back, they were right.

"So, if the key or the Pexa Stone had remained lost..." said Tara as a lead-in for him to continue.

"If the Key of Bridei and the Pexa Stone hadn't been found and brought together, these folk would've stayed a tale of myth and legend. But now..."

Angus wiped away the formation of tears in his eyes. "Pardon me." He cleared his throat of the welling-up emotion.

Tara and Brent stood patiently and smiled at the man, appreciating the attachment he had to his ancient past.

"But now we are gettin' to know them—I'm getting to know *me!* And you're gettin' to know *you,* Tara!

She smiled brightly.

"The stories... the *hundreds* of stories that we are startin' to translate... This is just beyond my ability to take in."

"So, the name," said Tara. "The key has the name *Bridei.* But you're saying that it was likely commissioned by King Uurad. Wasn't King Bridei alive hundreds of years before the stone was created? Why would it have been given the name the *Key of Bridei*?"

"Tara, you need to leave Brent and come work for me," Angus said with a chuckle.

Tara laughed. Brent rolled his eyes and shook his head.

"Such good questions from both of yeh! Yeh're right, of course. And that shall remain a mystery, it would seem.

"There *is* an ancient text in Ireland, thought to come from the Abbey at Kells in the ninth century. It didn't use the word 'key', as we'd say it today, but the documented words, '*iarna Bridei*' are certainly close enough.

"Though the name of a Pictish king and *iarna* were scribed together, it is a fact that the key was created long after King Bridei. So, it remains a mystery. We, today, are just not sure that it *was* the original name of the stone."

Angus smiled a toothy smile, leaned into them, and whispered, "But it *could* be."

Brent and Tara laughed appreciatively.

Brent became curious about another large stone panel that stood within a ring of red velvet ropes nearby. "Angus, the other stone. Why is it being displayed along with the Key of Bridei and the Pexa Stone?"

Excitement and a big grin lit up Angus' eyes. "That, my dear friend, is somethin' grand! Come! See!"

Angus unhooked one length of the rope from a brass stand, letting the end drop to the floor, and escorted them into the ring.

"This stone comes from the very time the Picti were conquered! Likely commissioned one or two years before the murder of the last Pictish king, King Drust.

"Drust was king for a year or so before his reign came to a rather egregious end. Before him was King Uurad. We think he had this particular stone made as a commemoration to a specific great warrior named Drosten."

Angus led them to the far outside edge of the panel, where the three then crouched down. He pointed to an inscription.

"See here? Look at this."

Tara looked at it quizzically and asked, "Isn't that Latin?"

"Good eye, Lass! It's actually an odd combination of both Latin and Goidelic, or as you'd probably call it, Gaelic."

Brent chimed in. "Isn't that a bit unusual? I mean, I've not seen any other stones—at least in my own searches—that had actual letters inscribed into them."

"Aye, it's uncommon! And excitin'! We're not certain why this stone has non-Picti writin'. Likely, it's tied to the monks who brought Christ's name to the area after Pictland fell. Maybe they understood the importance of what was carved here."

"The Christians who came to Pictland clearly did so 'cause they cared for the folk and wanted 'em turned to Christ. So, it figures to me they carved this inscription years later to show they'd backed or somehow helped with the task King Uurad gave to the warrior before King Drust came to the throne."

All three of them looked at the lettering:

ᴅʀosᴄeɧ
iʀeuoʀeᴄ
eᴄᴄꜰoʀ
cus

Tara asked, "What does it say?"

"It reads, 'Drosten, in the reign of Uoret'—that would be King Uurad—'and Forcus.' Drosten is the warrior for whom the commemoration and commission were created. Forcus... well, we're just not sure."

Angus, followed by Tara and Brent, stood and walked to one of the faces of the large stone.

"It looks like part of the stone is missing," asserted Brent.

"Aye. Right yeh are. Some of the upper portion of the stone is broken away. A pity, really. The stone's in two pieces. The top bit, before bein' found and reunited with its lower, was abused as a step in some stairs."

Angus pointed to the lower section excitedly. "Look here! What do you see?" He didn't wait for either of them to respond.

"We've got amazin' details! See these two circles linked by parallel lines, split by a diagonal? That's the Key of Bridei!"

"It doesn't look like the key to me," questioned Brent.

"That's likely 'cause the stone's maker was told not to provide the key's true markings.

"Now look at this shape below—a dome or coverin'. That's the symbol for protection. To the right, there's the mirror and comb, meanin' 'to take personal responsibility for.' Then, a host of animals with a warrior symbol below. The warrior's got a bow and arrow aimed at a boar. Any guess at its meanin'?"

Angus gave them a broad smile.

Tara and Brent looked at one another. Brent shrugged. Tara looked back at Angus and responded. "Well, I'm guessing that Drosten was commissioned to put the stone under his protection."

"*Well done!*" said Angus, his voice full of excitement. "From the Key of Bridei down, the slab says somethin' like, 'The key is yours to protect. It's your personal duty, no one else's. Be like the animals of the land'—each, I think, showin' ways to hide, move unseen, or outrun a foe—'and guard the key from an oncomin' enemy,' shown by the chargin' boar.'."

Angus folded his arms across his chest, proud of his obvious ability to now translate a language that had been lost for well over a millennium.

Brent smiled and said, "So, Drosten successfully protected the key. He got it done."

"He did, Brent. He did. And history backs that up. There are other upright slab stones showin' the Key of Bridei's two sides below a shield, made *after* the last Pictish king's death.

"The Scots would not have known what the symbols meant, but any remainin' Picti would have known that the key to the survival of their culture had been faithfully protected from the hands of their enemies."

Brent shook his head. "All of this in order to protect their heritage. It's amazing."

"Not so surprisin', my dear lad," said Angus. "Look at our own tombstones, our monuments. How different are we from the Picti? We all want to be remembered. But for the warrior, Drosten, it was about *more* than just their heritage."

Tara chimed in. "Wait. I thought that's *precisely* what this was all about—Drosten's protection of their culture so that it could one day be retrieved."

"Aye, their culture, but not their old ways. Their heritage was pagan, at least in the north where Drosten had his task. As for the cross on the Drosten stone? Clues suggest it was carved years *after* King Drust, the last of the true Pictish kings."

Brent was trying to make it all make sense. "So, then how did it go from being the protection of their *heritage* to the protection of a *culture*, especially the protection of a culture that was about Christ, when Christ wasn't who they believed in?"

"That, lad, was answered on the back side of the Key of Bridei! The reason it wasn't fully translated for centuries at Trinity College in Dublin was that the symbols didn't line up with the Latin on the back, causing doubt about all the others.

"For five of the six sections, they could sort of make sense, but the sixth didn't match any Picti text or symbols on the front. I believe, and other researchers now agree, that Drosten rewrote that sixth bit. He was set on wipin' out the old pagan religion he once followed, erasinin' it from their language forever.

"Remember this, too… We did nah have the Key Stone. Those so-called Picts in your town of Pittston… If not for … what was his name, Brian Baird?"

Brent nodded.

"If not for him, that David MacKay fella, and their research, not to mention…" Angus cleared his throat and shook his head with some obvious contempt. "…their thefts from our community here, we wouldn't have the stone in which the Key of Bridei fit. Hate to give 'em credit, but they did what we never tried."

Brent's thoughts went back to David and what he hoped was a confession of faith the moment he died. *Hope he's with you, Father.*

"Drosten, as the last *known* Pict, got to decide what culture would be restored, if the chance ever came."

Brent, eyes wide with sudden realization, turned to Tara. "That means that what Brendan and Stephanie were trying to revive..."

"... It was all a lie," finished Tara. "It was all just a ruse. He *knew* the information was not there to reestablish that ancient religion! But he was certainly going to make something up!"

"Way to go, *Drosten!*" exclaimed Brent.

The aging curator froze, and a curious look appeared on his face.

"What is it, Angus? What are you thinking?" asked Tara.

"A thought just struck me. What if Drosten, who carried the Key of Bridei to Ireland, came back home?"

"Here, to Scotland? Rather, his former Pictland?" asked Brent.

"It's clear he became a Christian. Who's to say he didn't also help spread Christ's word here in the north of Scotland?"

Angus's eyes became wide, and his face beamed with the possibility. "What if the Drosten Stone wasn't created *before* his mission to protect the key, but *after?!*"

Angus began pacing, processing the idea. He was getting more visibly excited by the moment!

"What if Drosten himself had this stone made to tell the story of the key's protection? The Gaelic and Latin words here could be his own mark! Maybe he dismissed King Drust and commemorated King Uurad because he's the one who entrusted Drosten with the mission of protecting the key!"

Brent and Tara watched the man with no small amount of pleasure. Then he said, "My apologies, Brent and Tara. I'll be just a moment—I need to check my books!"

With smiles on their faces, they bid the man leave. Brent again approached the Drosten stone.

Tara told him that she was going to step outside for a little bit.

TARA WALKED OUT OF the discovery center and into the yard. Dozens upon dozens of grave markers surrounded the old church building. Walking among them, her thoughts again returned to Stephanie, and she sighed. Oh, the things she wanted to say to her just now.

Stephanie, you almost died, and now you're in jail, all for a religion that Brendan was ultimately just making up.

It was all *a lie.*

Brendan used you for his own glory.

She walked up to a low stone wall, a partition between ancient and modern, and looked at the village.

She pondered again, this time just above a whisper.

"Maybe Brian Baird truly believed there was power to be had. Maybe after all the work he had done, he felt he *had* to keep the belief in an 'Olde Faithe' alive, even after realizing that the evidence for it no longer existed."

Tara shook her head. So many people had trusted in him to lead them to an ancient source of power and a life of ultimate fulfillment.

Stephanie had been played and deceived right along with all the rest. *What a waste.*

The spark of an idea formed in Tara's mind, one that caused her to smile.

"Stephanie O'Leary," she said out loud, "at one time you were *my* teacher of all things spiritual. How about I now return the favor?"

THE WHITE VEHICLE WITH government plates approached the home of Brent and Tara Lawton and slowed to a stop just short of the driveway. The driver barely took notice of what he was required to deliver, yet confirmed that the address was correct.

He looked at the address on their mailbox: 10113. It was definitely the correct location.

The man reached his hand through the window and pulled down the door, placing within the box a pile of mail.

Delivery complete, he drove his vehicle another sixty feet or so to the next mailbox on his daily route.

Contained within the Lawton mailbox, amidst three bills, two Happy Anniversary cards, and several pieces of junk mail, was an "Official Use Only" envelope addressed as follows:

> Village of Pittston, Office of the Mayor
> 5000 Robinhood Drive
> Pittston, OH 44058
>
> Mr. Brenton N. Lawton
> 10113 Belmeadow Drive
> Millsville, OH 44078

Within that particular envelope was an official governmental letter that began with these words:

> Dear Mr. Brenton N. Lawton,
>
> We would like to extend to you an opportunity to interview with our Mayor, the Honorable Marie A. Wilbur, for the position of Chief of Police for the Village of Pittston, Ohio. ...

COINCIDENCE OR PROVIDENCE?

At the outset of writing of this novel, I created a fictional character whom I named Drostan (with an "a"). He was to be the guardian of his people's history, culture, and religion. I enjoyed developing his background and personality. Then, in the midst of all my continued research into all things Picti, I came across an interesting description of a Pictish standing stone that is currently housed at St. Vigeans Museum in Scotland. Etched into the outside edge of one side of that stone is something that shocked me: *My character's name!* Immediately, I went back through my manuscript and changed the spelling of his name to match what was found etched into that stone.

One might start wondering if there once *was* a warrior, a guardian, a *hero* of the Picti people. A man named Drosten.

Side of the Stone   Front Panel

The inscription on the *very real* Drosten Stone:

ᴅʀᴏꜱᴄᴇɳ
ɪʀᴇᴜᴏʀᴇᴄ
ᴇᴄᴄꜰᴏʀ
ᴄᴜꜱ

BEHIND THE DARKNESS

BOOK 3 OF THE OTHEREALM SAGA

PREVIEW

PROLOGUE

It's about time I finally published this account. I've put it off for too long. I expect that, as I write it, it's bound to stir up many raw emotions. I just pray I can get through it.

My name is Brent Lawton. I'm the chief of police for the Village of Pittston, Ohio. I have a wife, Tara, and three children: Jenna, Jamie, and Amy.

I love my life.

You'd laugh at that last comment if you knew half the things that Tara and I have been through. But this story—this situation—took place before our children were born. In fact, it took place before Tara and I were even married.

This past Thursday evening, I approached Tara in our living room as she sat reading on the couch. I told her that I had a story that I needed to share, one that I thought would capture her attention even more than Tosca Lee's latest work of prose.

Tara did me the courtesy of setting aside her book with a humored grin. I'm betting she thought that my awkward demeanor was the precursor to something worthy of an upcoming laugh.

Sitting in my favorite chair while facing her on the couch, I took a deep breath and released it, the whole time looking her in her eyes. Her grin faded.

"What is it?"

"I have something to tell you. Something that happened a

few years after the hike."

'The hike,' as we've come to call it, was the event that brought Tara to Christ—and me to Tara—back in 1987. A long time ago.

"Hon, do you remember back in 1990 when…" I paused. I didn't really want to say the words.

"When your mamaw passed."

I nodded. "That was also the year that my Grand Am got totaled, Dad lost his job, and all of our friends took off into their own lives."

"That would be a difficult year to forget."

"If it hadn't been for you, I'd have gone crazy."

Tara leaned over and took my hands. "That was a brutal year for you and your family, and if I recall correctly, I wasn't very much help to any of you. Somehow, it ended up that your trip down to Kentucky for your grandmother's funeral was what got you grounded again."

She became thoughtful for a moment, remembering. I wondered if she would recall…

"You said something to me when you got back."

I nodded my head and looked at the floor.

"Yep. I did."

"You said that you couldn't tell me what happened down there. Is that what this is all about?"

"It is." I looked back up into her eyes. "After all that we've been through in the past year or so, with Donna McNeill and the Picti people… Stephanie O'Leary and your frustration with her stubbornness as you continue to share Christ… It's caused me to reflect quite a bit about God's ability to control everything that's been going on."

Tara's green eyes peered deeply into my own. She gave me a single nod to continue.

"Well, I guess it took all of these recent events to get me to a place where I'm finally willing to talk about what happened that week in Kentucky."

"I still wish I could have gone with you to her funeral."

"It's kind of funny to think about now, but your inability to come with me was the camel that broke the straw."

She raised an eyebrow. "You mean the straw that broke the

camel's back."

"No, Hon. I pridefully thought I was the camel, but God showed me very clearly, in the span of three days, that I was nothing but straw."

Venture *Backward*
into
The Otherealm

"The foolish plan of God is wiser than the wisest of any man's plans."
1 Corinthians 1:25

Control is a delusion... a tantalizing mirage pursued by all, from the mighty to the meek. Can it be bartered, bought, or seized? And if captured, how much power does it truly grant?

Pittston Police Chief Brent Lawton is about to share a story with his wife that will affect their lives forever. Hear the tale unfold as she learns of a twenty-five-year-old man—hostile toward God—who is unexpectedly bestowed with extraordinary supernatural powers and charged with the perilous mission of protecting the life of a pre-born baby ... without the mother knowing.

Journey into a hidden domain where spiritual beings—unseen by most—clash in a relentless struggle for the souls of humanity. Can one man's resolve and good intentions prevail when a sinister, ancient evil attempts to intervene?

Who—or what—truly governs the threads of life and death?

A Note From The Author

In writing these first two novels of my career, I have striven to be intellectually honest when it comes to true practices of witchcraft. As a former practitioner of the occult myself, I have had several of the experiences that are portrayed in the lives of my characters.

I've often been asked by people who have found this out about me, "What did you do?" and "Is it real?"

The answers I've given have been, and will continue to be, "I did stuff that I wish I hadn't, and got tangled up in darkness that I didn't want." And, "Yes. It's quite real."

There is a section of dialogue that I had written and wanted to incorporate into a discussion between Stephanie and Tara in *When Darkness Comes*. Unfortunately, the discussion never happened.

Who knows, though? Maybe the conversation will take place now that we know that Tara is intending to reconnect with Stephanie O'Leary.

Anyway, I want to use the dialogue now in order to make something *very* clear about witchcraft, especially to those who are *engaged in*, *dabbling in*, or thinking about *getting involved in* any form of the practices:

Tara looked straight into Stephanie's eyes, doing every-
thing she could to emphasize her next point. "The demons are following rules that *they* made up. It's their game.
Do you really think they are being controlled and manipulated by ceremonies, by incantations, and by religious objects?

"It's a *game!* A game with *eternal* consequences!

"Don't you see? You are lured by the idea of power and control. But it is a deception; a trap. If you believe that you can be in control, then in your mind, you will never need God's help. If you believe that you can control the spirits of the Otherealm, then in your mind, you will never need God's Word for knowledge of truth. Then, ultimately, by believing that God and His Word are unimportant, you will never see your need for a Savior.

"It's really that simple. God loves you. The Enemy of your soul does not. God wants to bless you with everlasting joy, peace, and life, and the Enemy—*your gods*—want to keep you from it."

That is the truth about witchcraft. The practitioner is trading the truth for a lie. He or she is given just enough by the Enemy to keep him coming back for more. Lots of promises are made by demons—*fallen angels*—but what benefit is there even if a practicing witch *could* gain the world, but sacrifices his soul? Hell is a real place, and God does *not* want anyone—that includes you, my dear reader—discovering it as his or her eternal existence; especially after He provided an escape from it through Christ!

Additional Information on the History Portrayed within *When Darkness Comes*:

First things first...
My greatest desire for the group of Picti antagonists was to

have them be practitioners of something "real" yet also unknown. I knew that I wanted it to be a form of witchcraft, so I started looking into *all sorts* of crazy stuff. I owned way too many books for the sake of researching the occult, witchcraft, demonism, etc. But I found one subject particularly interesting: *Pecti-Wita*.

It was supposedly derived from an ancient people called the Picts who had once ruled what is now Scotland. I had heard of these people before, but didn't really know much about them. But what I did know—or *thought* I knew—intrigued me enough to decide that the Picti people would be the predecessors of the "Olde Faithe" that was to be resurrected by Brendan Cadeyrn.

Boy, was I excited!

Then ... not so much.

When it came to the culture of the Picti people who would be portrayed through Drosten, I had to almost completely fabricate everything!

So little is known about them, and as a result, the research was both frustrating and enlightening; heavy on the frustrating. I wanted to add as much realism as possible to the life that Drosten had led, but as it turned out, I was left with just two major relevant pieces of history in which to catapult the story of *When Darkness Comes* forward.

First, the Picti people were able to stop the advancement of the most powerful army in the world. Because of the loss of the Roman Ninth Legion and other stunning Roman defeats at the hands of the Picts, Emperor Hadrian had a wall constructed that spanned the entire width of the Island of Britain, proclaiming it to be the end of the known world. (Remnants of that wall can still be explored even today.)

Second was the killing of King Drust and the remaining heirs of the Picti crown by the Scotti King, Kenneth MacAlpin, which was the beginning of a swift end to the Picti people. The rest was mainly from my imagination.

An aspect that I'm sure many of my readers expected to hear or "see" about the Picts was their tattooed skin. I could not find any real evidence that these people, outside of painting themselves for war, spent the rest of their lives covered with tattoos and dyed skin, so I decided to play it safe and not include the tattoos in any form, instead allowing imagination to take flight. So, for those of you who had never known about the legends of a highly-tattooed culture, you didn't miss anything. For those of you who did know the legends, I'm sure there were all sorts of imagined designs covering the skin of these ancient warriors.

The tattoos that each of the modern-day "faithful" had on their shoulder blades or under their arms, in addition to the ceremonial "tattooing" rite that was conducted by Brendan and Stephanie, were tributes to the word *picti* in the language of the Romans, Latin, meaning tattooed or painted.

The honor given to the MacKay Clan around the ceremonial mound at the farmhouse goes back to a discovery in my research that the MacKays of today keep as a long-held belief: that their lineage goes back to the ancient Picti people. The story of the 1486 A.D. Battle of Tarbat actually occurred between the MacKays and the Rosses, though there is no evidence that it had anything to do with the MacKays' Picti heritage.

The transfer of the *Book of Kells* from the Island of Iona to the now famous Kells Abbey *may* have occurred. Some historians believe there is a chance that the *Book of Kells*—a *magnificent* piece of work, by the way—may have Pictish origins, based on the artwork contained within its illuminations, but it's inconclusive. So, instead of going there, I decided to go with one of the more plausible theories for the creation of the book, that it was created, at least in part, by the monks at the Abbey of Iona, which really was headed by Abbot Indrechtach.

Some of the archaeological information about the standing stone pieces that were brought together for the reconstruction of the Pexa Key Stone (a creation from my own mind) is true.

Though the key stone never truly existed, there are pieces of broken standing stones that have been discovered in masonry work within and around the Tarbat Old Parish Church. These large fragments sparked my mind in such a way as to have a viable means for the Pexa Key Stone to be transported to America. After all, a large standing stone such as the Key Stone described in the novel could never have realistically been smuggled out whole.

These two novels have been a true joy to write. They started back in 2006 as a single novel. The second novel was finally completed in September of 2011. There were nearly two years in which nothing was written … because I had gotten stuck.

Having gotten past my own personal story, fictionalized in Part One of *Deliver Us from Darkness,* I began to doubt that I was capable of writing a good dramatic tale moving forward. But the burn to complete the *Otherealm* story stayed in my heart and mind, and I finally started writing again in earnest in late Spring of 2010, completing novel number one in November of that year.

With the completion of *That Dark Place* in 2021, the characters that I've written, that you have hopefully come to love—*and to despise*—have been my companions for fifteen years, and are not now easy to put to the side, especially my character Brent. He is the man that I aim to be in real life.

My other favorite characters to write (both good and *really* bad) were Tara Baker-Lawton, Karen McGlaughlin-Stanton, Jenna Lawton, George Chamberlin, Pastor Jonathan Sagan, Kyle Russell (novel 3), Elizabeth (novel 3), Drew Parks (novel 4), and Stephanie O'Leary.

May some of them find places within your heart, as well.

Thank you for investing both time and money into reading my stories. I hope to produce many more in the months and years to come that will also be blessings to you.

IN HIS GRIP,

W. Franklin Lattimore

THE APPENDIX

Footnote 1:
Pexa:

Most researchers now agree that *Pexa* was a tribal name from which the name *Picti* or *Pecti* was later derived. This seems to be confirmed by the oral traditions of the Scots, who call the ancient people *Pects*. It used to be believed that Picti came from the Romans, who used the same word that, in Latin, means "painted " or "tattooed."

To continue reading the story, turn back to **page 16**.

Footnote 3:
Pecti-Wita:

Also known as simply Wita and/or Pictish Witchcraft, this is the *supposed* pre-Christian religion of the Picts. I say supposed, because the current practices of what is called Pecti-Wita can only be traced back to two modern-day individuals who supposedly know its true ancient past: Aidan Breac and Raymond Buckland.

Two websites make these claims about its beliefs and practices: "Pecti-Wita is concerned with all aspects of prosperity, growth, abundance, creativity, and healing, and honors the Celtic Deities. The main tools in Pecti-Wita are the Staff and the Athame or Dirk. Pecti-Witans use a "Keek-Stane" which is, in effect, a scrying stone or the equivalent of a crystal ball."

And "Scottish Solitary tradition passed on by Aidan Breac, who personally teaches students in his home at Castle Carnacae, in Scotland. The tradition is attuned to the solar and lunar changes, with a balance between the God and Goddess. Meditation and divination play a large part in the tradition and it also teaches several variations on solitary working of magick."

Quotes taken from:
1. solitarywitch.yuku.com/forums/96#.Th9jNmXh6So
2. echosfate.tripod.com/4.html

To continue reading the story, turn back to **page 19**.

Footnote 4:
The Biblical Gift of Discerning of Spirits:

The Biblical gift of "discerning of spirits" (not "gift of discernment," as there is no such gift mentioned in Scripture) is a spiritual ability described in the New Testament, specifically listed among the gifts of the Holy Spirit in 1 Corinthians 12:10. This gift enables a person to distinguish between different types of spiritual influences—whether they originate from God, the devil, or human sources. Below, I'll break down what this gift is, its purpose, and its significance in the Christian faith.

What Are Spiritual Gifts?

In Christian theology, spiritual gifts are special abilities given by the Holy Spirit to believers for the purpose of building up the church and advancing God's work. These gifts are outlined in passages like 1 Corinthians 12-14, Romans 12, and

Ephesians 4. Examples include teaching, prophecy, healing, and, of course, discerning of spirits. Each gift serves a unique role in the spiritual life of the community.

What Does "Discerning of Spirits" Mean?

The gift of discerning of spirits (sometimes called "discernment of spirits") is the supernatural ability to:

- Identify the source of a spiritual influence or message.
- Differentiate between divine, demonic, or human origins.

This isn't just about intellectual judgment or intuition; it's a Spirit-empowered insight into the unseen spiritual realm. For instance, someone with this gift might:

- Recognize whether a prophetic word is truly from God or a deception.
- Sense the presence of an evil spirit affecting a situation.
- Confirm the authenticity of a spiritual experience.

Why Is This Gift Important?

In the Christian faith, discerning of spirits is vital for several reasons:

1. Protection from Deception: The Bible warns of false prophets and misleading spirits (e.g., 1 John 4:1: "Test the spirits to see whether they are from God"). This gift helps believers avoid being led astray.
2. Spiritual Clarity: It ensures that the church follows genuine divine guidance rather than counterfeit influences.
3. Safeguarding Faith: By identifying harmful spiritual forces, it protects individuals and communities from

confusion or division.

The gift of discerning of spirits is a powerful tool in the Christian faith, rooted in the Holy Spirit's work to guide and protect believers. It's not about suspicion or judgment but about seeking truth in a world where spiritual influences—both good and evil—are at play. If you're exploring this topic further, scriptures like 1 Corinthians 12:10 and 1 John 4:1-3 offer a deeper look into its Biblical foundation.

To continue reading the story, turn back to **page 29.**

Footnote 6:
The Book of Kells:

The Book of Kells is a stunningly beautiful manuscript containing the Four Gospels. It is Ireland's most precious medieval artifact and is generally considered the finest surviving illuminated manuscript to have been produced in medieval Europe.

Some believe that the book was created as a tribute to a monk by the name of Columba. It was he who began the monastery at Iona, which, in turn, led to much of the Pexa (Picti) nation coming into the fold of Christianity.

The manuscript was never finished. There are at least five competing theories about the manuscript's place of origin and time of completion. First, the book, or perhaps just the text, may have been created at Iona, then brought to Kells, where the illuminations were perhaps added, and never finished. Second, the book may have been produced entirely at Iona. Third, the manuscript may have been produced entirely in the scriptorium at Kells. Fourth, it may have been produced in the north of England, perhaps at Lindisfarne, then brought to Iona and from there to Kells.

Finally, it may have been the product of an unknown monastery in Pictish Scotland, though there is no actual evidence for this theory, especially considering the absence of any surviving manuscript from Pictland. Although the question of the exact location of the book's production will probably never be answered conclusively, the first theory, that it was begun at Iona and continued at Kells, is currently widely accepted. Regardless of which theory is true, it is certain that the Book of Kells was produced by Columban monks closely associated with the community at Iona.

The majority of text taken directly from:
www.thoughtco.com/the-book-of-kells-1788410

To continue reading the story, turn back to **page 45**.

Footnote 7:
The Battle of Tarbat:

First, let me, the novel's author, make clear that there is no evidence that anything about the *Battle of Tarbat* was related to an attempt by Clan Mackay to reclaim anything associated with their Picti heritage. The Mackays are believed, though, to descend from the ancient Picti people.

In 1486, the Battle of Tarbat took place. The Clan Mackay and Clan Ross had long been at feud, again and again the Rosses had suffered molestation of their lands by their enemies and when at last, driven to desperation and thoroughly infuriated, they gathered their forces and marched against the Mackays, they were in the mood to teach them a severe lesson. The Mackays, with Angus Mackay of Strathnaver at their head, were defeated by the Rosses and sought shelter in the church of Tarbat, where many were slain. The church was set on fire, and Angus Mackay and many of his clansmen were burned to ashes. This was followed by the Battle of Auldicharish: To take revenge on Clan Ross, Chief Ian Mackay, helped by a force from Clan Sutherland, marched south, invading the territory of Clan Ross and began laying waste to it. Chief Alistair Ross gathered his force of 2000 men and engaged in a long and desperate battle with the invading forces. In the end, the battle went against the Rosses, with the Mackays and Sutherlands gaining the upper hand. The Ross chief was killed along with many of his clan. In 1493, the Mackays invaded the Rosses again and took much spoil.

To continue reading the story, turn back to **page 62**.

Footnote 8:
Pictish Witchcraft Ceremonies:

The ceremonies depicted here are supposedly true to the original Pictish faith and are taken from the book *Scottish Witchcraft & Magick, The Craft of the Picts*, by Raymond Buckland, Llewellyn Publications, 2005. However, archeological and anthropological evidence would argue that no history of true Pictish belief systems has been discovered, which, in turn, would indicate that these ceremonies were created very recently.

Some researchers into witchcraft indicate that these practices are actually fewer than 200 years old and possibly under 100 years old. Regardless of the age of these ceremonies and occult practices, they are still a practiced form of witchcraft called PectiWita.

Witchcraft is witchcraft. Even though Pecti-Wita and Wicca, and other forms of witchcraft would emphatically declare their practices to be safe, positive, and for the betterment of oneself, they are declared by God to be detestable. All forms of witchcraft are a trap created by the Enemy to deceive people into believing that they have some sort of control, be it over nature, elements, and/or spirits. Even other people.

The Enemy has set up an illusion of power to draw people in, and this same Enemy will *seemingly* play by its own rules when it comes to the safety practices taught in the varied forms of the occult. An example of this would be Tara's "circle of protection" in Part Two of *Deliver Us from Darkness*. In reality, there is *nothing* about the circle she places herself within that prevents an evil spirit from attacking. However, the *illusion* of protection is maintained by the Enemy so as to keep people believing they are safe and, in turn, keep their eyes and minds trained away from God and his saving grace through

Jesus.

To continue reading the story, turn back to **page 70**.

Footnote 12:
Brent & Tara's Spiritual Warfare Research:

Much of what Brent & Tara have been reading and commenting on, comes from the actual website *Spiritual Warfare and Deliverance Ministry* (spiritualwarfaredeliverance.com). The site is not fully comprehensive, and I believe that there are a few aspects of the site's teachings that can be questioned when it comes to spoken authority.

This site still exists. It should be understood that the information that the Lawtons would have perused came from this actual online source back in 2011, when the story took place.

To continue reading the story, turn back to **page 94**.

Footnote 13:
Awareness in Warfare Situations:

Lest we forget, we've got a cunning Enemy. And since we cannot see them with natural eyes, we need to be cognizant of the fact that demons will take advantage of any observed weaknesses that we may display. One weakness that we have in the United States and most of the Western Hemisphere is "If we feel it, it must be natural."

Remember, the Enemy's function in the life of any Christian is to make him/her ineffective. If the Enemy can latch its claws, talons, hands upon a Christian and simulate some natural-feeling anomalies in the body, he will. Once we're convinced that something is physically wrong with us, what will we do? We'll turn our attention away from our missions from God and start to self-focus.

Now, let me qualify all of this. Just because you get sick or have a headache in the midst of a spiritual struggle does not *necessarily* mean that a demon is involved. But this *is* where awareness is essential. One thing that will never hurt is to pray.

One thing that *can* hurt is to assume that it's just another physical ailment.

Pray and use your Christ-given authority over it, then, if it persists, take precautions that may involve seeing a physician.

Another element that our Enemy enjoys using is distractions, e.g., a child who had been enjoying his day, all of a sudden starts throwing a tantrum. Or you get the thought that you could turn on the TV for just a little while, resulting in spending the day doing nothing but placating a desire for entertainment. (Nothing wrong with entertainment if it's not interfering with your purpose.)

It will never hurt to pray and verbally use your authority in Christ to protect your children, your spouse, and your environment. Use *spoken* authority to keep the hands of the Enemy from being effective in pulling you away from what God is calling you to do.

To continue reading the story, turn back to **page 150**.

Footnote 14:
Words of Knowledge and Words of Wisdom:

Here we have yet another gift from God the Holy Spirit. This is a gift or a happenstance that can occur out of the blue. Suddenly, you have insight into another human being or a situation. But with knowledge comes responsibility. God may speak into your spirit that a certain individual is going through a certain circumstance. Don't think that God gave you that tidbit of knowledge so that you can sit on it. God is not a gossip! If He speaks a word of knowledge to you, pray about what you've learned. Ask the Lord if He wants you to approach the individual that He spoke about. Maybe He wants that person to know that He cares, and speaking to that person about something you should have no knowledge about may be the key that opens the door. It may be that a person is going through a difficult time and has no way of knowing if he'll make it through. God may want you to just let that person know that God sent you to speak comfort to him; that he's not forgotten.

Words of wisdom work as a gift in a similar fashion, but

this involves wisdom from God that is imparted to another individual (or even to one's self). God gives wisdom to those who ask, according to the book of James. Sometimes, though, God uses another individual to speak wisdom into a person's life.

Why? God knows the impact it will have when a willing vessel (you or I) explains what God has given him to share.

The point is that God can use these gifts however He wishes, but you've got to be willing to ask for and operate in these gifts.

To continue reading the story, turn back to **page 163**.

Footnote 15:
Checks in the spirit:

Checks within the human spirit are a sort of interruption in our comfort when we're about to do something that the Holy Spirit wants to keep us from doing. In my own experience, I feel it as a sort of grab in my chest. It is sudden and very recognizable. It's enough to get me to stop what I'm doing (or about to do) and reflect or even pray. It's comforting to me to know that I'm being watched out for by God, even when I don't know the reason for his sudden "No" or "Don't."

A check in one's spirit is something that many don't want to receive. In our lives we tend to think that we've already got too many restrictions, and the last thing that we want or need is God *officially* and *directly* saying no to us about something.

However, if we are willing to accept two things, we'll be just fine with these checks: The first is to draw near enough to God that you could feel the checks when they are given by the Spirit. If you are willing to have an intense relationship with God in which He keeps proving Himself and His love to you, you'll yearn daily to experience His presence. Second, understand that God is all about your protection, not about chains. He's not looking to bind you up so that you can't enjoy life.

He has given you. However—and this is vitally important— He does expect you to understand that He is the God and you are the creation. We are not here for ourselves; we are here for Him. And part of being here for Him is letting Him love us with His guidance and protection while we pursue the purposes for which we were created.

To continue reading the story, turn back to **page 231**.

THE COMPLETE OTHEREALM SAGA

Deliver Us from Darkness

A cunning witch vows to prove herself to her mentor by destroying the reputations of two "Christlings." She lures Brent Lawton with seduction and Marta Rosales with deception, targeting their faith during a southern Ohio backpacking trip. Can Brent and Marta's faith withstand her assault, or will their lives shatter under her spell.

When Darkness Comes

A small-town police officer and his wife uncover a chilling plan for a human sacrifice in a neighboring town. Driven to save the victim, they risk his job and the safety of their family. But will it be worth either? What if they are unable to outmaneuver the darkness before it claims a woman's life?

Behind the Darkness

A young man, furious at God for his grandmother's agonizing death, dares to shout a challenge at the sky: "I'd have done a better job!" God responds, placing him into a scenario to prove his claim. Can he protect a pregnant teen's pre-born baby against her will, without her even knowing he's involved? Or is control over circumstances just wishful thinking?

That Dark Place

A teenage girl, ensnared in a secret life of pornography, stumbles into a predator's manipulative hands. Charmed by his deceptive mask, she doesn't see the danger. Will she realize the danger, uncover his identity, and find the means to escape before it's too late?

ABOUT THE AUTHOR

W. Franklin Lattimore is the creative force behind the gripping Otherealm Saga, a series published under Direct Impact Books.

A U.S. Air Force veteran and Kent State University alumnus with a B.A. in Political Science, Frank's firsthand encounters with the occult during his teenage years fueled the vivid, suspense-laden narratives that define his first four novels, drawing readers into a world of spiritual intrigue, intense emotion, and causes worth fighting for. With more thrilling stories in development, Lattimore aims to inspire his audience for years to come.

Beyond Frank's writing, the Lattimores are deeply engaged in their vibrant church community and volunteer efforts. Frank's passions include teaching, reading, fishing, ziplining, roller-coaster thrills, and indulging in crispy BBQ wings.

Together, he and his wife, Lynn, enjoy hiking, camping, road trips, biking, target shooting, and especially being around their growing family. They reside in Central Ohio.

Biography Photographer: Christy Brothers
Christy Brothers Photography—Columbus, OH

Notes